Lucky Girl

Lucky Girl

A Novel

Irene Muchemi-Ndiritu

The Dial Press | New York

Lucky Girl is a work of fiction. Apart from the well-known actual people, events, and locales that figure in the narrative, all names, characters, places, and incidents are the products of the author's imagination or are used fictitiously. Any resemblance to current events or locales, or to living persons, is entirely coincidental.

A Dial Press Trade Paperback Original

Published in the United States by The Dial Press, an imprint of Random House, a division of Penguin Random House LLC, New York.

Library of Congress Cataloging-in-Publication Data
Names: Muchemi-Ndiritu, Irene, author.
Title: Lucky girl : a novel / Irene Muchemi-Ndiritu.
Description: New York: The Dial Press, [2023]
Identifiers: LCCN 2022022123 (print) | LCCN 2022022124 (ebook) |
ISBN 9780593133903 (trade paperback; acid-free paper) |
ISBN 9780593133927 (ebook)
Subjects: LCGFT: Bildungsromans. | Novels.
Classification: LCC PR9381.9.M733 L83 2023 (print) |
LCC PR9381.9.M733 (ebook) | DDC 823/.92--dc23/eng/20220725
LC record available at https://lccn.loc.gov/2022022123
LC ebook record available at https://lccn.loc.gov/2022022124

Printed in the United States of America on acid-free paper

randomhousebooks.com

9 8 7 6 5 4 3 2 1

Book design by Diane Hobbing

This book is dedicated to my mom and dad.

In our culture, we don't say the words "I love you" enough. You brought me into this world and did the best you knew to do for me. For your love and sacrifices I am forever grateful, and forever, I will love you.

Kupenda sio kitu, Kupendwa ni kitu. Lakini kupenda na kupendwa ni kila kitu.

To love is nothing, to be loved is quite something. But to love and be loved is everything.

—Swahili proverb

Part One

Chapter One

Every morning throughout my childhood, at five forty-five A.M., Mother knocked on my bedroom door. I climbed off my bed, knelt, and kissed the floor. "Serviam. I will serve."

Still kneeling, I made the sign of the cross—Father, Son, and Holy Spirit—then started on the rosary, repeating the sequence of the Apostles' Creed: one Our Father, ten Hail Marys, one Glory Be—altogether five times.

I kept my morning showers short. Mother said many other Kenyans had no water to drink and most bathed with ice-cold water. While I scrubbed my feet with the pumice, I prayed for the Holy Father's monthly intentions—one month for the church's deacons to be good servants, another month for the refugees, the next month for world peace, for the sick and suffering—all year round.

Mother wanted me to do those things.

Everyone in our neighborhood knew Mother for her devotion to the Catholic faith. But she was not one of those Catholics who only had doings with other Catholics; Mother was like the old-day missionaries. She visited people in need, like the Abdullahs, the Somali family with seven children who rented a cottage at the back of a wealthy family's mansion down the street. Mother brought them baskets of hot buns covered with a white napkin.

"Those poor children are always so hungry; no sooner am I at their front door than all the bread is flying out of the basket," she sympathized. "The landlord's children have more than they can eat, but he won't give Mr. Abdullah even a cup of beans to feed his children."

She smiled with the Shahs, a Hindu surgeon and his plump wife who dressed in exquisite saris. When the Shah daughters brought payasam to share with us over Diwali, Mother received it graciously. When Mrs. Shah asked if the five-day lighting of fireworks was a nuisance, Mother said, "Nuisance? What nuisance? Anything for your gods!"

Mother kept me indoors. "There is too much evil out there," she said. I longed for a sibling, someone to play with. I read books, practiced piano. I sat by the window of the study where I could watch the children from the neighborhood. Sometimes, they played a game of rounders, dozens of kids swarming around the players' circle as if they were bees around a broken hive. Sometimes they raced on their bicycles, flying over pebbles and potholes. I saw that they stayed outside until the shadows of the jacaranda trees in our neighborhood disappeared.

I loved the escape of nursery school, all the hours I spent under the shade of the purple flowers of the grand jacaranda trees on the playground. I loved Princess, our housemaid, who raised me since I could remember. She hugged me often, and told me she loved me. She was always at the school gate waiting to scoop me up with arms wide open. She wore a head wrap and kanga and hummed as we strolled beneath the canopy of jacaranda trees that lined our street, and all the gardeners in the neighborhood followed her with their eyes as she walked by. Trailing three steps behind in my checked uniform, I wished I did not have to go home, that I lived at school, where I could play endlessly and without fear.

I didn't understand it, but I feared Mother. My father died on my fifth birthday. My vague memory of that was a stain I couldn't bleach out. Mother's stiffness with me made my fear even harder to understand. My aunts told me that before my father's death, Mother took me everywhere with her, like a trophy, singing to me while she planted her roses in the back garden, doting on me. After his death, she turned distant. She took on the life of a stern businesswoman.

My father owned a successful biscuit mill that he had grown from a storefront bakery to a household brand sold in supermarkets. After his death, Mother ran the business. She worked furiously, perhaps out of grief or the fear of failure. She sat on the board with men who had answered to my father, and she commanded their respect ruthlessly. By the time I was ten, she'd quadrupled the business's value, sold it, and invested in real estate and hundreds of acres of land for commercial farming used for coffee and roses. She was a millionaire many times over and for every extra shilling she made, her determination to mold me into a good, humble Christian girl increased. She had to be stern.

Every lesson she taught me growing up tied back to modesty. Though we had domestic workers, as did most middle- and upper-class Kenyans, Mother insisted I contribute to the household. Cooking, tending to her vegetable patch, and polishing the bumpers of her bright yellow Peugeot until I saw my brown eyes reflected back.

Mother had Musau, her beloved gardener, build a small poultry farm for eighty chickens in our backyard. She also brought in rabbits. Then the chores started. Saturdays at dawn, even before my prayers—"Kayai, wake up! The chickens won't feed themselves."

Kayai, little egg. That's what she always called me. Her only child, who she overprotected, doted on obsessively so I wouldn't fall and break, yet for all her care, she struggled to show her emotions. I longed for birthday parties but Mother said they were a waste. Instead, she would buy me a single present, always something practical and useful. I longed for a hug, a kiss. I got none.

Saturdays inside the coop were spent sweeping, changing light bulbs over nests, and picking up eggs. Sometimes, she did these things with me. As we cleaned the barn side by side, I'd yearn for stories of my father, my papai. I wanted to hear about Mother's childhood: why my four aunts and my kokoi, my grandmother, had come to live with us, why, even though Mother was so smart, she hadn't been to university. Most of all, I wanted to know the biggest secret: how my papai died. No one ever told me.

Instead of telling me stories, Mother worked in the chicken coop with the same steady focus she always had. She swept steadily, soaked in a strange silence that barricaded her from me.

Kokoi and my aunts, Mother's younger sisters, and Princess, made my world whole. They filled the house with chaos, dancing, laughter, and gossip when Mother wasn't home. I loved my kokoi more than anyone. Although she was only in her fifties, a tough life had taken its toll on her body and Kokoi was frail. She looked a decade older than her years. At fifteen, she had been circumcised and married off and soon after, given birth to Mother. Mother was named Nalutesha, *born on a rainy day,* and Kokoi gave her the pet name Nalu. After that, Kokoi lost five pregnancies and had one stillborn in the span of a decade.

During those years, my grandfather beat her often, though never inside the house, as a Maasai home is a sanctuary of procreation and prosperity, a place where children are conceived, born, and nurtured. Barrenness in women was a sign of disorder. To cleanse the disorder, he beat her more viciously over the years. Kokoi was scolded by her mother-in-law too, and her father-in-law wouldn't allow her to serve him a meal.

"If a woman cannot produce children, what then are they there for?" my grandfather's family asked her.

When her husband took a second wife, Kokoi was glad. He could finally have all the children he deserved. He stopped beating her and beamed with pride while talking about his new wife's pregnancy. Perhaps it was Kokoi's relief at seeing her husband finally happy, or the end of the beatings, but suddenly she fell pregnant. This time, she delivered a healthy baby girl she named Naserian, *brings peace,* or *peaceful one*. Then she fell pregnant again and had another healthy daughter, and then a third. Naserian, Laioni, and Rarin all came crashing in, one after another, like sheep that had been let out of their barn for morning pasture.

My grandfather, growing restless around two wives with a horde of children, had started to have a dalliance with a woman he met while working in the city as a cook for a British family. Eventually, he abandoned Kokoi and her co-wife.

As the eldest, Mother had to quit her education to find work. Mother dropped out of her economics degree at only twenty and registered for a six-month secretarial course. Within a year, she had learned shorthand, dictation, and typing. She said that she could type faster than her mind could think, and she started to become afraid of her fingers, wondering if they had a life of their own. Two years later, as she was working overtime to put food on the table, my grandfather returned home, saying he wanted to atone and bring his family together. Kokoi found herself pregnant again with a fifth daughter. My grandfather, absolutely sure this surprise baby would be a boy, was so gutted that he left Kokoi for good. That was how my youngest aunt, Tanei—beautiful, flamboyant—showed up like an unexpected thunderstorm nearly a decade after Kokoi's middle three daughters.

Mother was livid. She had already become the family's matriarch, responsible for more than she could bear at only twenty-three, and now there was a new baby in tow. When Kokoi told the girls they shouldn't carry hate for their father because he would always be their father, Mother was clear that he was never to be welcomed home again.

"Forgiveness can be granted, but a snake is a snake even after it sheds its skin," she said.

Now, decades later, Mother treated my aunts—responsible Naserian, cheerful Laioni, bookish and serious-minded Rarin, and wild Tanei—more like her daughters than her sisters, partly because she had helped raise them and partly because imperiousness was part of her nature. She tolerated no nonsense as long as they lived under her roof, even with Aunt Naserian and Aunt Laioni, who were in their late twenties. They had both studied business and accounting at the university, and they helped Mother with her businesses, both at the farms and in the factories.

They never brought home any boyfriends, even though I often heard Kokoi tell Mother the girls were past marrying age. Aunt Rarin, the fourth born, was Laioni's Irish twin, only eleven months younger. She studied law in Nairobi. It seemed when she wasn't in her books, she was in her head, dreaming of bigger things for herself. She declared that she would get a clerkship at the International Criminal Tribunal for the Rwanda Genocide after she passed the bar, to which we all rolled our eyes, and she did. She said she'd win a scholarship to continue with her master's degree in international criminal law and that she would study in Scotland, and she did. I loved my aunt Rarin. I wanted to live a big life too.

Tanei was only six years older than me. Mother's greatest frustration was her youngest sister's rebellious behavior, developed by the time she was in high school. Often, as Mother scolded Tanei, she appealed to Kokoi to intervene. "No," Kokoi said. "She's your daughter now. Who am I to say 'Close your legs' or 'Do this or that' when we eat your food and take shelter from the rain under your roof? Let everyone know that if it weren't for my firstborn daughter, my Nalu, this family would be nothing, nomads, beggars."

Kokoi meant to appease Mother, submitting herself to demonstrate loyalty. After all, Kokoi lived by Mother's generosity. And so it was this family of vibrant women who gave my early childhood color and joy. But with Mother, other than the hours we spent cleaning the chicken coop together, her warmth remained caged far away.

. . .

When I turned seven, I began attending a prestigious all-girls convent school across the city. Mother decreed the school bus unsafe, and instead, she hired a driver. I called him Mzee, Swahili for a distinguished old man. He had skin like onyx and wore Islamic prayer beads around his wrist every day.

We didn't speak much, mostly because I had never spent any time with any man and didn't know what to say except for an exchange of pleasantries. Our drive home was far more interesting. Even as a child, I was always intrigued by the disparate sections of the city. Going from the quiet, leafy suburb where my school had sat for sixty years since the Irish nuns built it from the ground up, to crisscrossing through the chaos of a township where the tin roofs lay so skewed it was a wonder they didn't slide off in heavy rain, to then finally entering my family's neighborhood where residential homes were resort-style mansions guarded by twenty-four-hour security companies. That was Nairobi—a captivating tilted society of haves and have-nots, where many lived on less than a dollar a day and walked miles to and from work in the broiling African sun, while others only shopped overseas for their clothes and shipped in European furniture.

At five P.M. on the dot every day, Mother phoned home to make sure I'd made it back safely.

In those primary school years, I started to really feel my father's absence. At my new school, fathers seemed suddenly to appear everywhere, at swim meets, tennis matches, and field hockey games, yelling out their daughters' names in deep, rumbling voices.

I thought I was ready to know the big secret of how my father died. Kokoi wouldn't tell me and neither would my aunts. They skirted around it like blowflies over a dead carcass. The older I got, the more my frustration grew. Kokoi told me, "With time, my beauty, with time. Some things heard by a young ear change the soul forever. The only thing you need to know about your papai is how much he loved you. He craned his neck like an angry ostrich over any imbecile who said, 'Don't worry, next time it will be a boy!' "

My aunts told me stories about my father that Mother never shared. They said when Mother went into labor on the warm January night of my birth and was rushed to the hospital, my father couldn't be reached. Mother complained through the night to all the nurses about his absence, though her bouts of anger were interrupted by bouts of worry and weeping.

"She fretted that something horrible had happened to him; she was inconsolable, but as soon as she wiped away the tears and blew her nose, she would stiffen up again and threaten to strangle him the second she laid eyes on him," said Aunt Rarin.

My aunts said that I was born at five A.M., small but pink and loud. A day later, I still had no father. On the second day, he arrived disheveled and dirty. His Volkswagen Beetle had crashed into a ditch on a remote country road, forcing him to walk miles and hitchhike to find help with towing. Mother was overjoyed. She told everyone that she had prayed to God and bargained with him: If He let her husband come back alive she would bite her tongue forever, no matter what Father said or did. No one could have predicted that on my fifth birthday, God would renege on His end of the bargain, and she would lose my father for good.

By the time I was ten, I begged everyone who would listen to tell me the truth about what happened to my father, but my tantrums brought no results.

"Soila, you are driving me crazy," Aunt Naserian complained. I hounded them while they folded meat into triangles of pastry, while they beat the rugs with brooms outside on the veranda. I circled them relentlessly, like a flock of hadadas. Naserian was the second oldest after Mother, and the other aunts followed her lead. If she broke rules, they did too. If she wavered, they did too. On this she remained silent, so the others did too.

At only sixteen, Aunt Tanei broke all of Mother's rules as if they didn't apply to her. If anyone would tell me something I wasn't supposed to know, it was her. But even she stood firm. "Soila, please! I'd rather die."

I searched for answers in the framed photographs of my father that littered our living room, staring back at me. I studied his eyes, his smile. They were as impersonal to me as the pictures in Mother's *Drum* magazines. I couldn't remember the moments captured in the photographs: my father holding me on his lap on a wooden stool in a photo studio or standing next to me in flared pants while I posed on a red tricycle. I squinted at his face in the photos. *If Mother won't tell me, maybe he will.* After all, Kokoi always said the dead tell stories.

I had only a vague memory of the period around when he died, like a broken vase I couldn't quite glue together. There was going to be a party for my birthday. I had a pink cotton dress ready to wear and Mother was fussing around me and bubbling with excitement. The next clear memory was Mother screaming and me being kept away from the closed door of her bedroom when I called for her.

At school, when my friends asked why I didn't have a father, I made up stories that became more colorful over the years. One day, my classmates and I were eating lunch, and the topic of my father's mysterious death came up yet again. "He drove his car into the back of a truck and his body was flat as a pancake when they dug him out," I replied.

"No, he didn't."

I had never liked Salome, the girl who blurted this out accusingly.

"That's a lie," Salome continued. "You've always got a new story."

The other girls were silent and wouldn't meet my eyes. They all knew something I didn't. The warmth of embarrassed tears stung my eyes.

"Yes, he did," I argued, packing up my thermos with my beef stew half-eaten. "And why would you say that he didn't? What do you even know about my family?"

"I know that he died inside your house," she said, taking a bite of her bologna sandwich. "Everyone knows."

"Stop it!" Jumping to my feet, I tilted forward to smack her in the face but the screeches of the other girls woke me from my anger. Could it be true what she said?

I couldn't bear the humiliation. I ran off clutching my lunch bag, blinded by tears. By the time I made it to the brick arches of the school chapel, I could barely catch my breath, choked by sobs. None of the other girls had stood up to Salome. None of them came after me, cared to comfort me.

"What in the heavens is the matter?" Sister Pauline hurried over to me.

"Nothing," I said, hiding my face with the sleeve of my school cardigan. All of the Irish nuns terrified me. They moved invisibly, only to appear just when we were at our worst behavior. Sister Pauline scared me most. She was head of school and head of the other nuns, who bowed their heads when they crossed her path. "Nothing, I'm fine."

"You're not fine," she said. "Let's go to the office and have a glass of juice, shall we?"

Mother always said, "Soila—if I ever hear that you have been called to Sister Pauline's office for bad behavior you will sleep with the chickens in the coop." And I believed her. Yet here I was, in Sister Pauline's office, sitting on a hard chair, staring at the wooden crucifix hanging on the wall in front of me while she poured a glass of fresh orange juice and set it on the table. "Now tell me, my child, what is the matter?"

"Salome says my father died in our house," I said, blowing my nose with a tissue from the box on her desk.

"Well, how would Salome know? Does she live in your home?"

"No, Sister Pauline," I answered, still sniffling.

"Well then, why do you let her make you so cross? You can't always worry about what other people say about you."

"Yes, Sister Pauline."

"Do you not know how your father died?" she asked, after a slight pause.

"In a car accident," I said.

"Who told you that?"

"No one. I just know it," I said.

"Well, well, my child," she said. "Perhaps it is time you asked your mum about this matter?"

"She won't tell me. But I know it's what happened."

"I think you're done with school for the day," Sister Pauline said. "I'll call your mother now to collect you, and in the meantime, go get your things from the classroom."

Mother didn't come to school. Instead, just like always, it was Mzee.

"What's happened to you?" Mzee asked, as I stuffed my backpack into the back seat of Mother's Peugeot. "Are you ill?"

"No. Where's my mother? The headmistress called her to pick me up, not you," I said sullenly.

Mzee answered with a shrug and turned the volume up louder on his favorite Swahili music station. I closed my eyes and allowed the sound of the East African drumbeat to fog my misery.

The phone rang in the hallway at precisely five P.M., like it had for years.

"Are you home?" It was the same cool tone that she used when buying vegetables at the market.

"Yes, I'm home."

"Start on your homework, then. I'll be home in an hour."

At six P.M. I heard Mother's footsteps move slowly up the stairs to my room. I imagined her bursting in with a sharp rebuke for getting myself in trouble at school. But then she entered, perfectly composed, upright, serene.

"So—you want to know how your father died?" she said, without greeting me first. I curled up on the bed, thirsty and puffy-eyed from crying. She sat beside me. "Sit up. I don't think you're old enough, but God knows if I don't tell you the world will."

I scooted away from her and leaned against my wooden headboard, putting distance between me and her mercurial temper, still expecting her to tell me off. Instead, Mother finally untied the blindfold from my eyes.

In the early morning hours of my fifth birthday, my father went into the bathroom, saying he wanted to get ready for work. Mother said it was unusually early for him to go in to the office on a Saturday, but he said he wanted to tie things up early at the mill before coming home for my birthday party in the afternoon. Mother fell back to sleep. It wasn't until she woke up again several hours later that she found the door locked and water streaming out.

"We had to use an axe to break the door," she said, her voice flat. "He used his shaving razor."

"His razor, for what?"

Mother rubbed her palms together and breathed a deep sigh. I searched her face, still uncomprehending.

"Soila, what I'm saying is that your papai killed himself. He used his razor and cut his wrists and allowed himself to bleed out and drown in the bathtub. Do you understand it now?"

I felt waves of shame crush my body. I didn't know my father at all, but imagining him drowning in the bathtub in bloodied water and Mother screaming over him, shaking him, begging him to wake up was numbing. That was the moment that I, in my newfound grief, began to understand why Mother was Mother.

Her grief, which had always frustrated and confused me, was bigger than I had ever known. I knew from my aunts' stories that Mother had been different before my father's death, but this was more than I imagined. My father hadn't just died. He had killed himself. And he had left Mother behind to torture herself with all the questions about why he had done it, for all these years.

Maybe Kokoi had been right when she said my ears were still too young and it was better left untold. Mother sensed that I didn't want to hear any more. Without saying another word, she laid her hand gently on my cheek for just a moment.

"I'm so sorry, Kayai," she said. Then, as if she hadn't just shattered my childhood, she stood up and left the room as serenely as she had walked in.

. . .

That night, dinner was served at seven P.M. just like it was every other night. But instead of obediently going to the table, I remained in my room until Aunt Tanei came to get me. She leaned on the doorframe with one hand on her hip.

"Soila, how long must we wait for you?"

"I don't want to eat," I said. I turned over and faced the wall.

"Excuse me, your highness," Tanei said. "I know you had a bad day but sulking about it won't make it better. Besides, your yeyo is giving me a hard time about my marks and I need your mopey face to deflect her from the nagging."

Mother loved dinnertime. Every evening, Princess brought out dishes of meat, or collard greens, or beans boiled with maize, or chapati and lentils. Our dark wood dining table, laden with food, was too formal for our informal family, an extravagance with eight curved legs with solid brass tips. Mother used dinnertime, when all of us were gathered together, to expound on the importance of a Christian woman's conduct in the outside world, and the joy of living in God's grace and daily pursuit of his mercy. Tanei's poor grades were another frequent subject of conversation at the dinner table.

Tonight, Mother didn't turn to me until we had finished eating and were clearing away the dishes.

"Kayai, leave the plates," she said, nodding at Princess and my aunts to finish up. "Sit down, I want to talk to you." I sank back into my seat. "You need to understand, Kayai, your father's death devastated me. Then, your kokoi reminded me that I still had to get out of bed for you. What you know now about your father's death doesn't change anything. You have to move on with your life, with the people who are here today."

Had she moved on? I was afraid to ask. She still wore the look of a widow. When my father was alive, I was told, our home was full of life and laughter. After he died, the mood became somber and she refused to change anything in the house. What she could have modernized remained antiquated—the red velvet couches, heavily printed carpets, busy wallpapering, the yellow-tiled kitchen with green appliances and yellow Formica countertops. She still slept in the same bed she had shared with my father that his family had bought as a wedding gift. Our house wore the look of a vintage wedding gown. Mother froze the house in January 1981, the year my father died.

To me, it seemed as though she expected my father would return someday and perhaps not be able to find our house if it had changed too much. I had heard stories of restless souls haunting houses, searching and lost, unable to free themselves from purgatory. I prayed that my father's spirit would know where to go to be free. I didn't know it then, but as I grew older, I realized that what I wished for my father was what I most wanted for myself: I wanted to discover where to go to be free.

Chapter Two

I expected the revelation of my father's suicide to shake the foundations of my life, but days passed as they always had, adding up to years. As I entered my teenage years, I began to chafe against the rigidity of our family's traditions.

Most of all, I hated that Mother whipped herself. I was only six or seven when I first heard it happen. When I was that young, I slept in a smaller bedroom next to Mother's. Mother often came in after I was already in bed to pray for my dreams.

She would read to me from the Bible, and sometimes when she was too tired, she asked me to read to her from one of my storybooks as she lay on my bed with heavy eyelids. I was always eager to show off my reading skills but soon my eyes would shut too. Once I woke in the middle of the night to go to the bathroom. Through the wall, I heard the sound of the whip.

After each blow, a whimper, and I counted them—seven. The first time I heard it, I ran to Mother's locked bedroom door and called for her, worried somebody was hurting her. The next morning when she woke me up for school, she wore a light cotton nightdress and I saw the marks, red and angry, on her upper back.

It wasn't until I was thirteen that Mother explained it all. I was sashaying back into my bedroom after a particularly long hot shower to find Mother sitting on my bed. I ran for a towel and came back into the room, mortified that she had seen the growth of hair that was starting to sprout in between my legs.

"Soila, what have I told you about taking long showers?" Mother scolded. "I've been sitting here for ten minutes and all I see is steam rising out and I don't hear you scrubbing your body, just singing. Children in this country don't even have water to drink."

"Yes, Yeyo," I said, sitting on the bed next to her.

"I take cold showers," she said. "Did you know that?"

"Yes, Yeyo. I know I'm supposed to. I'm sorry."

"Soila, we live in such a materialistic society that people can't understand you'd actually make yourself a little uncomfortable to be more mindful of God."

"Yes, Yeyo."

"Many people diet just so they can be thinner. Yet they wouldn't bear any suffering for God."

"Is this why you sometimes whip yourself?" I asked.

"Yes." She answered directly. "It's my penance. It's what I choose to do, to live fully in the spirit. The pope does it with joy, Mother Teresa does it, Saint Josemaría Escrivá did it."

I didn't agree with Mother, but I knew how important her faith was to her so I tried to understand. But what I couldn't understand was why our Christmas celebrations had to be so dull. I wanted to celebrate Christmas with pomp, like the students in my class who bragged about ripping open presents from wish lists. But in Mother's house, there was no exchange of presents.

"Christmas is a celebration of the birth of Christ but the world has made it about Father Christmas," Mother would say while we watched television families unwrap presents.

Kokoi never let anything stand in the way of her celebration. She dressed to the nines for the Christmas Mass. Kokoi grew up in the colonial era, when the "white man" came to the villages and brought forth his good religion about a prophet boy who was born to a virgin, who went on to perform miracles and die for Kokoi on a cross. Until then, the God Kokoi knew was Enkai.

Enkai lived on Ol Doinyo Lengai, Mountain of God, somewhere between Mount Kilimanjaro, the White Mountain, and Mount Meru, the Black Mountain. Enkai was all-loving and merciful, male and female, but also vengeful and murderous. Kokoi's parents had sacrificed their lambs to him at the mountain, and the synergy they had with nature, their cattle, and their harvest was tightly sewn in with their faith in God.

Kokoi still believed in these things. She still called God "Enkai." But she also believed in this new strange god that the missionaries had brought her, even if she questioned why she had been so quick to accept him.

"Why would I believe a white man would die for me?" Kokoi would ask sometimes as I read the Bible to her in Swahili, a language she understood but couldn't read or write. "Why do I believe these people? A white man wouldn't even let me learn, but he will die for me? How?"

Still, she loved Christmas. She wore her red fascinator with floating peacock feathers, so tall she had to remove the hat while she rode in the car. At church, she stopped by the Christmas manger and offered boxed foods that the parish would distribute later to the needy families.

Later, when we hosted a few extended relatives for lunch, Kokoi, still in her hat and pearls, talked about her Enkai and her Jesus—two unlikely heroes of her life—as if somehow she had found a way to get them to play along together and was willing to offer lessons to others who were struggling with her dilemma.

. . .

On Sundays, Mother was different. She smiled and sang in the car all the way to church and back home. After Mass, Mother let me do anything I wanted. I could lie in bed and read with leisure, splash in the pool for hours, eat as much ice cream as I liked, play my boom box a little too loud.

Her evenings were spent having tea with Father Emmanuel, Mother's priest and counselor. Mother ordered us not to dawdle around the living room while she served the priest homemade sponge cake with tea in the china she used only for special visitors. Not even Kokoi was welcome while they sat behind closed doors.

"Everyone knows they are more than friends," Aunt Tanei gossiped. She was nineteen years old to my thirteen, and more outspoken than ever. "What kind of a priest goes to a widow's home for tea then drags it on to supper and then to late-night coffee?"

The insinuations always made Kokoi snap. "Who is 'everyone'? I ought to put you in a potato sack and whip you till morning. Your sister has sacrificed herself to care for this family, and this is the thanks she gets? These things you say about her are wicked and I won't have us all kicked out of her home when we have no place else to go."

When the sun set on our relaxed Sundays and rose on Mondays, the ambience around the house grew stiff again. Mother's mood was like broken glass. I was eight years old when Mother slapped my cheek with her open hand so hard that it sizzled, after she opened the rubbish bin to find a whole serving of rice and lentils tossed inside. I shouted for my grandmother amidst tears. I knew I was special to Kokoi. She always told me that I was her first grandchild and therefore I would always be her special eng-akwi, granddaughter, no matter how many more came after me. She said that in Maasai culture, grandchildren were important because they kept old folks from aging. "A grandchild is a new lease on life after your children have left you. A grandchild makes your feet light with play, your memory sharp from the tales you must pass down, and your heart soft from all the love they give you."

"Enough, Nalu," Kokoi said as I held my burning cheek with the palm of my hand. "You're beating her out of anger. There's no wisdom in that. Come, there are other things to worry about." She pulled Mother to the living room by her arm. Something was happening on the news.

On the screen, crowds of Black people fled from an army of white men with giant guns strapped across their shoulders. They ran through clouds of tear gas. Some people fell and lay still, like our dog Simba after the mamba struck him in our garden.

"Just look at South Africa," Kokoi murmured, sadness in her voice. "It's 'eighty-five and still they're treated like animals."

Mother walked past me to the freezer and threw several ice cubes into a small plastic bag and handed it to me with no pity. Then as she moved toward the booming television she looked back at me as if to say, *I am not finished with you*. I flinched. "Soila, if I see you throwing food out again . . . Do you hear me? People are dying in the world," Mother said. "Don't be wasteful."

. . .

I started high school when I turned thirteen. My body was changing in ways I hadn't expected. Mother didn't talk to me about sex and I didn't dare ask. The nuns didn't either. Instead, they put up posters of male and female anatomy. The older girls told us horror stories of a documentary on childbirth that scared them enough to swear never to get pregnant, but no one warned me just how excruciating my period would be. The shock of seeing my white bedsheets soaked bright red in the early morning had me wailing for my aunts, my kokoi, anyone who could hear me. Finally, it was Aunt Tanei who burst through the door, to see what was wrong.

"You mean it's just your period?" She laughed. "My God, I thought you were on fire! It's just your period!"

"It's so sore. This can't be normal."

"Oh yes, it's normal! You're a woman now. Get in the shower and stop moaning. How will you scream when you give birth, if this is how you cry for your period?"

"Shut up! I'm dying." I'd never endured real pain before—never fallen out of trees, fallen off a bicycle, broken a limb. I had suffered Mother's whackings, but even those had dwindled as I grew older.

Tanei ignored my tears and seized the moment like she had been waiting for it her whole life. She gave me thick padding and taught me how to stick it on my panties and gave me aspirin for the pain. She pulled down the wall calendar with the photograph of the Maasai morans, warriors, lifted up in the air while they danced the adumu, and taught me how to count the days until my next period. She explained how I could fall pregnant, which days were "safe" days, and which days I would have to ask my boyfriend to "pull out." Then she helped me change my bedsheets and I curled up with a pillow between my legs. A film of cold sweat covered my back like hot breath blown on a cold window and waves of nausea crushed me, leaving my mouth watery with too much saliva. There was so much I didn't understand—so much more about my body was unknown to me than I realized.

"Sex is great, but you absolutely cannot fall pregnant because your yeyo will for sure kill you," Tanei said. She slid a finger across her neck. "You'll be dead, and we will come to your funeral."

"But I don't even want to have sex," I said.

"You say that now, but trust me"—Tanei winked—"it will feel so good, you won't know whether you're coming or going. Your mind will shut down, your mouth will scream, and your body will completely betray you."

I already felt betrayed by my body, by the blood. I didn't want more.

That evening, Mother sat me down on the cast-iron garden bench under our lemon tree and between us she placed the Catechism and her black leather-bound Bible that was as old as me. Mud from the rainy season coated my shoes. Mother's bright roses perfumed the air. The lemons drooped heavily and formed round shadows on the bench. I wanted to be in my bed, but Mother insisted we talk in the garden, her favorite place.

She had planted the lemon tree shortly after my father died. Through the years I had seen her quietly pruning it, spraying its stem with oil to keep pests away. I saw her talk to the tree, and wipe tears off her face the same way she did at the cemetery. The lemon tree had grown with me over the years, from a thin twig to a formidable tree with enough cover to read or nap under on a hot day.

As I winced in pain, Mother read to me from the Catechism about chastity—all Christ's faithful are called to lead a chaste life, she said. She closed her eyes and led me in a prayer to the Virgin, asking me to repeat the lines after her, but I was distracted by the ache in my abdomen. Mother tapped my wrist impatiently while continuing to say the prayers.

"Kayai, my small egg, you're old enough now to know that I have been celibate since your father died," she said. "Now that you have become a woman, you will be confronted by the pleasures of the body.

"After your father died, I struggled with my faith," she continued. "Back then I wasn't a strong Christian. I went to church now and then, but I wasn't really devoted. A friend I hadn't seen since before I got married heard about your father's death and came to the funeral.

She told me that not only had she never gotten married, she had also stayed a virgin. I couldn't believe it. She told me what a joy it had been to serve God with volunteerism and good works. She said that with time, she forgot about her physical needs and became completely fed by the spiritual world. She saved me. Looking back now I realize I would have died of self-pity, going from husband to husband, trying to fill your father's shoes. I learned to keep my mind on God's work and not chase after the pleasures of the body and the fleeting things of this world."

Mother stood to pick a lemon and peeled it, throwing the peels into her flower patch. She offered me a segment, but I shook my head and she shrugged.

"You should eat lemons—I tell you all the time," she said, dividing it into small sections. "They ward off diseases."

She held each section between her lips and sucked out the juice, then crushed it in her mouth. I winced.

"Men will use you only for one thing. Now that your body is mature, sometimes you will be filled with lust and you'll be tempted, but remember that lust is ungodly. Keep your mind on God and your hands on work that fulfills your purpose on this earth and keep your body chaste.

"The Apostle Paul admonished the Corinthians to run from the sin of sex," said Mother. She placed her blistered Bible in my hands and made me read and reread the words. "Repeat after me: 'My body is the temple of the Holy Spirit, who is in you, whom you have from God, and who owns you,'" she said, and I echoed her words dutifully.

. . .

Despite Mother's intentions in the garden that day, I gradually began to learn the pleasures Tanei hinted at. At night, with a pillow between my thighs, I found waves of sensation, all through my body, begging for release. Afterward, I felt sinful and dirty, and I feared Mother would kick me out of the house if she discovered my perversions. I recited the mantra: *My body is the temple of the Holy Spirit. My body is the temple of the Holy Spirit.*

. . .

Mother had always been fiercely protective, but now she grew overbearing.

"Pull that skirt down—it's not supposed to be a miniskirt," she'd chastise me. "And there's no reason for you to dillydally in school if there are no activities. All those girls do is chatter about boys and plan sleepovers."

While my classmates spent weekends at cinemas and slumber parties, I worked with our church in orphanages, or sold produce from the farm at the local market to raise money. I had private piano lessons at home with a crotchety seventy-five-year-old English woman with arthritic fingers who had once played with the Oxford Philharmonic Orchestra. Every afternoon, she brought out a round silver clock her father had used in the war. I didn't know which war. She'd place it on the same spot on top of the piano and scream, "Sit in middle C!"

What I detested most were the mission visits to refugee camps. Each trip was full of despairing eyes. Children with bare feet and tattered clothes ran behind the missionary cars, cheering us. It ate at me, the way the children would stare at me like I was a film star while I unpacked the gifts of clothing and books for them, the way their small, coarse hands touched my long hair and my face.

I was sixteen when I got my first glimpse of a life other than what Mother dictated. That year, I met a professional photographer associated with the missionaries Mother worked with. Jason was a scruffy young American with golden curls held in a ponytail. He sometimes wore the same pair of khaki cargo pants for days.

"Don't let these white people fool you into thinking they're poor just because they look homeless," Mother said, wagging a disapproving finger. "Jason finished university and chose to come here and take photos instead of getting a job. That should tell you that he's from a very rich family. Americans have no problems in life."

"But he's happy," I said. "I want to do something I love too, something that makes me happy; I don't care how much it pays."

"We don't do frivolous things like that—do you hear me? We work, and we work in real jobs, and we work until we're dead."

"But what is the point of working until you're dead doing something you loathe, when you can work until you're dead doing something you love?"

Mother glared at me, astonished by my newfound fearlessness.

Jason taught me how to take photographs and how to process them. Mother may have disapproved of him, but he always showed her great respect, calling her ma'am, taking off his rugged boots at the door, and enjoying whatever traditional Kenyan meal was put in front of him. He told Mother photography would be a good hobby for me and she believed him.

"There's something godly about documenting nature and hunger, war, the touching moments as well as the grim ones," he said. "It's humbling."

Mother bought me my first Canon for my sixteenth birthday. She said I deserved it and listed the reasons why while I tore into the box and fought to pull the camera out of its Styrofoam packaging.

"It'll keep you busy and away from all that nonsense the girls at school get up to," she said. "And you can take photographs of our mission trips." I barely heard her, enraptured by my beautiful camera. The camera was a Canon Panorama with the name *Autoboy* in red italics and a rectangular flash on the top right side. It had a shiny metallic exterior. It had a zoom and real-time release on the shutter speed, so that I could take a picture at the optimum time, like at the exact moment when the girls would dive off the diving boards at the school's swim meet, their heads down and backs bent, swallows lifting off from their perches.

Mother said I should drop off the used film rolls at the Kodak shop in town, but I couldn't. I imagined the gruff Indian shop owner mishandling them. A cigarette perpetually drooped from the side of his mouth, and I worried the ashes would dust my precious images. Instead, I made a small darkroom, just like the American had taught me, in an empty chicken coop. I was happier in that darkroom than anywhere else, with its smell of bleach and prints soaking in warm-water baths and the negatives hanging on pegs over my head. I took the camera everywhere. For the first time in my life, I had found something of my own, something that brought me joy.

Chapter Three

I had only one aunt who wasn't afraid of Mother. Tanei was fearless and with her beside me, I could be a little rebellious. Mother said that when I was around Tanei, I grew horns.

"Why can't you be a good role model?" she asked Tanei. "Like your sisters. You're ruining Soila. I wish I could throw you out of my house."

Mother's hovering over me became far worse as Tanei grew more rebellious. By my last year of high school, it was nearly impossible for me to have any semblance of a social life. At school, I was frustrated because I was one of the only students in my class who hadn't been out "clubbing," as the girls called it. I had never worn a miniskirt, relaxed my hair, or worn shimmery eye shadow. I'd never kissed a boy. I begged Tanei to take me with her to the popular nightclub Rave. But Tanei flatly refused. The weight of trouble she would face if we got caught was knee-buckling.

Tanei had gone to clubs and had boyfriends since she was barely sixteen. Back then I was only ten and I thought she was a superhero. She would wait until she saw the lights go out in Mother's bedroom and she'd slip on her tightest leather miniskirt and ripped-up tank top over a black bra, fishnet stockings, and black high heels. After smearing on heavy eyeliner, she'd lift her frizzy hair and tie a large bow on the side with a shimmery cloth and finish with a waist-length puffy-shouldered black leather jacket. She had a large Madonna poster on one wall, and on the other, Whitney Houston, Janet Jackson, and Michael Jackson—all of them in leather jackets, as if they were in uniform.

"This room has so many demons, even a priest would be afraid to step inside it," Mother would say, her feet aligned outside the door. "I dare not come in."

As I was finishing high school, Tanei was twenty-four and had enrolled in a nursing program at Mother's behest. Nursing did not suit Tanei. She wanted to study fashion. Since Tanei was in primary school, she had filled whole sketch pads with drawings of girls in voluminous ball gowns, wedding dresses, bolero jackets, culottes, baby doll dresses, maxis, and everything in between. She told Mother she wanted to go to a fashion college but Mother wouldn't hear of it. She could be sickeningly stubborn. So stubborn that she was blinded from seeing when things didn't fit together; she believed she could force them to.

Tanei dropped out of nursing college in less than a year. She said she couldn't stand the sight of one more bedpan and would apply to a fashion polytechnic instead, but Mother said there were no job opportunities. Tanei insisted that she could start her own business. She dreamed of making wedding dresses. Mother gave her an ultimatum—"Go back to nursing college or leave my house." Tanei stomped off to her room and emerged an hour later with two suitcases. She left the house with a respectful but lukewarm goodbye. Kokoi sobbed in her room for two whole days. Tanei went to live with a couple of girlfriends who let her sleep on their couch. But after a few weeks she had a massive row with one of them over a man. The other one refused to take sides. Her clothes and shoes were thrown out of the apartment's third-floor window. That night she called Mother and apologized. She had nowhere left to go. Mother listened quietly while Tanei rattled on about her problems: the polytechnic fees Mother refused to pay, which was holding back her dream career, the lumpy couch, the jealous friends. Mother told Tanei the only help she would give her was to pray for her.

"These are the moments that build character, that teach you to dig deeper," Mother said. "There's a better person in there. Find that person. Until you do, you're not coming back to this house."

That night and for the next several weeks, Tanei lived at the downtown YWCA. My aunts visited her every day. They said Tanei had shrunk to half her size and was gnashed to bits by the mosquitoes. But it was clean and safe, and at least she wasn't on the street.

My aunts said Tanei was sorry and they begged Mother to let her come home, but Mother would walk right past them. Mother didn't want to hear about Tanei anymore. She forbade me from meeting up with her. After a while, Tanei moved out of the Y and stopped asking for money altogether. She told them not to worry, she had a boyfriend—a married wealthy lawyer who was taking good care of her. She had an apartment, a car, spending money for a wardrobe, and she was taken out for the occasional holiday when he told his wife he was on a work trip. He even offered to pay for tuition at the fashion institute. Naserian and Laioni scolded their sister about her choices, warning her about the spreading HIV wildfire.

"How many girlfriends do you think your sugar daddy's got—do you think you're the only one?"

Naserian and Laioni didn't dare tell Kokoi the truth. Instead, they told her that Tanei was doing well and finding her way out in the world. Kokoi said, "I thank God. I know with time my Nalu will forgive her, and she'll come back home."

. . .

I understood how exasperated Tanei must have been when she left home. I too wanted to escape. More than half of the girls in my class were applying to universities abroad. At first it seemed like a far-fetched idea, but as I became a young adult, I felt even more haggard from the encumbrance of Mother's dominance. Other girls may have wanted to go to study. For me, it was so that I could finally breathe.

November rolled around and we sat for the national high school exam. A high pass meant I would gain admission into any program of my choice at the elite University of Nairobi. A low pass meant I would be restricted to less prestigious and lower-ranked public universities. An under C+ average meant I couldn't go to university at all and would have to settle for an apprenticeship or a polytechnic like my aunt Tanei.

None of it bothered me. I didn't care if the Kenyan government considered me smart. I just knew that I wanted out. In my bedroom I pored over the American university catalogs I collected from the study-abroad center in town. They featured photographs of students walking or sitting cross-legged in circles, with backpacks and folders in their arms. The campuses were strewn with brick buildings that framed wide lawns. The trees in the pictures had leaves that were orange, yellow, and red, and vines climbed the buildings. It all mesmerized me.

I dreamed of America, but I didn't dare tell Mother.

"My heart skips a beat just thinking about telling her," I confessed to my aunts. "She'll never agree to it."

"Why don't you just study here for now and then you can go overseas for your graduate degree, like Rarin?" Aunt Naserian was always the most pragmatic one, the one who gave the fail-safe option in every argument. "You're too young to go off to a foreign country on your own."

When I spoke to Aunt Rarin on the phone, she didn't agree with Naserian.

"Leaving home was the best thing I ever did. Working for four years in Rwanda and then studying in Europe changed my whole view of the world," she said. "I wish I had done my undergrad overseas, left much sooner. I don't intend on coming back until I have more years of work experience outside of Kenya. You have to get out of your comfort zone and see how much the world has to offer and no, you're not too young."

I started to write my application essays, all due in January, but I wasn't really sure what I was doing. Jason the photographer was the only American I knew and he was nothing like the captivating Americans portrayed on *Dallas* and *Dynasty,* the television shows I watched with wide eyes. I was entranced by the people on those shows, their ostentatious lifestyles and unapologetic quest for money. While the slums in Nairobi, with their poverty and hunger, seemed to sprawl out wider every time I drove past, in America it seemed human suffering was nonexistent.

I asked the nuns in school for recommendation letters. I still needed money to pay for the SAT, for the college applications, and to courier the packages to the universities. The only option I had was to ask my aunts for help.

Naserian and Laioni both worked in Mother's business, managing the rose farm and the coffee plantations. Mother paid my aunts reasonably and bought each of them a used car. It was just enough compensation to keep them unmotivated to find other jobs. Single in their thirties, they didn't want to pay for rent and food and all the expenses that would come with their independence.

Afraid I too would come apart from the years of pent-up restraint and end up in the same circumstances as Tanei, Naserian and Laioni were determined to help free me from Mother's imperiousness.

When I asked them for money for the SAT, they paid for it. When I asked for fifty dollars for each of my college applications, totaling two hundred dollars, they forked it over with no complaints or ultimatums. It was as if, for everything Mother had done for them over the years, they felt compelled to fulfill my dreams, to somehow pay it forward.

In February, my grades were out. I earned an A average and could attend any public university in Kenya and study for the degree of my choice. Mother was elated. This was the worst outcome for me. Mother had always dreamed I would study at the University of Nairobi, and I knew convincing her to let me go to the States would be nearly impossible. Undoubtedly, Mother was extremely intelligent—she had built a small empire with nothing but a degree in street smarts and a secretarial course. Everyone she met in the business world was taken aback by the fact she hadn't had a higher education. And now, she wanted me to have the education she never had but she wouldn't be ready for me to get it so far away. I didn't have the courage to tell her that the University of Nairobi was not for me and that mentally, I was halfway out the door.

In March, the packages started to arrive. The first one was a fat envelope. The second one was a thin one. I learned quickly that a fat envelope meant I was accepted and a thin one meant I was rejected. The third envelope walked into the house in Mother's hands.

"Soila, you've got a big package here from a school called Barnard College. Do you know what it is about?"

I knew this was another acceptance, but where there should have been a bubble of joy inside me, I felt dread. This wasn't the way I had wanted Mother to find out.

"Soila applied to universities in America and so far, she's been accepted by one and from the looks of it, that is another one," Aunt Laioni said, breezing by with a cup of cocoa. "We are so proud of her."

Laioni had never been able to keep a secret, and for the fact she'd kept this in the vault for months I was thankful.

Mother sank onto the sofa still in her shoes, her bag next to her, like she was waiting at a station for the next train.

"I can't believe this," she said. "Soila, you applied to universities overseas and you did all this behind my back? Why?"

"Because she didn't think you'd let her go," Laioni said. "But she came to us and she spoke to Rarin, and we encouraged her."

"And who gave you the right?" Mother demanded, her eyes darting furiously from Laioni to Naserian, who had heard the commotion and appeared in the doorway.

"Soila is very smart and ambitious," Naserian jumped in. "She's going to waste her best years at the universities here with all the student protests and the professors' strikes; she'll be so demoralized. What is the point of all that when she can go so far in life?"

Mother asked for a cup of tea and I scrambled to the kitchen to boil the water. I paced up and down the kitchen biting my cuticles. This wasn't the way it was supposed to go.

Mother called me back to the living room and ordered me to sit. My aunts were gone. She asked me about it all over again, as if Laioni and Naserian hadn't spoken at all. I had practiced this speech one hundred times. I knew Mother only ever listened to facts. As I gave my defense she listened quietly, sipping her tea. When I was done, she asked me to bring her the other envelope, the first acceptance. I ran upstairs and grabbed both the acceptance and the rejection.

"Put them there," she said, pointing at the coffee table. Without even touching them, she said she would think about it.

Over the next few weeks, the fourth package arrived and it was an acceptance. In all, I had been admitted to three universities. Mother still said nothing.

The deadline for making my college decisions was looming and I was unraveling with anxiety. Mother insisted she wasn't ready to make the decision.

"The University of Nairobi won't kill you. Many have gone there, including your three aunts. I don't see why you can't go there for now."

"But uni here doesn't start until next January and we are only in April. I can't sit around for ten months waiting. What am I going to do with myself? I want to go in September."

"You have more than enough to do! You can work with the orphans at the mission, work with your aunts, there's plenty to keep you busy."

Rarin's voice of reason, my loudest advocate so far, receded into the background. Naserian and Laioni, already taking blame for scheming behind Mother's back, refused to antagonize her further, and even Kokoi, who had chimed in when she realized how desperately I wanted to go, refused to continue to push no matter how much I begged her to.

Perhaps the one person with the influence to change her mind was Father Emmanuel. After spending every Sunday at our house, he knew Mother better than anyone. If I put my trust in him, he could help persuade Mother that going to school in America was the best thing for me, I thought.

"You have to talk to my mother. Please," I begged the priest while crouched in the confession box at St. Francis of Assisi. "She won't let me go."

Father Emmanuel pointed to the shut door behind me. "Let's step out of the confessional, Soila," he instructed me. I thought I saw an odd gleam in his eyes.

"I understand how badly you want to go study in America, but you must know how difficult this will be for your mother," he said, as we sat on the second pew. I had never been alone with the priest like this, side by side with no confessional wall between us, but his presence was comforting. "Why don't you ask the university you really like to give you a deferral—one year for everyone to think this out. Nothing good ever comes out of rush decisions."

"But it's not a rush decision for me. This is what I want to do. I won't go to the university here. I won't go even if she throws me out, like Tanei."

"There's no reason for such talk," Father Emmanuel said. He spoke in a measured tone that calmed me. I saw that he had a gift, a way with counseling and guidance. He gave me pause and I found myself wanting to see the world through Mother's lens.

"God will guide her and you must accept her decision, knowing it's what's right for you. You're a lucky girl, to have a mother who cares for you so much."

I nodded. He was right. I was lucky. I had a mother whose life revolved around me since I could remember. She made sure I never lacked for a thing. She loved me so much that at times I worried if I died she would die too. But her intense love over time was so constricting it was like a python wrapped around my neck.

Father Emmanuel couldn't have known how I really felt. He knew only what he saw. On the church bench, he stretched one arm out behind my shoulders. His other hand moved over my knees. "I will talk to your mother. You can trust me. I am on your side and together we can work this out."

The thick gold ring set with a purple stone he always wore on his ring finger trailed up and disappeared underneath the fabric of my cotton skirt. Then he slid it farther up until he found the most private part of me. I tried to shove him away and run out of the church, but my legs refused to stand. His words bounced around my mind like an echo, *I am on your side*. I parted my legs wider for him and felt myself rock to his rhythm until my whole body shook with convulsions, and then I was pummeled by an avalanche of disgrace. Father brought his hand out from my skirt and placed it back gingerly on my knees.

"You're a good girl, Soila." Then he took my hand in his and cupped it over his crotch. It felt like a brick between my trembling fingers. He had his eyes shut. He leaned his head back, letting his senses drive him. A feeling of disgust slapped me hard. I snatched my hand out from underneath his and slid across to the far end of the bench. When he opened his eyes, he smiled at me.

. . .

After that, I spent most days in bed, sick with worry. Sleep was all I wanted to do; it eased the anxiety. I couldn't get the image of myself sitting in the church pew, back arched, head tilted back, legs wide open, out of my mind. My thoughts haunted me. How could something so dirty, so immoral, feel so good? Why had Father Emmanuel done this to me? He had to know that it was wrong. Why did I blame him? I was the one who sat there, I had done nothing, said nothing. These thoughts swirled around in my head all day and all night; like a pendulum, my brain shifted back and forth—*You're dirty! No, he's evil! You're weak! No, he's evil.* I didn't know what to believe, who or where to go to for the right answer. One thing I knew for sure was now I had not even the slightest chance of getting into heaven.

"What's wrong with you?" Mother asked, hovering over my bed. She would come to my bedroom every evening after work. "It's days now that you won't get out of bed or eat. I'm ordering you to get out of this bed."

I turned around and faced the wall.

Aunt Naserian was like a second mother to me. It took all my resolve not to open up to her. She would look at me differently. If

Tanei still lived at home, maybe I could have told her. But she was a loose cannon. I didn't trust that she wouldn't march up to the altar at St. Francis of Assisi on a Sunday morning when the pews were full, wielding a panga at Father Emmanuel just as she had done to her cheating ex-boyfriend years earlier.

"Did she tell you what's eating her?" I heard Mother ask Naserian outside my bedroom. "If you're hiding it because she's asked you to, you're not helping her. You need to tell me what it is you know."

"Argh! I know nothing," Naserian snapped. "She won't even look at me. She looks at the wall."

How could I tell them that Father Emmanuel had done this, and would they believe I wasn't to blame? I had brought it on myself, visiting a celibate man alone, tempting him with my youthfulness. I had worn a knee-length skirt and a fitted strappy top with no cardigan or shirt covering my shoulders. I hadn't stopped his hand from swimming up my thigh, I hadn't threatened him, or tried to run off. I told him that I needed his help.

More than a week after I visited Father Emmanuel, Mother came into my room and sat on the edge of my bed. "If this is about going to America then you may go," Mother said. "I won't have my only child dying from depression over this. Your father always said he wanted you to study in the best universities in the world. Maybe God's answering his prayers from the grave."

I turned around to look at her, not believing what I heard. The Mother sitting next to me wasn't the stubborn woman I knew. This Mother was yielding, even tender. Maybe she was afraid.

"Why did you think that you couldn't tell me that this is what you wanted?" she asked. "Am I such a monster that you would go to your aunts and ask them for advice and money, rather than come to me?"

"No, Yeyo," I said. "I just didn't think you would want me to leave; you won't even let me go to the cinema."

"That is not the same," Mother said, shaking her head as if in disbelief. "Going to university and going to the cinema with your silly classmates are not the same things." She sighed. "Part of me doesn't know if I can trust the universe with you, but the other part tells me that you have already shown yourself to be truly mature by doing all this by yourself. I have to believe that you won't let me down."

Father Emmanuel had talked about miracles from the pulpit. I realized that I was watching a miracle unfold in front of my eyes.

"Which one do you like best?" Mother asked, holding all my acceptance letters in her hand.

I told her that I liked the all-girls college. I wasn't sure whether it was because I had attended an all-girls school since I was six, or because it was in New York City, which seemed to me like a place where I could finally escape.

"Good," Mother said. "I like this one too. There's only one thing. I don't want you to go this year. I've prayed over it and meditated. You're not ready. You're too young. Let's give it another year."

Underneath her collar I saw the bright red welts on the back of her neck. The joy that had swept over me just a moment earlier, joy that I never seemed able to hold on to, was leaving me once again.

"I just can't. I can't be here another year," I said. I started to cry, bawling uncontrollably. Weeping had become second nature, like breathing, ever since Father Emmanuel had put his hands on me. "I can't survive another year here, not with him around me."

"Who? Who are you talking about?" Mother said, straightening her back, staring down at me like an uncoiled cobra.

As soon as the words left my mouth, I knew I should have never mentioned it. Mother was scary in her lightest moments. In her upset moments she was terrifying. The room filled with a frightening darkness, like a solar eclipse.

"Who is 'him'?"

"No one. Don't worry about it, it's nothing," I said.

"Is there a boy who's bothering you? Soila, may God give me strength if you have been messing around with boys."

I lay back down and turned to face the wall like I had done for weeks.

"I'll be twenty next year. I'll be the oldest first-year college student in the world."

"Soila, if you don't start to behave and act your age, I'm going to change my mind about all this. I don't respond well to tantrums—you know this well. I want you to make yourself busy doing something worthwhile for the next year. There's no hurry. Next September you'll be ready to go away on your own."

She laid the letters and catalogs next to my head on the pillow and walked out of my room in silence, the same way she'd walked in. I got up tentatively, for the first time in days, and followed her downstairs.

Father Emmanuel was visiting. He was sitting in the living room in his black shirt and white collar, a glass of fresh juice in front of him. When I saw him, I took a step back to hide behind the door. The sight of him swallowed me up, buried me in a new wave of guilt and shame. He was nodding as Mother served him up a heavy dinner of pork and potatoes. Unable to bear the sight of him, I went back upstairs and lay back in my bed, thinking about a place where I would never have to see him nodding and smiling with Mother again. A place, I imagined, where the people were always happy, where the lush trees billowed over vast landscaped lawns, where the air wasn't dusty and the roads weren't sinking, where nobody seemed tired from the weight of the sun and their daily struggles.

At the same time, Mother, Kokoi, my aunts, my morning prayers, and Mother's lemon tree in our back garden were the only things I had ever really known; it terrified me that in a year I would leave them all behind. But for now, the only thing I could do to keep from getting ill at the slightest thought of Father Emmanuel was to keep myself so busy that nineteen would turn to twenty seemingly overnight. There was one other thing I would have to do. Mother would hate it, and we would fight over it every week for a year. She would call me a sinner. She would threaten to rescind her promise to let me go. She would stay silent at me and not even say good morning or good night. I didn't care. If I was going to survive the year, I knew that I could never set foot in the church of St. Francis of Assisi ever again. I also knew that I could never tell anyone why.

Part Two

Chapter Four

Mother didn't take me to America. I told her that I didn't need her to bring me to school like a five-year-old on their first day of kindergarten and she didn't fight me. For most of the year I kept busy to distract my mind from flashbacks. I got my driver's license and volunteered in the mission orphanage. I studied Spanish, and took hundreds of photographs of wide-open landscapes and the tiny faces of the orphans. If they could be happy despite everything, I knew I had to try to move on, to forgive myself, to be happy too. As my departure approached, Mother lost her appetite. I overheard her tell Kokoi as they sat in the living room one night that something had shifted in me. "She's got a darkness in her and a sorrowful spirit," she said. "And for the first time since she was born, I don't know how to help her." Another time, I heard her cry to Kokoi that nothing that had happened in her life until that moment had ever required more courage, but she would respect my wish to travel alone.

At the airport we all cried, except Mother. Kokoi buried her face in her cotton kanga and swore she'd be dead before she saw me again.

"Nobody is dying," Mother said, rolling her eyes at Kokoi.

Mother's fierceness had always been my stronghold. I watched her standing tall, the constant anchor of my family, next to my sobbing kokoi, aunts, and Princess, who was a tearful mess. Mother wore an embroidered black chiffon scarf I had made for her in a high school home science class. I had picked out the fabric myself at a Punjabi shop in the garment district. I used delicate satin threads in different shades of red to embroider roses across the length of the fabric and stitched in a sprinkling of pearls. It took a whole school term to finish it. When I gave it to her, she was so proud of it. She wore it to formal dinners and it added a simple yet extravagant detail to her modest clothing. That night at the airport, she had it draped loosely over her hair and then thrown over her shoulders, like a grieving widow. Yet, while everybody crumbled around her, she didn't shed a tear. She was everybody's vessel, everybody's life jacket.

I always believed nothing bad could happen to me as long as I had Mother. But then Father Emmanuel took advantage of me. He knew I needed his help and took something in return, something that he knew I never meant to give him. I could have confessed in that moment, but I wasn't going to let myself weigh Mother down with more than she already had to deal with from halfway across the world. Leaving my home felt like a rebirth. I was being severed from her womb all over again. I was being swept away from her all over again, just as I had when my father's death left her a shell of a woman incapable of hugging another human being. The thought of it all made me break down in tears. Then, uncharacteristically, Mother pulled me into her arms, held me close to her bosom, and urged me not to cry.

"You're going to be okay," she whispered. "There will be so many other international students there, all of them just as far away from their families. You'll see. You're starting a whole new life. How exciting! Think how many people would kill for a chance like that?"

It is true, I thought. I was getting a fresh chapter. Of course,

Mother didn't know that I was carrying with me a secret bigger than my suitcase, one I wished I could just leave behind.

. . .

I was twenty years old when I set foot in the chaos of New York City on a late-summer morning. The first several weeks at college were spent acclimatizing. Everything was different, from the bar food to the casual American way of dress. At home, the British had left us with a buttoned-up culture of suits and ties and stockings worn every day. I struggled with the rolled tongue of the American accent that made every word sound slurred. I hated having to share a dorm room because I'd always had my own bedroom. My roommate, Kirsten, was an Asian girl from Minnesota. When her white parents walked into our dorm room on the first day loaded with pillows, sheets, and towels, I realized she had been adopted.

"We emptied the whole store, honey," her mother said. They started to bicker about how much stuff she'd need and what could realistically fit into her closet, until I cleared my throat to let them know I was in the room.

"Oh my! Who's this?" the woman said, turning around. She was mousy looking and both she and her husband seemed too old to have a child Kirsten's age. "I'm sorry, honey, we didn't even see you there."

I introduced myself, saying that I was from Kenya. No, my parents hadn't brought me. Yes, I had found my way to Bed Bath & Beyond and bought my own bedding just fine, and yes, I was finding my way around campus fine too. Yes, I could understand the Metro map. Yes, I spoke very good English. Yes, I was articulate.

"Oh my! Isn't it just exceptional," Kirsten's mother said, looking over at her husband, hands together as if about to clap. "I mean, who would have thought. Isn't it amazing, honey? Kirsten, you're going to be living with someone all the way from Africa!"

Kirsten turned away from her mother, wincing. Later, they invited me to dinner with them. I said I wasn't hungry. But the truth was, I didn't want to sit through another minute of her patronizing tone. I was shocked that this woman, who didn't know me at all, would assume that I was stupid and helpless in New York because I was from "Africa"—like it was one country and my Africanness made me less capable than she was.

When she came back from dinner, Kirsten sat on her bed and started to fold her clothing into separate piles of T-shirts, jeans, and dresses.

"Look, I'm sorry about my mom," Kirsten said awkwardly. "She can be so out of touch. She doesn't know many people who aren't white. I'm for sure the only Korean person she knows."

She laughed. I laughed too. I appreciated her apology on her mom's behalf. In a small way I empathized. I knew what it was like to have a mother who saw the world through only her lens and who said all the wrong things. After that Kirsten and I became friendly enough to have quiet conversations about our classes and discovering New York. She was studying biochemistry. She said she wanted to get into the drug research field. Kirsten was sweet, but deeply introverted. She sometimes wore her headphones in the room even when I was only reading a book and hardly making a peep. It was as if to exist, she had to be in complete isolation. I felt constantly that I was walking on eggshells when I was around her.

We managed to be friendly, but I met my first real friend at college a few weeks later. As the brochure Mother and I pored over had promised, the third week of September was when student groups on campus hosted social orientation week. The students set up booths along the pathways crisscrossing the quad, with neon posters advertising their activities. I trudged past all the booths, slumped under the weight of my heavy backpack and uninterested in any of them. But as I walked past the Organization of Soul Sisters, I noticed a girl wearing red sneakers and a red plaid shirt tied into a bow at her waist, exposing her belly button. She had long braids and twirled a lollipop in her mouth. *She looks like a hussy,* I thought spitefully. But in truth, she was strikingly beautiful.

"Hey! Pump the brakes," she said, stepping right in front of me. Her face was too close, and her voice cracked in my ears. She poked my shoulder gently. I didn't like it. "What's with the mood? Who peed in your cornflakes this morning? Where are you going?"

"To the African Students Association." I felt the urge to muffle her, to stop the words spluttering out of her mouth like a wet cough.

"What's that accent? Are you one of those Blacks who went to Andover with the WASPs and learned to speak the King's English?"

"I'm African."

"Okay. So, you're not African American—but are you Black?" she said. "You look Black to me."

I nodded. "My name is Soila."

"Cool. I'm Leticia. You can call me Ticia. I've been doing recruiting with Donna over there." She pointed her lollipop at an exceedingly tall woman standing behind the booth. Donna had the sinewy physique of a Kenyan runner. Her hair was styled in cornrows. She waved cordially at me, and I waved back reluctantly.

Leticia pulled me up to the booth, her lollipop jammed into one cheek.

"Grab these—our calendar is in there. . . ." She smacked a few brochures into my open hand.

"I don't know if I'll have enough time," I said coldly.

"Oh please, it's a social club," she said. Her lollipop was in my face. "Some people sign up for four or five at once."

"How long have you been at this school?" I snapped. "You seem to know everything."

"I'm a sophomore," she said cheerfully, undeterred by my aloofness. "But even before I started, I did the summer program here. I met loads of people and learned everything about the campus before I ever had my first lecture."

She said she was studying literature with a major in creative writing. I felt my impatience with her start to slightly wane. She stood too close and had poked me, but she was so confident it was electrifying. Almost against my will—I was childishly determined not to like her—I was curious about what she knew that I didn't.

"You're lucky," I said cautiously. "I feel so lost."

"Girl, don't worry, okay? I got you," she said. "Just like Donna did with me when I first got here. Come to our mixer tomorrow night at Donna's apartment. Her address is on the brochure."

"Okay. I'll be there," I said, smiling.

In a strange way, it felt like I had run into Mother. Leticia was direct, stubborn, and forceful—all the dynamics I had fled from seven thousand miles away. I wanted to never see her again but as I turned to walk away, I realized this was the first time I'd really smiled since I had arrived in America. Kokoi always said that most people spent their whole lives smiling with their mouths. "Only a few of us are blessed to find the kind of happiness that makes a person smile with their eyes," she said. In those first weeks in New York, I smiled with my mouth through the myriad of introductions and at the spectacular sights. Then, unexpectedly, Leticia came smashing through my walls. She rattled my nerves. Yet, despite my annoyance, I couldn't deny I wanted to get to know her. And even though I wasn't sure whether she genuinely wanted to get to know me, or if I was just another recruit for her student association, it made me smile from within. I smiled with my eyes and I couldn't wait to tell Kokoi about it.

. . .

In my first semester, I enrolled in a photography class. My first assignment was to interview a stranger about their life and take a unique portrait of them.

"What's unique is subjective," Professor Bergman said. She was uniquely beautiful herself, with eyes as round as coins and thick, straight brown hair. She was tall, with pronounced collarbones, yet she wasn't so thin that it made you want to offer her a meal. "Unique is what you want it to be—now go out into the city with open eyes and create art."

After my first class, I went to see Professor Bergman about camera options. She showed me a catalog with different digital cameras and kits for interchangeable lenses. She spoke about budget-conscious choices that were well suited to skill growth. Bergman searched my eyes for a hint of understanding, but I lowered them, even though I knew a little about cameras.

"You don't have to show everyone you know everything!" Mother had said. "Listen with your ears, talk less—you don't know everything."

"You don't need a super-expensive piece of equipment when you're starting out," Professor Bergman said, flipping the pages of the catalog. "You want an SLR 35mm camera with adjustable f-stops and shutter speeds, preferably high-speed continuous shooting—as many frames as you can get per second—and high precision. If you can afford it, a digital SLR would be best. You can avoid film altogether and process your photos on our school computers with Photoshop."

I nodded. It was a lot to take in and I was glad I had shut my mouth and let her do the talking, because I realized now that there was so much I didn't know. Unlike the Canon Mother bought me when I turned sixteen, these cameras had a small built-in color monitor on the back. "This helps you view your images on the go," Bergman explained. "You want something lightweight, and something that will be compatible with other lenses so that, as you get more advanced, you're able to change lenses."

When I got my old Canon, I had stared all night at the camera sitting on my dresser, worrying that if I shut my eyes, it would all have been a dream when I awoke the next morning. But now, my little treasure paled in comparison to the new-generation cameras in Bergman's catalog. I had brought it with me to show her I already had a good camera but I didn't dare pull it out of my backpack and I readily lied that I didn't have a camera.

A few days later, I stood armed with Bergman's information at a shop on Broadway, looking at the cameras. Nikons, Canons—they were the only two I would consider, but they were also the priciest. The salesman chirped in my ear about 45-point Area AF and EOS and power boosters. I imagined Mother standing behind him with a camera in each hand as though she were sizing up the plumpest pumpkin.

When my choice was made, I walked right past Mother's apparition and purchased the most delicate yet resilient Canon. It had a two-tone exterior, silver and black. It was compatible with all other Canon lenses, and even popular with professional photographers. Best of all, it didn't require film. As much as I had enjoyed being lost in my thoughts in my darkroom, I also couldn't wait to experience the instant gratification of snapping an image and being able to view it immediately.

. . .

I found inspiration for the portrait assignment in photographs I had seen of the Meatpacking District from the 1980s. One early Friday morning, I took the train from 116th Street down to 14th and spent hours wandering around. It was hard to believe that this was the same neighborhood I had seen in those photographs. Now, more than a decade later, I saw the signs of gentrification all around me. Burly men in blood-smeared white aprons slung large sides of beef over their shoulders in the early-morning light and the streets were lined with delivery trucks and forklifts. But most of the meat factories had shut down. Empty, derelict buildings were being remodeled as residential lofts, high-end stores, and nightclubs. Rents climbed as investment bankers scooped up the units, and the owners of businesses that had stood in the neighborhood for years were worried about their future.

"Giuliani is determined to take us out like trash," the owner of a deli told me. "Koch sanitized us. He cleaned out the dingy bars and S and M dungeons. He ripped the soul right out of this neighborhood. But in the end, I suppose all things must change."

Still, even sanitized, the neighborhood hadn't lost the beating pulse of the city's underbelly. I photographed the deli owner in the light of day, and when I visited again at night, prostitutes posed in their stilettos and fishnets and bone-straight wigs, walking the cobblestone streets in front of his shop.

I submitted a manila envelope of my Meatpacking District photographs to Professor Bergman's cubbyhole. Whatever her feedback would be, I was proud of the work I had done. A few days later, I received a call from Bergman. She wanted to see me, she said, in her tiny office on campus.

"There's an anonymous donor," Bergman began when I sat down in her office. "A wealthy family. They want to offer a grant to an African student. I suggested you. I haven't seen this kind of talent in a long time. I mean, the way you shot the deli owner, the girls on the street . . . you could pitch this to *Life* magazine."

Bergman was dressed in a long beige cashmere turtleneck that dropped all the way to her lower thighs, thick dark leggings, and an expensive pair of tan horseback riding–style boots. There was something about her that seemed wealthy, even if she wasn't trying.

"Is photography something you'd consider for a career?" She studied me carefully. When I hesitated to answer, she pressed, "Is it because you don't think you can make a good living from it?"

"Professor Bergman, it's not that simple," I said. "My mother sent me here to get a business degree. Photography isn't an option for me."

"But has your mother even seen your work?" she asked.

"She has," I said. "I took a lot of photos back home. I've done portraits of malnourished families and dying animals, landscape photos of dry rivers, everything. I even once photographed a camel with no hump."

"What do you mean, no hump?" she said, removing her glasses and looking at me with curious eyes.

"It was emaciated, skin and bones, and its hump was deflated," I said. "It would have been the saddest thing if I hadn't met the family who owned it. They were dying too."

Tears filled Bergman's eyes. It was something I had to learn to get used to in this new country, the softness of hearts—grieving dead pets, catching and releasing spiders and fish. In Kenya, we stomped on spiders and swept them out of the house with brooms. I didn't want to tell her that it would take one hundred times more than a dying camel to get me to shed a tear.

"I'm sorry, I don't mean to cry," she said, perhaps sensing that her tears surprised me. "But the pain, the poverty, in Africa is just so raw."

"It's okay," I said, not really sure what I was excusing—her tears, or the poverty in my continent.

"Well, keep taking good photos and pitch them to magazines, to newspapers. As far as the scholarship, I'll advise it goes to a student who's doing this as a major. I think it's only fair, don't you think?"

"Absolutely," I said, relieved.

A few days later, I was still excited enough by my professor's praise that I made the mistake of mentioning our conversation to Mother when we spoke on the phone.

"I want to do this," I said. "Photography gives me a sense of satisfaction that I don't get from anything else. Professor Bergman thinks I could be very successful with it."

"Professor Bergman thinks?" Mother asked, and I clenched my jaw. "Honestly, Soila, absolutely not. Those Americans are going to fill your head with all kinds of ideas. Next week you'll take a class in tap dance and they'll tell you that you have potential and then you'll want to perform in a circus. And it's not about the money either. Money is not the issue here; they only think you need it because you're African. This is about your future, Soila. Taking pictures is no way to make a living. You will study business, as we discussed."

A few months later, I shot a photograph of a late-night candlelight vigil for a med student who'd jumped in front of the 1 train at Cathedral Parkway station. The story was newsworthy because the victim had been a young, high-achieving African American man who had succumbed to the pressures of his medical school residency. I had lived in New York long enough by now to understand that someone who looked like him was more frequently in the news because of crime or police brutality, so I was interested in what the vigil would be like. The young man's mother was covered in black lace under the moonlight, the light from the candle she held casting a shadow on her face. Her husband was slim and agile, speaking with quick gestures and clipped words. He said his son would have made a good doctor. He didn't say why or how he knew. He just knew.

I sent my photographs to the *Post* and the *Daily News* on a dare when Leticia said she could guarantee one of the papers would buy at least one of them. That evening, I got a call from the *Post*. It was a sleepy-sounding editor who said he was fact-checking the details. He said they already had photographs sent in by newswires and freelancers. I refused to get my hopes up but still, sleep came fitfully. At dawn I ran down to the newsstand in my pajamas and bought the *Post*. My photograph had made it in. My name, which most Americans couldn't pronounce, was printed in black-and-white in the caption and I would get paid. I finally had proof that this was no hobby. I mailed the newspaper clip home to Mother. I never heard a word from her about it.

. . .

At the end of our first semester, Leticia and I decided to get an apartment together. I had made more friends over time, but mostly, I loved my friendship with Leticia. She was smart and easygoing, unpredictable yet reliable. We spent evenings eating cookie dough in her dorm room, or buying nail polish in silly, glittery colors from Duane Reade at midnight. We had become practically inseparable. And we were both happy to leave our current roommates.

One night, Leticia announced that she needed some Swedish Fish immediately, or she would die. We headed out on one of our late-night trips to the bodega. As Leticia and I roamed the aisles in search of sweets, her face grew tense. I noticed her glancing out the corners of her eyes at the shop clerk who was trailing us around the store. I understood her irritation. In Kenya, I had grown up watching Mother boycott stores owned by Indian merchants. She had grown up in a colonial generation where Indians were more important than Black people in the social hierarchy and she had seen the unfair treatment that was meted out to poor-looking Black customers, including having their bags searched. As a child I had been with Mother in an Indian-owned jewelry store when she was dressed in unassuming clothing. She had asked about the price of an item that was in the window display and was immediately told she couldn't afford it. I had seen her walk out insulted yet amused, saying, "Does he know I can buy that whole shop if I wanted to?" But it wasn't always like that. In fact, most vendors trailed after us, nagging, offering us discounts on goods, the choicest produce, and best cuts of meats.

Leticia was chewing on her tongue holding back an angry outburst. We purchased our snacks and left the store. As soon as we were on the sidewalk, Leticia began to fume.

"Did you see that guy? Following us around? I hate that, people always assuming Black people in their stores are there to shoplift."

"Don't let it bother you. Some Indian store owners in Kenya treat Blacks like that as well," I said, shrugging it off. "Especially if you look poor."

"What are you talking about? This isn't about class. I could have strolled in there with a Harvard stamp on my forehead. Oprah could have walked in there and if they didn't recognize her, it would have been the same. And by the way, it's crazy that you don't think it should bother you. It's racial. It only matters that you're Black. Don't touch anything unless you're going to pick it up and buy it. And if a store clerk accuses you of shoplifting and tells you to leave, just go, because you won't win by mouthing off about your innocence."

I was stunned by Leticia's take on what seemed like a soft issue. Store clerks had followed me around in New York, now that I thought about it, like when I had gone to Bed Bath & Beyond to purchase my bedding. But I couldn't be sure that was racial bias. Surely these situations were more nuanced than Leticia painted them, I thought. I wanted to tell her that it didn't always have to be racism. I wanted to trust my own perception. But maybe she was right. After all, we were just a couple of girls in jeans, decent brand-name sneakers, and school sweatshirts. We certainly weren't raggedy. So why had we needed a set of eyes fixed on us? I was confused by the experience, mostly by why I couldn't seem to get as upset as Leticia. Why wasn't I as incensed? Why was she so offended? Why was she burdening herself with a small gesture of discrimination? Wasn't it tiring to walk around picking on every unfairness? I didn't want to live a life where I second-guessed every moment—Did I not get the job because I was Black? Did I not get served first because I was Black? Those were the things I wanted to say. But I didn't want to upset her further than she already was so I nodded in agreement and stuffed my mouth with Swedish Fish as we walked quietly back to campus, each of us lost in our own thoughts.

Leticia and I moved out of the dorms in the break between semesters and into a grimy apartment on the fifth floor of a building on the Upper West Side near campus. Our apartment had a lopsided kitchen sink and lime gunk that wouldn't come off the tub tiles.

"Honey! You have to put your back into it," Leticia's mother, Mrs. Hopkins, said. Leticia's parents had driven down from Upstate New York to help with the move.

Mrs. Hopkins had the same build as Leticia, just enough bust, petite, yet with curves and athletic shoulders, and in her cream-colored capri pants and red patent leather flats, she looked half her age and was just as spirited, though more assertive. Mr. Hopkins, with his salt-and-pepper goatee and a tweed flat cap and brown leather jacket, trailed quietly behind, seemingly not wanting to get caught in any situation that might arise between mother and daughter.

Together, Leticia's parents were so attractive they could have been prom king and queen in high school in their heyday. Leticia was their only child and they regularly drove five hours to New York City "to see our baby girl," Mr. Hopkins said.

"Why can't you just stay on campus and request a new roommate?" Mother had said when I'd called her to say I wanted to move out of the dorms to share an apartment with Leticia. She asked about the safety of the neighborhood, the proximity to the subway, and if the apartment had a gas stove.

"Too many people have died from burst gas cylinders. And no using pressure cookers either. Those things can kill you."

"Yeyo—the gas is piped here; it's not like at home," I said. "The pressure cookers aren't dangerous either. Everything's upgraded here."

"Don't give me an attitude because you're in America," she said. "I'm not going to fly my daughter's body home in a casket. Honestly, I can't see what's wrong with the dormitory."

I knew that Mother would love Leticia. I talked about her on the phone endlessly. I said she was confident and loud, but she was also hilarious and smart and that with her, I felt safer. "Even the boys won't come near her. She cares for me like I'm her younger sister, even though we're the same age," I said.

"This is how those Black Americans are," Mother said, on the phone. "Shyness is not one of their qualities. But I'm happy that you have found a loyal friend."

Leticia took me with her to Rochester on the Greyhound bus for Christmas. It had only been four months since I'd arrived and I couldn't wait to experience an American Christmas. Leticia and I spent the night in her childhood bedroom. Her parents hadn't changed it much. The walls were still hot pink. There were trophies and framed photographs of Leticia with other girls standing on a platform in her swimsuit receiving a medal, in her cheerleading outfit on a human pyramid. Giant posters of the Backstreet Boys and Boyz II Men were plastered on one of the walls in her room. It was hard to make Leticia believe that somewhere on the equator, on the East African coast, I had been crazy about the same boy bands. I recited the boys' names, pointing at each one's face like they were my brothers, and Leticia squealed with delight. We looked at Kodak albums of her life from back when she had thick pigtails and Chuck E. Cheese birthday parties. There was her prom night, when she wore a frilly, peachy dress and big hair with a dazzling slide comb. She went with Darius Knight, captain of the football team, top student, all-rounder. Leticia said Darius wasn't her first kiss but she let her parents believe he was, because he was the only boy they thought worthy of her.

That night, lying next to Leticia on her childhood bed, listening to her breathing softly, I thought about how different our worlds were. We had ended up at nearly the same place in most ways—we were both ambitious and driven. But Leticia had grown up with birthday parties and prom dresses and she had been smothered with hugs and kisses. I had never had a birthday party that I could remember except from old photographs. I hadn't attended prom, worn a big dress, or slow-danced with a captain of anything.

Leticia said her mother would shamelessly kick up dust at Leticia's school for the slightest persecution, like when Leticia was ordered to run around the soccer pitch ten times. Her teammate had been red-carded for her hot temper and punished with five laps around the field. Leticia, frustrated that the coach was being unreasonable, mouthed off at him and received ten laps.

The school principal explained that Leticia wasn't made to run longer because she was Black, but because talking back to teachers was unacceptable. It didn't matter to Leticia's mother. As far as she was concerned, the white girl had gotten off easier. Mrs. Hopkins's notorious protests at the school embarrassed Leticia, but Leticia knew they came from a place of immense love.

On Christmas, there was no gloomy meditation garden. The Hopkinses had the kind of celebration I had watched on television growing up, with wrapped gifts, stockings, and a giant feast for dinner. Leticia's father, dressed in a large denim apron printed with DAD's

WORLD-FAMOUS BBQ, kept vigil over a gigantic turkey he was roasting in the oven. Every twenty minutes he would saunter into the kitchen, pick up the turkey baster, and fill it with liquid stock then pour it slowly over the turkey and say, "Ah . . . looking good!" It made me chuckle—the way he congratulated himself. In such rare moments when I spent time with other fathers, I would think about my own. I knew he used to cook in the days when men didn't dare step into a kitchen.

Mrs. Hopkins had given us a list of tasks to take care of while she ran to collect all the grandparents and bring them to the house for the day's big meal. Leticia, in turn, had promoted herself to head chef and was ordering me to cut this and that while stirring a pot filled with collard greens and ham hocks.

"Are you okay?" Leticia said. She'd stopped stirring and was placing the lid back on a heavy cast-iron pot that her grandmother had passed down to her mother. One day it would be passed down to Leticia.

"I guess sometimes when I see other dads, I kind of miss mine," I said.

"I'm so sorry to hear that," Leticia said. "It must be hard."

"I barely remember him. It's kind of silly that it even bothers me at all."

The rich aromas circulating in the kitchen made me nostalgic for the times I had cooked with my aunts and Princess, laughing and gossiping, their eyes tearing up from the onions and their foreheads gleaming with sweat while they rolled thick dough for chapati.

Suddenly there wasn't enough oxygen in the room. I stepped out through the kitchen door into the cold winter breeze. So many memories were bubbling to the surface, triggered by everything about this holiday. Though it was nice to be welcomed into someone's home, unsettling feelings were piling up in a crescendo so loud I thought my brain would explode. Mr. Hopkins and his fatherliness, reminding me of the dad I never had. The idea of Leticia's relatives coming over to her house to sit around a table for a large meal and give thanks just like we did at home. Father Emmanuel. I shut my eyes against the memory of the priest's hand on my knees.

"Hey, what's the matter?" Leticia had stepped outside to check on me. "I'm worried about you."

"Nothing," I said. "I think I'm feeling a little homesick."

"Is that all?" she asked, rubbing my back like I was a colicky child. "You're not yourself, all of a sudden."

I hesitated. I had only known Leticia for four months but here in the kitchen of her family home, I felt safe enough to tell her the truth.

"Seeing your dad made me think of the dad I always wanted to have. When I was growing up I had someone who is a close confidant of my mother. I thought I could trust him but in the end it turned out he wasn't . . ." I trailed off.

"What do you mean?" Leticia asked, tightening the ties on her mother's apron. "Did he hurt you?"

"He's my family's priest," I said. "He is the first person she goes to for counsel. When I got accepted to come to school here, I was worried that she wouldn't let me, so I went to him to ask him to talk to her, and everything went wrong."

"What do you mean? Did he rape you?" Leticia asked.

"No, no, I mean, he . . . kind of touched me. I was so ashamed. I still am."

"Soila! My God, don't you understand that you were molested?" Leticia's hands were on her cheeks, her eyes as large as an owl's. "That's what all the victims say—that it was their fault, that they're ashamed. It wasn't your fault."

Once again, the pendulum was swinging back and forth in my mind. Father Emmanuel didn't have a gun to my head. I wasn't a young child. Yet for the life of me, I couldn't explain why I hadn't been able to stop him. His words, *I am on your side,* still played like a soundtrack in my mind. I remembered the feeling of frozenness, limp legs, being unable to scream, unable to slap the lust off his face.

"I was an adult. I could have stopped him," I said. "I should have. But I didn't."

"No, no, no," Leticia said frantically. "You're the victim, *you* are. He's the predator. It's not your fault."

"You don't understand. It's complicated." I closed my eyes and took a deep breath. "I kind of liked it," I admitted, hardly believing the words were coming out of my mouth. "So, what does that make me?"

"Soila, this is not your fault," Leticia said, covering her face with both palms. "Yes, of course you liked it. Your body responds involuntarily. That doesn't make it right. Why didn't you tell someone? Why didn't you tell your mom?"

"Like I said, I wanted to come to the States, and he's the only one my mom listens to," I said.

"So, he used you," she said. "Why don't you see the college counselor? This kind of shit could affect you your whole life. You should talk to a professional."

"No. I'm definitely not going to tell some stranger all my secrets. How will that help me?" I said. "I mean, I know he deliberately used me but I let him."

"What do you think would happen if you told your mom?"

"I honestly don't know. When it happened, I was sure my mother would be furious with me, because she's very religious and he is her confidant, her rock. Would she take my side, or would she say I had tempted a 'pious' man?" I said. "Then I started to think of it as a self-preservation thing—I couldn't rock the boat when I was so close to having my dream. I keep telling myself, well, I can always tell her one day, but not today, not this year. What good would it do? What's done is done."

"No, it's not!" Leticia said, slapping her hand hard on the kitchen screen door. "He shouldn't be around other young girls. You can't be sure that he's not done this before or isn't doing it again."

"But this would crush my mother. I wouldn't want her to feel that she failed somehow. Or I failed her."

Leticia walked up to me and hugged me gently. "I'm so sorry, Soila."

I didn't know if I'd done the right thing by telling her about Father Emmanuel. I wanted so desperately to just begin a new life in America, but the past was haunting me. Later that evening, as I sat with the Hopkins family around their brick fireplace drinking eggnog and half-listening to them reminiscing about stories I didn't know, I saw how Leticia looked at me and I couldn't be sure if she was judging me or pitying me.

Chapter Five

The second semester of my freshman year was over before I knew it. I had enrolled in several introductory business and economics courses as part of my business degree. I knew Mother was pleased with what I was learning, but I found the classes deadly dull. Still, I felt accomplished to have reached the end of my first year of college, and with good enough grades that I would be allowed to take on three courses that summer and additional courses for each semester of my sophomore year. Finishing my freshman year at twenty-one bothered me and I was determined to graduate with Leticia, who was already a school year ahead of me at twenty years old. I was so insecure about my age that I refused to acknowledge my twenty-first birthday even to Leticia, who only found out because she walked in on me having a phone conversation with Aunt Tanei about what I was doing on my big day.

I whiled away my days that summer attending lectures and working a minimum wage job selling hooded varsity sweatshirts and other school merchandise at the campus bookstore. Leticia was working as a camp counselor near her parents' home in Rochester for the summer, and so without her on campus, I was spending more time with my other friends, especially the African students. We would bring a picnic to Central Park on the weekends, feasting on traditional dishes from our childhoods, supplementing ingredients to make up for what wasn't available in American stores. The Nigerians couldn't find yams, cassava, or palm nut, so instead, they pounded sweet potato and ate fufu with creased faces.

"It's better than nothing," they'd say, and we all would nod silently, as if agreeing with an ancestral spirit. "It's better than completely throwing away our traditions."

We ate lounging on picnic blankets and talked about our memories of our homes, and about being in America. While Leticia remained my closest friend, the African students gave me a sense of connection to childhood experiences only they could understand.

I spent the rest of my free time that summer taking photographs in the city. It was the way I studied New York, first around the parks, museums, and Wall Street. I shot the lanterns in Chinatown, Bethesda Fountain, the sketch artists at Grand Central Station. I shot Lady Liberty at dusk from the Staten Island Ferry with the sun falling behind her and then got back on the ferry and shot the city's radiating nighttime skyline.

On clear days, I took photographs of the *Charging Bull* of Wall Street and the New York Stock Exchange Building with the giant statue of George Washington. I walked down the narrow paths between the historic banks, taking photographs in frog perspective so that all the buildings appeared to mesh together like planted spears.

It was only after I downloaded the images for editing a week later that I realized I hadn't paid attention to the humans in the photographs. The people on Wall Street were different from the rest of the New Yorkers. They walked with their faces down, hurried, and their clothing was darker. I imagined myself in the photographs, rushing to work in a gray pantsuit, entering a big building through rotating doors. I couldn't imagine ever being happy dressed like that, or sitting at a desk all day. But that's what Mother wanted for me. That drab, dour existence was completely different from the rest of New York—bright colors and the chaos of Times Square and wonderment of the art.

With time, as I got bolder, I traveled to the outer boroughs, becoming enchanted by the cultural enclaves, the way different ethnicities occupied a space and made it fully their own. Mother would never understand why I loved being out on the complicated streets of New York with my camera, but I wanted to make sense of this city. It seemed to me like an impossible place. Nowhere else in the world would a glassy-eyed homeless-looking man share a park bench with a clean-shaven man in a pressed suit and gold watch whose face was buried in the wide pages of *The Wall Street Journal*.

I found myself riding the subway to far-off neighborhoods, strolling through a Hispanic neighborhood in Queens, eating empanadas at ten A.M., soaking it all in. On the F train to Brooklyn, the conductor called Bedford-Stuyvesant. I had never been there but had heard it was something to be seen. I found Carl Jefferson, owner of the oldest barbershop in a beat-down section of Bedford-Stuyvesant—JEFFERSON CUTS, SINCE 1930.

"I'll never leave this block," Carl said, hands trembling on an electric shaver over a little boy's head. The boy's father was listening to Carl's stories, seemingly unbothered by the shaver teetering too close to his son's ear. "It's all about gentrification now. It's whitening the place, is what it is. I've been cutting hair since Hoover was in the White House. They'll have to come over here with a digger and dig me out. Only person who'll get me off this block is Death himself—put that down next to my photo when you get it printed."

Carl said he'd met more famous people than he would have remembered had they not left autographed black-and-white photographs on the wall.

"Look at this place—losing it will mean losing all these memories." He pointed at a photograph of a light-skinned Black woman with soft curls. "Lena Horne was so beautiful I could've eaten off the chair she sat on."

A few men, waiting for a haircut with their newspapers folded in their arms, bent over laughing.

"I would have washed her feet if she asked me to, that's how beautiful she was."

I shot Jefferson in black-and-white. He didn't need more color.

. . .

My sophomore year started and life was busy again. Leticia and I had decided to stay in our little apartment and I was taking extra coursework to accelerate my business degree. First semester flew by, then I spent another Christmas with Leticia's family, who continued to welcome me with warmth and generous portions of food. Then, shortly after my twenty-second birthday, when we returned to campus in January, I met Alex. Ashanti, a Ghanaian friend from my African Students Association club, invited me to a party at the apartment of a Kenyan cellist who had landed a position with the New York Philharmonic.

"Hey, I have met a lot of cool Kenyans working in New York that you should meet, plus it will be good to make more African friends. I know your roommate is a very good friend, but she's not one of *our* own, you know?"

I wondered if that's what Leticia's "own people" were saying to her, about me.

Ashanti said she'd meet me at the party—an apartment building near NYU—at seven P.M.

By seven-twenty she still hadn't arrived, and as I waited outside the building, my face felt frozen by the wind. I looked down at my feet. I had wanted to wear my suede boots that were lined with shearling, then shoved them aside for classier knee-high black leather boots. Who knew what this crowd would look like? I knew there would be a number of students like me, the ones whose stars had aligned either by birth or luck to offer them an elite education. It seemed like there were two groups of Africans living in the States: students like myself, and the other group—"the ones who do the asylums, the ones who do the grannies," as Ashanti would say mockingly.

Since I was little, I knew Kenyans who went overseas with the sole mission of working to send money back home to their families. The strategy was to get a visitor's visa and once it lapsed, they would remain in the United States undocumented. Others raised money for a year's worth of tuition and qualified for a student visa but after the year was done, they dropped out of college and worked illegally. Each year, our church held fundraisers for plane tickets and tuition and a bit of starting-off money for several people who were going to do this.

Even though I had been in the States for more than a year, I still hadn't met any of these Africans. They mostly lived in the working-class suburbs. Many of them had university degrees from back home, but in the States they worked menial jobs alongside Americans who looked down on them. These Kenyans spoke their own language, a language of a community who lived together, cooked together, fundraised for weddings and funerals together.

Mother urged me to build friendships with them.

"They have heart. You fancy ones in the city—if you die tomorrow, there'll be no one to come to your apartment and cook a stew and mourn together and fundraise to bring your body back home."

"I don't want a stew," I said.

"Well, there you go," Mother had said. "You won't get a stew, and you won't get anyone trying to help me get your body home either."

Standing in the cold on the corner, I tilted my foot to examine the thin sole of my boot. I couldn't feel my feet. The six-pack of beer I was carrying felt heavier with every minute as the cold continued to numb my hands.

I decided I might as well go upstairs and thaw my frozen body. As soon as the door opened, I felt relief at last from the warmth inside. The apartment was packed with so many people, it didn't matter if the host knew me or I knew him.

In the tiny kitchen, cramped by an oversize fridge, I sampled the guacamole on the counter, opened one of the beers I'd brought, and let myself be absorbed into the crowd.

A clinking on a glass silenced the room and then a tall man with dark skin and a New York Yankees cap climbed onto a chair. Could this be the Kenyan cellist?

When he spoke, it was in a healthy American accent. As it turned out, he was the cellist. With a charm that couldn't be cultivated by the best acting coach, he talked about his middle-class parents, his life as the child of immigrants.

"They don't let live," he said. "They can't just enjoy the present because all they can dream about is the life they will have when they finally go back home. But it's been twenty-three years. They ask me, 'Don't you want to know where you came from?' No, I don't. America is my country."

"Hear, hear!" some of the crowd chanted, their beers in the air.

"And everything I've worked for is in the present. Many of you know how many times I've auditioned, how many Greyhound buses I've been on to Boston, to St. Paul, to Cincinnati. Rejection, rejection, rejection. When I took the subway that morning to Lincoln Center, I had ninety dollars in my bank account. I wasn't sure how I was going to pay my share of the rent this month. And here I am, saying to you now, newbie African students, it's possible, guys, it's possible. You can be anything you want in this country if you work hard, and just go for it."

The room belted out "For he's a jolly good fellow, which nobody can deny," which confused me, because at home the nuns had taught us that it was "For he's a jolly good fellow, and so say all of us." I muddled it up like I had everything else that had come out of my mouth even though it had been more than a year since I'd come to the States.

A slender white man in a white V-neck T-shirt who looked like the men I'd seen in photographs on the big electronic billboards at Times Square offered his hand to help the cellist down from the chair. Then he guided his face to his, and to my surprise, they kissed each other warmly. The whole room erupted in wild cheers.

In Kenya, I had never seen two men as much as hold hands. I was told homosexuals didn't exist in our culture and if they did, they were mentally ill, or were teen boys misbehaving in boarding school. But now there were two men snogging right in front of my eyes and one of them was from my culture. This was a lifestyle so foreign to ours that not even Tanei with her wild and infinite wisdom had thought to prepare me for it.

The fact that this cellist was a Kenyan made no sense to me. All I could think was, *Do his parents know?* And if they did, I wanted to know what rare part of Kenya they came from where they had learned to accept him, because in *my* Kenya, the parents I knew, like Mother, would have coped easier with a three-legged child than they would a gay child.

A far-fetched idea had broken free and shown itself to me in a new light. Despite everything I'd been told, gay people really did exist outside of television. Their love was tangible and real. They weren't something rare. They weren't mentally ill and they didn't need an exorcism or a prayer meeting. They were regular people, cellists, going about their ordinary lives.

As the party resumed, no one talked to me. I was a voyeur. I noticed a man across the room talking to a frail-looking woman with waist-length golden hair. She wore white jeans. *I could never pull off white jeans,* I thought. She was leaning in to him with her hands on his shoulders, but he seemed uninterested, sipping his beer and barely touching her.

Eventually, I decided to leave the party as invisibly as I had entered. Ashanti never arrived. As I was slithering through the tight crowd to the front door to make my escape, someone tapped my shoulder. When I turned back, I saw the boyfriend of the blond fashionista. He was light-skinned with a head of fluffy brown curls like small chunks of cotton balls, but what struck me were his green eyes.

"You're Kenyan, right?"

"Yes," I responded, still making my way toward the door. He had a beautiful girlfriend, and the apartment was hot and crowded. I wasn't going to stop and talk to him just because of his green eyes.

"Me too," he said, trailing after me.

Fine, I thought. *Follow me if you want but I'm leaving.* "I wouldn't have guessed it," I said out loud.

"Why, because I'm point five?" he said, Kenyan slang for a mixed-race person. We both laughed. "You can't leave. I've been watching you standing by yourself all evening. I'm Alex. Come on, stay and have some fun."

He dragged me by the hand, turning me back in to the crowd. Then came introductions all around the circle of the cellist's friends.

The cellist was named Mo. He had been born in Kenya, but he came to America when he was a toddler. His parents were both tenured professors at NYU.

He had studied at the prestigious New England Conservatory of

Music in Boston, spending his whole life first on the violin and then the cello, though he said he dabbled in the trumpet.

"It's those large lungs on him," his boyfriend said, stroking the cellist's razor-shaved head. As I had guessed earlier, the boyfriend was a model. His face was beautiful, impeccably symmetrical and androgynous. I wasn't sure whether to call him handsome or pretty.

The cellist gave me his phone number.

"Anything, honey, anything," he said. "I'm New York–raised. If you ever need anything in the city, call me. And Alex here is my ride-or-die buddy so any friend of his is mine."

"I'm not Alex's fr—" I started to say, then stopped myself. Instead I thanked him for his generous offer.

I headed to the front door, Alex following closely behind. He continued talking to me about himself—he was a first-year med student at NYU and had been in the United States for ten years: four for high school at a boarding school, four for his pre-med bachelor's degree, and some "wasted time in between." I nodded but I was secretly wondering where his blond girlfriend had gone. Why was he so intent on talking to me?

I started to walk down the stairs to the street, and Alex, as if we were going home together, followed me, although he wasn't wearing his coat. He was dressed in a Yankees sweatshirt with a hood, which he had pulled over his head. He hunched his shoulders, his hands stuffed deep in his pockets.

"I haven't heard that term 'point five' since I left Kenya," I said, pulling down my beanie to cover my ears. "I'm pretty sure it would be considered derogatory here in the States. You're biracial now."

"No, now I'm just Black," he said.

"Which one of your parents is white?" I asked.

"My mother," he said. "She's American. My father was studying here when they met in college."

A few blocks down, my body was growing furiously cold. He

must have been freezing, yet he kept trudging on next to me, jumping over heaps of dirty snow on the ground.

The subway station entrance was right in front of us and I bid him farewell, but still he followed me inside. I could hear the train approaching as I swiped my MetroCard, whisking past the turnstile, and once again I bid him farewell, but he pulled out his wallet, took out a MetroCard, swiped it, and joined me on the platform.

"Are you also going home?" I asked, perplexed.

"No, I'm seeing that you get on the train safely. It's late, you know," he said.

"I think you should get back to your girlfriend," I said. "I'm a grown woman. I can get myself on the train."

"She's not my girlfriend, she's just—"

"It's okay," I said, moving closer to the platform and waving him off.

The train doors flung open and I stepped inside, unsure of what else to say. When the train bucked and lurched to move ahead, I looked out the frosty window and saw that he was still standing there, ears hidden by his lifted shoulders. Then he turned back around and jogged away, still with his hands burrowed in his pockets.

I wasn't thinking about dating. It had been more than a year since I'd arrived in the United States but I still felt like I was getting my bearings. Everyone spoke too fast and there were so many dialects—the Southern drawl and the African American speech that Leticia told me was called Ebonics and the thick accents of native New Yorkers. The English language had become nearly foreign to me. Early on, I didn't understand common phrases. The differences between "yeah no," "no yeah," and "yeah no totally" never stopped making my head spin. When I said "can't" I got blank stares. So, I said "ken't" to fit in. My written essays were returned with red circles and exclamation marks on every word I spelled with *ou*.

"*Caliber,* not *calibre*! Please use the dictionary!"

I was floundering, I told Mother.

It could have been the long distance, but something had softened her. Her tone on the phone was tender. Sometimes, she'd ask to speak to Leticia. Leticia would take the call and talk to Mother like she'd known her for years. I could hear it in Mother's voice that she liked Leticia, though she asked me once if Leticia smoked marijuana.

"She sounds a bit much. But I suppose *they* tend to be like that."

. . .

A couple of weeks after I went alone to the Kenyan party, Leticia dragged me back to that same neighborhood. She said she had found the "perfect LBD" in a vintage shop in Greenwich Village to wear to the "perfect date." I didn't know what LBD meant until I saw Leticia excitedly buying a little black dress. The dress was fine, I thought, though I didn't understand the big fuss. "Now we have to find the right something or other to dress it up—that's how you get away with vintage," she said, and I nodded.

It was growing colder as the sun started to go down, and we decided to stop at a Starbucks to warm up. We were debating mochas over regular hot chocolate, looking around for a spare table, when I saw Alex. He was sitting hunched over a small laptop computer. If Mother were here, she would have poked him hard in between the shoulder blades and screamed, "Sit up straight!"

"That's him," I whispered to Leticia, cocking my head at Alex.

"Who?"

"The guy I've been telling you about. From the cellist's party—the one who followed me down to the train without a coat on like a psycho."

Leticia gasped loudly. "Oh! The one you blew off at the party with all the Kenyans?"

Alex, as if he'd heard her, lifted his head and looked straight at us.

When I gave him a subtle wave, his shoulders rolled back into a straight position and his eyes widened, the eyes of a child who had been offered a chocolate bar. He made room for us at his table and, after we all sat, Alex wanted to know what we were doing all the way down in Greenwich Village, so far from our campus uptown. Leticia giddily talked about her LBD, and said he had to see the exciting dress. She took it out of the brown recyclable bag the saleslady with all the tattoos had folded it into and straightened it out in front of Alex like she was displaying artwork.

"Ah, yes, I see." Alex nodded, looking at the strapless bodice and the long slit on the side of the dress. "This guy, whoever he is, will be totally into you."

Leticia gushed all about the date, and I found myself staring at every inch of Alex, his dark stubble growing over his handsome face, his fingernails that looked manicured. When I spoke with Leticia, I could feel him watching me intently, and my ears burned. When Leticia and I were leaving the coffee shop, Alex asked for my number.

"Come on; give him your number," Leticia said. "What are you waiting for?"

"I'm just not interested in dating at the moment," I said.

"I'm not asking to date you; I just want to catch up, maybe have a coffee sometime," he said. "Come on, how many cool Kenyans do you think you're going to meet in the city? Let's hang out."

Leticia goaded, "Come on, come on," and eventually, I gave in.

. . .

The weeks after that turned effortlessly into months. Alex and I saw each other nearly every weekend. The simplest moments, like having a bagel with lox and cream cheese in a deli, became spellbinding hours of conversation. Everything was a high. He took me to my first New York Yankees game. We watched from the bleachers at Yankee Stadium with his college friends, wearing baseball caps and jerseys, eating hot dogs, and screaming with joy as we tried to catch foul balls. We wolfed down guacamole, tacos, burritos, and corn dogs, and we stood in line for half an hour for barbeque wings, giant burgers, and onion rings at American restaurant chains. I finished up my portions and licked my plates even though when I first arrived I'd said Americans ate like gluttons, and it made Alex laugh.

His apartment in the West Village was a renovated one-bedroom in a prewar building. The first time I went to his apartment, I took Leticia with me and Alex joked that I didn't need a chaperone. We couldn't believe that he rode in an elevator to the second floor, while we had to walk up a dark stairwell to our fifth-floor apartment. He had a spacious kitchen with a granite counter and stainless steel appliances, while we had a tilting kitchen sink and a fridge that hummed away day and night. He had built-in washer and dryer units, whereas we sat and read for hours on end at the corner laundromat. He had exposed brick walls, high ceilings, an oversize kitchen window that brought in plenty of natural light, a massive closet with overhead storage for his suitcases, and a view of the Hudson River from atop the roof deck, where he often held parties. The building had a sparkling marble-tiled lobby. It sat on a tree-lined block of townhouses. I could not fathom the difference between his lifestyle and mine. I shuddered when I found out how much rent he paid. I did quick mental math and realized that a month of his rent could cover six months of mine.

"I can't believe you live like this," I said, while Leticia and I walked around the kitchen in a mutual state of awe. We mostly kept our hands in our coat pockets, afraid our fingerprints would smudge the shine on the stainless steel appliances. I opened the fridge door and reveled at how wide and well lit it was inside. "Our fridge light doesn't even turn on and the freezer has this thick layer of ice that we have to defrost every Sunday, just to get anything to fit inside."

Alex's parents were well-known in the expatriate and socialite circles in Nairobi. They hosted ambassadors, anybody who was somebody, at parties with waitstaff, and they set off fireworks on New Year's Eve on their sprawling lawn.

Unlike Mother, his parents didn't spend all their time and money on church missions. Instead, they enjoyed holidays overseas, saying that travel was the best kind of education for Alex. When he turned fourteen, Alex was enrolled in a private boarding school in New Hampshire; because his parents traveled so much, they said they didn't want him to be lonely.

"Oh yeah, so basically, he kayaked and fenced—or whatever sports bougie people do—with the Bushes and the Kennedys and the Mellon grandkids," Leticia said, when I told her about Alex's upbringing. "He's playing in a totally different league from us. He has networks. We have none. He just has to make a phone call and he's got himself a job."

As different as our upbringings had been, though, we were similar enough that our relationship felt easy and familiar. We were both studious and highly organized. We gave each other the space we needed during the week to study and then got together to see each other mostly on weekends, at his apartment.

Alex was extremely popular at NYU. He was charismatic, like a politician or a church reverend. He hosted parties at his apartment with chips and dips and pizzas. At the end of the night, as we collected beer cans and stacked the dishwasher, Alex would say that he didn't know half the people who had been there.

He was as American as any American. He held citizenship passed down to him by his mother. He spoke the lingo and had adopted the tongue-roll accent. He enjoyed the ribbing when I called him a phony, while he told me I wasn't ever going to get anywhere if I didn't conform.

"Every immigrant here has to do a bit of code-switching," he said.

"You have to adapt at least a little bit of the lingo, try to relax your *t*'s a little, allow the Americans some comfort around your foreignness."

I worked harder at that but still I found my identity difficult to shed. It wasn't a pair of boots I could just leave at the door and pick out another pair. When I was in his apartment, I cooked a lot of Kenyan food to chase away the nostalgia. The smells of coconut and cardamom were so pungent we had to open the windows. When we walked in the corridors of the building, the Americans threw us spiteful stares.

"I can't wait for them to say something one day," I said to Alex, fuming, as we walked out of the elevator to find a trio of smartly dressed white women staring at us in the lobby. We were headed to a party at one of the dorms around Washington Square Park. The women pursed their lips and forced their mouths to smile and we heard them whispering after we had walked past.

"Okay, take it easy," he said, putting an arm around my shoulders as he steered me out of the lobby. "I don't want to get kicked out of the building. I really like this neighborhood."

"Frankly, I don't give a toss," I said. "It's too upscale anyway. Do you not see the wide-eyed stares of most of the students who come to your apartment? And your building only has snobby women with strollers. The other day some lady asked me in the elevator who in the building I work for because she is looking for a good nanny. I didn't even know what to say. I guess I should be flattered that I seem decent enough to be poached."

"Well, if you want to talk about spending, I think you're ridiculous," Alex said. "You'll walk in the rain to find the nearest subway to save ten dollars on a cab, even though you can afford it. You buy Payless shoes and wrinkly Old Navy shirts, even though you can afford to shop at Macy's. But that's your thing. That's who you are. I don't judge you. If I want to live in a decent apartment, why do you judge me?"

It really didn't matter to me what Alex did with his money. Yet, somehow, I felt having a fancy apartment, taking trips to Kenya every time he pleased, was wasteful. "I'm not judging you. I'm just saying that it wouldn't kill you to have some awareness."

By the time we had walked the ten blocks to the party, Alex and I had fallen silent. We mingled with the other students in the room separately, as if we didn't know each other. Later that night, I refused to go back to his apartment. It was our first big fight.

But mostly, Alex and I got along. He supported and encouraged me. He allowed me to feel like I could begin to step out of Mother's shadow. So that spring, I enrolled in more art classes.

Mother's resistance to my interest in photography only made me want to veer further away from economics. With the arrival of the second semester of my sophomore year, I had pored through the course catalog looking for more lectures in the arts.

"Are you really taking Intro to Art?" Leticia said, bending over to look at a hardcover title on medieval Asian art on my desk. "First photography, now art; what are you trying to do to your mom?"

"I need an easy grade," I said. "Besides, I want to know *something* about art. Whenever I go into these galleries, everyone is oohing and aahing and I have no idea why or what I am even looking at. Last week it was the rectangles made with different colors at the Met. I feel so insecure every time I walk into a museum, like I don't belong there."

"Rothko!" Leticia said, chuckling. "I don't get him and his boxes either. But Soila, who cares if you don't 'get it'?" She sketched dramatic air quotes and I laughed. "Look, not 'getting' art isn't a reason to feel insecure. When I was in high school we came to the city on a field trip and spent a whole day at the Met. Before that, I didn't care about art at all. But now I have some interest. You know what, take the class if it'll give you more confidence."

My Introduction to Art class was an eclectic mix of students and, surprisingly, there were many who, like me, weren't art majors. They were future doctors, lawyers, and political science majors who I found more interesting than the subject itself. They weren't afraid to thumb their noses at multimillion-dollar artwork, especially the abstract expressionist pieces that none of us could make out.

My professor, a minuscule older woman named Professor Kowalski, had a voice too big for her body and wore her hair in a tight chignon every day. She constantly urged us to dig deeper.

"It's not enough for you to say 'A five-year-old can draw that.' Really look closely, see the way the light falls on it, the layers upon layers of paint, the less evident colors slipping through the thin layers of the primary paint, the fine textures, the precision, the simplicity of it yet the feeling that it engulfs you when you're so close to it. Look at the way the artist refuses to label the pieces. And then I still dare you to show me a five-year-old who can produce such work."

"I'm really, really looking," I said, frustrated, feeling as if the floors of the gallery were buckling under me. "I just don't get it. Maybe I'm too dumb to get it."

Kowalski walked up to me; her eyes pierced mine.

"Do you know what Pablo Picasso said?"

I shook my head.

"He asked, Why does everyone have to understand art? Why not treat it like the song of a bird: just enjoy it! When I say really look, I mean that you must enter into a mind space where no words or voices or recognizable symbols exist. Take your mind out of the box and play with it like a toy, let your mind go where reality as you know it doesn't exist."

Kowalski brought in contributors to class. These were people who she said were way more learned in their craft than she could ever be. Japanese artists who showed us thousand-year-old ceramic bowls and explained kintsugi, or golden joinery, where the repairing of cracks birthed even more beauty. On a morning when I overslept and crashed through the doors a few minutes late, I found the lecture room darkened for a slideshow. An artist who, according to the lecture sheet, had been on digs with archaeologists in the Middle East was standing at the platform explaining a collection of document seals from 1300 B.C. Egypt.

"See here, this symbol is the name of the throne, so we know that this is the reign of Amenhotep III," he said, tapping his pencil on the image on the slide. He explained that the Egyptians at the time used mud to seal the papyrus.

"Akhenaten has studied this time period in immense depth," Professor Kowalski said, speaking loudly over the artist as he talked us through the slides with a calming voice.

The fluorescent lights flickered on and I saw that the artist was at least two feet taller than Professor Kowalski. She was so small next to him that he could have easily hoisted her onto his shoulders if he had to rescue her from a flood. His hair was in Bob Marley–length dreadlocks, though much neater. He wore a tight-fitted denim shirt that showed off his broad shoulders over loosely hanging cargo pants and a long, silky black scarf around his neck. I looked at the artist's note printed at the bottom of his lecture sheet next to an inset of a black-and-white portrait.

> Akhenaten Morrison is a modern art sculptor who uses bronze, stone, wood, and gypsum to explore several media and styles—from classical realism to nonobjective and abstract expressionism. He has studied ancient Asian and Middle Eastern sculpting. His works of over five hundred bronzes and stone carvings are in collections in the UAE, England, Turkey, Japan, Costa Rica, and the United States. After living and working in Egypt for several years, he is now based in Tokyo.

When the class was finished, students walked over to meet the artist in person. I saw him shake hands warmly with the gathering group and from where I stood I noticed he had rings on his fingers. I wouldn't know what to say to this man. I was not interested in sculpture. Perhaps I had reached my quota of appreciation after being raised around the wooden carvings of masks and warriors and rain and fertility gods, I thought. His clear interest in ancient Egypt—he had the name of an Egyptian pharaoh—was also off-putting to me. Even as a child, I knew that Egyptians famously refused to consider themselves Africans.

I tried to guess how old the artist was. Akhenaten. What a ridiculous name. If he'd really been to Egypt, he would know that they would call him *samara, blackie,* or *zarboon,* a slave, behind his back.

Despite all of that, I had to admit that he had accomplished an impressive amount. The sheer dedication and grit it must have taken for him to perfect his work and garner such respect in the art world was unimaginable. I was envious of that kind of purpose and ambition, to not be afraid to pursue the thing that you really love. If Mother were here today, would meeting a man like this, who was so successful, change her opinion of artists? Would it open her eyes to the opportunities I could have with my photography?

I didn't know. The only thing I knew for sure was that I wanted to keep taking photographs because they made me happy. And Mother didn't have to know about it.

. . .

I couldn't wait to go to Alex's apartment that weekend and complain about the Black American wannabe-Egyptian artist with a pharaoh's name who had lectured my class.

"What irks me most is that a person would have the cheek to wake up one day and change their name to whatever exotic preference they choose. This can't possibly be the name his mother gave him," I said to Alex. "This is serious cultural appropriation."

"What about all the Black Americans with Swahili names," Alex said. "Why doesn't that bother you?"

"I don't know. Somehow it just feels different," I said, itching to grasp why I was so worked up over a man I would probably never see again. "The racism against the Nubian community and darker-skinned Egyptians is a huge problem. He says he's been to Egypt and clearly, he loved it so much that he named himself after a pharaoh. Isn't there a disconnect? Some ignorance? He really can't honestly believe his skin color is popular over there."

"What's the difference if he connected with Egypt and wants to be a pharaoh? People who have never even been to the Middle East convert to Islam every day and change their names to Mohammed. What's your actual beef with this guy?" Alex was lying on the couch in his sweatpants, looking at me with bewilderment. "Black Americans are just trying to connect with their roots any way they know how. They can't change their last names but they can do something about their first names."

"It's the pretentiousness with this guy," I said. "Well, I'll give him one thing. At least he has worked hard and made something of himself—unlike all these Black American men who blame the world for their problems."

Alex sat up, visibly upset.

"Soila, whoa. It's shocking that you would say something like that out loud. That is what all the ignorant Africans I've met here say. I thought you'd be different."

"I'm not trying to be mean. It's just confusing to me, what poverty can look like here. Poor people in Kenya have literally nothing. Have you forgotten? They would weep with gratitude to have the lives of poor people in America. And then I see people here complaining of poverty who still somehow wear expensive sneakers. None of it makes sense."

"Poor Kenyans can't afford expensive sneakers because they have no access to minimum wage jobs, or housing, or food benefits. That doesn't make poverty here any easier. It's just as brutal here but it presents itself differently. Come on, Soila, you've got to see that it's not that simple," Alex said matter-of-factly. "It takes a ridiculous amount of willpower and drive to get out of a cycle of poverty. It's incredibly hard. Not to mention the systemic inequities that perpetuate poverty and criminalize race. You should educate yourself about why things are the way they are in the States. What if Leticia heard you right now?"

"I'm not trying to generalize and I'm not an idiot. I get that there's a tough history—"

"Excuse me, did you say 'tough history'?" Alex shot back. "Soila, that is a gross understatement. Black Americans have been through a special kind of hell for hundreds of years. Don't you read any Black literature? Should I give you a reading list? There's actually not a fitting verb to describe the horrific magnitude of Black history in this country."

"I don't understand how it always comes back to slavery. I don't understand why not just move on. In Kenya we know the Brits screwed us over, and it's horrible, but we get on with our misery. There's no choice, really, because there isn't any help coming from the government for the poor and the Brits aren't coming back to rescue us—they up and left us to languish. But here, the government is doling out benefits that poor Kenyans would die for—free education, housing, clean water, jobs, and still, why are there so many Black people in prison in America? Why are so many Black people here out of work? Why are they the ones who seem least interested in school? Why are they peddling drugs? What's all that got to do with slavery?"

Alex leaned back on the couch and shut his eyes. I saw now that I had revealed too much of myself to him, too much of what I didn't understand about Blackness in America, and speaking out loud suddenly made me feel ashamed of myself as a Black person, a fraud. He called me ignorant, unempathetic, a Black-on-Black racist, an elitist. It was the first time that I began to question my ideas and realize I was wrong. What had I missed? What else didn't I understand?

"I hope that in your years here you continue to meet more Black Americans from all backgrounds. I had Black friends in high school who kept their heads down the whole time just because they knew: They'd be the first ones to go if there was ever any trouble. The most valuable lessons I've learned in this country have been from my Black guy friends because I've seen it firsthand. Black kids have to learn to live their whole lives to fight even when they're the best in the room. So when you complain about a Black man who's made it big in his industry—picking on him for something as petty as his name and doubting his pedigree—that says a lot about who you are, not who he is. If a white artist with a stupid name had lectured that class you wouldn't have blinked twice. For some reason the white artist is given the privilege but that Black artist is not?"

"I definitely believe that there's a rampant cycle of poverty that makes things difficult," I said. "But it seems to me like poverty should motivate you to succeed in school and find a good job, to lift yourself up. It makes no sense to me that poverty would make you give up."

"It makes no sense to you because you're not coming from that oppressive history," Alex said. "When you've got four hundred years of psychological shackles holding you back, it's a miracle you can even get up from under all that. I saw what it was like for the kids who managed to get scholarships at my high school. It was rough enough for them to just believe that they could do it, that it wasn't some kind of prank. That's because they'd never known anyone growing up who did it before them. They needed insane drive and courage to survive such a foreign environment. Can you imagine what it must be like for the kids who never get the chance?"

Alex was so angry with me he couldn't even look at me. He said he wanted to go for a run even though it was gray out and threatening to drizzle.

"Don't go, I'll go," I said. "It's fine that you're angry with me. I get it."

"Do you really?" he asked. "Because if you don't, I can't be in this relationship. I can't be in a relationship with someone who believes Black people deliberately want to be lazy, or stupid, or in prison."

On the subway, my mind was churning. I felt ashamed of what I had said to Alex. And yet, I had spoken what I believed to be true: In Kenya, poverty was a motivator. It had certainly motivated Mother and hundreds of thousands of other Kenyans to get an education as a way out of villages and townships. I struggled to grasp why in America, a country with so much wealth and government support, a poor person would be unable to break out of the cycle.

When I got home, I went straight to my room and hoped I wouldn't see Leticia that night. I was afraid my argument with Alex was plastered on my face, or that she would read my betraying thoughts. It would have broken Leticia's heart and our friendship. I realized I needed to do a personal stocktaking about the stereotypes I was carrying around if I was going to remain in a relationship with Alex, if I was to stay friends with Leticia, even if I was going to stay in this country. What had my mother raised me to believe? What had my privilege—all that luck I had been born into—made of me? Mother had agreed to send me to America on the condition that I study business, but now I was realizing just how much about the world, the way it worked, and its people I really had to learn.

Chapter Six

I stayed on campus again for the summer after my sophomore year and spent my days crunching three more courses and working at the college bookstore. Alex was also in the city, and we spent every free moment together. Though he and I sometimes clashed, we were completely committed. And after our fight, I resolved to pay more attention to what I had misunderstood about Blackness in America. That summer, Alex and I were so happy together—in fact, I thought I had never been so happy in my whole life.

My only co-worker at the bookstore was Sandy Cortelli, the manager. Sandy was a melancholic senior majoring in poli-sci. She had piercings in her brow, lower lip, and tongue and her short-cropped hair was dyed orange. She wore combat boots in the peak of the summer. Sandy knew she wasn't ever going to get a job in her major when she graduated, so she spent her time applying to graduate school and she let me run the store, lifting her unkempt head from her laptop only when a pesky customer insisted on seeing the manager. With my eyes opened by Leticia and Alex, I saw clearly now that some of the nastier customers asked for the manager because they didn't want to deal with a Black person and it hurt me a great deal, even though a mere two years before it wouldn't have grazed my skin at all.

On the seventh of August, I opened the store at nine A.M. followed closely by a disheveled Sandy, who was holding on to her take-out coffee cup like it was a raft.

"I'm so hungover. I was at a party in Brooklyn until five A.M.," she said. "I can't feel my tongue, that's how many shots I had last night."

We immediately got busy, quietly unpacking new boxes of clothing that needed to be tagged, hung up on clothes hangers, or folded, when out of the blue Sandy grabbed my arm and shook it hard.

"Holy shit! Soila, oh my God!"

I looked up from the sweatshirt I was folding. Sandy reached her arm tight around my shoulders, as if she was ready to hold me if my knees gave in. With her other hand, she was pointing to the television at the corner of the ceiling. It was breaking news. There had been a bombing in Nairobi at the U.S. embassy. Nobody knew how many people were dead.

Sandy picked up the phone and held out the receiver to me, but I was too afraid to dial. If I didn't call, I didn't have to hear the news that someone in my family might be dead.

"Hey! You dial, or I dial. I'm going to take shit for this phone call because it's long-distance but I don't even care. You need to reach your family."

I reluctantly dialed while Sandy stood waiting. On the television, a female reporter who seemed to be perched on a mountain of rubble was struggling to get her message through.

"It happened at ten-thirty A.M. East African time," she said. "It's four-thirty P.M. here in Nairobi now. It's been already six hours and all we see is utter chaos. This is not a city with the resources for a trained rescue operation. We have mostly volunteers, as you can see, risking their lives to enter what's left of this shaky building to find anyone who might still be alive. They are digging out rocks to find signs of life. It's an appalling situation here on the ground. . . ."

I looked at my watch. It was nine-thirty A.M. and New York was seven hours behind Nairobi. While I was tucked warmly in my sheets in a foreign city, while I took a hot shower and ate my favorite American cereal this morning, my homeland was being annihilated. Why had no one called me? Were they all dead?

I hit redial on the line several times until finally I heard it ring, my hand heavy with fear. Someone was speaking but I couldn't make out whose voice it was. It was as if I were in a noisy restaurant struggling to hear what the person next to me was saying.

I realized I was screaming in Maa in front of a panicked Sandy, so I took the receiver to the back of the store. Just then, the noise evaporated and the voice on the other end became clear so that I didn't need to scream. Mother wasn't going to come to the phone, Princess said.

"Princess, what's going on? Where is everyone?" I asked. Behind Princess's voice, I heard wails. They were rhythmical, melodic, and I could see it now in my mind's eye, women rocking back and forth on their knees as they released guttural, animalistic cries.

"Princess, who is it? Who died? Just tell me," I said, surprised by my own strength.

"That's the thing . . ." Princess said. "We don't know yet. We are so worried. Aunt Tanei—you know she's got that sugar daddy boyfriend who is a lawyer and his office is in the Ufundi building, and that building has been flattened to the ground. God help us. We don't know where to reach her and she hasn't called us. The worst is Kokoi. She's lying on the ground. She can't survive this. Father Emmanuel and some of the nuns are all here praying with her."

I heard Aunt Naserian ask Princess who was on the phone. Princess said it was me.

"Soila, don't worry," Naserian said, her voice coming on the other end of the line. She was trying to be brave but I sensed her terror. "We're going to find her. I'll call you as soon as I hear from her."

When I got off the phone, my ears were still ringing with the wails behind Naserian's voice that rocked me like a punishing soundtrack. Sandy said something as I handed her the receiver. I shook my head that I had no news, picked up my backpack, and left the bookstore.

On my way home, I phoned Alex, who didn't answer, and I became more anxious than ever. Could he have lost a family member? Was he too distraught to answer the phone? My mind was everywhere. Leticia was home reading, her face directly in front of the fan. She had decided that summer that she would read all the "Black American literature every Black American person should read." I remembered Alex's comment during our argument about making me a reading list and wondered if I should start reading James Baldwin and Zora Neale Hurston too.

I sat on a large cushion on the floor and felt all the tension in my body slip away and I started to cry. Leticia closed her book and turned off the fan.

"Okay, why the face? Did someone die?" she said jokingly. There was no way for Leticia to know. We had no television; we couldn't afford one.

"There was a bombing," I said, the words heavy as cement blocks on my tongue. "In Nairobi."

Leticia looked sucker punched.

"It was the American embassy," I continued. "God only knows how many Americans are dead as well. I saw it on CNN at the bookstore. The building is gutted."

Leticia's phone rang and I lunged for my bag, thinking it was mine—either Alex or Mother trying to reach me. No messages, nothing. It seemed like years since I had talked to Princess and Naserian, but it had only been a few hours.

"Yes, Mama," Leticia said, nodding at her phone. "We've heard about it. She doesn't know much. We are still waiting to hear. Yes, she's holding up. I'll let you know, okay, as soon as we know."

Leticia wanted us to go out for a walk, or to head over to Alex's apartment and make sure he was okay. She thought it would do me good.

All I could think about was the mountain of toppled bricks and stones on the television, of the men who were digging through the rubble with their bare hands looking for bodies. An image of Tanei lying mangled under large stones flashed in my mind like a frame in an old-fashioned movie reel, except it wasn't in black-and-white. I saw her covered in blood, her head smashed, her eyes wide open staring at the blue Nairobi sky. I squeezed my eyes shut and rubbed my temples, hoping to erase the image.

"You are not okay," Leticia said. She had been watching me closely. "Come on, we are leaving. Let's get some fresh air."

We had only walked a few blocks, mindlessly, unsure of where exactly we were headed, when my phone finally rang. I looked at it singing and vibrating in my hand. I'd been waiting for this one call desperately and now my hand was frozen, and I couldn't press the green button.

"Come on, pick up!" Leticia said, grabbing the phone from my stiff hand.

Finally, I put it to my ear. The sound of traffic in the city was too loud, so I stepped into a small mom-and-pop record store, which I had never spotted before even though it was only one block behind our apartment building. Leticia stood next to me with expectant eyes, while thumbing through a collection of vintage vinyl albums.

"Soila, it's Yeyo. I'm calling from the hospital. Tanei has been found. They took her to the hospital, and she asked the nurses to phone me. She was walking around town, going to see her boyfriend, the lawyer, at Ufundi House. My assumption is that he's dead because that building is crumbled. Tanei has been badly maimed, Soila. She's burned. I couldn't recognize her. The glass flying from the buildings tore her body up. She's lost one eye. Her pretty face . . . is gone. She has broken bones because she was buried in rubble. She can't hear very well right now, but that will probably come back in time. But I thank God she's not dead. I thank God."

"Yes. Thank God she's not dead," I said. But in that moment, what I really felt was that God had smote Tanei. To her, being maimed was worse than death. She spent hours looking in the mirror, wearing different shades of eye shadow, styling her hair. Tanei loved being beautiful but Mother reminded her often that her beauty would one day fade.

"I can't believe it," I said to Leticia, when I was finished with the call. "My mother was so angry with Tanei that she never took her back in when Tanei begged to come back home. Then this happens."

"Oh no . . . your mom must feel so guilty now," Leticia said. "I know I would."

"My mother doesn't do guilt," I said. "She believes God makes things happen for a reason. Now she'll take my aunt back and care for her like nothing ever happened between them. It's all very African. People don't dwell; at least my mother doesn't."

"Yeah, I can see that," Leticia said. "It's the kind of thing my granny would do. You just do what you need to do and get on with it."

Leticia held my hand gently as we walked out of the record store, as if I were an old lady she had to help get on the crosstown bus. I could see on her face that she was aching for me, almost as if she was the one who had received grim news.

"Tanei has these big, light-brown eyes. Very unusual light-brown eyes that look like colored contact lenses. I can't believe she's lost those gorgeous eyes."

Alex called me later that afternoon. He had been in a summer lecture when he got a call from his mother saying there had been a bombing, but his family was safe. Leticia and I made our way to Alex's apartment to watch the news. By the next day, the death toll was trickling in: 100, 150, 200, and more.

Only two years ago, I'd been second in the queue with Mother at the U.S. embassy. I had been granted a five-year study visa and we had boasted to everyone. The queue was the kind of thing people would discuss at dinner parties. It started at the entrance of the embassy on Moi Avenue, and swung through corners and buildings in the disheveled engineering of the city, humans lined up like little ants marching for ten city blocks. The embassy opened its doors at nine A.M. and closed its doors at noon. Those who didn't make the cut would disperse like pollen in the wind and cluster back in line the next day.

When the U.S. embassy was bombed, I cried for my wild and beautiful aunt, the only one not afraid of Mother, now disfigured and half-blind at twenty-eight. I cried over the death of an existence where innocent human beings walked their children to school on busy city streets, and then went to work in tall buildings and laughed around the office water fountains about the trivial things that happened over the weekend. I grieved for the 213 people who died that day as if I had known each one. For me, the saddest thing was that when they had woken up that morning, they were blissfully unaware that a gang of men they had never heard of had decided that would be the day they died.

Chapter Seven

When classes began for the first semester of my junior year, I found it difficult, at first, to focus. The bombing was so recent, and being away from my family while knowing they were in pain was terrible. Alex and Leticia banded together to help me. Leticia began to schedule movie nights to lure me out of my room, where I had been spending hours sitting at my desk before an open textbook, my eyes unseeing and my mind focused on my faraway family. Her favorites were implausibly plotted romantic comedies where everyone ended up happy in the end. Happily ever afters were comforting, she said. For his part, Alex brought over take-out food in enormous quantities. Slowly, I felt the fog of sadness that had fallen over me lift. By the end of the semester, I felt like myself again.

I returned home that Christmas for the first time two and a half years after I left. The oldest of my aunts, steady, responsible Naserian, had met a man. After all of Kokoi's fretting that her daughters were old maids, Naserian was getting married. Kokoi said God had finally heard her prayers. The wedding was planned for Christmastime and Aunt Rarin would be home too, from Europe. It was a family reunion, a wedding, and a holiday, all in one.

For me, it was bittersweet. I looked forward to seeing my family again, but I dreaded seeing my youngest aunt. It had been only five months since the bombing. Mother had been careful not to include any photographs of Tanei when she sent me letters and cards. I longed to see her, but I worried about what I'd say when I was met with her unfamiliar face. When I came out of arrivals at the airport, my aunts Naserian and Laioni were waiting. They came at me like high-speed trains and I stumbled backward, falling over my pile of luggage. They picked me up off the ground, bent over laughing, and then we made our way to Mother, who was standing behind the throng of anxious families waiting for their loved ones. Mother was composed, but when she held me close, I felt her arms tremble. I remembered all the days growing up when she had phoned home each afternoon to make sure I had survived the drive home from school.

The crisp nighttime Nairobi weather braced me as we walked quickly to the car park. Aunt Naserian was thinner than ever, in preparation for the upcoming fitting of her wedding gown. She said she'd been taking a Brazilian pill that was renowned for quick weight loss.

"It's great, I tell you, I've never felt so good," she said, puffing her chest and lifting her shoulders high.

"Look at the way she's strutting." Aunt Laioni pointed her finger at Naserian's behind like she was aiming at a target. Naserian walked ahead of us dragging a large suitcase. "All she needs are colorful feathers and she'd be a peacock."

Naserian paused her hurried walk and turned back with a frowning face.

She'd forgotten her jacket and wore a sleeveless top with a pale blue silk pashmina draped over her shoulders—the same way the Maasai morans wore their red-and-blue shukas. She shivered a little when a brisk wind fluttered the cloth over her bare skin.

"Laioni, you know you're just jealous because you've been dieting for months and still can't get rid of your big bum," Naserian retorted. She was tall like Mother. Laioni, who was the shortest of the sisters, had always been jealous of Naserian's graceful height. Naserian was not as busty as Mother, though everyone said that would change once she had children. She had a tiny waist and voluptuous backside, which her younger sisters poked fun at. It was no wonder she had taken to diet pills for her wedding, even though she didn't need them. Though Tanei had been "the pretty one" before the bombing, I had always thought Naserian was beautiful.

"Ha, ha, ha. . . . Naserian, please, you sit on the toilet with the runs all day," Laioni said. "If that's how I have to lose weight, then let me be fat."

I angled to look at Laioni's behind. She had always had wide hips and a classic pear shape.

"Aii, I know I'm a fatty," she said, pushing me to the side. "You don't have to stare at my bum like you're inspecting a new heifer."

Mother smiled and shook her head as she walked slowly behind us. She looked the same as I remembered her.

Not much had changed in Nairobi either. We had the same dictatorial president; the roads were in even worse condition than I remembered. I asked about Tanei, admitting that I was anxious to see her. Naserian said what was concerning wasn't what she looked like, but that she had fallen into an insurmountable depression.

"Even the antidepressants don't seem to work," she said. "To think she used to be so happy—nothing could spoil her mood—and now, she won't even get off the couch."

"What about her friends?"

"Of course, only a couple of her friends stood by her," Naserian said. "And it didn't help her spirit that her boyfriend was killed in that building."

"You can't show someone something they're not ready to see,"

Mother said. "Until Tanei's done feeling sorry for herself, until she sees how much God loves her and what He wants her to do with her life, it's pointless."

"Yeyo, you weren't always a Christian," I said, hearing, even as the words came out of my mouth, how bold and un-Kenyan I sounded, talking back to Mother this way. Mother was sitting in the front passenger seat and she unhooked her seatbelt and turned back to look at me like she couldn't believe her ears. I realized that now I had to commit to my argument. "Early on, after Papai died, you weren't such a big Christian, but you found your way. Aunt Tanei will find herself in time. Besides, not everyone is like you."

"Whoa! Soila, I see America has given you quite the motormouth," Mother said. "I know the bombing was only five months ago and it's sad. But it's not the end. She doesn't understand that there are people who are worse off than she is. Even with that bombing, some died, some are paralyzed, some don't have the money for physical therapies, skin grafting, prosthetics. She locks herself up in her room all day, when there's so much she can still offer the world. Tanei needs to just get up and put one foot in front of the other."

At home, Kokoi was the first one to receive me. She jumped up and down, calling out loudly as if she were talking to someone who was upstairs. "Toto! My toto! You're home." She had always called me her baby.

I found Tanei sitting on a chaise in the corner of the room by the faux Christmas tree. As I walked up to her, I saw her lips try to curl with laughter but the thick skin around her mouth imprisoned them. I knelt before her to give her a hug and felt her body, weak and fragile, in my arms. I worried she might disintegrate if I embraced her too tightly. She placed her bony hand, now mangled, fingers knitted together by skin, over mine.

I looked up and saw that her face with its one blind eye was pleading for me to treat her the same way I had before the maiming.

Though Mother said the first round of skin grafting had made the scarring a great deal better than when she'd first come home, it was still horrific to me.

But in the early evening light, by the Christmas tree, Tanei was stunning. She only needed to see herself, I thought, to see how much she still had to offer the world. I took out my camera, wanting to capture that for her. That was the photograph I snapped in black-and-white and had framed for her as a Christmas present.

The mood around me was sheer excitement. The women rushed around bringing out plates and bowls, even though I had already eaten on the plane. "Nonsense!" Mother yelled. "If you think that is food, then you should eat a foot."

I sat next to Tanei and watched her as she observed the joy in the room, suspended like a balloon, unattached, unable to join in this happiness.

. . .

Naserian was marrying a man she'd met while on a trip to South Africa for one of Mother's businesses. She was in her late thirties, a virgin, marrying her first serious boyfriend, whom she'd known for just over a year. The groom's family wasn't wealthy, or from our tribe, the Maasai. His name was Kamau and he was a Kikuyu. There was an unspoken air of discomfort about this from the elders, but they were happy Naserian was finally getting married.

The Kikuyus were the largest tribe in Kenya, the ones who owned most of the land and held economic power. The smaller tribes felt like the Kikuyus rubbed our noses in their preeminence. The scars of land loss between tribes, resettlement, and marginalization of smaller tribes like ours, the Maasai, remained, the stories recounted through generations. By the time Naserian was getting married, though, we were living in a generation that was less tribalistic, where people knew about but didn't feel the wounds of history and fell in love with whomever they wanted. But they walked into intertribal marriages aware of the difficulties they'd face.

Naserian had allowed her wedding to go to her head like cheap whiskey. At her dress fitting, when I went to touch the fabric of her elaborate wedding gown, she fretted over her dress. "You're going to rip the organza!" She slapped my wrist off the garment.

I had come to Naserian's fitting because I wanted her advice. I asked her if she thought Mother would ever let me switch from business to a photography major. "Don't forget," Naserian lectured me, "your yeyo didn't have much for herself. She dropped out of university to work as a secretary. She wants better for you."

"Then she should want me to be happy," I said.

"Soila, don't be naïve," said Naserian. "You might be the daughter of a millionaire today, but you were once the daughter of a secretary, and you're the granddaughter of a white man's cook who ran out on his two wives before that. We've come from far."

"This is nuts!" I said, pushing away one of the large boxes that littered the floor of the fitting room with my foot. "Why aren't you on my side?"

"Do you really want to take photographs?" Naserian challenged me. "Why don't you start with photographing my wedding; stand there for twelve hours and see how you like that, arranging people, shooting petals and champagne glasses close-up, and stubborn dancing grannies who won't listen. I'll pay you a sixteenth of what you'd make on your first month as a banker. Tell me how that feels."

"Argh. You don't get it. I'm not trying to be a wedding photographer. I want to have a serious career as a photojournalist or a fine art photographer."

I felt defeated and dropped heavily into a small velvet chair, fussing around with my camera, taking several photos of Naserian in her gown. It was elegant, though too swirly for my taste. She looked like a cone of soft-serve ice cream. I flipped through the pages of a bridal magazine. None of the brides interested me—some looked too tightly wrapped to breathe while others looked like they were draped in toilet paper.

I tossed the magazine back on the table and slumped in the chair, my eyes shut. I wondered what Alex was doing right now. Could I see myself in a cupcake-y dress, running down a long aisle with Alex? I revised the image in my mind, this time wearing a simpler dress—no layers, no tulle, no train, no veil. Still, not me. All I could see was Alex, smiling as we walked together, his face nestled close to mine, his hand over my shoulder, protecting me on the streets of New York.

I hadn't seen Aunt Rarin in years. She had left for her education in Scotland before I went to America, and she'd graduated and worked her way up the ranks to counsel at the International Criminal Court in The Hague, where she had lived since completing her degree. When she'd visit Kenya, I was in college, and I missed her desperately.

In her recent phone calls, Rarin had mentioned to her other sisters, not Mother, that she had big news. But she wanted to tell them in person, and by the time she arrived, excitement was at a fever pitch. We fell asleep that night, my aunt Rarin and I, in the large guest cottage across from the main house. I had left underwear, socks, T-shirts, and jeans lying in a pile on the bed.

"I can't believe you still behave as if Princess is going to come and pick up after you, even two years after living on your own in the States. . . ." Rarin criticized, assessing the mess while I quickly threw things into drawers around the room.

Rarin was immaculate. I watched her remove her folded clothes from her suitcases in equal batches and lay them down in the same batches in drawers. What was creased she set aside for Princess to iron, and what was a gift she set aside in a large bag to give on Christmas Day. She folded every piece of underwear in a symmetrical triangle and every bra in half at the center. I watched her keenly and knew that this attention to detail she displayed toward something as insignificant as her wardrobe was the reason she was an international criminal barrister.

As Rarin and I fell asleep in the cottage, I told her that I needed just a hint of what the exciting secret was she was waiting to reveal.

"It's a guy," she said. "But it's so complicated, my baby."

"Why?" Lying faceup on my pillow, listening to the mosquitoes buzz outside the hovering net, I thought through all the complexities a man could bring into one's life. So far Alex had certainly changed mine. It was already almost a year since I'd met Alex at the Kenyan cellist's party. I hadn't slept with him yet. I knew it was something he wanted and even though he didn't pressure me, I couldn't shake the feeling that he mistook my reluctance for something more demure than the lingering demons of Father Emmanuel's assault. He often told me he didn't mind waiting, but privately I wondered how long that would be true.

"Is he married?" I asked Rarin.

"No, he's not married," Rarin said. "He's divorced and Scottish."

"Oh, come on, Rarin, our family is not that old-fashioned," I said. "None of that matters anymore. Besides, which Maasai guy are you going to find in the Netherlands?"

"I don't know, Soila," Rarin said. "I want to believe it, yet I'm so afraid."

The next morning, we waited until Mother left the house for early morning Mass, then congregated in the cottage with the door closed. Even Aunt Tanei was led slowly from her bedroom to come hear Rarin's news.

His name was Alisdair, a professor she'd met while studying in

Scotland. He was older and completely in love with her. She showed us a stack of Kodak photographs taken during her college years in Scotland. I found the scenes of Edinburgh more striking—the lush greenery, the fallen cherry blossoms in the meadows, the picturesque row houses painted in rainbow colors. Scotland seemed like an imaginary fairyland. Alisdair himself wasn't much to look at. I saw that my aunts thought the same, but none of us said it.

If Kokoi were here, she would have thrown up her hands in her usual theatrical manner and said that if life had taught her one thing, it was that the heart picks a frog despite the desperate pleas of the eyes. Alisdair had ginger hair, pasty skin, and big ears. His smile displayed a weak jaw and poor teeth. But he was tall and lean with athletic shoulders and he was sharply dressed in all of the photographs, wearing elbow-patched jackets and classy V-neck cardigans.

Rarin looked different somehow in the photographs—her smile had changed from how it had looked in my childhood. Her new smile seemed brave and free, not the guarded hand-over-mouth smile I'd always known. What made me believe she was truly in love was the way she leaned on this man, tucked into him, as if they were part of each other.

Afterward, I showed them a few photographs of Alex. Compared to Alisdair, there wasn't much to say about a Kenyan boy whose mother was white.

"Alex's dad was able to bring back an American woman to his family nearly three decades ago," I said. "If he could do that, you can too."

A gaping silence between my aunts billowed in the room. I sensed there was an exchange of awkwardness I wasn't privy to. Then Rarin, as if she hadn't heard me, quickly changed the topic.

"Have you slept with him?"

"Of course not!" My harsh reaction to the question startled even me.

"Well, do you love him, Soila?"

"I think so," I said.

"So what are you waiting for?" Rarin asked. "You said it's been a year. That's long enough."

"Hey!" Naserian butted in, looking combative. "Does loving him mean she has to sleep with him? Soila, don't listen to her—if he loves you, he'll wait."

"Soila, you can listen to these thirty-year-old virgins or you can listen to me," Rarin said. "If you love him, tell him and show him or you'll lose him and only blame yourself."

Over the past year, Alex and I had found intimacy in our own way. When we were alone together in his apartment, I wanted to go all the way but my resolve always wavered. His hands and lips were addictive, and I wanted to follow the pleasure we found together, but my mind wasn't ready to embrace the needs of my body. Alex didn't pressure me and I loved him even more for that.

"It's not so simple," I said. The four women in this room loved me more than anyone, and I wanted to let out my dark secret. But I still felt dirty and ashamed. I had tried to find the courage to tell them, or Alex, about Father Emmanuel. But I couldn't. For now, I would let Alex believe that the woman he loved was a rare unspoiled virgin. Besides, I had Leticia. And perhaps, with time, I would find it easier to talk about my past.

. . .

Naserian's wedding was a society event, the party of the year.

A few days after Christmas, exactly one week before the wedding, we performed the aadung inkishu, the dowry ceremony. During the ceremony, only men were allowed into the negotiations. Because he was marrying a Maasai girl, Kamau's Kikuyu family had to follow our traditions. We had bargaining power because we had the bride.

Kamau, his brother, his uncles, and his father sat at one end of the circle, while Mother's uncles—some of Kokoi's older brothers who were still living—sat on the other end, all elderly men dressed in knitted sweater-vests and weathered mismatched suits. They were feeble and tremulous, holding on to wooden sticks, and the lot of them bore only four or five wobbly teeth between them, yet their presence was registered heavily. Without them, the negotiations couldn't begin.

Mother had hired chefs who sweltered in the kitchen in white overcoats smeared with the bright colors of carrots and beetroot. My aunts and I were busying ourselves with service, bringing in large bowls and balancing them on our knees while pouring jugs of warm water for the men to rinse their hands before the big meal. We served millet porridge in bowls. While the men ate, the conversation became friendly, the room buzzing with laughter. But after the plates had been cleared away and the last sip of water drunk from the clinking glasses, silence returned to the room.

Dusk had turned to night before a beaming Kamau emerged, giving a thumbs-up sign to his fiancée. The dinner that followed the negotiations was a more relaxed affair, this time with all of us gathered together, now that the two families had formally merged. At ten P.M., the Kikuyus climbed into their motorcade and made the left turn out of our driveway, disappearing into the night.

Mother's uncles, with the stoic nature of old African gentlemen, sat Mother and Kokoi down in the living room, while we stood listening from a distance to show respect. It was a fair deal, my uncles said. Our family wanted thirty cows as Naserian's dowry, and in the end, Kamau's family agreed to the monetary equivalent of twenty and several sheep.

"It's just so ridiculous," Rarin said later when we were all in the cottage, sighing from the fatigue of the day. "Too many dowry negotiations have gone awry. Too many weddings starting off under a dark cloud because the families couldn't agree over cows. I want my biggest problem to be how I will afford a Vera Wang dress, not haggling over the number of cows."

The night before the wedding, we held the kupamba, the official party held only for the bride, the olden-day bridal shower. We dressed Naserian in her wedding collar, a large flat leather necklace about twelve inches in diameter brightly decorated with different colors of beads. For her slender neck, it seemed almost too much for her to carry, but it was a rite of passage. The necklace had thin strings of smaller necklaces drooping down to her navel. Kokoi had beaded the tiny necklaces after the dowry was settled. Twenty shoestring-size necklaces symbolizing the number of cows she was worth. To offer cows for brides was something that would have been incomprehensible to an American girl like Leticia, I thought. This was the kind of thing that could start a revolution in America. But I loved it. The notion that a man would love a woman so much that he would be willing to give up his most prized possessions for a lifetime with her.

Naserian's friends all attended the kupamba. We gave them fancy beads, and we wore veils and pretended to be brides, only for one night. The married ones gave her household gifts—pots and pans, juicers and blenders, expensive linens, and their share of advice, which I didn't listen to at all. Mother didn't allow alcohol in the house, though a steady decibel of old-school R & B was flowing from the sound system. I looked over at Tanei. She was sitting on her chaise with a veil over her head and a glass of punch about to tip over in her crippled hand. She was fast asleep. Leticia would have called this party lame.

. . .

In the morning, Naserian woke us up at dawn. Her wedding wasn't until three P.M. but she was panicking about everything from the shade of her MAC foundation to the decorations at the country club and most important, if her dress would fit. By noon she had made herself sick. My aunts and I fanned her with woven trays and we managed to catch her just as she was about to pass out. We laid her in the tub, making sure to hold her head above water so as not to wet her hair and create another debacle. Rarin gave her one of her anti-anxiety pills.

"Trust me," she said, as we watched Naserian swallow the pink pill. "It takes the edge off. It calms the nerves."

"The edge off what?" Mother asked, alarmed, as she entered the scene in her dressing gown, a silk cloth wrapped around her head. "You people have drugged your sister on her wedding day! What is wrong with you?"

The makeup artist finally arrived and started with us; Rarin, Laioni, and I were official bridesmaids. We all wore different designs, each one suited to her own figure, but we had managed to match the same shade of pale rose.

After our makeup was done, our dresses zipped and fascinators in place, the work started on Naserian. We all watched in fascination as the makeup artist worked on her until, miraculously, it appeared as though Naserian had had a light touch of cosmetic surgery—thinning of the nose, cheek implants, and even an eyelift. Though she had nearly flawless skin, every subtle discoloration was concealed, every out-of-place brow hair hidden.

When her makeup was complete, her long, thick hair was styled into a neat bun.

She didn't need any jewelry apart from teardrop tanzanite earrings that were a gift from Mother. The only thing the eye fell upon was her face in all of its glory. After that, we gowned her, careful not to pull out the multitude of sequins and beading around the sweetheart neckline. She sucked her stomach in as we zipped the bodice, praying it would fit. The rest of the gown fell into place with layers of organza ruffles. In that moment, I looked at everyone in the room and I knew that we all wished we were the ones getting married.

On the street, Kikuyu women were banging on our gate, calling out for Naserian. It was their custom. On the wedding day, the women in the groom's family took to the home of the bride to sing wildly and cause a ruckus until the family of the bride gave in and let her go. Mother wasn't perturbed. Everything went on inside as slowly and steadily as if there wasn't any commotion outside.

When Naserian was dressed we all proceeded to the driveway, where all of Mother's closest church friends stood like cadets in honor of the most beautiful bride. A prayer was said, and finally the gate was opened for the zealous Kikuyus, who continued to sing songs begging for the bride.

They had brought kikois and kangas to be laid on the driveway, so the bride's feet wouldn't touch the ground. When she got to the waiting limousine, the women scooped her up and stuffed her inside like a meringue going into an oven.

At the church, the pews were lined with people. Mother and Kokoi walked in first, holding hands. They'd never looked so beautiful. Kokoi wore a powder blue satin dress with a matching coat, a gold clutch, and a pillbox hat. Mother looked stunning in an African-style dress made with an exquisite pink Yoruba fabric imported from Lagos.

The flower girls went in second, followed by Rarin, Laioni, and me. The organist changed the tune, signaling for the congregation to stand, and Mother's uncle, Kokoi's youngest brother, a spry elderly gentleman, walked Naserian down the aisle. She was beaming.

When Father Emmanuel stepped up to the pulpit, I felt my body stiffen. His charisma, his mild manner, and his adept skill at warming up a crowd of strangers, his booming laugh and piercing eyes—all the things that made him popular—now made me nauseous.

After the two-hour Mass was over, the bride and groom floated out into the fresh air. More family joined the wedding party to pose for photographs on the steps of the cathedral. I looked on in wonder at the crowd of relatives squeezed into each frame. Everyone seemed joyous to be a part of the affair, except for a few of the groom's family.

"We're just going to have to get through the day with their furrowed faces somehow," Kokoi said, while we were in the bridal party limousine driving to the reception. "It's not our fault they're not Catholics and had to struggle through Mass."

"I don't know what the Kikuyus expect," Mother said, unaffected. "It's far too late for them to imagine they'll get their way now."

"Kikuyus, Kikuyus!" Kokoi said, tossing her hands up. I could feel Rarin's thighs tense next to mine. I knew her nerves were threatening to snap. If this is how Mother behaved about Naserian marrying a Kikuyu man, how would she respond to her Alisdair?

"I don't want to hear it anymore," Kokoi said to Mother. "Show me the Maasai boy who has the education and the money to marry these girls. They are fewer than the white rhino. Let it be." I felt Rarin relax again at Kokoi's words.

As we walked into the country club, the large throng of Kikuyu women entered following Naserian, praising God in song and dance for the special day and the beautiful bride.

But at the entrance, a gang of morans, Maasai warriors, Mother had hired for the day stopped the throng of in-laws and quieted them with their own song and dance. The morans were wrapped in red sheets and flailed high in the air, dancing the adumu with upright spears. Their feet elevated to such height it seemed they might never come back down. The olaranyani, the leader, had such a strong and mystical voice that he immediately hushed the large group of Kikuyus, commanding them to listen to his song. His warriors followed his melody with a rhythmic throat singing, a sort of call-and-response in layered tones, and their heads tilted back and forth as they jumped, as if uncorked from their necks. It was stunning; I wished I had my camera. Leticia would have loved this. But when I looked back at the crowd of Kikuyus, silent on their feet at the doors, I wished I had a veil to hide from their unspoken ire. The warriors' dance was traditional for a Maasai wedding celebration; another thing the Kikuyus chafed against because they were sidelined.

At the reception, the country club served a spectacular three-course wedding dinner. While we ate, one member after another of Kamau's extended family spoke about commitment and honor. Uncles and aunts, cousins and grandparents, narrated stories about Kamau and the blessing he had been to his family. They offered gift after gift to the couple, from woven baskets to blankets for the couple's new bed, and envelopes of money.

As the Kikuyus continued to clap and roar, I saw Mother signal for the MC to make an announcement. The MC steered his way through the large crowd of Kikuyus onstage and took the microphone.

"Ladies and gentlemen, ladies and gentlemen," he said, wiping his brow with a pocket-handkerchief. "Thank you to the groom's family. We would now like to welcome our ancestral spiritual leader, our laibon. Please stand for Laibon Ololeiyot."

As he walked toward the high table from the back of the room, I gripped Rarin's hand.

"Oh my God, why would Yeyo invite a medicine man?" I whispered to Rarin, my eyes shut. "Kamau's family is going to think we're into witch doctors."

"I don't know what's happening in this wedding," Rarin said.

The laibon was wearing his red sheets, and his earlobes were stretched to his shoulders, his face streaked with white powder, charms around his neck. The couple stood and walked up to the podium, where the laibon waived his fertility horn and dusted fine powder on their hands and faces.

"Here," he said to Naserian, gesturing to the horn. "Cradle it like a child. It will bring you one."

Naserian, whose face was frozen with embarrassment, took the horn and awkwardly cradled it. The whole room burst into laughter. I was finally able to loosen my grip on Rarin's arm, and I could tell from her demeanor that Naserian relaxed a little too.

The laibon had prepared two amulets whose protective charms, he said, were activated when he spat on them, and he tied them around the couple's necks. Spitting was a sign of esteem, he said.

"This is how the Maasai have always joined two people for life," he said.

He anointed Kamau with a Maasai name, Nalangu—one who comes from another tribe. He then spoke briefly in Maa to Naserian about her role as a wife. She will always please her husband, even when she is not pleased, he said. Naserian shook her head quickly as he spoke, hoping to rush him off. Eventually, the MC showed the laibon away.

From the corner of the room, I heard a clatter; something or someone was falling. Rarin gasped and I looked over to see Kamau's father half off his chair, wrestling the people around him. He stumbled to the podium, where Kamau, who had dashed from the high table, grabbed him by the arm before he took the microphone. Still, his voice echoed in the room.

"Does she think we couldn't have also shown off our own dancers and spiritual leaders? Or that we have no traditions? We contributed to this wedding just as much as she did. How dare she show us up?"

I worried for Mother. She was sitting upright in her chair at table one like a queen on her throne. Naserian's face was crumpling and I knew she was about to cry. I whispered to Rarin and Laioni to help usher her to the bathroom. We locked the door and Naserian cried.

"Kamau's family loathes us!" she wept. "They think we're showing off."

"But we are," I said, exhausted, turning down a toilet seat lid for a chair. "Yeyo has completely hijacked this wedding. I mean Kamau has even been given a new name! I'm so sorry, Aunt Naserian."

"Argh, who cares?" Rarin snapped, as she dabbed away Naserian's tears. "Naserian, you got the wedding of your dreams, the wedding of the year. Don't let anyone make you feel bad about it. Besides, every wedding has drama. A wedding with no drama is no wedding at all and if it is, I daresay, the marriage will be boring too."

Back in the banquet hall, the MC announced that it was time to cut the cake. When the cake was wheeled out, it was decorated with a crown of Maasai beads and Mother smiled from ear to ear.

The mood relaxed as the crowd mingled, holding saucers of vanilla icing and fruitcake and cups of tea and coffee. Rarin and Laioni and I didn't have much left in us to work the room. I found myself daydreaming about being back in New York, away from the chaos of my family, but my thoughts were often interrupted by the other guests.

"When will you be done in America so you can come back and help your mother here, Soila?" someone asked. My heart dropped. I couldn't fathom coming back, let alone having to work for Mother.

"When are you going to bring us a good husband? Now, that will be the real wedding of the decade!" someone else said.

"Are you mad? Soila is busy studying, not looking for a husband," I heard Mother snap. I hadn't seen her standing behind me. That was the thing about Mother. She was always with me. Even when I was as far away as New York, I could feel her presence around me. I turned and walked away.

Outdoors, I found a fountain with a koi pond. The sky was cluttered with millions of stars. It felt like I could reach my hand out and scoop them up. The December night air was warm over my bare shoulders, a respite from the brutal winter nights I would be returning to in New York. I took off my heels and sat on the edge of the pool, watching the fish swim around me.

I thought about this place and what it meant to me. Here, I was someone acknowledged, missed, loved. In two days, I'd be back in New York, sometimes lonely, an outsider, yet independent and free.

Rarin came out and joined me by the fountain. "It's so strange being back home, isn't it?" Rarin said.

"It is," I said, nodding. "It's as if I changed, but nothing here has changed, and I don't fit in anymore. I can't stand everyone's expectations, the assumption that my life is going to go a certain way and that I'm going to run back home as soon as I'm done with school. Everyone assumes I'm going to work for Yeyo and have a big stupid wedding like Naserian."

"I can't come back and live here," Rarin said. "I love Alisdair. I can't give him up. I just can't. He doesn't want to live in Kenya, and I love my job and I'm happy there."

"I feel the same way," I said.

I felt a deep sense of loss. Somewhere between finding my way in college and having the freedom to do whatever I wanted to do without Mother breathing down my neck, I could no longer imagine a life in Nairobi. There was nothing left here for me.

. . .

In the second semester of my junior year, I finally realized that racism in the United States wasn't something I could shove away. It was heavily my burden. That February, outrage was roiling over the shooting of a young unarmed Black man, an immigrant from Guinea, who had been shot to death by the police just a few weeks ago. Amadou Diallo's murder had shaken me and my friends from the African Students Association. After my argument with Alex ages ago about what it was like being Black in America, I had gradually opened my eyes to a reality that was different than I had understood. But Diallo's death had made it even clearer to me that in America, being Black was dangerous. Diallo hadn't even been American. He was African, like me. Regardless of anything I did, I could have been shot like him too. Leticia and I had talked of almost nothing else for days, and in those moments I felt I fully understood the trauma that she could never seem to let go of. I understood better why she was always defensive when there seemed to be an extra set of eyes on us at the drugstore or the clothing store, when the movie theater attendant checked our tickets twice, when the registrar's office alerted us that the extra credit we wanted to do would cost us more in tuition and didn't we want to check with the financial aid office first?

These were the discussions I was continuing to have with Alex too. He admitted that being African, sometimes he didn't react in the same manner his male Black American friends did. His experiences were similar. Being undermined by patients—*Is there another doctor?*—and by some of the teaching staff who would already have picked out their star white residents even before the shift began. It was humiliating, to constantly fight for his turf, to work three times as hard in order to prove his ability, to hold his tongue when a patient blatantly refused to accept his care. A few wouldn't let him touch them or their elderly parents or their children. It was brutal, he said. But still, he was able to shrug it off, move on. These conversations had brought us even closer together. Someone close to me understood how I really felt about my different brand of Blackness in this racially charged society and I could speak honestly about it. We became inseparable. After too many times rolling away from him on the couch, sitting up to put distance between our bodies, I started to hear Rarin's advice ringing louder in my ear. Alex had been patient but I couldn't be sure how much longer his patience would hold.

I sought Leticia's take on the matter and she once again was exasperated with me. It wasn't just Father Emmanuel. It was my religion. Leticia didn't understand the way Mother and the nuns had indoctrinated me—chastity and purity above everything else. Leticia had lost her virginity at sixteen, as had most of her classmates.

"We were all trying out sex some way or another," Leticia said. "Sure, some people might have stopped at first base, but most of us—including moi—went all the way. It seemed like everyone was doing it."

I never understood why Americans used baseball metaphors for sex. It seemed to put the entire focus of sex in a context of achievement—winning, scoring, opposition. I wanted sex to be something I shared with Alex, something special for us to share together. I tried to explain this to Leticia.

"I'm worried that I will end up being a notch on Alex's bedpost."

"Good lord, Soila, how can you even think that?" Leticia exclaimed. "Alex has never been like that. Why don't you talk to him about what the pervy priest did to you and then he'll understand where you're coming from? Give him a chance to be a good guy."

"I can't tell him about that. I don't want him to look at me differently," I protested.

"He's not going to look at you differently," Leticia assured me. "Soila, you really need to give him more credit than that. Besides, most men wouldn't wait this long. If he was only after sex he'd be dating a girl who gives it up easier than you."

Alex had waited but he hadn't made it easy either. He argued endlessly what his American mother had taught him—that sex was something between two people who loved each other. That wasn't true, I argued back, because pretty much everyone around us was having sex and none of them seemed in love with one another. I had been taught that my body was a temple of the Holy Spirit—but then Father Emmanuel had broken in and desecrated it.

Alex walked into my life with his broad shoulders and greenish eyes, his long fingers, and his mad ambition that I found irresistibly attractive. I felt that maybe, he was worthy. Maybe, he could change the way that I felt about giving myself to a man.

On a Saturday night in February, a nor'easter hit New York with four feet of snow. An afternoon visit to Alex's apartment turned into a night huddled on the couch with him when the power went out, the cold seeping into our bones. I woke up before him at dawn to see the snow still falling quietly outside—a pristine white tablecloth blanketing the narrow streets of the West Village. The electricity was back on. I slipped out of our nest of blankets, careful not to wake him, to go make a pot of coffee.

A little bird with riveting red feathers flew briskly toward the kitchen window. I thought for sure it would smash into the clear glass. Instead, it perched on the ledge.

It tipped its tiny head as if it was watching me. It struck me how free the bird was. It flew wherever it wanted. It was as bright and light as magic. Unlike me. I was tired of all the restraints—trying to live up to Mother's expectations, carrying the shame of Father Emmanuel, worrying that I was failing God by succumbing to the pressures of the world, to lust.

My desire to be with Alex had overtaken my spiritual beliefs. Surely, even God himself could see that what Alex and I had was not purely driven by lust. God could see that we loved each other, and perhaps Alex would be my husband one day. I wanted to be free like the bright red cardinal that floated outside Alex's kitchen window. I wanted to feel I could fly.

Alex was still asleep on the couch, arms spread out as if awaiting a hug.

"I'm ready," I said, poking at his chest until he woke up. "I want to do it, with you."

"Really? Are you sure about it?" he asked, wiping the sleep from his eyes. "I don't want you to compromise something that you really believe in."

"I'm completely sure. I'm ready for it. I just want to know that you'll still be here and that I'm not just some trophy for you to bag."

"Of course I'll still be here," Alex said, looking at me like he couldn't believe that I would question it. "I've been waiting for a while now. If I wasn't committed to you, I'd have found someone else a long time ago."

"There's something else," I said carefully. "I had a . . . well, a bad experience as a teenager. It did my head in when it comes to how I feel about trusting a man with my body."

Alex wanted to know more, and I found that once I started to tell him about Father Emmanuel, the words came out easily and I felt lighter.

"I knew there was something," Alex said. "I felt like there was this wall that I couldn't knock through. I knew there had to be more than the Catholicism. You don't even go to church. I've never even seen you read a Bible. But, Soila, I wish you had trusted me enough to know that you could tell me."

"I never told anyone else, only Ticia," I said. "It's taken me a long time to work through it all, to not blame myself."

Alex was careful and tender. He said he loved me so many times that the words carried me through my fear and I felt as safe as I ever had. It didn't matter that sex was a sin, that I was a sinner. Me, the daughter of a puritan, raised in the church, whose body was a temple of the Holy Spirit. All I wanted was to lie naked in bed with Alex, eating Chinese takeout. All I wanted was for us to be together.

Chapter Eight

In the spring of my junior year, I had nearly completed all my required courses after piling on extra credit through two summers and my sophomore year. On paper, I was halfway through senior year. On top of a full schedule of economics classes and my relationship with Alex, recruitment began for internships at investment banks and management consulting firms. I barely had time to wander the city taking photographs anymore and my course schedule had no room for art classes either. When I spoke to Mother and my aunts on the phone, they praised my dedication and focus on my studies. But as much as my econ classes bored me, recruitment was a thousand times worse. The competition was so intense you could almost smell it.

Students knew slots at the banks went quickly. And we knew they would be recruiting at all the other top schools across the country, which meant thousands of students would be fighting for twenty to thirty spots—or fewer, depending on the size of the coveted bank. I bought the dullest gray pantsuit with a beige blouse, like I had seen women wearing when I took photos around Wall Street, and walked into the main hall on campus on recruitment day with a folder full of résumés. I saw all the recruiters sitting in allocated areas and the students milling around them with shameless desperation and instantly felt exhausted. But this is what I had to do. This was the career that Mother had ordained for me.

I approached the first desk with a weak smile. My résumé was so bare that I'd had to use a fourteen-point font and double-spacing just to fill out the page. There just wasn't much to say. I had been born, gone to school, gone to college, and now I needed a job.

The recruiter, a middle-aged woman with a hairline that mushroomed unflatteringly close to her eyebrows, sized me up like a cow at auction. I felt battered under her assault of questions about my desire to work long hours, my regard for hierarchy, and my ability to "play well with others." When she was finished, she tucked my résumé in a folder, gave me a business card, and shook my hand, flashing a toothy smile. I couldn't tell whether I had done well, considering how Americans always smiled like that.

The rest of the meetings were a blur, the recruiters all the same with their dark suits and unmemorable faces. By the end of the day I had three invitations to real interviews with banks in Manhattan.

My first interview was with a bank that employed thirty-four thousand people and had sixty offices around the world. I was told that I would be meeting with an associate and a VP. I felt confident. I had studied up on math questions all night and re-memorized the formulas.

"Are they really going to ask you all that?" Alex remarked with a condescending tone. He was heading out to a twelve-hour rotation at the hospital. "Surely they know you're coming out of college. You're overstressing."

"Hey! Don't patronize me. I don't make rude comments when you're up all night studying words that I can't pronounce on your flash cards."

"How am I patronizing? Plus, it's not the same. I'm studying ahead of a surgery that I know I'll be in the next day with a head surgeon who's going to be quizzing me the whole time. He expects me to know that stuff. You're studying something you've never done a day in your life, and those guys know that."

"Just go," I said, waving him off. Watching him leave the apartment with a shrug, I felt the sliver of doubt that was slowly becoming familiar. We had only been having sex for a few months, but I felt our relationship being overtaken by a strange dullness. Everything Alex did had started to irritate me: his choice of ice cream at Maria's Gelato—why was it always rum raisin?—the way he left cabinet doors open in the kitchen and the cap off the toothpaste, the way he left his shoes around the house for me to trip over in the dark. But the more I picked a fight, the less he fought back. Often, he just walked away, and that made me even madder.

While prepping for interviews with the investment banks, I learned that they had an unusual hierarchy. Unlike most other corporations, which boasted one vice president and one director, at investment banks, vice presidents and directors were littered all over the place. For every three years a banker managed to live through the horrendous working hours, they were rewarded with a more-important-sounding title. It started with analyst, associate, vice president, and finally after nine years of indentured servitude, bankers were named director. Everyone's job was to make the person's job below them harder and the person at the bottom rank was judged by how gleefully and dutifully they performed for their taskmaster. The interviews were just as torturous. For an analyst position like mine, an associate and vice president conducted the interviews together in one room, or at times in separate interviews. They behaved in strange ways. In one interview, the vice president signaled for me to sit and then looked at me for a few minutes without saying a word.

"Okay, I'm leaving," I said, picking up my bag. "I came here for an interview, not for whatever is happening right now."

"Good, good!" the VP said. "You've got spunk. You need that in this business. You need that innate ability to not get rattled, and to be confident."

Several weeks after the interviews, I was still waiting to hear from the three big banks, and I knew that several of my classmates had already received offers. Leticia was still out hunting for internships at magazines.

When I became completely desperate that I hadn't made it in with the investment banks, I decided to see the diversity recruitment counselor at school. She was a shrinking African American lady, retirement age, with silver hair and a layered necklace beaded with tiger's-eye stones. Her name was Dorothy Simmons. I ranted to her about my horrible interview experiences and she listened intently.

"Honey, I'm listening to you now and I don't think you'd be a good fit for the big banks," she said. She stretched her hands over the desk and put them on mine like she was shielding a delicate bird. "That environment is soul-consuming. I've got a contact at a boutique bank that's very focused on diverse hiring. It'll be a much better fit for you." Mrs. Simmons pulled out a business card and slid it on the table toward me, the way the dealer at a poker game does. The card looked familiar. I dug in my backpack and came up with at least ten cards, then shuffled through them. There it was.

"I know this lady," I said, slapping the desk with excitement. "I met her. She was here on recruitment day. She was the first person I talked to, but she didn't show much interest in me." I didn't tell Mrs. Simmons that it was the woman with a hairline that grew all the way to her brows.

"Oh really?" Mrs. Simmons said. "You don't worry, honey. I'll give her a call. You'll be hearing from her."

The email from Gloria Reuben, managing director at Cohen & Brothers Co., arrived a day later, inviting me for an interview. This was different. No senior person at any bank had ever personally invited me to an interview—it was always a human resources person.

I knew this bank focused on mergers and acquisitions, so I read up on that and why that particular area interested me. At nine-thirty the following Monday, I sat in Gloria Reuben's office. This was definitely not the woman who had been on campus on recruitment day. Gloria was older, more distinguished. Her dark hair was styled in a short coif more appropriate for a man. She wore no makeup and a plain black pantsuit. She was relaxed in the way she sat on her swivel chair, leaning back rather than upright, and that put me at ease. She said she had visited Kenya with her partner and shot out a bullet list of the places they'd seen, and when she said, "Anyway, let's dive right into it," I realized that I was completely calm and ready for the interview. The questions were rational and appropriate—no valuations, no math. She said she was "only interested in Soila."

. . .

I was hired as one of ten analysts for the summer internship at the boutique bank Cohen Brothers & Co. When the offer came through on email, I was sure I'd read it wrong. That summer I'd be taking home nearly thirteen thousand dollars. I printed out the email and took it home to show Leticia, who was brimming with her own good news. She'd been offered an internship at *Josephina,* an art magazine that featured the froufrou art collections of wealthy New Yorkers. Her internship didn't pay, but the editor had promised a full-time staff writer position after graduation, if Leticia did well.

"Soila, you're rich! This is crazy. Who makes this kind of money over the summer?"

"Apparently Wall Street people."

Alex didn't agree.

"This is minimum wage, don't you get it?" he said, shaking the printed email in my face. "This is a racket."

"I don't understand."

"Look, it's simple math. Investment bankers pull, what . . . a hundred hours a week. So do the math. Thirteen thousand dollars over twelve weeks at any regular forty-hours-per-week job would be twenty-five dollars per hour. But at one hundred hours a week, you're making like, ten bucks an hour. Even fishermen earn more."

I laughed a little, but I also felt the bile rise inside me. I snatched the printout from his hand.

"Well, once I start working full-time, I'll make a huge bonus," I said. "Besides, you won't earn much either."

Alex was about to graduate from med school. I knew he was under a ton of pressure.

"Yeah, but my poverty is out in the open. We go in knowing we won't make much for at least eight years after college. Banks, on the other hand, are showing you big numbers and keeping you comfortable, but in actuality, for the kind of labor they're putting you through, they're totally ripping you off."

"Argh, shut up," I said, frustrated. "Investment banks pay ludicrous bonuses."

"Okay," he said. "You'll see when you start working."

I pushed my feet into my shoes and grabbed my purse.

"Where are you going? I thought we were going out for dinner."

"Why are you so taken aback that I'm leaving? Were you not in the room the past hour or did you miss the hurtful commentary about my job?"

We were supposed to celebrate my offer with dinner at Phak Yun, our favorite Thai restaurant with the hot chili deep-fried fish served whole with its eyes, gills, and tail. We liked to eat it with our hands, carefully picking out the meat from the tiny bones, recalling stories we had heard in Kenya of people who had choked on fish bones. We would giggle about Alex doing CPR on me right there at the restaurant if I choked, and how ironic it would be if he was the one who swallowed a bone, since I couldn't perform CPR.

"I'm not in the mood for dinner. I'm going home," I said.

It turned out Alex was right about my internship. We were workhorses, plugging a hundred hours a week developing slides for pitch books that ran over hundreds of pages. Sometimes there would be two to three deals going on simultaneously that needed multiple pitches at the same time. The work was also cyclical. When we didn't have any work to do, we would have to sit around putting in "face time," which was essentially looking like we were working hard when we were really chatting online.

I spent a good amount of time watching and learning human behavior. I often felt more like an anthropologist studying a tribe than I did an investment banker. I had learned so much about Americans from Leticia and Alex, but these bankers were nothing like the college students I had met in the past three years. I felt like I was starting all over again, learning the rules of this new culture. Some people were more outgoing and garrulous, and they used that to get points with the higher-ups. I saw the expressions exchanged when an intern tried too hard, like Jodie Hale, who constantly offered to do the Starbucks run and make tea. She was pitiful. I learned the trick was to be seen as willing to get the Starbucks only if I was going, so I'd stand up, stretch, and say, "I'm heading to Starbucks—anyone want anything?"

Then there was Dave O'Neill. Dave came in at eight A.M. with a smile and Starbucks in his hand, and was told that he was late. Confused, he looked at his watch and said, "Well no, I was here till one this morning and I'm here at eight."

"Dave, I don't want to argue with you, but basically, you're late when I'm in the office before you," Angie Blythe, a first-year associate, told him coldly. She lived to make our lives miserable. She was rail thin and hardly moved her arms when she walked. Her black hair was cut to a blunt shoulder-skimming bob with severe bangs, and the interns gossiped that she looked like "Cleopatra, if Cleopatra had never gotten laid." When Dave came in "late" again, Angie didn't bother saying a word, and I knew that he wouldn't get a full-time offer.

On a muggy July day, Gloria Reuben called an impromptu meeting to discuss a pitch we would be making for the impending merger of two giant corporations. It had been a high-energy week for the entire floor because the markets were exploding. Internet start-up companies were being invented daily and the stock market was swelling with overpriced valuations. It was all built on a bubble. The American stock market had never had such a great year. What that meant for banks was competition for the initial public offerings and for mergers and acquisitions.

At the meeting, Gloria asked questions about feasibility—realistically, how quickly could we turn the pitches around given everything else we were working on—and who was working on what?

I quickly spoke up and offered a suggestion about creating consistent teams, saying that sometimes interns felt as if we were playing a game of double Dutch, jumping in and out of multiple projects at the same time. I said that it would be nice to be in a core team, able to chase one project from its initiation to the end. Gloria said that that was excellent feedback and perhaps consolidating teams might bring better cohesion and efficiency in the way we ran projects. I left the meeting feeling positive. I had contributed in some way. My small voice had been heard.

Back at my desk, Angie Blythe stood over me, arms folded over her waist.

"Who do you think you are? Where do you get off?"

"What are you talking about? What did I do?"

"You think this is how you get ahead? By throwing everyone else under the bus? You just made me, and all the other associates who manage you, look like bumbling buffoons. You just basically told us that we don't know how to organize our teams to get work done efficiently. Well, you've had your little moment in the sun. I hope you're happy."

The entire floor was stiff with tension. When Angie stormed away, I stood up and went to the bathroom, shut myself in one of the stalls.

I crumpled into tears. I was in there for fifteen minutes when I heard a light knock. Under the half door of my toilet cubicle I saw black patent leather shoes with block heels and the seams of well-ironed black pants.

"You gonna stay in there all day?" A woman was talking through the gap in the door. I stood up and inched the door slightly open to make out lips the color of the inside of a pomegranate. It was Molly, a petite, curly-haired associate.

I opened the door fully and came out of the stall, walking straight to the sinks. I washed my face and dabbed my swollen eyes with tissues.

"I'm Molly, I'm a third-year associate," she said, talking to my image in the mirror, rather than to my face. "I think we've met."

I nodded, while still dabbing my eyes. I realized now that she was more senior than Angie and I was touched she had gone out of her way to comfort a minion like me. "Don't worry too much. You made one mistake. In the future, just remember that it's the small things that matter. You don't need to open your mouth; quietly make the lives of those above you easier and they'll remember you for it."

That night, I couldn't sleep. I was on a rampage. I'd turn off my bed lamp, close my eyes, then sit up again, turn on the lamp, and rant to Alex.

"Soila, I'm going in at six A.M. for a twelve-hour shift," he said, covering his face with a pillow. "It's just office politics. Just figure out how to play the game."

"Alex, I don't need this stupid job. Okay?" I sniped. "I really don't! I could call Professor Bergman for contacts in the photo industry and have a freelance gig by the end of the month. I could be out covering the protests in East Timor, or HIV in South Africa."

"Soila, have you forgotten that Cohen's going to give you a permanent work permit after you graduate, if they offer you a job? So, unless you're sure you don't want to be based in the States anymore, you can't just up and quit."

"So what? America is not heaven," I said. "Besides, there are other ways to get a green card. I could marry you. I could ask my mom for a loan to invest in a franchise here and buy my way into residency. I could buy a 7-Eleven. Or a Dunkin' Donuts. She's all about business. She'd grab on to that idea like a dog with a bone."

"Okay, this is insane." Alex sat up and took a deep breath. "First of all, I'm not doing a green card marriage. When we get married, it will be for real. Second of all, you'd hate owning a Dunkin' Donuts."

He lay back down and pulled me toward him.

"You just had a bad day. It's a learning curve. Try not to let the daily shenanigans get in the way."

I fell silent. Overpowered.

Nonetheless, I heard Alex. And I heard Molly. She told me to be helpful, do more. I started coming in a half hour earlier than my usual seven A.M. and created *The Ten Things to Know This Morning* email newsletter.

For the first few days everyone scoffed at my newsletter, but within a week it was the first thing everyone read every morning. For stressed-out analysts and associates with barely enough time to finish their morning donuts, it beat scrolling through the entire length of *The Wall Street Journal*.

. . .

Keep Shining! Three weeks after starting my morning newsletter, I opened my inbox to find those words in the subject line of an email from Molly. When I swiveled my chair to turn to her cubicle, she was grinning broadly. Then she pumped two thumbs-ups in the air. In the end, showing initiative had come easily. All I needed was a compass in a new landscape to direct me which way, and Molly had done that with pleasure. Then I just applied the work ethic Mother had instilled in me as a child. I learned everyone's name and listened to heaps of unsolicited advice and slogged through the files of data they tossed into my inbox.

Mother had always said, "Every person, even the village idiot, knows something you don't—even the people you think are stupid know something you can learn from." All I had to do was work hard with no complaints. Finally, the lessons Mother had drummed into me about bathing myself with humility and patience and perseverance were paying off.

Meanwhile, Molly had become obsessed with styling me. It annoyed me slightly, but I knew she had good intentions.

"You have to look the part!" Molly said, snapping her fingers in my face. She was an easygoing Californian who had turned hardcore New Yorker. "I was like you when I first got here. I wanted to come to work dressed in my usual loose-fitting tops and open-toed heels. Then I realized nobody was going to put me in front of clients looking like that."

On a pleasant Sunday, Molly dragged me to Bloomingdale's, where she selected dark-colored pants, sweater-vests, jackets, and tailored shirts. She picked out handmade leather belts in brown and black, and then she put me in a pair of heels. I couldn't walk in high heels, even though as a little girl I had loved playing dress-up, hobbling around in Mother's fanciest pumps. Mother wore heels her whole working life. It was the same with makeup—she applied a facial mask every night and foundation every morning. I used the same tube of ChapStick for months. Mother said a little help goes a long way, but whoever Mother was, I wanted to be the opposite.

Molly and the frustrated salesladies—I had tried on ten different pairs of heels—made me take practice laps around the shoe department. With each pair, I hissed in pain and moved as if on stilts. Molly rolled her eyes.

"All right, you've made your point. Guess it's not so bad to be the only woman on three floors who doesn't wear killer heels," she muttered critically. She picked out three pairs of block-heel shoes; one black pair with a distinctive silver buckle I particularly loved.

We ended up at a high-end spa, where Molly described the treatments she wanted done on me in great detail. I felt invisible.

"We need to get rid of this unibrow," she said.

She was tracing the length of my eyebrows lightly with her index finger, inspecting them closely as if looking through a microscope.

"When was the last time you actually waxed your eyebrows? And *please* don't say never."

Molly mentioned the twists in my hair while we were in an elevator going up to our office on the fiftieth floor on a Monday morning. But my hair was something I refused to compromise on.

"Actually, Molly, I don't want to straighten my hair. I like that I can change my style every month if I want to. I love my braids, my twists, my Afro, and my bun. If someone wants to judge me based on my hair and not my work then that's too bad."

"Okay, fine—keep your hair," she said, raising her hands up in a defensive way. "It's clearly a touchy subject."

After an awkward silence, Molly turned to me and said, "Look, I get it—you want to express yourself. But banking is an environment where, sadly, you have to conform. I'd love to come in with flaming red hair tomorrow, but I can't. I'm just trying to help you."

"You've helped enough," I spat out, and felt the air in the elevator grow tense. Sleep-deprived bankers with their Starbucks cappuccinos in hand pretended not to hear us. "I'm not your African pet project."

When I told Leticia about the confrontation with Molly over my hair, she was outraged. "Oh my God, who is that white woman and what the hell is her problem?" she said. We hardly saw each other at home anymore. Leticia's job was more flexible, but it also required schmoozing. She spent a lot of her time at gallery openings, dinners hosted by socialites, and odd events, like parties held on boats. I left home at dawn and returned after ten P.M. We had taken to meeting up at coffee shops in the middle of the day, when I could sneak out for a bit. "I mean, seriously, I've been listening and watching over the last few weeks, but I can't hold my tongue anymore. Your bushy eyebrows didn't need waxing—okay, maybe a pluck or two—and your hair doesn't need straightening."

"No, Molly was trying to help," I said, feeling the urge to defend her. "I needed a serious crash course to survive this job and she stepped in to teach me. If I want to get a full-time offer, I'm going to have to play the game, fit in, dress the part."

"Fit in to what? This is classic de-ethnicization. Why do we have to dilute our heritage? Why should you have to straighten your hair to get a job offer?"

"Leticia! Don't be naïve—you know it's a white man's world."

"That's a world I refuse to live in," Leticia said.

"Well, I work at this bank and if I have to wear a suit or pluck my eyebrows to get a full-time offer, I'll do it," I replied. "But I'm not going to change my hair—that's where I draw the line."

"Girl, you should have been a writer," Leticia said. "At my job, no one can say anything about what I wear unless it's straight-up unprofessional. They don't pay me enough."

"Well, you're in the creative industry," I said. "I'm in the robot industry. God forbid a person stands out."

The next morning, I went to Molly's desk. She was happy to see me, her eyes bright and wide as always. "Listen, I didn't mean to be abrasive yesterday about the hair thing," I said. She started to speak but I stopped her, gently tapping her arm. "I know you're trying to help me, and I really appreciate that, but if I straighten my hair, I lose my identity. I don't know if that makes sense?"

"No, it's fine, I totally get it," Molly said. "I'm sorry I even suggested it. I overstepped."

As I walked back to my cubicle, I thought about Mother. Would she have been proud of me, standing up for myself? Or would she have rebuked me for sabotaging my chance to succeed in corporate America?

Molly and I worked late every day, sharing tubs of Chinese food while she told me about her childhood in California, her yogi mother who was also a flamboyant sex therapist, and how that had embarrassed Molly her whole life. Her boyfriend, Simon, was a comedian who performed stand-up at comedy nightclubs around the city. We'd catch his shows when we could after work. Alex too was working around the clock, and we hardly saw each other. By Sunday I was so exhausted I could barely get out of bed.

On the phone, when Mother asked about church, I said I attended the ten A.M. service at Riverside Church. In truth, it wasn't a Catholic church and even if it had been, I had not set foot in a church since I landed on American soil three years ago. But I could see its steeple from the window in my apartment and it gave me an inexplicable comfort.

If Mother saw me now, she would bemoan all the ways she had lost me to this new world. But I had not completely forgotten my past, certainly not Mother. Rather, I was putting aside my old me to make room for the new. I was like Mother's chickens in the coop that would stop laying eggs when their molting began and only recommence when their new feathers had grown in.

. . .

My last week as a summer intern at the offices of Cohen & Brothers was filled with sickening anxiety. The interns had been united in their torment for three grueling months, whining over beers about the inhumane hours, cussing out narcissistic personalities who ground us like we were coffee beans. But now hiring negotiations were happening daily in the conference room and the interns hardly spoke to one another. Jodie Hale wasn't going to make the cut; she had to know it. She showed no critical-thinking skills and was a pushover. We all knew Dave O'Neill wasn't going to make it either.

"She's got a stick up her ass," Dave said about Angie, one late night in the office. "And you know how it is—her voice will be a big factor in their decision-making. Whatever. . . . Banking's not for me anyway."

That left eight of us on the battlefield, but there were only five spots. I wasn't confident about a spot either. After Angie's and my run-in, it had taken weeks before she'd warmed up to me again, despite my diligence and extra initiative. Molly assured me that Angie liked me. I had to take her word for it because Angie seemed as cold as ever.

"She's like that with everyone," Molly said. "She's probably like that with her own husband."

I was shocked to learn she was married. I couldn't imagine her stiff arms wrapped around the warm body of another person.

"If I don't get it, I'll take it as God's way of telling me that banking is not for me," I fretted to Alex as the last week drew closer to an end.

"You're going to get it. You've worked hard. God's got nothing to do with it."

Deep down, I wished just a little that I would fail, knowing it could be the way out with Mother. If I was deemed not good enough to get a job in the industry, there would be nothing she could do. Maybe she'd finally allow me to pursue photography.

Midweek, when I thought the tension between the interns couldn't rise any higher, I was sitting on the toilet idling inside the cubicle, wishing Friday could come before Thursday and we could all be freed from our suspense. I heard the main bathroom door swing open, heels clicking toward me, and the voices of two women talking in low tones but not quite whispering. Kokoi would have said it's the way people talk "when they're busy sharpening their knives."

"Oh yeah, Stu's definitely in—his dad golfs with the CEO. It's totally unfair. Kiran's getting in too. . . . Let's face it, he's a minority plus he's brilliant. Steve's also a minority, so there you go. God, it's pointless these days if you're white."

"Wait, Steve's a minority?"

"Yeah, didn't you know? He's half Black."

"Oh wow, he totally doesn't look Black. I did think he looked a bit tan but figured it's the summer. . . ."

"God, Mel, you're kidding me, right?" the other woman said with a stifled laugh. I knew then that Shelly was the other woman talking. Mel and Shelly were fellow interns who had taken to each other since the beginning of the internship. I almost envied their relationship. I didn't have anyone in the office who I could lean on. I had Molly but she wasn't an intern. "Okay, so that's the three spots. What about the other two? I'm sure Soila. God she's such a kiss-ass, she makes me want to hurl."

"She's shrewd, though, you have to admit. Her morning roundup email is actually helpful."

"Yeah, but the way she hangs on to Molly—it's so transparent. She's buddied up with everyone who matters in the hiring process. It's nauseating. Angie can't stand her, though, so maybe she won't get in."

The women slipped out as casually as they had slipped in, their heels slapping on the tiles. They hadn't even used the bathroom, except to gossip and perhaps reapply their lipstick.

The Soila of three months past would have sobbed in the toilet cubicle. But the summer at Cohen had earned me a hard shell. I'd learned that intelligence wasn't enough. To survive I'd have to be strategic, form alliances, identify others' weaknesses, and avoid making the same mistakes. I wasn't going to let Shelly shame me for surviving.

I detoured past her cubicle on my way back to my desk. "Next time, check the stalls," I said without slowing my stride. Her face turned the color of curdled milk.

On Friday morning, I was the first one called in to the conference room. I was sure I was being let go. Gloria Reuben, managing director, Paul Dover, a vice president I'd chatted to often about the markets but hadn't worked with much, and Angie Blythe sat at one end of the long table. Gloria gestured for me to sit at the other. The polished expanse between us gaped.

"Soila, when I hired you, I saw great potential and you haven't disappointed me. You're eager, you show initiative, you're supportive, you're a team player. I know you'll be receiving a lot of offers at the end of your senior year, and I really hope you choose to come back to us."

Paul looked at me proudly, as if I were his daughter, even though he was probably only about ten years older than me. Angie tapped her pencil on a pile of papers. I knew that I never wanted to have another stressful job interview. I was familiar with this environment, and I had even made a friend.

"I'll stay on here," I said, matter-of-factly. "I want to work here."

"Wow! Well, that didn't take much convincing," Gloria said. "That's fantastic news. I'm so glad." She stood up and walked around the table with her arms wide open, held my shoulders, and looked me in the eyes. "Great decision, Soila. You'll be happy here. Good luck with what's left of your senior year!"

Paul stood up too, and shook my hand. I looked over at Angie. She was tugging at her collar absentmindedly, staring into the street all the way down from the fiftieth floor.

That night, the person I really wanted to celebrate my win with was Leticia. She had finished her internship too and received solid recommendations from her editors and she had cultivated a great network. She felt confident she would be offered the staff writer position before graduation.

Better still, I knew she'd be elated for me. She wouldn't do the math, and analyze whether it was worth it for me. That was what Alex would do, and I didn't want to hear it.

Leticia met me at Phak Yun, the Thai restaurant Alex and I loved.

"It's on me," I said, toasting with a tall glass of a rum cocktail that Leticia had ordered for us. "Can you believe it? All the other hired interns will come back to Cohen next summer after graduation, and I'll be starting in January—that's a whole six-month head start. I'm so glad I suffered through the extra coursework. It was so worth it in the end."

"Cheers! Okay, so check this out," she said, wide-eyed, as she pulled an issue of *Time Out* magazine from her bag. "I know you don't care about this kind of stuff, but I have to show you this. *Time Out* has done a profile of all the hot Black artists and photographers in the city. Isn't that amazing? Literally, the whole issue is like a tribute. I'm so proud of *my* people."

I flipped through the pages of the magazine and stopped when I saw a face I recognized. It was Akhenaten Morrison, the artist who had guest-lectured my Introduction to Art class in my sophomore year. He was photographed in black-and-white wearing all black, leaning on a white wall with his arms crossed over his chest. His dreadlocks were longer than I remembered. In front of him stood a life-size sculpture made from some form of metal. I struggled to read the article, or the caption, as the only source of light in the restaurant was the flickering candles on the dinner tables.

"I know this guy," I said, handing the magazine back to Leticia with the page folded back.

"Really?" She peered closely at the page.

I couldn't tell her that my relationship with Alex had nearly collapsed on the day I met the artist or that I was now, years later, completely mortified by the words that had come out of my mouth that afternoon.

"Yeah, back in that intro art class I took, remember? He was pretty weird, Ticia. He's named after a pharaoh, really eccentric. . . . But he's very accomplished. I'm not surprised he's been featured."

"Hah! Interesting," Leticia said, moving the magazine aside. "Maybe I can pitch to interview him once I start working full-time. Gosh, Soila, look at me. I'll graduate college in debt with a fluff degree that ain't worth shit but at least I'm following my passion, right?"

She'd say that often, sometimes as she did a pirouette, pretending to be a ballerina, or sometimes when she was feeling sorry for herself. But the way she said it always made me laugh.

"Soila, maybe your mom is right. Maybe you're better off getting a degree that will actually pay the bills, you know? I mean, look at us. . . . You'll end up with a six-figure salary really soon, and I'll make not even half that or be laid off, just going by how many magazines fold every year. I might end up a waitress. Maybe it's a good thing you shelved the photography dream."

"Don't say that," I said, trying to keep her spirits up as she started to look drained by the reality of the choice she'd made for her career. "You're a great writer, a better networker than anyone I know. I'm not worried about you."

"What about Alex?" Leticia said, taking a long sip of her cocktail.

"What about him?"

"Well, for starters, he's not here. Isn't that a little weird? You should be celebrating with him."

I shrugged. "He's so weird these days. It seems like all we do is irritate each other."

Alex was knee-deep in his medical rotation and we hardly spent any time together. He had decided that he wanted to specialize in pediatric oncology. He'd said that during the rotations, he saw so much sudden and unnecessary death—gunshots, car accidents, fires—and what saddened him most was that the families never had a chance to say goodbye, with the doctors wondering if they could have done more. But with the kids who had cancer, there was a greater chance for bonding and for closure for the families and the doctors, he said.

"I think maybe he's fallen for someone at the hospital," I told Leticia. The food had arrived at our table and I poked at it without enthusiasm.

"That's ridiculous," she said. "Where would he find the time between dissecting cadavers and suturing bullet wounds? Do you think he's making out with nurses? Girl, please! The brother is stressed-out."

"Why else would he become so distant? I don't understand why he's acting so different." I wished Leticia had never brought up Alex's absence. "We're drifting apart. Plus, his little quirks that never bothered me now drive me crazy. Like the way he never hurries. Not even the sound of the train when he's late for his shift stirs him. He never runs. He jogs slowly like he's carrying two suitcases, one in each hand—like a robot. It drives me nuts."

"It's just a phase," Leticia said, laughing at my impression of Alex. "You guys love each other."

"And the way he spends money! Who buys a two-hundred-dollar hoodie from Nordstrom? I don't feel we value the same things."

"Wow, okay, drama queen, will you stop it?" Leticia said. "We're all caught up with finishing school and starting jobs. Maybe your relationship has taken a step back, but Alex is a great guy. Don't give up on him."

Chapter Nine

My senior year began in September and as the students I'd met over the previous three years gathered back together on campus, it was clear we had all had a rough summer. Some of us had earned jobs through internships, while others weren't so lucky. Everyone wore strain on their faces. I slogged through the fall semester, finishing up my required coursework, and I spent another Christmas with Leticia's family. It had become a tradition to visit the Hopkinses for the holiday, and I found it much warmer and more fun than Christmas at home ever had been. In January, I turned twenty-four and started full-time at Cohen & Brothers and felt more mature than ever. Spring semester felt like a turning point from the exhaustion of the fall. We were four months from graduating from a top university with strong life prospects. Leticia and I felt buoyant. Nothing could sink our spirits.

That winter was one of the coldest I had experienced since coming to the United States. Despite Leticia's encouragement, Alex and I were barely spending any time together anymore and it seemed clear to me that the tight seams of our relationship were coming apart.

One Friday night, Leticia and I went to Papyrus for happy hour in an attempt to lift my spirits. The bar was warm, the onion rings toasty, and we were determined to enjoy ourselves and think about something else until we gathered the courage to venture out into the arctic temperatures.

"Why are you pushing your food around on your plate like that?" Leticia asked, taking a swig of her beer. "You do that all the time now."

"I haven't been feeling great," I answered, struggling to enjoy the same onion rings that I had loved eating for the last three years. "I've been feeling so nauseous and I have stomach cramps all the time. I think it's the stress of my new job, feeling so unhappy with Alex, graduation, and knowing my mother's coming for the first time and I don't even have a decent apartment to put her up in. I'm feeling anxious all the time."

"If I didn't know better, I'd say you're pregnant," Leticia said, putting down her beer. "Could you be?"

"Absolutely not," I said. But then I realized I couldn't remember the last time I had my period. "Oh God."

Leticia stood up quickly. "Get your coat, we're leaving."

At the pharmacy, there was nearly an entire aisle packed with pregnancy tests. I felt paralyzed. *How did I get here?*

"Soila! Stop daydreaming and pick a test—get two different ones just to be sure."

"I can't do this," I said, walking backward. "I need to go. I can't be pregnant; this can't happen to me."

"Fine, you want to run? Run," Leticia said. "But every minute you waste means you're losing options."

Leticia grabbed two boxes from the aisle and headed to the counter, unperturbed, as if she were going to pay for a pack of gum. As soon as the cashier rang her up, she took my hand.

When both sticks showed two clear pink lines, I sat on the bathroom floor and stared at the palms of my hands. Early in our relationship, on a dare, Alex and I had visited a diviner's Santeria shop in the Latino part of Queens. I remembered now how she had held out my palms and told me of my good fortune. She'd rubbed her cowrie shell beads, made me rub them too, thrown them around, studied my open hands, and told me of my ire, my blessed, fortunate future.

In the bathroom, I knew that this was nothing but bad fortune. I tried to cry, but the tears wouldn't come, so I heaved and heaved, my lungs needing more fresh air.

"Open the door, Soila, come on, open!" Leticia was banging frantically on the door. "If you don't open this door, I'm calling the super."

I crawled toward the door and turned the lock while still on the floor. Leticia looked at the sticks with their bright pink lines. She sat on the floor with me and laid my head on her lap, and we sat like that, not speaking.

The night passed slowly. After three cups of chamomile tea, still sleep wouldn't come. I lay in bed until it was nearly dawn listening to New York City as she marched on, awake through the night. Garbage trucks beeping, rogue car alarms, zooming motorbikes, a couple fighting in the street. When the winter sun warmed my face I opened my eyes and it all came back. My bad fortune, my hell to pay for fornication—it was really true. It hadn't been a dream. I was pregnant.

That morning, Leticia and I sat down at our tiny kitchen table and tried to come up with a plan. Leticia made coffee and placed the steaming mug in front of me. She put her hands over mine.

"What should I tell Alex?" I could hardly hear the whisper of my own voice. "I don't know what I'm going to say. How will I tell him? It's going to destroy him, his career—"

"Wait," Leticia said, cutting me off. She tipped my face up to look at me. "Are you even thinking about having this baby, Soila?"

"I don't know . . ." I said. "Just the thought of killing a baby. Maybe I should keep—"

"Whoa, whoa, stop," said Leticia. "Soila! This is your life, your entire life on the line. You're just about to graduate college; you've just turned twenty-four. You haven't even started your career. What are you going to do with a baby? Will you raise it in our apartment? Will you send it back to Kenya? Will you go back to Kenya?"

"I was up all night thinking about what I'm going to do about the baby—and even though the most sensible thing to do is to . . . you know . . . it goes against everything I believe."

"See, I don't buy any of that," Leticia argued. "You think it's hard now—wait until you have to give the baby away to your mom in Kenya. Or until you have to raise it here in the States and have to juggle work and daycare and pediatrician appointments as a single mom. It's really hard."

"Leticia, you're not the one who has to have an abortion," I snapped, stung. "It's so easy to say when you're not in these shoes. I would never tell you to have an abortion."

I shook my head. How would I ever know what was the right thing to do?

Alex and I met at a Starbucks in Greenwich Village during the kind of workday when I could barely get a bathroom break. I told Angie I had a doctor's appointment and would need an hour. Watching Alex walk in, in his usual slow stride, I felt sorry for him. His big green eyes, his soft, fluffy curls, his cappuccino skin, his spontaneous smile, his massive brain, and his love for medicine—these were all the things about him that I was about to ruin with my bad fortune. But these were also the things that our baby could inherit.

"What's wrong? You look ashen," he said, sitting down with a venti cup. "Have you not been taking your iron tablets?"

"What did you get?" I said, pointing at his oversize coffee cup.

"A caramel macchiato. Why?"

"No reason," I said, putting my hand over his. Alex knew that I hated that he spent hundreds of dollars a year on fancy coffees. In the early days, I had calculated the math for him hoping to change his mind. He didn't, and I complained about it incessantly. Eventually, I realized he would never stop his overpriced caffeine habit and my complaining turned into mockery. Now he was looking at me like he was gearing up for one of my deadpan comments, but the last thing I wanted to do was aggravate his mood.

"Alex, I'm pregnant."

The sudden movement he made to snatch his hand from mine shook the table hard. He accidentally smacked his cup and sent scalding foam and coffee over the both of us.

Alex ran to the counter and returned with a pile of napkins.

"How . . . I mean . . . when did this happen?"

"I only just found out," I said. "I guess I've been so busy with finishing up school and starting work that I didn't even realize I'd missed my period."

"You've been too busy? Are you kidding me? Who doesn't notice they've missed a period?"

"Do you really think this is the right moment to criticize me?" I was getting angry, but I was determined to stay patient.

Alex took a deep breath. "What do you want to do about it?" he asked quietly.

"I've thought about adoption but—"

"Adoption? Are you kidding me?"

"I know it's almost impossible to get a Black baby a good adoptive home. But I want to think I could help someone else who can't have a child."

"And could you really live knowing that you've got a kid out there, somewhere, in the universe? Besides, are you ready to work a hundred hours a week while pregnant and then disappear and come back after you give up the baby? Do you know how awkward that would be? Having to respond to 'How's the baby doing?' every day?"

"I'm not an idiot. But it seems the right thing to do," I said.

He was silent. I looked at him, hoping we could connect with our eyes, like we used to, before the distance started to encroach on us, but Alex had turned his head and was staring into the street.

"Look, don't make me the asshole in this situation, Soila," he said, grabbing his beanie and tan leather gloves. "End of the day it's your body, so it's your decision, but I've told you where I stand. This isn't something I'm prepared to take on at this point in my life."

I stretched my hand out to reach for him as he stood to leave.

"Don't go just yet," I said. "I need us to talk a little more—"

"No, I have to get back to work and you should too," he said, pulling himself out of my grasp. "Think really hard about this before you upend both our lives."

As I watched him slide out the door, pulling his beanie over his head, I felt the tears. The tears I hadn't been able to cry in my bathroom were finally here on display in public. A woman sitting behind me working on her laptop stood up and approached my table, handing me another napkin. Then she sat on Alex's chair and held my hand.

"Honey, he's not worth it, not even worth a dime," she said. She'd placed her closed laptop on her lap and, on top of it, a fiery red purse. She had a thick Afro pulled up into a high ponytail and when she smiled, strong dimples appeared. She was stunning. "I didn't mean to eavesdrop but these tables are tight." Suddenly, I was laughing and crying at the same time. "Listen, honey, you do what you want to do. Never mind him. I can tell you right now that he is not going to be there for you, whichever road you take. So you might as well take the road that has your name on it."

"He's right, though," I said. "Adoption is too hard. It's the right thing but it's just too hard. I'm going to have an abortion." When I said it, I felt relief surge through my veins.

"Are you sure?" She stared down at me, her eyes dead set, not blinking.

"Yes, I'm sure."

"Okay. Just remember, you can't have regrets. Always remember that you did what you had to do."

I picked up more napkins from the table and dabbed at my eyes, blew my runny nose. The tears were gone for now. I hoped they wouldn't come back. I turned around to get my purse from where I'd slung it on a hook on my seat and dug inside for a Kleenex.

"Thank you so much for your kind words—I feel much better," I said, still rummaging inside my bag. "I feel so much better. . . ."

Just like that, she was gone.

It was the kind of February day when the sun was out and the sky was blue, but the windchill was so cold I couldn't feel my face. Alex and I sat in the busy reception office of a Planned Parenthood on Bleecker that Saturday morning. He patted my hand every few minutes, almost as if he had to remind himself to comfort me. He had brought his laptop and was busy reading a new study on glioblastoma. When my name was called, he stood up and hugged me.

"It's going to be okay, I promise," he said.

I nodded but, inside, I wished I could strangle him. It was never going to be okay. Never. Once I lay on the cold bed in a flimsy hospital gown that exposed my bare back, I felt the shame seep in. It was shame so deep in my mind, crawling through every vein, every pore in my body.

"Count from five backward." A woman in a surgical mask stood over me, and, as if knowing that I was starved for comfort, she gently stroked my arm. "It's going to be okay."

After what felt like only a minute, I was awakened. I put my hand on my belly, but nothing had changed. I had never felt it, never a kick or a ripple. But I had fallen asleep every night knowing it was there. I'd patted my belly and wondered what it would look like—was it a boy or a girl? The doctor at Planned Parenthood said I was eight weeks along. I had only known about the baby for a few of them and still, they had been the cruelest weeks of my life. Yet now, after all of that anxiety and the tormenting deliberation, it was gone. It seemed like it had all been a terrible dream. Back at the reception, I was handed over to Alex, who led my woozy body to the front door. At Alex's apartment, he laid me on the couch and fed me painkillers with a glass of cranberry juice.

"Do you want to talk about it . . . how you're feeling?" Alex asked, sitting next to me with a mug of coffee. "I'm here for you."

"Are you really?" I asked.

"Totally," he said. "I want to be. I love you."

"I don't want to talk about it—ever," I said, firm.

Some of the hurt I felt was in my body, but more than that, the hurt in my soul was unbearable. I had lain in bed the night before, sleepless, praying for forgiveness, telling God I was sorry I had abandoned him in America, sorry I didn't go to church or pray anymore. I'd begged for His mercy.

God, you've given me this baby right now, and I don't know why. But I can't keep it. I know what this means for my soul. I know that I will go to hell. I'm begging you for mercy. Forgive me. Forgive me.

I prayed this prayer over and over, hoping God would perhaps whisper to me, or put His hand on me, or give me a sign, like a crack of lightning, or thunder, to tell me that I was forgiven. But that night, God said nothing at all and the guilt was crushing.

"Do you want me to order some Chinese?" Alex asked, flipping through sports channels. "Do you want to take another round of pain meds?"

I envied his painlessness. He would never know my anguish, and who could blame him? As far as he was concerned there was no such thing as hell. He hadn't committed a mortal sin, because for him, that was all baloney. He had gotten the hurdle moved out of his way as he wished, and his life would continue on as if nothing had changed. But my life would never be the same. I could logically justify it, jot down the reasons why I had to do what I had done, but emotionally, I would never really heal. Spiritually, I was terrified of what was waiting for me on the other side. It was February 26. The date would be etched in my mind forever.

Alex left for his night shift hours later. When he closed the front door behind him, the tears came. I cried through the night, enduring the merciless cramps, which I refused to ease with more medication. I wanted to feel the walls of my womb being wrung dry, like a wet towel.

I had blocked Mother from my thoughts in all of this. What would she have thought of me, if she knew? I had betrayed her and the lessons she taught me under her lemon tree. Worst of all, I would have to keep another dark secret from her, and the weight of this felt unbearable. For Father Emmanuel, Mother could possibly forgive. This, she never would.

As I mourned the choice I'd had to make, Leticia was there for me at every moment. She woke up to check on me when nightmares drove me from my bed to the couch, making me cups of tea at three A.M. and smoothing my hair. I knew I wouldn't have gotten through those months without her chivvying me out the door at dawn to make sure I got to work before Angie Blythe. She was my rock.

. . .

In March, the city sidewalks were still slick with ice. I arrived at the office and was unwinding my scarf from around my neck when I noticed a young trader walk into Gloria Reuben's office. He wasn't high enough in the hierarchy to warrant a face-to-face with the managing director—something else must have been going on.

Through the glass walls of Gloria's office across from the bullpen, I saw him sit down, tall and confident. But as Gloria talked, the trader's body deflated until he looked utterly defeated. After a few minutes, Gloria stood up and shook his hand and walked him to the door. It didn't look good. I felt my heart start racing.

Returning to his cubicle with his hands in his pockets and shoulders up to his ears, the trader turned his computer off, packed a few things in his bag, and walked out. Three other traders followed him out of the office and returned in a murmur of loud whispering. Like a game of telephone, the news passed from one person to the next until it got to me.

"Scott McNealy's been laid off."

After the whispering came silence. Everyone sat in their cubicles like we were in mourning. Our greatest fears were becoming reality. The financial industry knew for at least a year that we were sitting on a dotcom bubble, inflating the value of unprofitable Internet companies. Eventually, the stock market couldn't sustain the inflation and that spring, it all burst. My *Ten Things to Know This Morning* newsletter, which had become a daily staple in the office, highlighted the extent of the massacre. Every morning, I harvested news of imminent collapses and buyouts.

Finally, the inevitable layoffs that had been devastating other banks on Wall Street for weeks arrived at our door. We'd told ourselves that our firm was small, boutique, and with only nine hundred employees, there just wasn't enough fat to cut. For months, we had convinced ourselves that we were safe, even as *The Wall Street Journal* had printed numerous doomsday articles.

We should have seen our funerals coming. But we were caught up in the frenzy of the beginnings of the Internet. We were so enthralled by the *pshhhhkkkkrrrkakingschhhh*ding*ding* sound of the dial-up connection and the voice of the man who announced *You've got mail* every time we logged on. The pioneers of Internet capitalism were a bright-eyed, enthusiastic generation. But every business idea backed was more outlandish than the last. The end was inevitable.

Over the next week, fifteen people were fired, each of them going into either the human resources director's or Gloria Reuben's office and leaving with a cardboard box and their head down. Every day we would sit, numb with fear, waiting, wondering who would be next. If the fired employees had looked withered leaving her office, Gloria looked worse—she was shredded, mowed down. Each night, as I shut down my monitor to go home, I thanked my lucky stars. I was safe, for at least one more day.

By summer, the worst of the tech stock market bust had come to pass. At Cohen, the fifteen people who had been fired were just the beginning—a couple of months later, more than seventy people were let go. The office was so empty that the sounds of the printers and copiers reverberated around the room.

Somehow, Molly and I were still standing. Molly had always been the top performer in the associates pool. Not only was she bright, but she had a way with people. In the annual performance review, there was the question we all feared: "Does the employee play well with others?" In an industry like ours, being a difficult team member was the quickest route out the door. The preparation of big pitches was a shared fate. The trick was to shine individually, while being able to make your team and your vice president and director shine too. Molly did this effortlessly.

Angie Blythe, on the other hand, with her dull, unyielding persona, wasn't a great motivator. But she was a machine; she was a military leader. She came in first and left late. Angie got us to complete the job on time and meticulously. Gradually, my loathing for her had turned into admiration for her fortitude. And Angie, like the fighter she was, came out unscathed.

It was inexplicable that I still had a job. I was a mere analyst, a worker bee only two years into my career. But when I examined it more carefully, I realized that analysts had the best chances of survival. We were paid the least and we did the most work. Nonetheless, half our team was shown the door. The rest of us were left sitting in hobbled banks, holding on to the rails of a crumbling bridge, praying for mercy on our livelihoods.

Chapter Ten

With my previous summer internship salary and a signing bonus from Cohen, and Leticia's parents' financial help, we could afford a deposit on a new apartment. Leticia said that moving would be a new start that would help shake me out of my depression. We decided to move to Brooklyn after graduation.

"Just as long as it's not the ghetto part," Leticia's mom said on the phone after she wired the money for a deposit to Leticia's bank account.

"Mama, we're upgrading, okay?" Leticia had pushed back, belting out the theme song from *The Jeffersons*.

One Saturday in April, we had an apartment showing in Brooklyn. Leticia had the directions in hand and she steered us from Morningside Heights to Cobble Hill.

Leticia and I fell in love with the neighborhood before we even saw the apartment. I'd been mired in sadness for much of the spring, but now, for one of the first times, I was finding delight again. The streets of Brooklyn were charming.

Cobble Hill was bourgeois Brooklyn. Leticia called it White

Brooklyn. Bars and coffee shops lined Court Street and on a warm spring day, the residents were buzzing in and out of trendy boutiques and ethnic restaurants. The sign on a small pharmacy lined with graying men and women said APOTHECARY. Old ladies in overcoats with headscarves tied around their necks slowly dragged their shopping carts into bodegas for fresh fruit and vegetables. Small bookstores, record stores, costume jewelry shops, a small cinema with indie movies on show. It all thrilled Leticia.

"Can you believe it? An apothecary? And look, there are no hideous supermarkets. Fresh produce sold by your regular mom-and-pop. This is so hip; this is how I want to live. Don't you just love it? It feels like a little village."

The apartment was on the third floor of a brownstone on a street of row houses. The houses were beautiful, old yet dignified. They'd been there for at least a hundred and fifty years and we felt privileged to be standing in their midst, wishing we could learn their stories, the stories of all the people who'd once lived on the street, the stories of the immigrants who'd carved the stones. A line of tall trees flanked the row houses, a canopy of foliage hanging above.

Leticia closed her eyes and breathed heavily with delight. The landlady, Mrs. Rego, lived on the ground floor. She was in her seventies, from India, she said. Her husband had died recently of a heart attack.

The apartment had bay windows that brought in a warm glow of sunshine. The floors were hardwood, with black-and-white tile in the kitchen and bath. The appliances were new, a massive stainless steel fridge and a four-burner gas stove. The bedrooms were large enough to fit queen-size beds and the closet in one of the rooms was walk-in. But the other bedroom had better views. We'd have to battle it out.

Leticia said that we very much wanted the apartment, and to show good faith we were willing to pay for the first two months up front.

"And deposit also; don't forget deposit," the landlady said. "No boys in and out, no loud music! I won't tolerate bad behavior. I will evict you. God help me."

"I see you're Catholic?" I asked, pointing at her rosary. Leticia looked at me in such a way that I knew she was afraid I was going to mess it up.

"Yes, I'm Catholic. My family, we are from Goa. In Goa, we are all Catholic."

"Okay, Mrs. Rego," Leticia said, pulling me out the door. "See you soon."

As we walked down the street, arms entwined, Leticia couldn't compose herself. She was bursting with joy.

"Best apartment ever! We are so lucky, Soila," she said. "By the way, the walk-in closet is mine."

"I don't know about luck with twenty-two hundred a month in rent," I said.

Leticia laughed. "Tell me, why do you always need to know everyone's religion? That's weird to me."

"Is it? It feels natural to me—to want to find out where one is with God."

"No, it's absolutely not natural. It's prying. What if she'd told you that she's a Satanist? What difference would it make? You'd still want the apartment."

"If she'd said she's a Satanist, I can assure you that you'd be moving in on your own."

"See? Prying will get you nowhere, and it will definitely not get you a good apartment in New York. Why are you so fixated on religion?"

"It's just how I grew up. People in Kenya don't ask, 'Do you go to church?' They ask, 'Which church do you go to?' "

"If you say so," Leticia said.

Mother arrived for my graduation in May 2000. The flowers were already in bloom, little white and yellow trumpets blowing in the wind. The weather was warm. Bare thighs and painted toes were on display on the streets, and on the subway, people chatted more and smiled with strangers. I was anxious to the point of nausea before Mother's flight landed, knowing that she would see my life in New York for the first time. If she knew the truth, the things I had done, she would never forgive me. I anticipated a week spent tying myself in knots to seem like her good African daughter again. When Mother arrived at our apartment in a cab from the airport, she hugged me and remarked that I looked tired—the betrayal of my abortion wasn't written plainly on my face after all.

I had taken graduation week off work and it sped by in a blur. I was so busy I forgot to eat until a slight tremor in my hands would remind me I had skipped two meals. We collected our caps and gowns, and our final transcripts. Leticia and I were moving out of our grubby apartment building, and though we would miss all the idiosyncrasies of the dodgy neighborhood, we looked forward to leaving it behind. We were bouncing off the walls like sugar-induced toddlers. That week, we filled Leticia's dad's truck with boxes of clothes, books, bedding, and knickknacks we'd collected over four years. Mr. Hopkins worked tirelessly, disassembling the beds, stacking them in the cargo bed, and roping them. I'd asked Alex to help out, and the men carried the beds and boxes up and down flights of stairs from the old building to the new.

Our new apartment was freshly painted. Sunlight streamed into every room. The apartment had a light, joyous atmosphere and the newness of it all, from the smells of the wax on the hardwood floors to the lingering paint odors, opened up all my senses. It was like that first bite of a Popsicle on a hot summer day.

Mother and Leticia's mom fussed around the windows with chiffon drapes they had picked out at Bed Bath & Beyond. We struggled to sort out our bedding, which had gotten mixed up in the move. Then we went into the bathroom, where we laid out new fluffy mats and candles and hung a white shower curtain in the tub. Only Mr. Hopkins and Alex worked quietly, assembling the beds in our bedrooms.

Mrs. Hopkins complained our kitchenware was "pathetic." She had brought new pots, a box of plates, and matching coffee mugs and was arranging them in the kitchen cupboards. She gave Leticia a box of silver spoons and when Leticia received them, she cradled them close to her chest.

"Now it's your turn to have these spoons. Remember, they come all the way down six generations," Mrs. Hopkins said. "And keep everything sparkling. One never knows when they might need to cook for a young man. That's how you worm your way into their hearts. Just make sure it's the right young man. Don't be over here cooking all willy-nilly for any idiot who knocks on your door!"

Leticia howled with laughter as her mother talked.

"What a difference this place is," Leticia's mother continued. "The old apartment, you couldn't even see the tiles on the bathroom walls. It was all covered in grime. There was never any light in that apartment. I prayed for these two every night. I worried I'd get a call they'd been stabbed. Here, their downstairs neighbor is a lovely widow. Bless her heart."

"Hmm, at least you're only a few hours away," Mother said. "You can jump in the car if anything—"

"Oh absolutely, I don't even know how you do it, being on a different continent," Mrs. Hopkins said. "You must be very strong."

Mother crossed her arms and looked down at her feet, then quietly walked out of the bathroom and made her way to my bedroom. Leticia and her mother glanced at each other with a look of bewilderment and I followed behind Mother.

"People judge me," she said, sitting on the bare mattress. I tore open one of my boxes, beginning to unpack.

"No one is judging you," I said. "She is complimenting you, saying you must be very brave to let me go to a faraway place."

"No, there was something in her voice," Mother said. "I'm being condemned because I would part with my child; she's implying I must not be maternal enough."

"What does it matter what she thinks?" I asked. I was struggling to squeeze my fitted sheet onto the mattress, running through my mental to-do list, annoyed because Mother wasn't helping me. Her uncharacteristic whining was getting on my nerves.

"It's fine," Mother said, waving her hand in the air. "I am made of stone. Just ask your father's relatives, the way they fought me for everything when he died. I gave them all of your father's land, money, the only thing I had left was the business, and I didn't know if it would collapse in a year. Now where are they? Most sold off the land and are living hand to mouth. How they wish they had kept me in their corner so I could keep their pockets lined."

We fell silent, listening to Mrs. Hopkins and Leticia in the kitchen talking about boyfriends. Mother cleared her throat and tentatively inquired about my virginity. Even though she liked Alex, I was to remember that the scriptures stated quite clearly that to have sex before marriage was a terrible sin.

I told her we weren't having sex. The lie flew out of my mouth easily. In moments like this, where my life depended on Mother's approval, I barely had a conscience. Mother breathed a heavy sigh of relief, and I knew lying to her had been the right thing. My relationship with Alex had dwindled down to a sort of obligatory friendship and the timing of our relationship's end couldn't have been better for the purposes of Mother's visit.

He had received offers for residency in pediatric oncology at Tisch Hospital, where he had completed his med school rotations, and Boston Children's Hospital. I knew Boston was his top choice, but I wanted him to fight for us. He didn't. Instead, he said, "It's a great opportunity, totally the right path for my career."

"What about us?" I'd asked, the morning he told me he had made his decision. This was only a few days ago, right before Mother arrived. "You have the opportunity to work here at Tisch and be with me—isn't that enough?"

"We can still see each other," he said half-heartedly. "Boston's an hour-and-a-half flight. It's nothing."

I could feel that this was it, the final break, but it wasn't easy to admit. I was surprised at how unemotional I felt. I was once so in love with him. I remembered how my heart would flutter. But now I was only tired, wearied by the time we spent together. Slowly, not meeting his eyes, I shook my head.

"Alex . . . I'm not interested in a long-distance relationship. And this"—I gestured at the gulf of space between us in the bed—"isn't working anymore. Is it?"

He heaved a huge sigh. For a long moment, he didn't speak. I watched him, feeling empty. "Yeah," he said. "I— You're right." He got out of bed and moved sluggishly to the bathroom and after a few minutes I heard the sound of the shower. I got up and went to the kitchen to start the coffee machine. When he walked into the living room, he was already dressed in his scrubs and wore a spring jacket with a brown leather collar that he liked to wear upturned. I had bought it for him one Christmas and it warmed my heart that he still chose to wear it despite our crumbling relationship.

He poured himself coffee in a silver travel mug inscribed with his name, gave me a light peck on the cheek, and touched my hand. "We'll always be friends, Soila. And don't worry, I'll help you with the move."

His attempt at lightheartedness drew a smile from me. As I watched him slip on his black leather backpack, I realized that a few tears had slipped down my cheeks. I went to the window and watched him step out of the building, walking in his usual slow manner down the street until he disappeared around the corner.

Our parents were about to arrive for graduation and we had already mentioned each other to them. It had only made sense to carry on for a few more days. And as he promised, Alex showed up to help with the move. I saw how he packed up the boxes and carried them down four flights of stairs and I knew that it was in these small ways that he was trying to make up for the loss he had seen me grieve, which he couldn't feel.

. . .

On the morning of our graduation, Leticia and I woke up early, like two brides on their wedding day. The commencement ceremony would kick off at ten A.M. in front of the library. We found seats for our parents, then gave each other a final hug and went off to join our separate faculties. The ceremony was predictably boring, and I caught myself nodding off under the hot sun until the university president started to call out the departments, and a wave of joy washed over the entire quadrangle. After each department was called, those students were allowed a few seconds of mad cheering and cap throwing, and then on to the next. Later that afternoon, there was a school ceremony. This time, I didn't have to wear my cap and gown. I could finally show off the sleeveless kitenge dress Mother brought for me to wear, so gorgeous it had thrown Leticia into a fit of jealousy.

After a short speech, we stood in a queue and one by one walked up to the podium to receive our diplomas. As I shook the dean's hand to receive my bachelor of economics, I looked over to see Mother standing at the bottom of the podium in her classic beige pantsuit. She wore the black chiffon scarf that I had embroidered in my high school home science class tied around her neck like a Girl Scout. She was snapping photo after photo, the camera flashing. When I came down the steps, Mother shoved the camera into her handbag and held me tight, so that my head was thrust inside her heavy bust. When she let go, I saw the tears running down her cheeks.

"Thank you, thank you," she said, her chest heaving. "You've made me so proud."

. . .

That evening, Mother announced that she wanted to take me out to a special celebratory dinner, just the two of us. I chose to take her to Phak Yun, my favorite Thai restaurant where I had celebrated many milestones along the way. I wanted to bask in the feeling of her pride, knowing that finally, I had done enough to make her happy.

But once we were settled into our small booth, dishes of food before us on the table, it became clear that Mother had other plans for the evening. She set her knife and fork down after taking only a few bites and steepled her fingers.

"Soila, you have graduated from university now. You are no longer a child. You're a young woman."

I cautiously agreed, unsure where this conversation was about to lead.

"When we were speaking yesterday, about your father's brothers, and their resentment of me . . . There's more to that story. And I suppose that it's time you should know it. I can no longer shield you from the truth."

"What truth, Yeyo?" I asked quickly, beginning to feel alarmed.

She paused, looking down at her plate. She shifted her fork a millimeter to the left, then cleared her throat and shifted it back again. I hadn't seen her fidget like this since the day she told me about my father's suicide. "When your father died, it was decided by his family that your uncles should take everything and split it among themselves, never mind his own wife and child. Then, at his funeral, his brothers brought another woman to me. A white American woman. She had a child, a little girl. They introduced her to the family. They demanded that she also deserved a share because it's what your father would have wanted."

I wanted to gasp, but Mother's words had stolen the air from my lungs. I couldn't breathe. I set down my knife and fork, and placed my palms flat against the crisp cotton fabric laid over the table. "Are you saying that I've got a sister?"

"I don't know," Mother said. She crossed her arms and looked down again.

"What do you mean, 'I don't know?' " I could hear my voice rise an octave too high. She wouldn't like it. But she wasn't going to lecture me about respecting elders while she was shattering my world. "Stop looking down. I'm asking you, do I have a sister?"

"She was older than you, maybe ten, or younger. Seeing her standing there—the pain—it felt like my heart was being pulled out of my chest. Your father revealed as a philanderer from his grave. There was nothing I could do but pay off your uncles and the woman. I said I never wanted to see her again. I don't know what happened to them. I don't ever want to know."

"Them?"

"Yes, the mother, and the girl."

"What was her name? The girl?"

"Aisha, I think." Mother looked at me with great pity, but she didn't reach across the table to comfort me. She looked small and hollow. "Your father's brothers turned on me before his body was cold. His eldest brother, Oldonyok—that's the evilest one," she said. "He told me God's mercy on a bereaved widow could only go so far. Soon, I'd bring engooki on myself, a curse, reversed only by sharing your father's possessions with his brothers. Can you imagine?"

I couldn't. I sat stunned in the clattering, noisy restaurant, surrounded by happy people enjoying normal meals. I could almost breathe the sadness that emanated from Mother's words, from her memories. Mother was only thirty-four when my father died but she had lived through a lifetime's worth of grief. First dropping out of university to support her siblings, then becoming a widow, terrified she'd be out on the streets with a young child. Her husband had killed himself and she'd discovered he had another family all in the same week.

"It was time you knew, Soila. I am . . . I am sorry. I wanted you to think of your father as a good man for as long as possible but the truth is he had his faults."

Mother wasn't looming, daunting, fearsome. A whole barrier crumbled—suddenly. She was broken, arrested in her development, still that single mother fighting to protect what was hers. On the outside, her strong will was indefatigable. It was the only way she'd learned to survive. But then, as quickly as she had displayed her vulnerability to me, she put her armor back on, and lifted her knife and fork again. Unaffected in her demeanor, as if she hadn't just revealed that my whole life was a charade, where only certain facts were told and only certain characters revealed, she continued to eat her dinner.

I couldn't eat another bite of my meal. When we left the restaurant, we took the train back to my new Brooklyn apartment, where Mother took my still partly made-up room and I the couch. I was sitting in the dark when Leticia came home late that night.

"Soila, you okay? What's going on? Did something happen at dinner with your mom?" Leticia asked, seeing immediately how upset I was.

I was not okay. I was still stunned and confused and I felt physically ill. "I found out I have a sister," I told her, surprised by how quickly the words fell out of my mouth.

"What? Wait, what are you talking about?" Leticia sat beside me on the couch.

"The reason my mother wanted to take me out to dinner, it wasn't to celebrate graduation. She's just told me that my father had an affair with an American woman, and I've got a sister," I said. "I feel like I'm spinning."

"Why is your mom telling you this now? Did she just find out?"

"No, apparently she's known about it since he died," I said. "Nineteen years . . . and suddenly, today she tells me. I feel like I'm dreaming. What else do I not know about my family? Or rather, what do I even know? How could my father do this to her? How could my aunts keep this from me? I thought we were so close. My granny too. I feel so betrayed."

"So, you don't know where she is?"

"No, I don't. I really don't know anything."

Part Three

Chapter Eleven

The fortnight that followed my graduation should have been full of joy at what I had accomplished. Instead, I was in turmoil over Mother's revelation about my sister. And I quietly grieved the sad end of my relationship with Alex. Leticia had received an official offer from her editors at the arty *Josephina* magazine as well as a popular entertainment magazine and she was weighing the pros and cons of being a big fish in a small pond or a small fish in a big one. Either way her future was cemented. My excitement about our new apartment should have been at a high, yet no matter how much I tried to muster joy, it felt distant. After two weeks of spinning in circles, I had to make a decision. Mother had controlled everything in my life, from the time I woke up in the morning to when I learned about major events, like my father's suicide and his other family. I needed to take charge now. So I packed a suitcase.

Leticia lay on the living room couch watching her favorite series, *Soul Food*.

"I'm taking a trip home, Ticia," I said, coming in for a farewell hug.

"Wait, what? Did someone die?" she asked, sitting upright.

"No. I need to find out more about my sister."

"Well, of course you do. But jumping on a plane out of nowhere? Are you sure?" Leticia pressed.

"I have to do this," I said. "It's important to me."

"And Angie? How is she agreeing to a vacation five months into your job and with massive layoffs? She must be short-staffed."

"I just told her it was a family emergency and I need a week. This is something I have to do."

"Just be careful, okay? You're digging up family skeletons that have been buried for a long time."

After twenty-four hours of travel, I arrived at Mother's house in the early morning. When Princess opened the gate, the taxi driver was hauling my bags out of the trunk. Princess hadn't changed. When she saw me, she started screeching at the top of her voice.

"How can this be? What are you doing here? What a surprise!"

I followed Princess into the house dragging my black suitcase behind me. I had packed light. It was going to be a short stay, I'd told myself. I was here with a mission.

When I walked through the front door, Kokoi, who was having her breakfast, heard my voice and came toward me, wrapping me warmly in her arms. We were still hugging when Mother entered the room in her old blue bathrobe. She'd worn it since I was in primary school. Mother never threw anything out. Her wet hair was wrapped in a towel. Tanei followed Mother in, dressed in her pajamas.

"What on earth is going on?" Mother exclaimed.

She opened her arms to me, but I knew her embrace wasn't approval of my presence.

"I just saw you two weeks ago. Why aren't you at work?"

"I asked for a week," I said.

"So what holiday is this—unannounced?" she asked. I could lie, I thought for a split second. But this family had had enough of lies.

"I want to find my sister," I said, perhaps more boldly than when I'd played out the scene in my mind.

Kokoi sat back down, seeming regretful that she'd been so happy to see me. Aunt Tanei came up to me and touched my cheek with her disfigured hand and said she was going up to have a shower.

"It's good to see you—so glad you are home," she said, softly. My youngest aunt, who was once sprightly, now walked slowly with the gait of a ninety-year-old.

Mother wasn't budging. Why did I need to know about my sister? She repeated it on a loop, every time becoming more impassioned than the last, until she hit a crescendo, like an opera singer.

"Why—why did you tell me if you didn't want me to know?" I was shouting and restraining a flood of tears at the same time.

"Why are you crying? Have you gone mad, Soila? I should slap you right now, to wake you up from this nonsense," Mother shouted back. "You're not entitled to behave this way."

"I am entitled to know the truth about my family."

"Why? Your father lied to me. . . . He had another family—"

"Yeyo, this is not her fault," I snapped. "Your anger at him is keeping me apart from the only sibling I'll ever have. Your anger is punishing me and her."

"She's not your sibling," Mother barked, shaking her head. "She's not your sister. You don't know this woman. She could be a thief, even a prostitute. I'm trying to protect you."

"She's the only thing I have that's a part of my father. I want to know her, and I'm sure she wants to know me."

"Absolutely not," Mother said. "I won't let you destroy my family by bringing in strangers."

Kokoi was groaning and rocking herself back and forth on the couch. She stood up, her knees cracking, and came to me, cupping my chin in her hand.

"Listen, my child, you must never open up the scab of a healing wound," she counseled, pointing into my face. "Listen to your mother. Nothing good will come out of this."

"Kokoi, what wound? It's all been one big lie," I cried. "I need to know who my father really was. I need to know this other person, who is a part of him and also part of me."

"There's a wound," Mother said. "Just because we don't speak of it doesn't mean it's not there."

"Please. Please. She's my family. My sister."

"Your father kept it from me, his wife," Mother said, standing up straighter, as if to steady herself from the burden of his affair. "What makes you think he would have told you?"

I sat down, my head heavy from the fatigue of travel and the argument. When I left New York, I'd been confident that I was doing the right thing. But I didn't want to hurt Mother, if this really was such a painful wound. I felt lost and uncertain.

"I'm going to bed," I said, defeated.

When I awoke in the afternoon, I heard loud comings and goings downstairs. Though I didn't feel like it, I knew I had to show my face. Downstairs, my aunt Naserian jumped on me like a monkey let out of its cage. Kamau, Naserian's husband, was sitting on a lone Swahili bench by the front door. He seemed a hollow figure, a ghost watching over his living relatives. Several of Mother's friends, including, of course, Father Emmanuel, were also in the room, mingling and slapping one another's backs and laughing. I walked around the living room greeting each visitor one by one, curtsying for the elders. As I made my way to the father, I saw a wide smile cracking his mouth open, and bright, expectant eyes. When he laid his hand on my shoulder to greet me, my skin burned. "We have missed you, truly," he said, swinging my hand in his like he was my puppeteer. "It's been too long."

"Not really," I snapped quietly. "I was here less than two years ago, for the wedding."

"That is a long time, and sadly, we never managed to find the time to catch up," he said, loosening his grip on my hand. His brow showed a growing film of sweat. He took out a white pocket-handkerchief and wiped his face, still grinning at me, his bright pink gums gleaming. "I can't tell you how proud your mother is, with your graduation and your new job. Please, make time before you leave, come to Mass, come to confession."

Will you confess too? Will you repent? I wished that I had the courage to ask him. But I was a coward. Leticia would have said it. After all these years, I still hadn't learned to speak my mind like her.

I nodded, but kept my eyes averted lest he see the shame that engulfed me. Luckily, a distraction arrived when Laioni walked through the door and began screaming with excitement. She stole the room with her usual joyousness, swinging her wide hips from left to right.

"I want to know everything—everything," Naserian said, piling a plate with pilau, goat stew, and chapati, and then handing it over to me. "Eat, eat, you're too thin."

We all moved back upstairs, me helping Tanei climb up the steps one at a time, and the other two moving fast behind our heels. Finally, we settled in my bedroom: I sat at the desk where I had completed hundreds of assignments, where I had studied for the SAT and written my college admission essays, Naserian and Tanei on my unmade bed, where I had crashed after having a fight with Mother and Kokoi that morning. Laioni dropped her big hips onto an old beanbag in the corner and looked at me with a wicked grin.

"What's the matter with Kamau?" I asked. "He looks like he wishes his chair would carry him far away from here."

"Argh! Forget him. His moods change faster than a pregnant woman's, not that I would know," Naserian said. "Tell us about you."

There wasn't much they didn't know. Naserian and I talked on the phone most regularly and I knew she did a good job of passing on the news, because very little was kept secret between the four sisters. I told them about my new apartment, and about Alex and our breakup.

"Oh, Soila, I'm so sorry. I know he was your first love," Naserian said. "But tell us, we're dying to know—did you have sex with Alex before you split up?"

"I did," I said. "Don't tell Mother."

Naserian waved her hand. "Argh, please, you know we would never tell anyone, except Rarin," she said. Rarin was still working in The Hague, still secretly in love with Alisdair, whom none of us had ever met. "You know what, Soila—good for you. I waited and what has it done for me? God strike me dead for what I'm about to say, but Kamau . . . he's a terrible lover, the worst, and on top of it all, I can't get pregnant."

My heart dropped. My aunt would have done anything for a baby. I had gotten rid of mine. *You are going to go to hell when you die.* My mind went to that same dark place I'd been in right after the abortion, giving me just enough time to run to the bathroom and lock the door before the tears came. I ran the tap to drown out the sound of my sobbing. I splashed my burning face in cold water. In the mirror, all I saw were dead eyes staring back at me, the eyes of a woman who would murder a helpless being.

"Are you all right?" Naserian said as I came back into the room, standing up to feel my forehead for a temperature. "Maybe you caught a bug on the plane."

"I'm fine," I said, swatting her hand away. My mood had flipped to sour, and I saw that my aunts were baffled. "I didn't know you were struggling to have a baby," I said, trying to shift their focus away from me. "I just assumed you wanted to wait. Besides, it's been less than two years."

"Two years is a lifetime at my age," Naserian said.

"But how is he a terrible lover, when he clearly adores you?"

Aunt Tanei, who hadn't spoken till now, let out a small chuckle, covering her mouth with a mangled hand.

"Tanei, stop it," Laioni said from where she sat on a puffy cushion on the floor. She was pointing a warning finger at Tanei.

"What? It's true. His adoring her won't satisfy her needs in the bedroom, will it?" Tanei asked, raising her shoulders. "Their wedding night, he couldn't even perform."

"I can't believe this." I was astounded. "Surely something can be done."

"No, there's nothing to do. I could live without sex, if I had a baby," Naserian said, shrugging.

"What has the doctor said is the reason you can't have a baby?"

"Well, you know at my age it's going to be difficult for me anyway, but the doctor says my eggs are healthy and many women have babies past the age of forty-two. The problem is that Kamau won't go for a checkup so we will never know if it's me or him," she said. "He says real men don't have their manhood surveyed like a parcel of land."

We all sat quietly for several minutes, pondering the situation.

"Just divorce that silly man and move on," said Aunt Tanei, breaking the silence. We all laughed. "You can't live like the older generation, who stayed in pathetic marriages their whole lives. Can you really have bad sex for the next forty years? No, there're only two ways out of this—poison him or divorce him."

"This is why I'm so afraid to get married to Peter," Laioni interjected. Peter was Laioni's boyfriend, who was a general practitioner with his own medical practice. He was much older than her but had never been married. Laioni was sleeping over at his house more and more.

"Your yeyo fumes whenever I don't come home." She smirked. "I don't care what she thinks. I'm forty! Who on this planet is a virgin at forty? It's time to stop pretending."

"So, do you love this Peter?" I asked.

"Oh, I'm crazy about him," Laioni said. "But I'm not rushing into marriage. Things are good as they are."

"Alex being a doctor—that life just didn't work for me. He was never home, always at the hospital, so preoccupied."

"It's not like that with Peter," Laioni said, brushing me off. "He's in private practice. He keeps his own hours."

"Then why aren't you marrying him?"

"I guess I'm just not the marrying type." She shrugged. "Marriage is complicated with the haggling of the dowry, the in-laws, the elders who meddle. I just want to be with Peter without all the baggage."

"Laioni, you're soon going to be too old to have a baby," Naserian said. "You will regret these wasted years, when you find yourself unable to conceive, like me."

"Nonsense," Laioni said, standing up from her cushion forcefully. "This story of a baby—as if a baby is what makes a life meaningful—is such an old-fashioned way of looking at relationships. Besides, I know many women who've had children into their forties."

She plopped back onto the beanbag and studied her ink-blue-painted fingernails, a color that surprised me. The old Laioni would have worn a natural-looking polish. Sitting in front of me now, Laioni had Sisterlocks bleached at the ends like birthday cake sparklers. Rarin was the professionally ambitious one, and Tanei had been the wild child. Laioni had always been the middle child who followed after Naserian in being traditional and responsible. Now, at forty, Laioni had mutated into the old Tanei.

"What about me?" Tanei said. Until then, none of us had given a thought to Tanei's halted life. "I will never get married or have a baby. No man would ever look at me—who would dream of undressing me?"

We all started to speak at the same time, consoling her, reassuring her.

"How can you know what God has in store?" Naserian said. "You're only thirty."

"Tanei, if I could choose to be like any person on this earth, I'd choose you," I said. "You are so free-spirited and fearless. You have to go out there, do things, and be happy again. When you do that, you will meet someone who'll love you as you."

"But how will he see that, when Tanei doesn't leave the house?" Naserian asked. She turned to Tanei. "You can work with us, or go back to school, volunteer. But you refuse to do anything. Will a good man fall on your lap?"

We sat in silence again until Naserian turned the conversation toward my visit. "Anyway, Soila, why do you want to meet this half sister? How's it going to help you? Just let it go," she advised, sounding exactly like Kokoi.

"Why didn't you tell me about her, all these years? You lied to me."

"We didn't lie. It wasn't our place to tell you," said Naserian, wrapping her long arms around her chest, as if she were standing on a windy street in New York.

"Well, I'm here to try to find her," I said. "I know she's most likely to be in America now. Papai's brothers are the only ones who might be able to tell me anything. It's the only place I know to start."

"The other wife returned to America right after the funeral. Your uncles were the ones who brought her to your father's funeral and demanded that she should get her share. It was clearly done in spite—to show your yeyo she wasn't as important as she thought she was. I don't believe that woman wanted any money. She was here to see your father's other life, what he had dumped her for. I'll never forget that little girl, holding her mother's hand so tightly."

"What were they given?"

"A share of the business," Naserian said. "At the time, the business was standing on good legs, but it wasn't that big. So, it was more like a formality really. But when we got bought out by East African Foods she made a lot of money. Later she sold back her stake to your yeyo."

"How could I not know any of this?"

"If anyone so much as whispers any of it, your yeyo goes blind with anger," Naserian said. "She cut off all your uncles. No one would dare talk about it, let alone tell you."

"Where are they, in America? What does the girl do?" I was insatiable, needing more and more information.

"Soila, I don't know! You're right. The only way to know anything is through your uncles."

"Will you help me? Please?"

Deep silence followed as they all sat still. I saw them look at one another, coming to a decision in the unspoken language of family.

"We'll help you," Naserian said. "Of course we'll help you."

. . .

I hardly knew my father's eldest brother. That's how Mother wanted it. My uncles had little access to me. They never visited us at home, we never visited them. And they never called me. Mother didn't talk about them, and neither did my aunts or my kokoi. Growing up, I knew it was odd. But Mother was odd.

The day I visited my uncle Oldonyok, we arrived at his rural home in Narok at noon. A strong breeze bent the branches of the blue gum trees. Heavy clouds had gathered over the city that morning, hovering, tailing us, as we drove west to Narok. When I opened the car door, a sweet, pungent zing rushed up my nostrils. It was the smell of rain coming. Since I was a little girl, I could smell rain a few hours before it hit the ground. The smell soothed me.

Naserian had driven Laioni and me from Nairobi. An hour into the journey, we arrived at the breathtaking Great Rift Valley. We slowed down to pull to the side of the road, where the majestic escarpment gaped in front of us like the open jaws of a crocodile. The stop was an overlook for the rift and from an angle one could get a glimpse of Menengai Crater, the massive caldera formed by volcanic activity millions of years ago. The area was crowded with camera-wielding tourists and farmers running among them with their reed baskets to hawk their produce. I gave a young woman in a leopard-print headcloth money for a bunch of Lady Finger bananas. She had a sleeping toddler strapped on her back like a baby koala and a basket of bananas balanced on the top of her head. I watched as she dug inside her bra for a bigger bundle of cash and counted out my change. As she handed it to me, her mouth widened into a grin. "Barikiwa!" she said as she ran to her next traveling customer.

"These are the things I miss most when I'm in New York," I said to my aunts while peeling a banana.

"What? Baby bananas?" Aunt Laioni asked, shading her eyes with her hand as she looked over at the vast horizon.

"Yeah. But mostly just these little moments of gratitude that we take for granted here. In America I might get a 'Bless you' when I give a homeless man money. But for the most part, people only say 'Bless you' if you sneeze."

My aunts laughed.

When we returned to the car, I rode shotgun, my thoughts whirling about the meeting with my uncle.

"I don't know how Yeyo survived it all. I cannot imagine Yeyo agreeing to give my father's mistress a portion of the business or letting her brothers-in-law take the land her husband had owned. That just doesn't seem like something she would do. The woman I know is not a pushover."

"Well, she wasn't a mistress. She was his lawful wife and that was what made it so painful for both of them. This woman had an actual claim that your yeyo couldn't deny. And you don't know what your uncles were like," Naserian said, turning down the radio. "They were worse than hyenas. Back then, there were no property laws for women. There were no financial planners and your father had no will, no executor of the estate, nothing! The odds were against her."

"How did he make so much money by the time he was forty-six?"

"He was very lucky to have money saved up when he returned from America. The first thing he did was buy land. Then he started with his cookies. Nobody believed in him—he asked for a bank loan but got nothing. In those days, men didn't cook but your papai could bake any cookie imaginable—with oats, cocoa, coffee, nuts, and even berries. They were so big and buttery. Then he taught his recipe to a few bakers he poached from white households. He started to open pop-up stalls in the wealthy neighborhoods where the rich could go and collect fresh cookies. I wish you had been there to see it—white people waiting in a queue for their cookies while roasting in the sun. Anyway, back then it was simple, not like today. You simply brought your food to shop managers for a taste. Your father did that with his cookies. He would say, 'I'll have a hundred of these for you every week, if you hire me.' Supermarkets made so many orders that within a year, he had to move into a small factory. Within three years, he was moving into the mill."

"But why cookies? He should have been entering government, not selling cookies."

"It's a funny story," Naserian said, tightening her grasp on the steering wheel as the potholes threatened to kick the car off the road. "When your dad returned from America, he realized there were no cookies here. We had biscuits. That's what the Brits had brought to Kenya, but there were no cookies."

Laioni, sitting in the back seat, shifted her hips around. She was chuckling. "Can you imagine? Life with no cookies?" The sound of her laughter bounced behind us as the car jostled over the potholes.

"He said it's what he missed the most about America," Naserian continued, looking at Aunt Laioni from the rearview mirror. "He said that fresh cookies had sustained him through long study hours and the harsh cold of the winter."

My uncle's house was built on a sprawling farm. A few black-and-white Friesian cows loitered around the compound, with rogue chickens at their feet. Mother and my aunts had told me that this was some of the land that had belonged to my father.

We'd phoned to let my uncle know we were coming, but I hadn't told him why. As I walked across the lawn to my uncle's front door, he came out of the house and waved joyously. In the sun, his gray eyebrows and beard were illuminated so that his face shone like an angel's. But what kind of angel would steal from his brother's widow, I wondered.

His wife, a woman I didn't know at all, waited for him to release me from his embracing arms so she could embrace me in hers. After I'd been set free, I sat on a crinkled gray leather couch. A plush carpet brushed the soles of my bare feet. My aunts sat across from me.

Glancing around their living room, I searched for something familiar, something that could connect me to my father.

"Take a look at these photographs of your family," my uncle said, handing me a dusty cardboard box. Inside, there were stacks of photographs, vintage black-and-white prints that were so old they were yellowing. "These are all the people who've watched you grow, who've longed to know you but haven't found a way."

I took the box and flipped through ancient photos of my father as a baby, of his mother, my other grandmother. In one snapshot, my grandfather was wearing old-fashioned Western clothes. The photograph was crinkled and streaked brown with water damage. It was dated 1937.

I had looked at nearly all the black-and-white images when I caught a glimpse of a color print at the bottom of the box. When I pulled it out, the photograph showed my father like I had never seen him. He was leaning on a bright red Chevy, a white woman with dark wavy hair embracing him. She wasn't strikingly beautiful, but there was a softness in her eyes, and she had plump cheeks and a genuine smile. They looked happy in a way that made me feel ill. Behind them, I saw the gray sky, the fall foliage, and a vast lake. This was the other woman my father had loved. The photo wasn't dated. At the bottom there was only a scribble—*Purdue*.

"This is Indiana," I said, feeling slightly light-headed. "When was this photo taken?"

A blanket of silence smothered the room.

"Tell me, when was this?"

"I would say late sixties, maybe," my uncle said, clearing his throat. "That was after his university years."

"Who is this woman? Is this my sister's mother?"

Another prolonged silence.

"Please," I begged. I was so close to the truth. "The secret is already out. You don't have to hide anything."

"Her name was Elizabeth. Elizabeth Ackerman," my uncle said. "She's since passed on."

"Tell me the whole truth—you do realize I'm not ten years old anymore?"

"Yes. That's the woman. They met in university."

"And what then?"

"Oldonyok, please just tell Soila what she needs to know. The past is the past, and now she's a grown woman," Aunt Naserian said.

My uncle straightened himself up. Then he stood and walked out of the room.

"What! Is he mad? Where's he going? Where are you going? Come back here!" I was screaming at the old man in a way no African child would dare speak to an elder. I had unraveled.

"Soila! That is enough," Aunt Naserian exclaimed. My uncle's wife gasped. Naserian put a hand on my back to calm me.

"Get your hand off me," I said, wiggling my back to move it away.

"Who are you? I've never seen you this way," Naserian said.

I bolted through the front door before the tears spilled out. I didn't know where I was going but I knew I had to get away from everyone. I went to Naserian's car and leaned my palms on the hot metal of the hood, filling my lungs with deep breaths of fresh air. From the doorway, Laioni called me back.

"Come back, get back here; there's something we want to show you."

Inside, my uncle stood in the middle of the room. He directed me back to my seat.

"Soila, we have tried to shield you from this because what good is it when you have never met a man to hear only the things that would make you hate him? But I knew this day would come. I had hoped your mother would tell it to you, but the woman has the strength of a waterfall and once she has decided on something, nothing will change her mind."

He handed me two more photographs. These weren't in the box. In one photograph, my father was dressed in a purple velvet suit and next to him was the raven-haired woman in a white lace dress. She held a bunch of pink tulips across her arm, like they were a newborn baby. *1969*.

Once again, there it was—the happiness plastered on their faces was so wild, so infectious. In the second photo, he was asleep on an orange armchair, shirtless, with an infant snoozing on his bare chest. The child wore nothing but a diaper. The back of the photo read *Aisha, summer 1971*.

The tears I had fought hard to keep behind floodgates were now streaming down my face and my nose was dripping unstoppably.

Aunt Laioni dug in her purse for a tissue. I wanted to hold on to the idea that the American woman was a mistress. But there was no denying it. He really *was* married and his other family *was* a real family.

"Yes. Now you see why we spared you the pain."

"Then why didn't he stay there, in his happy life?" I was seething.

"You don't understand it now, because times have changed," my uncle said. "Back then Africans wanted to come back home. President Kennedy's government was offering a special scholarship program for Africans in the late fifties and early sixties called the Airlift. Africans were offered a university education in the States so they could return and decolonize their countries."

"So what? As a child I had many classmates with mothers who were European and American. He could have brought her back."

"There were very few African students who brought back their wives," my uncle said. He had become animated, fighting hard to defend his dead brother. "Your father tried to get Elizabeth to come back with him, but she wouldn't. Her family wouldn't hear of it—their daughter off to a 'jungle.' Her only option would have been to leave against her parents' wishes but she wasn't brave enough."

"So, he just abandoned them?"

"Perhaps at first, because the relationship was strained, and he didn't have anything to offer anyway. But then he built his business and it picked up very quickly, and he promised he'd always take care of Aisha. Not that she would have ever starved. From what I heard, Elizabeth's family was well-off. That's why it was such an embarrassment for them that she had chosen this African. They didn't even attend the wedding."

"And what about my yeyo? Did anybody think to tell her any of this?"

"Soila, it wasn't our place," my uncle said. "Your mother and father were happy. They met in 1973 and within a year they were married, and then you came quite quickly after."

"Did his other wife know he had a new wife?"

"She did. She was no fool. She asked for a divorce, but it never happened. Later, we sent her a copy of his death certificate so she could have an annulment. We kept in touch for a while. I know she remarried. We didn't communicate for many years; then I received a letter out of the blue in 1992. She said Aisha had finished university and joined something called the Peace Corps. She was going to help build a water plant in northern Uganda. Aisha wanted to visit; she wanted to meet you. I called her and we spoke for a long time about Kenya, about you. You were in high school. I called your yeyo and told her about Aisha, but she called me many names then hung up on me."

"Do you know where Aisha is now? That's why I've come. I want to meet her."

"The last time I spoke to her, a few years ago, she was calling from Ghana. She told me Elizabeth had passed from cancer."

"Did you know all this?" I demanded of my aunts.

"No!" Naserian shook her head. "I don't think your yeyo knows all this either."

"No, she doesn't," my uncle cut in. "She doesn't want to know."

"I want to meet my sister," I insisted.

"Yes, okay," said my uncle. "I have her email address and the last phone number she had in Ghana. I don't know where she is now."

For the first time in weeks, since Mother had ambushed me with the news, I felt a semblance of relief. I was one step closer to connecting with my father, to knowing the parts of him that I had never had the chance to know, to forgiving him.

Chapter Twelve

Returning to New York after my visit to Kenya was a relief. Mother's fury that Naserian and Laioni had taken me to speak with my uncle had turned the house into an arctic wasteland, Yeyo had so completely frozen me out. When she hadn't spoken a word to me, hadn't looked at me, in two days, I changed my flight back to New York and flew out before the end of the week. I dived back in at Cohen for the first time without any distraction. The breakup with Alex, my abortion, graduation, Wall Street layoffs—all behind me. I was fully immersed and with the authority to ask the fresh summer interns for help when I needed it. Nothing else had changed. Angie Blythe still hissed about what she needed by the end of the day, I still scrambled to complete projects and stay in the loop, I still found the spreadsheets full of numbers as soulless and dull as ever. I went to lunch with Molly and filled her in on everything that had happened since Mother's mammoth confession and Molly encouraged me to email my half sister.

"Don't overthink it," she said, with a mouthful of her turkey sub. "Just say that you've recently tracked down her contact info and you'd like to connect. What's the worst that can happen? So, she doesn't reply, or she'll reply and say 'I'm not interested.' Either way, you'll know that you tried."

After lunch, I sat at my desk typing and deleting an introductory sentence for hours, while at the same time trying to crunch numbers on spreadsheets. In my email, I tried to introduce myself but shied away from using the word "sister." I had recently found out about her, I said, adding that I hoped we could get to know each other. Hardly an hour had passed after I'd sent the email when my inbox dinged. The new message was from Aisha. I took a deep breath to calm and steady myself before I clicked on it.

> *Oh my God! I can't believe I'm finally hearing from you!! You have no idea how long, how many years, I wanted to meet you and know you. This is the best day ever. Yes, definitely, let's connect!*

The euphoria I felt, mixed with relief, was incredible. I floated toward Molly's desk. "She wrote back, and she wants to meet," I said.

Molly got up and did a little cheer, making me laugh. She'd been a cheerleader in high school.

"So . . . what's the next move?" she asked, sitting back down.

"I guess we're going to email back and forth, until we finally meet."

"Maybe you'll go to Ghana?" said Molly.

I shrugged. "If she invites me, maybe. But West Africa is so humid, and their food is so hot it's inedible."

"You sound like one of those Americans who never leave their hometowns." Molly laughed. "Come on! Go for it. A month ago, you didn't even know you had a sister!"

I spent the next few days completely preoccupied with replying and expectantly waiting to open the next email Aisha sent me, filing away all the details in my mind like I was preparing to be quizzed. I wanted to know everything about her. She'd been living in Ghana for a while, working for a Norwegian foundation that supported urban development in Africa. She had a child. She wasn't married. She said she traveled a lot for her work, and she came to New York often. She said she was always racked with guilt about what she felt was absentee parenting. I talked about life in New York and banking and the shortage of decent guys I could date, which really was unfathomable in a city with millions of available men, I said.

I know all about it. It's an island of misfit men, Aisha wrote. She'd lived in New York for a few years, straight after college, before joining the Peace Corps for two years and then returning. She said she knew every corner of the city, and the men even better.

She sent me photographs of her child—a cocoa-skinned little girl with kinky hair that looked like a big rain forest growing out of her head. But she never sent me photographs of herself, so I was reluctant to send one of me. I imagined her skin was the same shade of brown as her daughter's and perhaps her hair had soft curls. We probably looked similar. That's what Naserian had said. I found myself smiling absentmindedly as I walked through crowded streets.

While I basked in the joys of newfound sisterhood, Leticia had taken it upon herself to match me up with several eligible men she'd met through her work. She herself was dating a man named Kevin, an African American professor she had met while I was in Kenya chasing down Aisha. She was enamored with his career accomplishments and swore he was the most brilliant man she'd ever met, that he was genuinely interested in her as a human being, not as a sexual conquest. She'd go out with him wearing casual flats and no makeup, whereas for everyone else she'd dated, she had always bought a new outfit, only for those relationships to fizzle out weeks later, usually with a slamming front door or the ignored buzzing of her cellphone.

"Somehow, I don't feel like I'm competing with anyone else who is smarter or prettier," she concluded. "I can just be me."

When I met Kevin I was taken aback by how different he and Leticia were. He was mild mannered, shy, hardly making eye contact as we shook hands.

"Are you sure he's a professor? How can a professor be so shy?"

"I can assure you that he's not shy in the areas that matter." Leticia giggled with a twinkle in her eye.

Despite their age difference and his introvertedness up against her butterfly spirit, they had found their rhythm. Because she had found love, Leticia was determined that I would too. She filled my calendar with dates. Men who bragged about climbing Kilimanjaro, working in Sierra Leone to help the limbless casualties of blood diamonds, volunteering to help those *poor blind dolphins* in Japan. *What do you say we go back to my apartment and open up a bottle of cabernet?*

"I swear, Ticia, all the dates end with that line. Why not just come out with it and ask me for sex? Where do you find these men, and why do they all drink red wine?"

My six months as a banker passed mostly this way: endless, grinding hours at the office, where I often felt both conspicuous and invisible, as the only Black person present most of the time, humorless bad dates on weekends. Kokoi and my aunts had slowly unfrozen Mother from her fury toward me, and we had resumed talking on the phone. I never mentioned, though, that I was in touch with Aisha. On weekends, when I would once have ventured out into the city with my camera, I did chores. I hated to admit it to myself, but I had stopped taking pictures after my abortion. I was punishing myself by denying myself what had once brought me joy.

On a frigid Friday night in early December, I wrapped up ninety hours of a grueling week and headed for the train. My bag started to vibrate, and I dug inside for my phone.

"I wouldn't make you come if it wasn't worth it," Leticia said. She was calling from an art show in SoHo. "He is hot, and he is single."

"Ticia, I would rather step in front of a bus right now than go on another date," I said. "I just can't do it."

"Please, you have to come," she said, her voice crackling on the phone. "You're not going to believe who is showing at this gallery. Come on, just for me."

I sighed, resigned to my fate.

Leticia was waiting outside for me at a small upscale gallery, her head peeking past the glass entrance door.

"Come on, come on! He just got back from Japan. He was living there for a while," she said, tugging me by my sleeve toward a table covered with white linen.

"Who?" I asked, becoming more perplexed by the minute.

There was a selection of wine bottles and slender glasses. A woman dressed in a white shirt and black pants stood behind the table.

"White or red?" asked the waitress.

"White," Leticia said, as if ordering for herself. She stuck the glass in my hand. Then, pointing with her free hand across the room, she mouthed, "Look. . . ."

I followed her finger to see a tall, broad-shouldered man with dreadlocks down past his shoulders, neatly tied back. I felt a hard thump in my stomach and nervous energy spreading outward. It had been years since I'd seen him in person, but I recognized him instantly—the sculptor who had lectured in my Intro to Art class, who Leticia had pointed out to me in *Time Out* one night, who had caused a fiery argument between me and Alex about stereotypes against Black men. Akhenaten Morrison. I had been working for years to unlearn the ideas that had so hurt Alex, but privately, I still thought the name was ridiculous. Vaguely aware of Leticia continuing to talk in my ear, I watched him gesture with his long-fingered hands as he spoke to a small knot of partygoers. He wore a navy vest over a gray turtleneck and dark blue jeans. Though I wanted to dislike him I felt my face grow warm and I took a sip of wine, hoping to calm my nerves. Of all the men in New York Leticia could have dragged me out to meet, why Akhenaten Morrison? My chest fluttered and I swallowed hard.

I barely noticed when Leticia took my arm and guided me toward him, interrupting his conversation. When he turned to Leticia, he held her hand gently as she spoke, and looked at her closely, as if reading her lips. As it turned out, Leticia had already scored herself an interview and with her schmoozing skills, she charmed him into conversation in a way that I could have sworn they'd known each other for years.

"Leticia, I can't do this tonight," I whispered, overwhelmed by the unexpected intensity of my attraction to this long-haired artist. "I'm going home." But Leticia grabbed my hand and turned back to Akhenaten.

"This is my friend Soila," she told him. "I've known her for years. She's Kenyan."

"Nice to meet you." He turned to me with a charismatic smile, so warm that I couldn't tell if I was just another one of his prospective buyers that he had to appease.

Akhenaten had a gentle voice and a mild manner. I remembered how his voice had surprised me when he lectured my class, because it didn't match his giant stature.

"Actually, I think we've met before," I said.

I let the moment linger, watching the artist search his memory. I could see that he was coming up blank.

"You don't know me, but I know you," I added, taking mercy on him for his confusion. "You visited an art class I took in college about three years ago. You talked about Middle Eastern sculpture. You had just returned from a dig in Egypt. Remember?"

"Oh! Professor Kowalski," he said. His eyes lit up brightly. It surprised me that the memory of teaching undergrads would be so joyous to a man who had traveled widely and accomplished so much. "Were you there? I don't remember you. I'd have totally remembered you."

"I didn't introduce myself to you in person," I said. "I left as soon as you were done."

"Really? Was I that unimpressive?"

"Oh no, I'm just not big into sculpture. And I've got a bit of a hang-up about Egypt."

"Wow—okay," he said. "You don't hold back, do you?"

I was weighing my words for an apology for having been too critical when he grinned and I saw that he wasn't really offended.

"Hey, people try to flatter me all the time, how my art is so brilliant, blah, blah, blah. I could use some honesty."

Leticia murmured that she'd spotted someone she really ought to talk to, and slipped away.

Akhenaten hardly seemed to notice Leticia's departure. His eyes were focused intently on me. He wanted to know what I did for work, but I didn't want to discuss all the ways Angie Blythe continued to make my days hellish. He asked what I thought of New York and I told him I enjoyed the anonymity of the city, which somehow made it feel even more inclusive. New Yorkers didn't care that I had an accent, just like they didn't care that there was a Black man in a Rasta hat and sunglasses sitting with a rooster on his lap on the morning train.

Akhenaten nodded with interest, as if what I had to say was the most fascinating thing in the world. The force of his attention felt like it was burning me up.

He started walking me around the room, one broad palm placed lightly on the small of my back, and my knees threatened to turn to liquid at the touch of his hand.

"I know what you mean," he said. "I've seen a naked guy trotting down Madison and no one as much as asked him if he needed clothes, or if he was nuts. No one called the cops. Or even bothered to cover their kids' eyes."

I laughed out loud, spilling wine on my beige wool overcoat, suddenly grateful Leticia had opted for white wine. Akhenaten hurried off to the server's table and brought back a handful of napkins. He started to press down on the fabric to absorb the moisture but the pressure of his hand on my thigh made me jerk, spilling more wine, this time on his tan boots. We both moved to apologize, falling into more laughter and then looking at each other in an expectant silence. Somehow, his hand was still against my thigh. I saw that he had two small gold hoops in each ear. He wore a black stone signet ring on one hand, on the other a large silver ring on his index finger, a gold clasp bracelet, and on his neck, a subtle gold chain with an Africa continent pendant.

"So, Akhenaten—that's an interesting name. What exactly is it?"

"Akhenaten was a controversial pharaoh," he said, eager to explain. "He started worshipping the sun instead of the Egyptian gods; he became the first monotheist. He had serious balls—I mean, challenging something that had been done a certain way for centuries. Anyway, the first time I went to Egypt in my early twenties I was so blown away by these people and their art that I came back a different person. It totally changed my thought process, my representation of art."

"Egypt is a sore subject for me," I said. "Egyptians say they're Arabs, not Africans. They only want to identify as Africans when they play in the Africa Cup of Nations, and it drives the rest of us mad. Especially when they win."

"I certainly haven't felt hated or unwanted when I've been over there," Akhenaten said. "But I guess I mostly hang out with archaeologists and academics at the university in Cairo."

"As part of decolonization in the African classroom, the Egyptian civilization was drilled into us. We were told that ancient Egypt should make us proud to be Africans. But how could it make me proud, when the Egyptians don't even consider me one of their own?"

"I'd love to travel through the rest of Africa," Akhenaten said. "And not as some 'going back to my roots' expedition, but really, to live in a specific country in Africa and actually get to know the place. I did the same thing in East Asia."

"Your art is definitely not the kind I'm drawn to," I said. "I'm not really moved by inanimate objects. I like portraits and landscapes and lots of color. But obviously I'm in the minority since your stuff sells faster than you can make it."

Akhenaten bit his lip. A sculpture of a bronze face whose wide-open mouth appeared to be giving birth to a spiral-like creature was in front of us, and we both stared at it in a silence that had suddenly turned awkward.

"This piece is about rebirth and the possibilities that can be harvested if only human beings allowed themselves to pursue their dreams," he attempted.

"I'm sorry—that was insensitive just now," I said quickly. "I didn't mean to imply that people are only buying your art because it's *in* at the moment. I'm saying I just don't know much about this kind of art—"

"I'm not interested in appealing to the masses," he cut in, agitated. "Of course, I don't want to starve either. I used to do traditional sculpting, but I wanted to move away from representational art. I wanted to make art that would challenge people to find their own meaning in the work."

"Do you know what it is you're creating when you start out? Do you know that it's a shoe, or a bridge, or a phallic symbol?"

"Sometimes I have a goal—to disgust, to trigger meditation—and sometimes I move like a neutral vessel with whatever my spirit is telling me and see where it goes."

I twirled my wineglass between my thumb and index finger as he continued to describe his work, and as I listened, I saw and heard only him—nothing else intruded on my attention, even though the room had grown fuller and noisier.

"Sometimes I know exactly what I'm making. See that figure there," he said, pointing to the image of a man with sculpted glass for a head and an elongated, misshaped body with a flying tail made from steel. "See how his head is so clear and brilliant, but his body is metallic and dull? With that, I knew I wanted to create a tortured man. I separated the textures and colors of the head and the body, to illustrate his brokenness. Do you know what I mean?"

"I think so." I nodded. "You're trying to show that even a brilliant mind can come apart." My attention snagged on his long fingers as he pointed. His nails were perfectly trimmed. My palms on the wineglass were getting hot and sticky.

"It's the same as abstract paintwork," he said. "Jackson Pollock's work lets you drink and breathe in whatever it is you're feeling. Sometimes I go to MoMA and look at a Pollock and it practically makes me weak. All I can do afterward is sit on a bench and stare at the world around me like I've never seen it before. I don't know if Pollock was dripping paint all over a canvas going, *Oh yeah . . . I'm going to make someone cry today.* I think he just wanted to make a beautiful piece of art and let it take us where *we* want it to take us."

Akhenaten watched my face as I took it all in.

"I take photographs," I confessed.

A youngish couple had walked toward us, wanting to speak to Akhenaten. I turned away, thinking to track down Leticia. I didn't want to leave his presence, but I worried that I had taken up too much of his time. I touched his arm. "I'm just going to find Leticia and—"

"No, don't go," he said. He gave the couple a business card and deftly saw them off.

"Isn't this part of your job?" I asked. "The selling? They're here to meet you."

"Honestly, it's the part I hate. Tell me about your photography," he said, eager to get back to me.

"There's not much to tell really, except that I've been interested in it since I was a teen. I made a small darkroom in a shed in the back of our house that my mother used as a chicken coop. Once I started, nothing could get me out of that darkroom, the smell of the dyes, and the negatives hanging on pegs over my head."

Akhenaten laughed softly and I watched his shoulders moving. "Really, a chicken coop? How big was that thing? What happened to the chickens?"

"Oh, the chickens were more like pets." I laughed. "They got to go wherever they wanted. They didn't need that coop. Anyway, I don't know why I'm telling you all this, I hardly talk about this with anyone."

"I'm glad you're telling me."

"Well, I thought about becoming a photographer full-time."

My face warmed.

"What stopped you?"

"I guess I was afraid of disappointing my mother," I said.

"My mom wanted me to become a university professor, like my father. It was her dream. A generation of Black men who had defied the odds and joined the ranks of the revered white academia. I didn't know what I wanted to do but it wasn't that. I was kind of a late bloomer. Anyway, she came around in the end."

"My mother is all I've ever had," I explained. "My father died when I was young. My mother put everything she had into me. It's difficult for me—you know, disappointing her." Akhenaten nodded and I melted further at the kindness and understanding in his eyes. I took a deep breath. "The kind of photography I'd want to do is to tell stories about things most people don't know about. I'd love to live with an ancient tribe who are going extinct, like the El Molo in Kenya—there are only two hundred of them left. Or profile dementia patients in Kenya who remain undiagnosed. I remember as a kid, I met my great-grandmother—I must have been six or seven—and found it strange that she couldn't remember anyone. She thought my grandmother was someone else and she called my mother another name. She became violent when they tried to take her to the bathroom, and then she wet herself right in front of me. I was mortified. The whole scene was film material. She had this stare, these vacant, dead eyes, like she had totally checked out. I asked my mom what was wrong with her and she said it was just old age. That's what they say in Kenya when the elderly start to become confused, forgetful—'It's just old age.' Of course, now I know it was dementia. But you can't imagine how many people are sitting undiagnosed in my country, with an empty, dead stare."

"Wow," Akhenaten said, his voice full of soft awe. "You have such vision. It's terrible that you feel you can't live an authentic life."

I didn't want to talk about Mother, yet it felt so natural with him—like I'd known this strange man forever. I wished the people in the gallery would disappear so that I could talk to him all night. I wanted him to peel off my cashmere scarf and heavy coat, unzip my dress, and lay me down right on the gallery floor. When I finally tore myself away from him, I got a cab home alone to Brooklyn. I wanted space with my thoughts. In the shower, I tried to run a mental list for my weekend—work a half day tomorrow, mani-pedi in the afternoon, laundry and grocery shopping on Sunday. When I lay in bed that night, I tried to think of anything other than the sound of his voice, the touch of his hand, the sheer magnetism of his presence.

No matter how hard I tried, I could not will myself to calm my mind. How bizarre life was, I thought, as I drifted off to sleep. One minute I was trudging through yet another mind-numbing day of fluorescent lights and spreadsheets. And the next, I was fully infatuated, intoxicated, consumed by the sheer presence of the strangest man I had ever met, a man I could never really be with. So why couldn't I stop thinking about him?

Chapter Thirteen

"I liked him. Actually, I really, really like him. But Ticia, I can't date him," I said over brunch that Sunday. "He's *too* out there. He wears more jewelry than I do! And that name!"

My mimosa sat in front of me unsipped, and I hadn't touched my French toast. "I can already hear my mother wailing when she meets him. *I sent you to America, and you brought me shame. Are you trying to make a mockery of me?*"

"Shame? He is such a catch; women beeline for him. I can see you want him," she said, jostling my shoulder playfully. "You have to go out with him. He has a very strong sense of identity, a *very* Black man, you know what I mean? Plus, he's well-read and well traveled. He's a globe-trotter."

"A globe-trotter?" I snorted.

"Yes!" Leticia was getting highly animated. "He's lived in Japan, been to North Africa, and been all over South America! Have you ever met a guy who speaks fluent Nihongo?"

"My mother would die," I argued. "Besides, it's like you said, he's probably propositioned by all kinds of glamorous women every day. He has no time for some boring investment banker."

"Why do you just assume he's only interested in sex? And who the hell cares who your mother likes? She's not the one dating him—you are!"

"You know, my aunt Rarin has been dating this Scottish guy for years, it's so sad. She can't tell my mother or my grandma. When I went home for my other aunt's wedding, I kind of mocked her about how silly she was to hide her boyfriend. Now I feel bad, because I totally get it. And that Scottish man seems tame compared to Akhenaten."

"Oh please." Leticia shrugged.

"Plus, Ticia, he's old! I'm twenty-four," I said.

"So he's in his early thirties, so what? We're all adults. Kevin's way older than me and it's never been a problem. It's time for a new chapter! A taller, sexier, smarter, older guy is what you need."

"Smarter than Alex? Really?"

"Alex is a nerd. Akhenaten is world-wise. Trust me, you want wise."

"I just feel so inadequate around him," I protested.

Leticia persuaded me to see him again, at least one more time. And despite my protestations, one date turned into a cascade of them. I couldn't deny that I was drawn to him. Akhenaten was more than six feet tall. Standing up straight next to him, my head barely grazed his chin. He admitted to having been in open relationships. He was fluent in Japanese and Spanish. He played the sanshin banjo, and he did it without looking like a fool. When he recited Bashō's haiku by heart, I was in awe. He loved to play dusty vinyl records on an old LP player. He told me what the blues meant to him. I said it sounded depressing. He didn't give up on me. Slowly, I was able to distinguish Muddy Waters from Count Basie, Duke Ellington from Thelonious

Monk, and I enjoyed it. He told me stories about his dead father, a professor in New Orleans.

Every conversation with Akhenaten broadened my ideas about art, music, race. "For my father to be a professor was rare at the time, especially in the South," he told me one evening at the Italian restaurant across the street from his SoHo apartment. I'd lost count of how many dates we'd been on in only a few weeks.

"My folks didn't want to stain my world, give me bias. They said, 'You're as smart, you're as talented, as anyone else.' It was tough, because I was great at basketball, but also nearly top of my class in school. So I was isolated from Black kids in school, who thought I was pompous because I could spell 'pompous.' My parents started to bus me to a public school in a very wealthy white neighborhood, and then I was competing in class and in sports with the best of the best of white kids. And I started having more white friends and started to believe that I could blend in with them, that if I fit in with the white kids, then the world would extend to me the same privileges and safeties they had. But then I got older, and I saw white women hold tighter to their purses when I walked by. I saw them lock their car doors when I crossed the street. That's when I realized I could go to the whitest college, date the whitest woman, but when I'm out there on the streets, none of it matters."

"I talked about some of this with my ex-boyfriend. When I first came to this country, I thought, like I think a lot of Africans do, that all the talk of racial profiling in America was exaggerated. I've met a lot of African guys in the U.S., including my ex, who tell me they definitely feel the profiling but it doesn't cripple their lives; they take it as it comes but it doesn't color their whole world," I commented. "I completely get that what you feel is not imagined but I sometimes wonder if the heightened reaction is from growing up in a racially charged society?"

Akhenaten nodded as if with pity. "Where I come from, what it's like for me, is not something you would ever understand because you grew up in a country where everyone is Black." He pushed his steaming bowl of minestrone away. "If you didn't grow up with racism, it could hit you in the face and you wouldn't even know it."

"I do see it. I just choose not to let it consume me. The African guys I knew when I first got here didn't talk about it, and that started to make me think Black Americans just have a chip on their shoulder, sorry to say. I really regret that. But over the years, I realized that of course they were experiencing it just as badly as Black American men but they just chose not to talk about it. The standard line with Africans when they get here is 'I don't want to make race an issue; it's not always about race.' But with time we learn that race is the issue. I understood it especially when Amadou Diallo was killed. Now I know why Black American men are so triggered when cops tell them to pull over on the road, whereas an African guy will just pull over and thank the cop and move on with his day. For Africans it takes a while to learn that the landscape has changed. In the beginning, a Kenyan guy wouldn't even expect a cop to be racist because in Kenya, it's not like the cops are white—everyone has the same skin color, so race just doesn't come into it. But then he'll get pulled over repeatedly and he'll start to connect the dots and then he'll start to fear for his life. But the fear is not organic for us. It's learned over time, and also our reaction to it is somewhat dissociated—we think we can walk away from it all, like it's not a burden—which now I know is of course not true at all."

"Yeah, that's the difference. It's infuriating because it's something we've had to endure from birth, to have to learn how to talk and behave around someone because they have the power to annihilate you is so disempowering and dehumanizing, terrifying, and it makes us feel so hopeless as well because this is our country—it's not like we can pick up and leave. Do you know that just two days ago a cop car pulled up to me while I was just minding my business, waiting for you to come down, when we were going to go see that movie? Cop car pulled up to me, beefed-up cop rolls down his window and says, 'Sir, waiting for someone?' I said I was waiting for my date and pointed up to your building. He asked if I was from around there. I said no, very politely. He gave me this *look,* like, sideways, and left. There were two of them in the car. That scenario could have gone very differently, if I didn't know how the game is played. When I was a kid, I wasn't afraid of the cops, even though they were always somehow around me, asking me, 'You live around here?' One day, I went nuts and ran my mouth. I was cuffed and put in a cop car. I was fifteen. Longest six hours of my life. They booked me but I didn't know what for—they said 'disrespecting a police officer.' My dad came down to get me, signed me out, and did not say a word. Not even 'How you doing?' We walk a couple blocks to the car, then he stops and punches me in the mouth so hard I thought he broke my jaw. He said, 'Son, I'm only gonna say this once. You are a Black man in America. Do you understand that? This is what's going to happen. From now on, when a cop asks where do you live, wants to pat you down, you are going to comply. No running your mouth, no running. No wearing a hoodie after dark and no going around to fancy neighborhoods at night, unless you've got a real good reason to be there.' "

His voice was cracking. His pain was real, and I felt helpless. What was broken was so much bigger than anything I thought I could fix.

"Why didn't you tell me that the cops bothered you?" I finally asked. "I mean, I live in Brooklyn. I thought it was safe there. For you and me and Leticia."

"Not your part of Brooklyn," Akhenaten shook his head. "Your part's bougie."

I reached across the table to hold his hand. The layers of stereotypes and skepticism I had been trying so hard to unlearn about Black men were being peeled away. I loved Akhenaten, and I was determined to open my heart and mind to whatever he had to tell me about his own lived experience. And I believed him.

"Well, I'm glad you told me," I said. "Please keep telling me things like this when they happen."

. . .

Akhenaten owned two lofts in an old building and had knocked through the wall between them to create one large apartment with an adjoining studio where he worked. On my first visit, he poured me a glass of wine and put a jazz record on the player and we sat talking on the couch. I surprised myself. When the buttons on my pink shirt started to pop open, when the zipper on my black pantsuit came down, I didn't fight it. This wasn't who I was, I told myself.

"I have an early day tomorrow," I said in between kisses, his mouth on mine, and on my face and neck. But I knew then that I was his. Akhenaten had snatched my temple from the Holy Spirit. He'd crashed inside and taken ownership with merciless passion. The sex we had was not the neat and tucked-in-a-bed kind of sex I had known with Alex. It was as messy and confusing as my feelings for him. This sex had no rules. I was coloring outside the lines. Akhenaten had me in the kitchen, in the shower, on the floors, up against walls. Every time, my mind said I should be quiet, be a lady, but my body would give in to madness.

Days with Akhenaten moved seamlessly into months. Winter turned quickly into spring and everything that I had dreaded before Akhenaten came along became tolerable. Angie Blythe, the endless hours of spreadsheets, sitting invisibly in conference rooms that were often filled with all white men.

That March my aunt Rarin was getting married in Kenya. Rarin had fallen pregnant with twins and finally found the courage to tell Mother and Kokoi that she was going to marry a Scottish man named Alisdair. Mother's fury, I heard, had been terrifying. After everything Mother had taught us about chastity, integrity, and honesty, Rarin had kept her relationship a secret for years and had gotten pregnant before marriage. Mother said it was unforgivable. Rarin said she was forty and it was ridiculous that Mother would believe a woman her age who was not a nun was still celibate. Mother responded by freezing out Rarin for weeks.

Kokoi, on the other hand, was overjoyed that she was finally getting a second and third grandchild all at once. Finally, Rarin announced that since Mother wasn't interested in meeting Alisdair and his family, the couple had decided to have the wedding in Scotland. That was all it took for Mother to change her mind about everything. Rarin said she wasn't going to put Alisdair through the haggling of cows. Mother said a very small Catholic wedding with only a few guests was best and we all knew that she was trying to keep the pregnancy as quiet as possible.

I couldn't go to the wedding. The pressure at my job was hellish, and I nearly broke out in hives just imagining asking Angie for time off. To keep myself from homesickness, I buried my head in work and then spent the rest of my waking hours with Akhenaten.

Over the past year, while my aunts and I exchanged emails and phone calls about Rarin's situation, I also told them about Akhenaten. I sent them photographs of him attached to an email headed *I think I've met the one*. I told them that I had met a Black American artist in the summer. I said we couldn't get enough of each other. I said I had never been as happy in my life.

A few days after Rarin's wedding, she was on a plane back to Scotland, and Naserian phoned me to tell me all about the details I'd missed. We also talked about Akhenaten.

"He looks like us," she said. "Maybe his people came from the Maasai."

"Don't be ridiculous. You know they came from West and Central Africa."

She said her favorite photograph was the one taken in Washington Square. We were wearing sunglasses, and he had his arms wrapped around me from behind.

"Oh, your yeyo will die. She's not ready for this kind of thing—this Bob Marley type. No way she'll accept him. Especially after everything that has happened with Rarin, she's had about enough."

"Well, this isn't the man I expected I'd end up with either. But here he is."

"Don't give me that. Race, culture, and class are everything. A marriage is not an isolated planet. You need your family when the challenges come, and they will come," Naserian warned me.

"So, tell me, how is the family helping you now with having a baby?" I challenged her. "At the end of the day it's you and Kamau and you're the only two who can solve your problems."

"Oh, you are so naïve! How I wish you were here with us to see Rarin and Alisdair and his whole family. Sure, Rarin and Alisdair looked happy. But there's so much more to a marriage. The old women shook Rarin like a farm basket, saying, 'Rarin, marriage is like a coconut! You have to crack it to see what's on the inside. Don't be fooled by the fantasy.' I watched Alisdair's people roasting in the sun—my God, I worried they'd melt—as we held the festivities to welcome them. You should have seen them the day before the wedding, when the young men slaughtered the steer. Their faces turned to chalk. When the elders sipped its blood from a calabash, the white people looked like they were going to vomit. When the morans pulled Alisdair into a circle to teach him the adumu, they jumped straight up like spears, but he jumped from side to side, like a limp ostrich. We adorned them with our beaded necklaces and wrapped them with matavuvale cloth, but they smiled fake smiles. Rarin told us that she wants to come home for a visit after the babies are born, but Alisdair won't hear of it. He says the babies will catch typhoid. Is he crazy? We are a hundred times wealthier than the people in his small village in Scotland."

"Akhenaten isn't like that," I argued. "He can't wait to visit. If we were to wed in Kenya, he would love it."

"Is he a Christian?"

"No, he's agnostic."

"Haiyayaya . . . he doesn't even know for sure that God exists? Soila, how will it be? A believer married to a nonbeliever?"

I ignored her, saying instead, "I wish my papai was still alive. He would have loved Akhenaten, I just know it."

"This is true." Naserian sighed. "Your father would have allowed you to marry a goat if it made you happy. But he's not here. Soila, you know what they say—be careful when you try to kill the fly that perches itself on the scrotum. You must decide whether this guy is worth the stress you will endure."

A few days later, I called Aunt Rarin to congratulate her on her marriage, but then the conversation steered to Akhenaten, and I told her Naserian wasn't encouraging of the relationship.

"Oh! Who cares what Naserian thinks?" Rarin sounded ecstatic. I couldn't tell if she was happy for me, or still riding a wave of excitement since her wedding. "Soila, those photographs! My God, he is stunning," she said. "How lucky can you be? A famous artist who looks like a god?"

"Well, she thinks I should drop him."

"What does she know? She married a Kenyan guy—is she happy? He's not able to make her pregnant but mopes around and makes her feel bad, like it's her fault. Doesn't want to adopt a baby either."

"Well, I don't think I have the guts to bring it up with Yeyo. What if she completely hates him?"

"She'll moan about it for a few years and then she'll get over it. What can she do? She can't cut you off—she loves you too much, you're her only child."

"But what about you? Weren't you terrified when you found out you were pregnant? To tell Yeyo that you're dating a foreign guy is one thing. To tell her you're pregnant—where did you find the strength?"

"For years, Alisdair begged me to introduce him, and for years I just wasn't ready," Rarin said. "I saw how much it hurt him to hide our relationship, but I couldn't face it. Then I fell pregnant and I had no choice."

"Did you ever consider not having the babies?"

"Oh no! Absolutely not," Rarin said, sounding shocked by the thought. "I wouldn't have dreamed of not having them. I've never understood how a woman can choose to have an abortion. How would I sleep at night?"

"I'm sure with time you'd sleep fine," I snapped.

Rarin didn't speak for a minute or two. She had always been the most intuitive of all my aunts. Naserian was a busybody, always handing out unsolicited advice, never quite listening. Laioni was a leaky bucket and I constantly worried she'd slip up unintentionally. Before the bombing, Tanei was extremely self-absorbed. Mother always said she hoped that Tanei would never have children because she would forget to feed them. Her wish had come true. Rarin, on the other hand, was a good listener and pragmatic adviser. These were the qualities that made her a gifted lawyer. Anyone else would have missed it, but not Rarin. As soon as I snapped at her, I regretted it.

"Sorry, I didn't mean that. I'm just saying that the decision to have a child isn't as easy for everyone as it is for you," I said, as calmly as I could.

"Soila, is there something you want to share? Because you know you can tell me anything, and I would never judge you."

"Um . . . I think you already did, though," I said, tears welling up—releasing a flood of emotions I hadn't felt in a long time.

"Soila, I'm so sorry," Rarin said gently. She was the first person in my family who I had told, inadvertently, and she would probably be the only one. The relief of one person in my family knowing was like a boulder lifting off my chest. "No, no, don't cry, my baby. How awful that you had to go through that all by yourself. You know that if you had called me, I would have gotten on a plane to New York. You didn't have to suffer alone."

"I wasn't alone," I said. "And I have made my peace with it and I don't really want to talk about it. Let's talk about you. Are you going to be happy with living away from home for the rest of your life?"

"Soila, this is our life now—me and Alisdair and the twins. He's my family now. My life is in Europe now, not in Kenya, and I'm okay with that."

I understood Rarin. Being with Akhenaten was fulfilling enough. I couldn't imagine leaving him to return home. He was clear about what he wanted. He wanted me. I continued to fall further in love with him. I was vulnerable in ways I had never been with anyone. I talked to him about my confusing childhood, learning that my father had committed suicide and later that he had a secret family I never knew about. I told him the strange way I had been loved immensely by Mother, yet had never been allowed close to her heart, never held in her arms. I fretted about an American sister whom I'd never met, the burden of an African family, and what was expected of me—to return home, to continue building my family's legacy, even though it wasn't said out loud.

I talked about lying in a lonely room with my feet in stirrups wishing I had the strength to get up and walk away but instead succumbing to the anesthetic and waking up to an empty womb.

I told him about Father Emmanuel. How much I hated him, and

how, even though Leticia tried to convince me that the priest was the monster, I still couldn't accept that I wasn't complicit.

"It's not an age thing," Akhenaten said. "You could have been nine or nineteen or twenty-nine years old. What remains is that you were disempowered. Men in power get away with this predatory behavior, and a woman can't fight it. I didn't really grasp the power a man can have until I became somewhat of a name in the art business and saw the vulnerability of young female artists around me. Some of them will give up anything to find some success. I would never take advantage of that. That priest absolutely took advantage of you. Do you want me to kick his ass? I can totally go to Nairobi and kick his frock-wearing ass, if you want me to."

I knew Akhenaten was joking. He would never resort to violence. But his protectiveness made me feel loved and cherished as I had never been before. Sometimes in the middle of the night, I found myself wanting to stare at him until the alarm clock next to my bed counted down to three, then four A.M., and I had to force my eyes closed for at least an hour before I had to be up for work. I'd lay my head on his chest and listen to his heartbeat, slipping my hand over his, chuckling quietly at how long his fingers were next to mine.

I was happy in a way that scared me. I could fall off a ledge and he'd be there, ready to grab me before my body hit the ground. I imagined getting pregnant. The thought didn't terrify me the way it once had. I wouldn't hesitate to have Akhenaten's baby. I imagined our daughter bursting through the door in her pajamas to climb onto our bed. I'd raise her with the hugs I was never given. I'd talk to her about men, about love—the kind of unexpected love I'd found in her father.

But then, always, I thought of Mother and a prickly sweat would run down my back. I was in a relationship Mother wouldn't approve of. She would never accept him. I should stop this now, before I break his heart, I told myself.

Still, how could I give up this kind of love? What I couldn't grasp—and I tried—was why this man was so deeply in love with me. I was different from the women he'd been with, the people he knew. I couldn't get comfortable with being kissed in public. I couldn't wear a minidress, even though Akhenaten said I had beautiful legs. All I saw when I looked at myself naked in the mirror was a flat bottom, small breasts, and pencil-size legs that seemed to grow out of my rib cage to the floor.

I hadn't traveled the world like Akhenaten and his friends. When they talked about the humble joy of riding the rickety train across India or debated the value of paying fifty thousand dollars to hike up Everest, all I could do was nod and play with the olive in my martini.

He bragged about me to his friends—how I'd left home as a teen to come to a country where I knew no one, about my experience with poverty, photography. When I would fidget with nervousness at eclectic dinners, he would stroke my hand under the table and whisper in my ear, "You okay? Let me know if you wanna get out of here."

I knew that to him nothing mattered more than me, and, to him, I was pure brilliance. I trusted Akhenaten never to hurt me. Finally, some tight, cold thing that had been stuck in my heart for more than a year began to fade. After a few months with Akhenaten, thawing from lingering sadness into joy, I took my camera out again. The clattering, colorful city I had loved when I arrived five years ago was still there. When I pointed my lens at interesting blocks or crowded parks, I saw through the viewfinder that the bright colors inside me were still there too.

"I have never seen you this happy," Leticia said. "With Alex, it was you constantly trying to please him, going out of your way to make him happy. With Akhenaten, you're so balanced. You're not cooking up a storm for him, trying to be a good African wife. You're just you."

Leticia and I were on the couch in our apartment, painting our toenails together.

"I know, I'm so happy. But sometimes, I feel our differences are too big," I said. "Like, even on the subway, I feel like we're stared at. People expect a similar set of people together. When we hold hands on the subway in the evening, I'm in a pantsuit and he's in these bohemian pants that look like MC Hammer's pajamas. What do you think people are thinking?"

"They probably think you're his psychiatrist who has just signed him out of a mental facility," she said, laughing, putting her arm around my neck, and bringing me even closer to her. "Honestly, I could strangle you. You worry too much about what the world thinks. Your mother really did a number on you."

"It's not just my mother," I said. "African society is very conservative, and we still live in extended families, so I also have to worry about what my grandmother thinks and all my mother's friends. No one wants to be an outcast. No one with weird hair or tattoos or piercings fits in. No one wants to be out of the closet, or to be anything that our society doesn't deem *normal*."

Leticia listened intently. I continued, "If he were clean-cut with a career in something my mother respected, like medicine, or finance, law, architecture—anything but a bohemian artist who has dreadlocks—she'd learn to accept him, like she did with my aunt's Scottish professor husband. But my mother would literally die if she had to introduce her friends to Akhenaten as my husband. I get shivers just thinking about it."

"So, you're saying that in Kenya everyone is pretty much the same?"

"Pretty much. Or they pretend to be," I said.

She leaned her head back on the couch as if too exhausted by the weight of the conversation. "That is a sad society," she said. "A tragic society."

Chapter Fourteen

That summer, I arranged for Molly to meet Akhenaten for the first time at a buzzing outdoor restaurant. We were going to have brunch. Molly wore a frilly white skirt with a strapless pink shirt that was cut asymmetrically in the shape of a bandanna. She was fizzing with excitement about the purchase of a duplex brownstone she had put an offer on in Harlem.

"I mean, you won't believe this place," she said. "I know it's the worst time to be putting all my savings in a down payment—who knows if I'll have a job next year—but I really think it'll pay off. It's got two separate apartments, one on each floor, so I'll rent one out. I'll be downstairs. In all my life, I never thought I would ever be able to afford to buy an apartment in Manhattan, but here I am, buying a duplex!"

Akhenaten announced he owned an apartment in Harlem too, which surprised me. "There's some stuff you don't know about me," he said wryly, chewing on the end of a toothpick.

"The seller's going to make a killing," Molly said. "When he bought it, it was a tenement. He gutted it, stripped the floors—you have to see the floors! And oh my gosh, the bay windows are huge."

I saw Akhenaten's expression tighten. I could tell that Molly's comment had rankled him. He spoke to me often about gentrification displacing Black folks across the city, and I knew that white folks acting like they were helping historically Black neighborhoods when they moved in made him angry. "Why does it take white people moving in to finally get the garbage picked up, to make schools better, to get the police to do their job? White folks come into Black neighborhoods at cut-rate prices and claim they're *improving* the neighborhood, and then Black folks can no longer afford to live there," he had said to me on more than one occasion.

Molly twittered on about the cheap price of the building and how much money she would make renting it out. I made vague noises of interest as she talked, but I wasn't really paying attention to her. I was preoccupied by Akhenaten's aloof silence and worried he would break with anger, saying things that would leave my friendship with Molly in disrepair. When we were alone together, he had never shied away from these discussions, and when I didn't agree, he took me to task. I knew he had a lot to say to Molly, but he stayed focused on his plate and I wasn't sure if I was thankful or sad. The man I loved and a good friend I wanted to keep in my life were so divided in their worldview that the only relationship they could muster was one where one pretended they couldn't hear the other.

Eventually, Molly talked herself out. She gave me a kiss on the cheek, tucked her clutch under her arm, and left with a little wave to Akhenaten, who stayed stone silent.

"My God, what was that?" I exclaimed once she had left the restaurant. "I brought you here to meet my friend, and you didn't even say a single word to her."

Akhenaten shrugged, blasé in a way that made my blood start to boil.

"White folks are in denial," he said. "Did you see how out of touch with reality she is, all that shit she was saying about improving the neighborhood?"

"Then tell her that, kindly," I said. "Educate her; I'm sure she'd appreciate it."

"Are you kidding me? It's not my job. Besides, white people are so fragile. They don't want to hear the truth. The fact that you're sitting here asking me that shows that you still don't know shit about what it's like to be Black in America," he shot back. "We've talked about this a hundred times, Soila, and it's like you still don't hear me. I can't be on the Upper East Side after dark—white folks see me, they don't see *me*. They think I'm just a thug skulking around their neighborhood. It won't be five minutes before they've called the cops. And if I start challenging a white lady in the middle of brunch, all I'll get are a white woman's tears. And that is a shit show I can't tolerate. So, I keep my mouth shut because I know what will happen if I look angry. How do you still not get that?"

"Why are you attacking me?" I said.

I stood abruptly, kicking the chair behind me, and throwing my napkin over my hardly eaten crepes. As I walked away, I heard Akhenaten raise his voice, not in anger but surprise: "What? What'd I say?"

Leticia was home when I stormed into the apartment. I complained loudly, opening and closing the fridge door and the cupboards. "I mean, how could he do that? How selfish is he?" I yelled. "Couldn't he just smile and be nice to my friend?" When Leticia didn't answer, I walked back into the living room and found her head covered by a large pillow. "Ticia! Say something!"

Leticia slowly pulled off the pillow and looked up at me.

"First of all, you need to take down the decibels a notch," she said. "I have a hangover from hell. And secondly, you know what? I agree with everything Akhenaten said. Your friend Molly is a Park Avenue

Pollyanna who would've melted down the second Akhenaten challenged her. He was smart to stay quiet."

"What are you talking about? Molly is from California, not Park Avenue."

"That's not the point. The point is she's upper-middle-class white. She's never lacked for anything, and she's not used to people telling her she's wrong."

"Akhenaten also was raised middle-class!"

"Soila, the Black American middle class live in a totally different reality than white people. Our parents had to work twice as hard to buy a house in a good school district and they weren't exactly welcomed with warm muffins by their neighbors. They put away every penny, too afraid of having the rug pulled from under them. They were lucky if a bank was willing to grant them a mortgage. They know the struggle, and we've seen the struggle through their eyes. Molly's parents probably weren't the first in their families to graduate college, they may even have gotten cash from their parents for the down payment on their first home. That's generational wealth. You can't compare the Black middle class and the white middle class."

Later in the evening, Akhenaten rang the doorbell. He had come to smooth things over between us. "I know Molly is important to you," he said. "Why don't you invite her over and I'll try again?"

"Oh please," Leticia interjected, having overheard. "Why should you have to make nice when you didn't do anything wrong? White fragility is real, my brother. You can never really be honest with Molly, so you'll never really be her friend."

"White fragility. White privilege. Black consciousness. Until I came here, I never knew any of these terms. I know now that the assumptions I had about race when I first came to this country were wrong. I'm more sensitized and I've seen enough to know it's all very real and painful. I have moments at work where I feel tinges of racism directed at me. Remember when I overheard Shelly and Mel at work saying that I'd only get a permanent offer at the bank because I was a minority? Or all the times I was asked by customers at the college bookstore to bring out Sandy—as if I was too stupid to understand and only a white employee had the authority to explain why a worn item couldn't be returned. Even at work, I see how my feedback is disregarded and then a white guy will say the same exact thing and suddenly it's valid. But even with all that, it is still difficult for me to accept that I have to carry the constant weight of it. To survive, I shelve it away, because if I don't it'll become too much of a burden. That's where I see a clear difference between us. You're just not ready to let any of it go."

"Well, you tell me," Leticia said, voice raised. "How can we let it go when every day our men are being profiled by the cops, our grandparents are being pushed out of our old neighborhoods, we have to put our kids in the shittiest public schools where the teachers don't even bother to show up, and our boys are piled up in prisons? Like, who the hell does this Molly think she is that she can glorify white privilege and negate a Black person's actual life experience?"

"No one is denying the reality of things for Black folks and I'm certainly not minimizing the systemic racism and the trauma," I said. "But shouldn't we separate issues here? Molly is not trying to push down Black people and she isn't a white supremacist. She's just a single woman who is trying to buy a well-priced apartment in a city full of unaffordable real estate. Why begrudge her that? Why take it out on a woman who's worked her butt off to afford a property in Manhattan. Ticia, you know how hard it is for women. . . . Why can't you cut her some slack?"

"I think I'm gonna take off," Akhenaten said, easing himself off the couch.

"Nah, nah, dude, you don't get to leave," Leticia said, turning around to face him. She'd picked up the remote control to turn off the television and now she shook it in his face. "You're the one who brought up all this crap, ruined my perfectly peaceful afternoon with all this shit."

Akhenaten shrugged and lifted his hands up, then slid back down onto the couch. "Okay. It just looks like you got this."

"Do you know what my biggest fear is, Soila?" Leticia asked. Her chin thrust forward and she was still holding the remote control. "My biggest fear is that I'll have a son. Black boys are an endangered species in this country, and it doesn't matter how successful, how rich, I'll be by the time I'm a mom. When he's walking down the street, white people will only see a Black man. And that means all they're seeing is someone they think will rob them, shoot them, and rape them. Do Black men in your country get arrested for no reason at all? Just for being Black? No! They don't. So, what do you know?"

"Guys, I don't know what's wrong or what's right," I said. "What I know is that the poor kids in my country would kill to switch places with a kid here. Even poor kids in America have shoes and clothes; they go to public school. They have running water and electricity. Poor kids from my country would work their butts off to get a scholarship, any scholarship, to a better school. And if the security guard at the mall asked them to open up their bags, they'd open them, and then walk away, focused on survival, focused on tomorrow, because that is more important than proving a point, no matter how valid that point is. There are Kenyans who do this, who come to the States and live exactly this way."

"So, you're saying we should lie down and take shit?" Leticia fired back.

"No! No, I'm not saying that. But, Leticia, I've seen things I wish I could forget—famine and poverty so cruel that I can't even shed a tear anymore. I've visited the biggest slums in Africa. And none of the poorest people I've met have complained about being victimized or oppressed. They take the worst hand dealt and find ways to survive. I've seen oppression from my own Black people. The people who are supposed to govern us are thieves who live like kings, while their own people starve to death a few miles down the road. You've got a better life than your parents, and their parents. You've got a college degree and a great job. White folks can be as racist as they want to be, but I just refuse to let it consume me, and I refuse to take it out on Molly."

"But that's because they relate to you differently than they do to us! Don't you get it? You're a foreign Black. All your white friends tell you that Black people are still complaining about slavery and you nod your head and say, 'Yes, it's time to let go of the trauma.' That's why they're comfortable with you. Next time you see Molly, ask her how many Black friends she's got. I'm not talking about la-di-da friends who make her feel comfortable, like you. I'm talking about, I don't have one ride-or-die white friend, a white friend who doesn't defend a white cop every time a Black man is killed. . . . They go, 'White men are shot too, you just don't hear about it.' I haven't got one white friend who sees things through my lens. The fact you don't see it either—when you're Black—this shit hurts! I thought you got it—all this time."

I sat on the floor between the couch and the coffee table and rubbed my temples, wishing I could somehow evaporate out of the room. Leticia's voice was shaky.

"Soila, you are so willfully oblivious," she said, putting her face in her hands. "I honestly can't deal with you. You are a super-privileged Black woman with an English accent. White people talk and laugh with you because you make them comfortable. You see the other side, but you refuse to accept it."

Leticia turned around and walked fast to her bedroom, nearly tripping on her furry pink house slippers, and slammed the door behind her.

"If this was our old apartment, that door would have come off the hinges." I sighed. I looked at Akhenaten, who was now squeezing the bridge of his nose between his thumb and index finger.

"Man, she's worked up," he said.

"You started this whole thing when you attacked Molly. How can you not see that this stuff is poisonous?"

"Hey, now that Leticia is so mad at you, do you wanna move in with me?" He was half-laughing. "It's just a matter of time before she stabs you at night while you're sleeping."

My mouth dropped open but I had no words. Akhenaten was asking so casually that I was completely taken aback. Moving in together felt like an enormous step in our relationship. I knew I loved him, but the idea of living with a man whose existence Mother didn't even know about seemed insane. "I can't move in with you," I spluttered.

"Why? You're always at my place anyway," he said.

"No, it's too hurried. We've only been dating like seven months! And my mother . . ." I felt giddiness rush to my head and realized a smile had spread across my face.

"Come on, look at that smile," he said, pulling me onto the couch. "You know you want to."

I considered it, lying tucked next to him, staring at the fan on the ceiling. I thought of the days we spent together, visiting museums or going to restaurants, and the days we spent doing nothing at all but being near each other. I remembered the dinners we cooked together, how he paid attention to the flavors I liked and didn't like. I thought of how I snuck out of bed in the mornings to bring him coffee before he woke up, and found myself going all the way to the Upper West Side, far out of my way, to surprise him with cookies from his favorite bakery. I thought of how he praised my bravery and resilience and how he said he'd never known anyone like me before. And I thought about the warm bubble of joy that inflated inside my chest whenever we were together.

"I want you to live with me, like, all the time," he said. I turned my face to look at him. He traced a line down from my forehead over the ridge of my nose to my mouth, down the right side of my neck to the collarbone, then stopped. His eyes were flooded with kindness and adoration. "Besides, Ticia is maaaad. Think of it like I'm rescuing you," he said. We both laughed.

"What if she's right? What if you're both right? Do you really want to be with someone who doesn't understand where you're coming from? I'm not sure I'll ever really fully get it. I feel like a spectator most of the time. I don't feel the pain of it in my veins."

He looked at me intently then shut his eyes for a moment.

"I'm serious," I said, touching his eyebrow with my fingertip.

"Look, Soila, I think that we have a very different history. You're an empowered Black person. You went to private school with wealthy Black kids. You grew up wanting for nothing. Even though my parents were educated and middle-class, some things were so unimaginable, they didn't allow me to dream them. I've literally never heard a Black kid say, 'I want to be president when I grow up.' I can tell you that it wasn't something that ever crossed my mind growing up. How messed up is that? What Ticia is saying is that it can hurt when it is another Black person questioning the things you've endured. Your friend Molly is like most white people out there; she has a severe blind spot. She is not capable of seeing the world in any other way because it's been presented to her her whole life in one sort of way. You? You're different. You have questions and strong opinions. One of the things I love about you is how you want to see what you've been missing. Do I think you and I can't be together because we come from different places and have some different opinions? Of course not. I also think that things could change in your life that will really shake you. Maybe you'll have a son, and it'll fully come together when you have to see how painful life can be through his lens."

As we lay together on the couch, I felt the room get smaller. A raging headache was cracking my head. I was angry, but also I was scared. The truth was out in front of me like never before. Here we were, all of us the same skin color, the same dark-brown eye color, the same hair—but our histories were so starkly different. I had nothing else in common with these two people whom I loved deeply.

Aunt Naserian was right. Culture, tradition, religion, those things *did* matter. In that moment, I longed for something I hadn't wanted in a long time. I longed to be back home, to be with my own, to belong, to be understood.

"So, what's the word? Are we moving in together or what?" Akhenaten asked after we'd lain in silence for a moment, each lost in our own thoughts.

"I can't afford to pay half for your place," I said.

"Save up your share and buy an apartment to rent out," he said. Then he laughed. "Maybe in Harlem next door to Molly."

I thought about Alex, my first love, and all the frivolous dates Leticia had sent me on. It felt like a lifetime ago. Akhenaten was different and I didn't want to lose him.

"I love you very much, Akhenaten Morrison," I said. "You're one of the good ones."

"So, what does that mean? You're moving in or what?" he asked, laughing.

"Yes," I said, worn-out. "I'll tell Ticia she can kick me out."

. . .

My relationship with Leticia had gone from easygoing to less than cordial since the fight. Most nights, I would come home late and she would be already in her room with the door shut. We didn't eat together anymore or chat, except for a quick hello while we both poured coffee into our mugs in the mornings.

All I could think about all week was how I'd bring up the topic of my moving out. I imagined Leticia saying, *Well, what are you waiting for then? Leave!* and slamming the front door in my face.

When I came home to find Leticia sitting on the couch watching a documentary on Liza Minnelli, I knew the ice was beginning to thaw because the living room—our one shared space—had been out-of-bounds for a week. She was already wearing her satin hair wrap and her oversize Minnie Mouse sleep shirt, so she was about to go to bed. It was a brutal summer with no respite from the humidity even after dark. I went to the air conditioner to turn it up.

"Since when do you like Liza Minnelli?" I asked as I threw my bag and keys on the kitchen counter.

"What are you talking about? I love Liza! I used to watch VHS cassettes of her onstage on repeat. She's got that *za-za-zu,* you know? That stage presence. I think you're just either born with it or you're not."

"Hey, Ticia, can we talk?" I asked. She sank back into the couch, deflated.

"Now? I'm in the middle of this. . . ."

"Come on, Ticia, you cannot keep avoiding me. I haven't been able to tell you that I am so, so sorry for the fight we had last week. It was totally my fault," I said.

Tentatively, I sat next to her, though I was afraid she would shift to the other end of the couch. "Molly is important to me. But in defending her, I hurt you, and I'm sorry. I don't want us to fight," I continued. I sifted through my mind for a minute, trying to find the right words. "Let me be clear that, if the situation were turned around, and I felt Molly had misjudged you, of course I would challenge her too. I know that I will never come close to understanding what Black people in this country have been through. But I'm learning every day, through you and Akhenaten, and—"

"Okay, stop talking," Leticia cut in. I swallowed hard, preparing for her to blow up like she had the week before. "Look, Soila, end of the day, you're like a sister to me. We've lived together for more than four years and somehow made it work without killing each other. My parents love you. I can't even imagine you not being there at my wedding. What was said was said and Molly is your friend, and you had every right. Now, can we just watch Liza?"

"Are you sure? Are we okay?"

"Yeah, I'm sure."

"Then why have you been locked up in your room every night?"

"I needed a bit of space, you know? But it's all good."

"There's something else," I said, feeling my hands go numb like they did before I walked into my job performance reviews.

"Let me guess. You're moving in with Akhenaten?"

"How did you know?"

"I figured. I'm happy for you. He's a really good guy, Soila. Don't screw this up."

"What do you mean?"

"All I know is, this man is completely in love with you. He would move to the moon for you. Don't take that for granted. It's slim pickings out there."

"I know, I know," I said, feeling lighter. "And Kevin. Kevin's a good guy, let's not forget to be thankful for him."

"Kevin's afraid of commitment," Leticia said. "I'm not rushing him, but I also don't expect that I'll be the one who miraculously changes him. So, when a man is begging you to move into his gorgeous SoHo loft, you jump, okay? You jump in with both feet."

"Well, I'm going to continue to pay my half of the rent here until we find you a great roommate." I laid my head on her shoulder and she tilted her head over mine.

"Hey, you want some ice cream?" She ran off to the fridge and came running back with a large carton of chocolate chocolate chip Häagen-Dazs and two of her most prized spoons, the ones she broke out only for special occasions. I remembered the day her mother gave the set of silver spoons to her, the day we moved into this apartment.

"When did you get Häagen-Dazs? I thought we couldn't eat ice cream since you started doing that Atkins thing."

"Got it a few days ago when I was still mad at you, and this is all there is for dinner so eat up!" she said, holding up one of the spoons to my face.

"Why are we using your special spoons?" I asked, scooping up a mouthful of ice cream.

"I've just been thinking about my great-great-great-great-great-great-grandmother and the stories I've heard about her over the years, and I realized I didn't want to keep these spoons locked up anymore. I feel like she would have wanted me to use them every day, use them fiercely!"

We both burst into a belly laugh.

Leticia wiped a smudge of ice cream off her lip, and then her face was taken over by a grimness I hadn't ever seen before. She wasn't laughing anymore.

"My mother spent years doing research, since she was in college, piecing together everything she could find out. Most Black Americans don't know anything about the history of their enslaved ancestors, so I'm really lucky my mom was able to find out so much through estate records, slave schedules, and wills," she said, her eyes boring into mine in a way that made me stop eating. "I think about her a lot. Here was this house slave whose mother died giving birth to her, her father was sold off and she never saw him again, her older sister who raised her was then sold, and her older brothers were allotted to another owner. They called it a 'chattel mortgage.'

"Can you imagine, watching your family being mortgaged off to someone else, a down payment on a human being? I think it's like, finally, she'd had it, something snapped. I imagine what it must have been like that last day when she ran away—walking with a straight back down the length of the dinner table carrying a big pot, serving white women, ladling soup from one bowl to another, her face like stone. Was it something she overheard them say? Maybe she overheard that she was going to get sold. . . . Maybe she got a whupping or was raped on that last day. Or was it the thought of living on that plantation for one more day, or one more year? And I imagine that later in the night while she's cleaning the kitchen, she wraps these lavish spoons engraved with her slave owner's name in a dishcloth and slips them inside her apron. Then she walks calmly back to her quarters, packs a small bag, and is never seen again."

"Wow." I was so enthralled by this story that I couldn't quite believe it. "Are you sure this all happened? It sounds like a movie."

"I don't know that it happened in that exact way, but these are the stories passed down in my family, and look, these spoons exist," she said, bringing her spoon closer to my face.

"What's this engraving here? *C?*"

"No, that's the other thing! The *C* must have been her slave owner's initial! Isn't it lucky that she was never caught? She was carrying solid evidence of theft. But what's even more outstanding is that she had the smarts not to sell off the silver, even though the money would probably have helped. Isn't it amazing that this is who I come from?"

"Wow" was again the only response I could muster. I had heard Leticia talk about the spoons, but never in this way. Her voice was so bitter I could almost taste the tartness in her mouth.

"She was one badass bitch. I feel so grateful for her existence, even though I've never seen her face. I feel her strength in me. I am so emboldened as a Black woman, you know? Like, even though she was a thief, at least she tried to run, refused to have her heart or her body broken one more time, and she took something with her that could have totally got her killed. I can't imagine being so pissed off, so tired, so desperate, so done that the consequences of whatever may come pale in comparison."

"What happened to her? Where did she go?" I asked, hungry for any little bit that she wanted to share with me.

"My mom always heard the stories from her own mom about a grandmother six generations down who fled the Cobb Plantation in Missouri, and who married a freed slave in Chicago. When she was a slave, her owner wasn't super wealthy, I think he only had about fifty slaves, which sounds like a lot of people to, you know, *own,* but apparently it wasn't. So Cobb was her slave name, and then that was lost to the Simmons slave name when she got married, and that's pretty much my mom's legacy—and this set of silver spoons. How crazy is that?"

I looked down at the tub of ice cream and realized we'd stopped eating. I felt nearly responsible for Leticia's heartache.

"You know, one thing I've been thinking about a lot since I came to the States is how the Africans were just as scheming as the Europeans in the transatlantic slave trade." I cleared my throat. "I tell myself that I am East African and that *we* were traded by the Arabs and therefore the transatlantic slave trade has nothing to do with me because that was all in West Africa. But more Africans are beginning to acknowledge how morally complicit we were. Last year, the Benin president fell on his knees in front of a Black church in Baltimore and begged them for forgiveness. That's something at least. But for the most part, Africans just want to forget."

"Hmmm . . . kind of convenient to forget, don't you think?" Leticia said. "It's the same thing that white folks say today, you know, 'It wasn't me, it was three hundred years ago, it has nothing to do with me.' "

I'd known Leticia for years, and we'd shared our deepest secrets, but this, this part of her, she'd never allowed me this far inside. Listening to her talk about a legacy mired in trauma, I now felt so contrite, so deeply ashamed. She was the first Black American I'd ever really known who had told me these things—the things I read about in novels and watched in Hollywood movies. I saw then where all the Molly drama had come from. It wasn't really about Molly. It was the intergenerational trauma, the torturous visions Leticia had of her great-great-great-great-great-great-grandmother, the stolen spoons, and the pain of not knowing anything about her mother's side of the family. We sat in silence for a while, the television still muted, each of us lost in our own thoughts.

"It must be so nice to know what your name means, to know where it comes from and that it's lived before you for centuries," Leticia said, moving the tub of liquid chocolate ice cream from the couch to the coffee table. "To know that it was not replaced with 'Cecily' and capped with the last name 'Washington.' That would be enough for me."

"I really don't think it's that simple," I said. "In Africa, we haven't got proper record keeping. I don't even know what year my great-grandmother was born, let alone my grandmother six generations ago. The fact you can trace that yours was born about twenty years before abolition is amazing! Old Africans speak of birth dates using historical events . . . things like 'It happened during the great famine.' But even that's not helpful, because it wasn't a global event like a world war. There are no dates on century-old tombstones. Perhaps we are able to say that our ancestors were medicine men, or blacksmiths, or whatnot. But not all Africans know these historical details. The families that have a lineage of chiefdoms and royalty have a much easier time tracing their ancestry because their ancestors were known widely in communities. But in the end, without record keeping, tracing ancestry is like hitting a wall. We didn't even have photography until the whites came, so the earliest photograph you'll see in a Kenyan museum might be dated like 1890. My grandmother says she saw a reflection of herself for the first time as a little girl in the river. After that, she saw herself in a black-and-white photograph the missionaries snapped of the children in her village. That was the 1930s. She couldn't recognize herself. The priest had to point to the image of each child and say to the kids, 'This is you, and this is you, and here you are.' And let's not even get into how we lost our religion. My grandmother was taught that God was androgynous, both masculine and feminine. But when the missionaries came, they taught her that a white man with long golden hair died for her on a wooden cross, and for that she owed him her faith. And then, the colonial masters took land from the Africans, all the while smiling at them, bringing them new medicine, introducing a cash currency, and offering them work so they could earn it. It's like owning a pet snake, feeding it mice, and all the while not anticipating that it'll strangle you while you sleep."

Leticia nodded along, her eyes grim and sympathetic.

"I mean, it's unbelievable, T!" I said. "The colonization of property, body, and mind—to this day, I have no idea why we drink afternoon tea when it's boiling hot outside. Why we name our kids Geoffrey."

"Oh, what the hell!" Leticia said, standing up and bustling toward the kitchen. She threw her hands up and looked up at the ceiling. "Lord! All this suffering on Black folk for centuries. Why?"

When she got to the door, she looked back at me. "I can't believe you're moving out. Who am I going to have heart-to-hearts like this with? I'll really miss you."

Chapter Fifteen

Over the past eight months, as I fell in love with Akhenaten, and eventually moved in with him, I had been keeping in touch with Aisha over email. She arrived back in New York at the height of late summer, just a few weeks after I had moved the last of my boxes into Akhenaten's loft. Aisha and I arranged to have an early dinner at an Italian bistro. I was shivering from nervous energy. At the end of August, everyone was clamoring to get a seat outside. Aisha was already there when I arrived. She had a seat at one of the coveted tables, and was waiting in a sleeveless red floral-print maxi dress. I wished Akhenaten were with me so I could jab him with my elbow to show him I'd been right when I'd fretted that Aisha would be the pretty sister. She had café au lait skin, the longest eyelashes I had ever seen, and jet-black wavy hair. Why on earth had my aunts told me that I looked just like her? Even harder to believe was that I was twenty-five and she was thirty, but she didn't look a day older than me.

"Look at you! My God, you're as cute as a button," she squealed happily. "I love, love your Bantu knots. I so wish I knew how to do them for my daughter. She's got the same hair."

I settled across from her, starting to feel a tinge of disappointment. Since I'd learned that I had a half sister, I'd dreamed of a person just like me. But that was slowly splintering with the realization that we didn't even look like distant relatives.

She had ordered a cucumber cocktail.

"Here! Taste it," she said, passing the glass over to me. "Taste it. I promise it tastes better than it looks."

I'd really never liked cucumbers, but I didn't want to come off as difficult only five minutes into our relationship, so I ordered one too. She was chatty, and it made me glad, because I was worried that despite our easy rapport on email, we might be awkward in person.

We were nothing alike. She was self-assured in the typical American manner, something that I'd struggled to adapt to over the years. She steered our conversation like an orchestra conductor, speaking knowledgeably about her microfinancing work in Africa, though not in a self-aggrandizing way, or worse, with a savior complex. Her work clearly wasn't a stunt for her résumé, or a "finding yourself" mission. She genuinely cared about her work in developing countries and driving development from the inside out. She wanted to create jobs and nurture talent within communities, rather than simply export expatriate intelligence.

"When I was in the Peace Corps, I was so eager to go out and save Africa," she admitted. "I cringe now just thinking about how self-righteous I was. It took me a minute to realize I was a part of the problem. A lot of well-intentioned people come to Africa and fail because they haven't addressed the deep-rooted problems, just the symptoms. People want to save Africa. You can't save Africa. Africa has to save herself. When I realized that, I knew what I wanted to do. For me, it came down to women.

"If a woman has an income, she can build a nest egg. She doesn't have to be dependent on a man, she can break free from domestic abuse and raise her own kids and break the cycle of poverty. So—

I started investing in women. We've given seed money so far to four hundred women in Accra—most of them single mothers—to open bakeries, hair-braiding salons, organic farm stalls. And guess what? More than ninety-nine percent of the loans we give are paid back within a year. Women are increasing the household income, serving three meals a day to their children, and sending their kids to better schools. Women are brilliant, they're incredibly hardworking, and they do not disappoint!"

Aisha's passion blew my mind. She seemed to have already achieved her dreams at only thirty.

She showed me a photograph of her daughter.

"It's weird how you and I didn't know our dad, and she doesn't know her dad either," Aisha said, tracing her finger over the child's face. "Maybe history really does repeat itself."

The child's name was Nuru, Swahili for light.

"Was that something you just came up with?" I asked. "I've noticed that Black Americans often give their children African names."

"I don't identify myself as African American," she said sternly. "There's nothing about me, in my history, or my life's experiences that's African American. My whole family is Jewish—I had a bat mitzvah. I was always the only brown person at our dinner table at Thanksgiving. I always felt like an intruder. So, I tick Black in the race box, but I wouldn't appropriate Blackness in the American context because I'd feel a bit like a fraud. But now I've got this cappuccino-skinned daughter, and maybe that's why it's easier for me to be in Africa, because I don't feel equipped to raise her as a Black child in America. You know how different it feels to be Black in Africa than in America. I guess I feel better raising her there because she doesn't get pigeonholed because of her skin color the way she would here. I think I've always tried to connect somehow with my father. It's as if I'm always trying to find something—anything—I can grab on to. I gave my daughter a Swahili name so she'd know that a part of her is Kenyan."

She talked a lot about her daughter, offering anecdotes about Nuru's love of dolls and her after-school soccer league, the difficulties of managing ethnic hair, which she herself had never had to deal with because she had loose curls. "It doesn't always look like this, trust me," she said, giggling. "This is after a half hour of blow-drying this morning. But still, it's nothing like my little girl's, and I just worry that all the magazines and books out there glorify blond hair and light skin, and she's going to think she's not good enough. I'm running around like a crazy person overcompensating, buying her ethnic dolls, buying her storybooks like *Nappy Hair, Don't Care* that I didn't even know existed before I had a kid. My mom never did any of that!"

The waiter had returned with our meals—black linguini with clams for me and tagliata for Aisha. She dug into her meal quickly but I was still too nervous to take more than a few bites.

"Tell me about yourself," she said between bites. "Are you close with your family?"

"Yes," I said, surprised at how fast the word spilled out. "I have four aunts who pretty much raised me because they lived with my mother and me for my whole childhood. When I was younger, we had a different relationship, but now that I'm older, we talk about everything and they're more like older sisters. I'm very close with my granny because she also lived with us. My mom never remarried. It was a house full of women, which I now realize was very empowering for me."

"Wow. Do you miss him?" Aisha asked. "Our dad, I mean?"

"I struggle to remember him," I said. "He died on my fifth birthday so celebrating my birthday has never really been my thing. Do you know how he died?"

"Yeah," Aisha said, unaffected. "I think I was fifteen when my mom told me that actually he had killed himself. I had a friend at school who committed suicide and it affected me terribly. I guess she decided it was time I should know the truth about my father. I was shattered. But that was probably when I stopped hating him. He treated my mom and me unconscionably. But it must have been hard on him too, making those decisions, or he wouldn't have been in a place to take his own life."

"Well, my family hid it from me too until I was ten and I honestly believe they would have hidden it longer," I said. "All the memories I have of my father, really, are stories that have been told to me so it was a real shock to hear that this man I had built up in my head as a saint was actually a very flawed, struggling human being. I don't miss him. But when I was a kid, I'd see the other fathers and wonder what it'd be like to have one. When my mother disciplined me, I'd cry myself to sleep wishing I had a father who would put her in her place. But as I get older, I guess I'm understanding her issues better."

"I don't remember him that well either," Aisha said. "I remember my mom crying a lot, not getting out of bed, when he left. I honestly thought he'd left for, like, a vacation. I didn't realize I'd never see him again. My grandmother made it worse. She heckled my mom endlessly. . . . *We told you so, we told you he was no good.* And then of course I didn't see him for years and then was told he had died, and that we would be going to the funeral. It was all very confusing. I was very aware of what was happening around me, but I didn't really understand all the nuances. I remember being at the funeral. It was so hot the minute we got off the plane. The roads were so dusty and chaotic. There were so many people—more people than I'd ever seen. I remember thinking, *How come everyone is brown?* My mom told me you were my sister, which I think was weird for me because I didn't even know I had a sister, and you looked nothing like me. I think my mom wanted to go so that she could see this other life of my father's—this other woman that he'd chosen over her, this other child who was more special to him than her daughter. That trip was what she needed to get some closure."

"So, you hate him?" I asked, feeling suddenly defensive over a man I hardly knew myself.

"I don't hate him. I definitely did at first," she said. "Later I realized he did actually love us, but had other pressures. I guess he just wasn't happy here and he couldn't get my mom to leave with him."

"For sure," I admitted. "Leaving you and your mom must have been part of what made him depressed enough to commit suicide."

"I just want to know what made him make the choices he made," Aisha said. "Actually, I do know. I know, because I've experienced it with my daughter's father."

"Oh, is he really not in your life at all?" I said, then winced, worrying I'd stepped too far.

"Nope!" She pushed her plate away, only halfway through her meal. "Turns out I wasn't good enough to marry. My daughter doesn't know her father and that's on him."

I was perplexed, though I tried to hide it. The conversation had taken an awkward turn, first with what felt like a shot at Mother—the woman who'd stolen Aisha's father away. Then, I had ignited a whole new fire by inquiring about her daughter's father.

"I apologize if I've upset you," I said. "You don't have to talk about it."

"No, not at all. I'm not upset. It's just that my father ditched my mom in the exact same way my ex ditched me. My ex is Nigerian. I met him at Harvard, moved with him to New York for a few years. Then I joined the Peace Corps and he stayed here, but we didn't break up. Anyway, I was good enough to date for years, but I wasn't good enough to marry."

"That's awful, I'm sorry. Did he refuse, literally, to marry you—even though you had a child together?"

"Yes. I know that his parents know about Nuru," she said. " 'The baby he has with the American woman' is probably what they call her. As if that part of his life was a mistake, like some sort of redacted document."

"Is he here? In the States?"

"No, no," Aisha said, waving her hand. "After the Peace Corps I came back to the States and found a great job here in New York and we were still in a serious relationship. Nuru was born here. I figured we would make a life here. Then he ditched me, moved to Lagos, and is apparently engaged to a Nigerian girl he met while I was in the Peace Corps. So why did he not just go out with her then? Why did he waste years of my life?"

"I don't know," I said sympathetically. I reached my hand out and put it over hers. Somehow, it felt like the natural thing to do. She didn't move her hand away.

"He was happy when I got pregnant. But then he started to get iffy the closer the due date came. He was flaking out, so I tried pressuring him into giving me a commitment. I wasn't asking for a proposal, you know, just some sign that he was committed—like introducing me to his parents. But the more I pushed, the more distant he became. Finally, just a week before the baby was due, he said to me, 'I'm sorry, but I can't.' Just like that—'I'm sorry, but I can't'—as if he was changing his mind about buying a car. Then he went into a long spiel about his family being very close-knit and them having expectations about the person he'd marry. Six years, and he hadn't figured out that his mom and dad might not be on board? It didn't help that my mom had just passed away. I felt like she was the only person in the world who'd have understood what I was going through. It was the shittiest time of my life, yet the happiest because I had this beautiful baby."

"Wow," I said. "You're so strong."

Aisha smiled. "When Nuru was born, one of my ex's sisters who lives here in New York came to the hospital to see the baby. As she was leaving, she said to me, 'You're an amazing person. I adore you—all my sisters do. But my brother is the good son. He will do what will make my parents happy. They will never be happy with a foreign woman. To you, curtsying for our dad is probably beneath you, but to a Yoruba girl—even one with an Oxford degree—it wouldn't be an issue.'

"I remember thinking that was the meanest, coldest thing anyone had ever said to me in my whole entire life. That I was too stupid, or too arrogant, to learn a new culture. It was such a harsh rejection. It was also a cop-out. I have several Nigerian friends in interracial and intercultural marriages. I have several American friends in Ghana who are married to Ghanaians. It's not a culture issue. He could have had the balls to come out and say that I wasn't good enough for his parents. He didn't have to blame it on culture. I tossed out the Nigerian name I had picked out and opted to go with a Swahili one. I needed some light in my life at the time. It was the perfect name."

"Look, I'm not making excuses for him," I said, finding my voice. "But it can be extremely difficult with African parents. It's universal too, I think. It's petty racial and class and cultural bullshit, and some families are just not as accepting. Could be a wealthy, blue-blooded family in Connecticut saying no to a Black or Latina person. Or your Jewish grandparents refusing to let their daughter marry an African man. Some of us win the lottery with parents who get it and some of us are cursed with parents who only care about what their families are supposed to look like to the outside world, not their children's happiness."

"Well," said Aisha, half-smiling, then sipping the cucumber cocktail. "It's okay. I dodged a bullet, really—there's nothing worse than a mother-in-law who's got it in for you. It pains me that he doesn't have a relationship with Nuru. She deserves a father. But that's his loss because she's a really amazing kid."

I lifted my green drink in the air and she raised hers too. "Cheers to that."

Aisha insisted on picking up the check, and we left to walk around the neighborhood and find gelato.

As we strolled, we talked about New York, and Little Italy, and how much smaller it had become over the years. She knew so much more about the city than I did but she brushed my insecurity off quickly.

"You've got a corporate job," she said. "You're in early and out late. You haven't got the time to go traipsing around town. For my job, I have to connect with people who will help me with funding and all that. A lot of my work is having lunches and dinners with wealthy folks who want to throw money at poverty."

We stood in a short queue at a gelato shop on the corner of Mulberry, waiting for a couple with their young children to finish sampling different flavors.

"Tell me, did you want to leave Kenya? Is that why you came here?" Aisha asked. "I only ask because for me, I have to say, I needed to get out of the Midwest. I couldn't wait to graduate high school. I applied to colleges that were as far as possible from Indiana. I moved to Boston for college and have been out in the world since."

"I just needed some independence from a very overbearing mother," I said. "I think it's been good for both of us to have some distance. She's had to let me go a little."

We each chose a different flavor of gelato and walked down Mulberry exchanging cups so we could eat a bit of both. We talked about Aisha's dating life, which she said was dead in the water.

"It's hard when you have a kid and a job," she said. "I don't want to waste my time with losers because every minute I spend elsewhere is a minute I'm not spending with Nuru. What about you? How is it going with Akhenaten—I love reading about him in your emails."

"Actually, I have news," I said. "I've just moved in with him."

"Whoa!" Aisha said, stopping in her tracks. "Wait, how do I not know this? You didn't say anything on email."

"I wanted to tell you in person," I said.

"Oh, Soila, that's so sweet," she squeezed my shoulders. "You must love him. You don't seem like the type to move in with a man you aren't sure about."

"Actually, I haven't been this happy, ever. I sit next to him on the couch with my book and feel like I've always been right there, right next to him. Somehow, I know that he's not going anywhere. He just seems so content with me as I am. Oh! And he cooks. He makes the most amazing seafood gumbo, the best jambalaya. He's basically just amazing in everything he does."

"Geez, sounds like the real deal, huh?" she said, sounding a little envious. "So your mom and your aunties must be really happy for you then?"

I paused, a little ashamed. "I haven't told my mother," I admitted. "I don't know when I'm going to tell her."

"You haven't told her?" I thought I heard a tinge of *I knew this was too good to be true* in her tone. "I'm sorry, why?"

"I don't know. It's hard. She's a little imposing, so I navigate her delicately."

"Delicately? Why do I feel like I'm rewatching the movie of my life?"

"I know. She *is* a problem. She's going to complain that he's too eccentric, because he's an artist. Never mind that he's really successful. All she'll see are his dreadlocks and that will be enough to send her into a tailspin. Frankly, she'd kill me if she knew I'm living with him. It's so complicated."

"If you love this guy, be with him," Aisha said decisively. "If you don't love him enough to fight for him, then you need to leave him now. I know what it's like to be led on for years and then have your heart ripped out. Don't do it to this guy."

"I know. . . . I won't," I said. We were standing at the end of the street. I noticed a wedding party streaming out of the doors of a Catholic church. The building was nondescript, with a stone façade and no external architectural bells and whistles—no tall spires, ornate wooden doors, onion domes, or even a steeple. The bride and groom stood on the steps and were being showered with rice by a small crowd.

"Look at that wedding," I said, directing Aisha's eyes to the fanfare. "No wedding in Kenya is that small. It's the same with funerals here."

"Do you know what church that is?" She was chewing on the end of her plastic ice cream spoon. "It's one of the oldest Catholic churches in New York. Some of the scenes in *The Godfather* were shot there. There are actual catacombs in there. It's a tourist attraction."

"Seriously, how do you know so much stuff about this city? Next to you I feel like I know nothing."

"I just do," she said, shrugging and laughing at the same time. "I know a lot of things. But—I don't know how to keep a man."

"Sure you do. You just haven't met the right one," I said. When I leaned in to give her a hug goodbye, I could smell lavender in her hair, and inexplicably my eyes filled with tears. Aisha looked at me with confusion and concern.

"I'm sorry. Meeting you for the first time, and really liking you, is overwhelming," I said. "I feel like I've known you my whole life, but I also feel like I was robbed of this relationship."

"Well, we have the next seventy-something years to make up for it," she said, tugging on my shoulder.

Across the street, the bride and groom were being whisked away in a vintage car roped with tin cans that banged loudly as they drove down the street. The guests stood together in a tight crowd on the steps of the church, cheering. The joy was palpable and as I watched the whole scene I couldn't help but smile. I felt like I was a part of their celebration, even though I hadn't the faintest idea who any of these people were.

"Oh my God, look at you," Aisha said. "I think someone's itching to get married."

"Oh, stop," I said, feeling caught out. "I'm not thinking about that at all."

"Please—who are you kidding? You want to get married. You do, don't you? And you're afraid that for whatever crazy reason, you can't have that."

. . .

That night, I called Mother. I couldn't shake the conversation I had had with Aisha. I didn't want to do to Akhenaten what Nuru's father had done to Aisha, what my father had done to Aisha's mother. My stomach was churning with anxiety when I thought about the news I had to deliver, but I wasn't going to be able to live with Akhenaten if I was hiding it from Mother. It would be a lie, to him especially. A fantasy I didn't think was fair. I told Akhenaten that I wanted him to talk to Mother. It probably wouldn't go how we would want it to go, but at least we would be able to live our truth, I said.

It would be seven A.M. in Nairobi, and she'd be getting ready to head off to Sunday Mass with Kokoi in tow. I planned that first I would talk to her and then hand Akhenaten the phone, so he could introduce himself. I asked about Kokoi, Tanei, and Princess, like I always did. Mother said everyone was doing well. Tanei was taking a counseling course. She had decided she wanted to work with victims of trauma, like herself. Mother said the locusts were back and decimating produce on commercial farms. She fretted about her rose and coffee farms, which were her largest sources of income. It didn't look like she would be exporting much of anything this year, she said.

"What about you? How is work going?" she asked.

It was always the same question, as consistent as a trained parrot. It gutted me every time I had to answer, because I hated that I had to lie to her every time. This time, I didn't say anything.

"What's wrong? Is something wrong with your job?" she asked.

Again, I couldn't find my scripted answer. Instead, I blurted it all out.

"Yeyo, I have something to tell you, about my life, not my work. I have been in a serious relationship with a man I love for nearly a year. We have decided to live together."

Mother was silent for a little while. Then she cleared her throat.

"Are you calling me on a Sunday morning to inform me you are living in sin?"

"No, I'm calling you to have an honest conversation with you about my life, because I don't want to keep a big part of my life hidden from you, because I don't want to have to lie to you for years like Rarin did."

"Is he African?"

"No, he is African American."

"I'm afraid to continue this conversation, Soila. What does he do?"

"He's a well-known artist," I said. "A sculptor."

Another excruciatingly long silence, where the only sound between us was the static and hissing of the phone line.

"Don't you want to know his name?"

"I don't even want to imagine that you have slept with this man," she said, dismissive. "Please tell me that you have not. Please tell me that you're still celibate. That he is at least a good Christian who has not ruined your modesty."

"Yeyo, I am a grown woman," I said. "I'm living with a man. Obviously, I'm not celibate."

"Is he a Catholic?"

"No."

"So, what is your plan with a foreign man, who is not a Christian? Will you bring him back home? Or will you live in a foreign country for the rest of your life, like Rarin? I can't imagine you have thought this through."

"No, I haven't thought through all that," I said. "All I know is I'm happier than I've ever been."

"That's the other thing. What kind of a man lives with a woman who he hasn't married and a woman whose family he has never met? If he wants to live with you, he should marry you."

"Yeyo, we don't need to rush into marriage," I said. "We are simply living together because we are together all the time when we're not working. It's the next step in our relationship."

"And how do you know he won't get you pregnant then leave you high and dry? Soila, this is not how I raised you."

"Well, I'm sure about him," I said. "I know his character and you shouldn't judge someone you've never even met. I want you to know him and talk to him."

"I will do no such thing. If you want to live in sin and even get married to this man, you can go ahead. But I won't be involved. I don't know him, where he's from, who his people are, and, frankly, you have nothing in common with such a person. What sort of a person is this that you're bringing me? Are you trying to humiliate me?"

"Humiliate you? Are the opinions of your friends more important than your own daughter's happiness?"

"What is this song you keep singing, 'Being happy, being happy . . .'? Do you understand what you're jeopardizing? Even if you think you want to marry this man, you should know that it can't work out. Marriage is long and hard. It's a sacrifice and a compromise every day. It's not about the fun time that you think he's giving you now. I thought your life was finally on track since you graduated and got a good job. You have a good career. Why are you throwing everything away? Where are all the values I taught you all these years?"

"I don't really understand what you're talking about," I said. I was angry. But I would never lose my temper or insult Mother. It wasn't something I knew how to do. "What has me loving a man who makes me happy got to do with my career?"

I listened quietly while she trampled on my self-worth and belittled my choices. But then, vengeance started to build up inside of me like the clouds gathering before a storm. I knew that I could punish her. I could sting her, so badly she would whip herself for hours, pleading to God for answers.

"By the way, Mother, you know what? I met Aisha," I said, in the coldest voice I could muster.

"Who is Aisha?"

"Don't play dumb with me, Mother. You know exactly who Aisha is. She was in New York for a few days for work and we spent some time together, and I will continue to talk to her, and get to know her better."

"Soila, why are you saying these things? What have I ever done to you that has made you want to hurt me in this way? You have gone and made a relationship with that girl even though I asked you not to. . . ."

There was a shuffling and then I heard her muffled voice. "Where is Tanei?"

"It's me," I heard Tanei speaking in the background. "I'm right here."

"No, I mean, Tanei?" Mother asked. "Where is Tanei?"

"It's me! It's me, Tanei."

There was more shuffling then she was back on the line.

"Tanei, you're making a huge mistake."

"Why are you calling me Tanei? This is Soila."

"What?"

"It's Soila," I said, shouting. "You called me Tanei."

More shuffling. Then she hung up.

Akhenaten had been waiting outside, listening through the door, and he hurried in as soon as I hung up. When he walked in, I shrugged, defeated.

"What can I do?" he asked, sitting next to me on the bed.

"Nothing. Nothing." I sighed. "She's so selfish. I love my mother but she's so selfish. She's angry that I met up with Aisha after she forbade it. She's mad that I'm living with a foreign guy who she's never met. But what am I supposed to do? She doesn't accept or respect anything that I do, so I constantly have to do everything behind her back, but I'm done living like that."

Akhenaten was looking down to the floor. "Soila, I want to be with you for a long time. Is that something that's even possible? I know how important she is in your life," he said, seemingly unable to look into my eyes.

"Listen to me," I said, cupping his stubble-bearded face. "For the first time in my life, I absolutely do not care what my mother wants. I would want her to get to know you for you and respect our relationship and bless it. But it is what it is."

Akhenaten sighed. "Give her time. She might surprise you. She might come around."

"Something else was weird," I said. "At the end of the call she got my name mixed up. She was speaking to Tanei, but she was asking for Tanei. Then she got back on the phone with me and she called me Tanei. My mother doesn't ever mess up like that, definitely not with names."

"Maybe she was so upset from the news that she lost it," Akhenaten said. "Maybe it's too early in the morning."

I shook my head. I wasn't sure.

"I never rebelled as a teen; I have done all the things that she asked me to do for my entire life. Until now. And she still wants more, but I have nothing more to give."

"Boy, your mother is badass," he said, shaking his head. "Hoooo! She is badass."

When he said that, for no reason at all, we both burst out laughing so hard we couldn't breathe. Kokoi always said, "When things are so absurd and you've cried so much that you have no more tears left, you might as well have a good laugh." It was true.

Chapter Sixteen

Akhenaten had worked all night in his studio, and the emptiness on his side of the bed felt enormous. I couldn't fall asleep for hours. Thoughts popped in and out of my mind like little bubbles rising to the surface. It wasn't work-related stress. The layoffs had eased and I was starting to feel confident my job was safe. But I couldn't stop thinking about Mother. She had refused to talk to me after our last phone call, the same way she had cut Rarin off when Rarin told her she was pregnant and getting married. She refused to answer my calls. It bothered me much less than I ever thought it would, but that wasn't the same as not being bothered at all. I loved Akhenaten. Just lying beside him at night with my head buried inside the crook of his arm made Mother's resistance easier to endure. I pulled his pillow close and buried my face in it to breathe in his scent. Finally, I was able to fall asleep. But when my eyes opened to the soft morning light, I turned around to look at my clock and couldn't believe the time. It was seven-thirty A.M. My clock hadn't buzzed, and Akhenaten hadn't come to bed like he usually did when he worked late. There was a note on his pillow—he had slipped in without waking me—

S, lots of work to do. See you tonight. Love, A. I rushed out of bed thinking about the long string of client meetings that lined my whole day. Worse still, I would be late for the first one.

On the subway, I glanced at my BlackBerry every few minutes. For sure, there'd be at least one email from Angie, reminding me, with poisoned sweetness, that I was late. I couldn't get a signal underground, but I continued to scroll the screen as if my email might somehow appear. When I finally ran up the stairs out of the subway it was already almost nine.

At the top of the stairs, a group of people were looking up at a Nairobi-blue sky. But then I saw, directly in front of me, a thick cloud of smoke puffing out of the top floors of one of the towers of the World Trade Center. A murmur spread through the crowd on the street; everyone was wondering where the smoke was coming from. Some responded confidently, like they were experienced firefighters, saying it was probably just a small fire and would soon be handled. We all shrugged our shoulders and scattered in our separate directions.

I walked into the office a little before nine. No one was at their desks. There was a large sealed window on the east wing of our office where I had stood over the years when I needed a break from the glare of my desktop. I liked to sit on its wide ledge and stare down at New Yorkers the size of ants walking in and out of the shopping center across the street. Everyone in our office crowded at that window, the same way everyone coming out of the subway had been crowded around me just a few minutes earlier.

"A plane went into one of the towers," a young man I didn't recognize told me. He was talking to me, but his eyes stayed glued to the window.

I opened my mouth to ask what he meant—his sentence sounded like nonsense—when I saw the tail of a large airliner as it blew through the back end of the second tower. I saw it and the image froze my brain. I couldn't think, couldn't process. Chaos. Shouting. Crying. The ground trembled and the building began to shake.

I looked for a face I knew. Not just knew, but someone whose hand I could hold. Where was Molly? Molly would tell me that it was going to be okay and I would believe her. The ground shook again, this time even more violently. I rushed back to my desk. Everyone was on their cellphones, dialing and cursing. I tried to call Akhenaten using my desk line but I heard only a relentless busy signal. Still, I couldn't stop dialing, over and over. Molly. Akhenaten. Leticia. I needed someone to know what was happening. Finally, I saw a face I recognized. Angie. She was at another desk in the traders' section of the office, dialing and redialing the phone. I tried to talk to her, but she put her hand up in my face. I felt like she wouldn't have spared a moment's thought for me if I hadn't shown up that morning.

"Angie! I can't find Molly. Is she in yet?"

Angie's eyes darted behind me, as if I didn't exist.

"I don't know, I don't know, okay?" she said.

I was made of stone and none of this was real. Where was Molly? She was always one of the first people in. She always sent me a message if she wasn't going to be in, if she was calling in sick, which was close to never.

I had no bars on my cellphone. I went back to my desk and uselessly kept dialing from my phone extension. I didn't know what else to do. What was I supposed to do? If only I had gone down to the studio to kiss Akhenaten goodbye before I left the apartment that morning, I wished. I refused to think about Leticia. She worked in Midtown and took the F train every morning all the way from Brooklyn. But her schedule was erratic. She was often not in the office. Mostly, she was walking from one meeting to another for interviews in the sprawling apartments of wealthy socialites, or with gallery owners, artists, and musicians. She could have been anywhere in New York. I wouldn't let myself imagine the unimaginable.

Everyone around me was lost in their own anxieties, clinging to their phones. Some people were holding on to a desk, a wall, in silence, steeling themselves for their next move. Some women were sitting on the floor crying, saying things I didn't want to hear. . . . *"There are people jumping out of the building."*

All I could focus on was finding Molly and I ran to the bathroom in one last attempt. Maybe she'd gotten stuck in one of the stalls. While I was in the bathroom calling out for her, I heard shrieking and then a thunderous roar. I came out just in time to see one of the twin towers falling to the ground.

Everyone around me was insane with terror, screaming at an even higher pitch, and cold fear washed through me, but I wasn't going to cry. I wasn't going to scream. Mother's discipline beat like a drum in my head. Help someone else. Be useful. But how could I possibly be useful right now? I felt so alone that I couldn't find the strength to offer anyone else support. Sure, there were other human beings around me, but no one in this room knew real things about me—whom I loved, or by whom I was loved. Akhenaten, Leticia, Mother, Kokoi. In the midst of the screaming chaos, I was completely alone.

A group of men, faceless, nameless, in suit jackets and ties, organized the rest of us near the stairwell. We had to get out of the office. They told us we had to take the stairs all the way down from the fiftieth floor. I thought it sounded completely insane. Who could go down that many stairs? But I didn't hear a word of complaint from anyone. I didn't know this side of New Yorkers, who normally complained about everything. Looking at the brave resignation on the faces around me, I understood that this was what I could do to be useful. I could be orderly and not protest and put one foot in front of the other.

A chalky white substance descended on us, dust-like, but ashier, thicker, and blinding. I couldn't make out anything more than an arm's length away. We had to get out—without Molly.

Once we were lined up at the stairs, we moved respectfully. At every floor, a new rush of people crammed into the stairwell, like a tributary joining a great river. The men were kind. They would allow women to move up in front of them. Women took off their heels and stuffed them in their bags. They unbuttoned their shirts, revealing lacy or simple cotton bras, and the men didn't even care to stare. There was an overweight man standing in the corner on the landing at about the thirtieth floor. His skin was pasty, and his white shirt was glued to his chest and back by layers of sweat. He couldn't make it, he said. Several people walked past him but a man who was climbing down behind me stopped and held his hand. He pulled him, quite aggressively, and forced him to walk ahead of him. I could hear the heavy man's grunting behind me, but every time he stopped, the man guiding him would push him forward again.

"No one's getting left behind, buddy," he said. "You're going home."

The line began to slow to a near standstill, and I realized we were getting closer to the ground level.

"What's going on?" people yelled from above me.

"Hang in there, guys." A New York City firefighter pushed his way up the stairs with heavy gear and a light mounted on his helmet. A wave of relief washed over me at the sight of him, so strong my knees nearly buckled. "It's the lobby. The rubble's come all the way to the revolving doors. It's going to be a while but we're doing our best to dig you out."

With barely a grumble, everyone cooperated. I didn't understand what it meant that rubble was blocking the doors. How high would it be? How hot would it be? I didn't want to ask. I remembered Tanei telling me how hot and blistering the debris from the embassy bombing was on her skin.

It took half an hour to get us down to the lobby. And just as we stepped out of the building, the second tower ripped open from the top and fell to the ground in a cloud of dust. This time, I cried. Not knowing how many were trapped inside, knowing that no one could possibly survive that—my despair was insurmountable. But once again, I had no time to process what was happening. I saw what was in front of me, but I wasn't making sense of it because one moment didn't leave room for the next. There was rubble flying through the air. With the helicopters, the sirens, the police officers lining the streets, the air so blazing hot, musty, clogged with ash and debris and smelling like the inside of a jet engine, the bloodied and injured New Yorkers—I just could not believe that I was in Manhattan. *One foot in front of the other,* I heard Mother.

Defiantly, the firefighters remained in the chaos, unstopped by the torrential rubble and the human stampede. They were invincible. They directed us toward the Brooklyn Bridge.

"There is no other way out of the city, if you're here in Lower Manhattan," I heard one of them explain.

We walked in a tight crowd on the Brooklyn Bridge. Over us, the dark-green military choppers circled in a way that felt more predatory than protective. I blocked my ears. A woman walking beside me wept, "I know he's dead, I know he's dead." I held her trembling hand in silence. Together, we walked across the bridge and the East River beneath us looked dark and ominous.

The only place I could go to in Brooklyn was Leticia's, but I didn't have a key anymore. I rang the bell even though I knew she wouldn't be home. I sat on the stoop, dazed. On my walk through Cobble Hill, I'd seen crowds of people gathered around neighborhood sports bars, watching television while quietly sipping on their beers, and it wasn't even noon. It seemed that anyone who'd survived the morning didn't want to be home alone. All I wanted was to be home with Akhenaten, and to know where Leticia and Molly were. When I heard the little chain in the door behind me unclasp and saw Leticia's face peering through, I began sobbing uncontrollably. When she opened the door, I fell into her arms and we collapsed in a heap on the floor, crying together. Leticia had come down with a stomach bug and called in sick to work that morning. She said she had tried to call me for hours and hadn't been able to reach Akhenaten either to ask about me. She had been able to reach her parents in Upstate New York by hitting redial relentlessly all morning, but getting through to anyone inside the city was next to impossible. I sobbed that I hadn't been able to find Molly. Leticia said Molly probably overslept and just never managed to make it downtown from Harlem and couldn't reach me. I believed her. I had overslept too.

In the shower, I couldn't wash out the dust. It was wrapped around my hair and my eyelashes, and the more I scrubbed, the pastier it got. I cried once again, uncontrollably, in the shower.

"It's the shock," Leticia said, as she handed me a cup of chamomile tea. We sat on the couch, watching the reel of the crumbling buildings on CNN on repeat. It was five P.M. when my phone rang for the first time that day. Akhenaten's name lit up the screen.

"I didn't know, I didn't know how I was going to get past this, if I'd lost you." I could hear his voice crack. "Your office is so close, and my mind was just all over the place. I just kept wishing I'd said goodbye this morning."

We didn't know when we would be able to reach each other again. The grids were locked. The subways were closed.

"Your mom must be beside herself," Akhenaten said. "I can't even imagine it. My mom finally got through to me in the afternoon. She was so worried about you."

"I don't think my mother wants to hear from me anyway," I said, despondent.

"Don't be crazy, Soila. She's probably sick with worry. We have to find a way to tell her you're alive."

I promised him I'd try to call home until I got through.

After we hung up, I lay on the couch while Leticia baked something chocolaty to calm our nerves. A copy of *Walden* sat on the coffee table.

I had read Thoreau in college. It seemed like a century ago, but the memory I carried of his essays was that human beings had to break free from conformist notions of the good: *I learned this, at least, by my experiment: that if one advances confidently in the direction of his dreams, and endeavors to live the life which he has imagined, he will meet with a success unexpected in common hours.*

A pink laminated bookmark peeked out. On the back, Leticia had scribbled her name and the date: 1999. I slid it out and read the quote printed on it. *My life is short. I can't listen to banality. V. S. Naipaul*

Now, the same feeling gripped me as when I'd stood in Alex's kitchen years ago in the middle of a winter storm. I remembered how I'd watched a riveting red bird fly all by itself, over the bareness of the winter. How mesmerized I had been by its boldness and freedom of flight. If a little bird could do it, I could break the mold too, be the person I really wanted to be deep inside. I could fly free.

"Ticia, think about all the people who went in to work today, to another day at a job they hated. And then didn't come out alive. What was it all for in the end, no matter how much they got paid?"

She was in the middle of pouring her chocolate mix into ramekins. She paused and set the bowls aside.

"Sure. But there are also a ton of people who went to work today, to jobs they loved, like the firefighters, and they didn't come out alive. What was it all for in the end, no matter how much they loved it? They died heroes but they won't see their kids grow up, graduate college, get married. Was it all worth it? If you don't like your life, change it. There are no guarantees."

"I hate my job," I admitted. "And then today, I saw those buildings come down, so many people die right in front of my eyes. I don't want to live this life that I don't love anymore. I don't want to live my mother's dream. I want to live for me."

"Soila, you've been through so much today. Take some time to process before you do anything drastic," Leticia said.

At ten P.M., my phone buzzed. I still couldn't peel my eyes off CNN no matter how much I tried to close them and shut off my brain. I answered automatically.

"Soila, I have been so worried," Mother said. She was nearly incoherent. It was four A.M. in Kenya and my heart broke for her that she hadn't been able to get ahold of me for twelve hours since she had seen the towers fall on television. "I really thought you died. I tried to call Leticia, but I couldn't get through. I couldn't believe that God could do this to me all over again. All the ladies were here, and Father Emmanuel, and we prayed through the night. Everyone told me not to give up, but seeing those images on the television . . ."

I let her speak, because I knew it was her way of unburdening her own guilt. But I didn't have much to say. She had punished me with silence. The day's events hadn't undone that. If anything, they hardened my resolve to live life on my own terms. When Mother was done, I asked to talk to my aunts and my kokoi.

"It's going to be all right," Kokoi said. "You're going to hear from your friend. It's going to be all right."

I didn't stop calling Molly all day on September 12. Initially, the lines were busy. But by the next day, her phone would ring and ring and then send me to voicemail. On the third day, her phone didn't ring anymore.

A day after the towers fell, the grids opened up again. I returned home to Akhenaten, and we held each other and spoke very little. On September 14, I got a company-wide email from the Cohen CEO. There were three names. Gloria Reuben, the managing director who had hired me and believed in me; Paul Dover, who had cheered for me when I got a job offer at the firm; and Molly Gehrig, one of my best friends. All three had gone to a meeting that morning on the one hundredth floor of Tower 1 of the World Trade Center. I couldn't bear to read the rest of the email.

Why didn't Molly tell me about the meeting? We always exchanged notes about our days, the week ahead. Why didn't she mention this? Had she tried to call me? There were so many questions haunting me.

I left my BlackBerry on the kitchen counter and climbed into bed. I couldn't bear the sight of food, the forced sips of water Akhenaten tried to get into my mouth tasted metallic, the honey tea was nauseating. The only thing that I wanted to do, that I could do, was sleep. In the depths of my dreams, I could keep Molly smiling. In my sleep, I could keep her walking down Fifth Avenue with me on a warm Saturday morning.

Gloria Reuben's family chose to have a private memorial, but there was a joint public memorial for Molly and Paul after the towers fell. Paul Dover had been a likable VP at the firm. He was good friends with Molly. She had said that Paul knew how to make a woman feel like she was part of the boys' club, even though she knew she would never be. I couldn't bear to watch Paul's wife, pain-racked, and their six-year-old twins crying. Their little faces were blanketed by confusion—like mine had once been as a child, watching my own grieving mother.

Molly's parents came from California. They cried in the front pew, looking at an oversize canvas photo of Molly's ever-smiling face, with the falling curls and freckles and the pomegranate-red lipstick.

At eight-fifty A.M. on Tuesday, September 11, I had just run out of the subway station, climbing four steps at a time. I had seen the smoking building and spared a small thought for those inside. At eight-fifty A.M., while my good friend Molly was dying, I was thinking only of how late I was for a job I didn't even care about.

Part Four

Chapter Seventeen

"Ma, I'm so afraid I'll come home and find her hanging from the ceiling," I heard Akhenaten whisper to his mother.

She had arrived the day before Molly's memorial, as soon as travel was allowed into New York again. I liked Akhenaten's mother. She had included me in the birthday card that she sent her son that year, adding that she couldn't wait to meet me, even though Akhenaten and I had only been dating for several months. She'd send me sweet emails signed off *Love, Estelle Maude,* as though her first name was worthless without her middle name. On the phone her voice had the power of a gospel vocalist in a spirited Black church. She often said, "Now, is my boy treating you right?"

She had been planning to come for Thanksgiving, but after the towers fell, Akhenaten was worried by my darkness and sought his mother's help. I took three weeks off after the office opened again, which was an incredible risk in a crumbling economy, but I didn't care. I spent most of my days staring at my bedroom ceiling. Leticia visited and simply sat with me, hardly speaking, and her comforting silence was exactly what I needed. Mrs. Morrison took the guest room and spent her days cleaning the already clean apartment and baking bread, muffins, cornbread. She made me hot chocolate—one mug after another—and patted my back as I lay facedown on the couch.

I was curled up on the couch, on a gray, meaningless, nothing day in early October. Akhenaten was speaking to his mother in the hallway, just within earshot. "It's just everything. First her mom completely rejects me, and then her friend dies. Where does it end?"

"What are you planning on doing about her mom?" Estelle murmured. "She's a piece of work, this woman. How can she be so unsupportive of her only child?"

"I don't know, Ma," Akhenaten said. "Their relationship is so complicated. Her mom should be here, dealing with this, not you or Ticia. I've never seen her like this. I didn't know she could sink into this intense kind of depression."

"What about therapy?" Estelle whispered.

"I think it would help her, but she would never go."

I heard him sigh deeply and then his feet shuffled toward me. I pretended to be asleep.

It was mid-October when I finally let Akhenaten lead me out of the apartment for an afternoon walk. The purpling and yellowing of the leaves astounded me. When had it become fall? The air smelled so crisp, like fresh mint. I had only a few days left before returning to work.

"I want to go to Molly's apartment," I had said to Akhenaten the day before, while I lay on the couch. He took off his reading glasses and looked up from his PowerBook, where he was constructing strange three-dimensional shapes on digital art software.

"Oh, Soila." He closed his computer and placed it on the coffee table. "How is that going to help?"

"I don't know," I said. "I need to see something that helps me believe she's not coming back."

"And you think looking at her townhouse from the street will do that?"

"Maybe. I need a grave. I need something."

"Okay," he said, leaning back on the wingback he sat on. "But I'm taking you up there. I'm not letting you do this alone."

The next day, Akhenaten and I set off early on the subway, uptown to Harlem, holding hands, saying nothing.

The butterflies in my stomach turned into bees the closer we got. I bit hard on my nails and pulled on the cuticles. Akhenaten slipped my hand out of my mouth like he always did, discreetly, so as not to embarrass me.

"It's just a building, on a pretty tree-lined street," he said, squeezing my hand tighter. "There's nothing to be afraid of."

We got off the train at 125th and walked hand in hand toward Central Harlem. Molly's townhouse was on West 121st, tucked a block off Marcus Garvey Park. In the beauty of autumn, surrounded by so much history, we barely felt the city around us.

As we turned the corner to her street, I saw a moving truck parked outside and men moving in and out of Molly's second-floor apartment with boxes and equipment. Molly's father was standing outside, talking on the phone. I recognized him from the memorial, a sight I'd never forget. At the chapel, he had sat, eyes glazed over, while his wife crumbled apart beside him.

"That's Molly's dad," I reminded Akhenaten. We had stopped at the corner, watching the scene. Molly's dad paced the street. "I'd like to say hi."

Akhenaten nodded and followed behind. In the last month, he'd been more supportive than I could have imagined. He had let me lie in the dark, not take a shower, talk when I needed to, and when I fell quiet, he did too. He had been this person before, for his mother, after his father died. And he had learned with time, through his own grief and hers, what to say, when to push, and when to fall back and let me have my way.

Molly's dad watched us approach him on the narrow street. His body language turned apprehensive as we neared; I could see he didn't recognize us. I was surprisingly less anxious than I had anticipated. Perhaps the walk through Harlem had eased my spirit, released my fears, I thought. I wasn't sure what to say in this terrible scenario, where there were no words that would help a man who had lost a child. But, as respectfully as I could, I introduced myself and told him that I had worked with Molly and she was one of my best friends.

"Oh, it's wonderful to meet you," he said. "Molly lived away from home for so many years that we never really got to know all her friends. Gayle! Come out here. There's a young lady who was Molly's friend."

A short woman popped her head out of the front door and started slowly down the stairs. She wore black leggings that highlighted her lean legs. I remembered Molly describing her mother as a carefree yoga instructor. Her slender physique fit Molly's description but her carefree energy had been stolen away. She wore a heavy poncho-like cardigan over her leggings and rugged brown suede boots. She had Molly's curly hair with strands of silver sprinkled inside like confetti and freckles like Molly's too. She gave me her delicate hand and looked into my eyes for so long I became uncomfortable and gently slid my hand out of her grasp.

"Mrs. Gehrig . . ."

"Please, call me Gayle," she said, pushing a flyaway hair behind her ear. "Tell me, tell me, how did you know my daughter?"

"I worked with Molly and we became very close. When I first started out, she took me under her wing. She really looked out for me. I absolutely loved her. She was so proud when she bought the townhouse. I looked up to her so much. I wanted to be like her. She wanted to go with me to Kenya, for a visit."

"Oh! Kenya? Wait. Are you Soila?"

"Yes."

"Oh my goodness! Molly talked about you a lot. She loved you. Oh, how lovely that we get to meet you. What brought you here?"

"I don't know. . . . I just felt I really wanted to be here one last time," I said. "I can't explain it."

Akhenaten had introduced himself to Molly's father and, while they spoke in the background, Gayle told me that they had thought about keeping the townhouse, but the logistics of managing it from California would be too complex.

"We've had to stay in the city for a while now because of all this legal and financial stuff. And how do you leave when you haven't got anything to remember your child by? We have a death certificate, but no part of her to take home. I went to Ground Zero thinking that maybe if I looked really hard, you know, from behind the fence, that maybe I'd see her shoes, or her purse. All I saw was rubble. Even now, I keep thinking she's going to call me. I keep checking my phone. . . ."

When she choked up and started to cry, her husband walked back to us and held her. Akhenaten and I stood in front of them like boulders shielding them from a harsh wind, watching quietly.

"I'm so sorry," I said, unsure of whom exactly I was talking to. "She was happy. She was really happy here in New York. I just want you to know that." Tentatively, I reached out and hugged each of them. "Goodbye, Mr. and Mrs. Gehrig."

We walked down the street quickly, not wanting to look back at that kind of grief. It was grief so dark, so grim, and like a vortex, ready to consume anyone who came too close. When we turned the corner, Akhenaten and I stopped walking and stood as if glued to the street at the crosswalk. Then, feeling too tired to begin the journey back home, we found a coffee shop and sat, each of us absorbed in our own thoughts.

...

I returned to work a few days later. Despite my bold proclamations to Leticia about quitting banking to pursue my passion, I still wasn't brave enough to walk the path of nonconformity. It was a good thing at first. The spreadsheets were methodical, they were columns and rows and they balanced out right, whereas my life made no sense at all. For ten hours of my day, stuck in a cubicle with CNBC blathering about the NASDAQ and DOW somewhere in the office, I at least had control over my life. The staff was different too. Gloria Reuben had been a managing director at Cohen for years, and she had made the company feel like her own family. She garnered an incredible amount of respect from her staff. Without her, morale was terrible. She had been replaced by a younger MD with poor people skills, brought in from the London office. I knew that I could work at Cohen for ten years and he still wouldn't know my name. Gloria had been completely the opposite. I missed her dearly. No one had replaced Molly. The economy was already shaky before the attacks. Afterward, we were lucky to have anything. The worst part of my day was walking into the office in the morning to see Molly's empty cubicle. It didn't matter how hard I tried to retrain my brain. *Don't think about Molly. Don't think about Molly.* My thoughts betrayed me every morning.

Even though I kept working, I also began taking photographs with much more seriousness than I had in a long time. It could have been the grief, or it could have been what Leticia said about being realistic about how to pursue my dreams. If I wanted to do this for a career, I had to take my time—collect good shots, create a portfolio, build a brand, in order to be successful. And New York had always been the perfect canvas. I talked to Angie Blythe about cutting back my hours on the weekends and surprisingly, she agreed. I wanted to be outside capturing life with a camera, perhaps writing a travel blog about humans around the world, how we were all so different and yet the same. I didn't want to be in fluorescent-lit office spaces crunching numbers for the rest of my life. I understood that Mother would be furious. She'd spent forty thousand dollars a year on a world-class American education and in turn I was giving her well-shot digital prints.

When I started taking photographs again, they were disconnected and wandering, like my thoughts. Most were shot in black-and-white, the numbness I felt in the moment. My favorite was an image I'd shot in color of sixty-five-year-old identical triplets celebrating their birthday at a local park. They sat together on a bench with their feet sheathed by piles of fall leaves.

They were all wrapped in black coats and red knitted scarves, their faces turned toward the soft afternoon light as if they were heeding a voice calling from the sky. Their silver hair shone against their toffee-dark skin. Their sullen eyes and the deep shadows around their cheekbones made the sisters appear striking yet ghostly. I blew up the photo and mounted it under clear glass in the kitchen. They reminded me of my aunts.

November, December, January, February. The first-year anniversary of my relationship with Akhenaten passed with no fanfare, the holidays had come and gone, my twenty-sixth birthday, which I refused to have acknowledged. Time merged into a haze. Estelle stayed with us and I loved her more as the days became months. I loved to come home to her care and comfort at the end of my workdays. She always waited up for me and warmed me a plate. I told her African wives did that for their husbands.

"An African woman must always get up and warm her husband a

plate with a smile, even when he comes staggering home at three A.M. from the bar," I said. Estelle laughed so hard that she woke Akhenaten, who came to the living room to see what the hullabaloo was about.

On weekends, I spent hours walking through the city with my camera, buying cup after cup of Starbucks coffee until my hands trembled from the caffeine. I had once judged Alex's expensive coffee habit so harshly, but now, I was just as wasteful. I stopped at hot dog trucks and pretzel stands. I sat in unfamiliar cafés and ate bowls of clam chowder while looking out to the street. I ate, often, for no reason at all but to sit and chew mindlessly while watching the city go by. It was a strange winter. Something bigger than losing sunlight had darkened the city.

New York was desolate all winter and the stench of death still hung heavy into March. The house was quiet too. Akhenaten didn't play his music loud anymore. He treated me like a dying bird. We mostly read in front of a fire that Akhenaten would build in the evenings. In early spring, his mother went home to New Orleans. Her absence in the house was palpable.

The week after Molly died, I had told Mother that I was struggling to return to work. It was too painful. Besides, I didn't want to be in banking anymore. Once again, Mother refused to hear me. That not even a trauma as horrific as losing my best friend on 9/11 would evoke her empathy was the end for me. When she'd call me to say that Jesus suffered on the cross, that death is not the end, I put the phone on speaker and my mind on other things. It had taken twenty-six years of my life, but finally, I was done listening to Mother.

After that, I refused to answer the phone. She called four or five times a day, and every time I ignored it. Then Naserian, Rarin, and Laioni began calling me, begging me not to freeze her out. They said Mother was destroyed, unable to talk about anything other than the fact that her daughter in America had cruelly abandoned her.

"You shouldn't dwell on this," Naserian said. "Your friend is gone and there's nothing you can do. If you dwell on this, it's going to break you. You saw what grief did to Tanei."

Aisha called too. She pleaded with me to visit her in Ghana. It would be good for me, she said. Then Mother started to send text messages—increasingly dramatic, almost hysterical ones.

I'm the only mother you're ever going to have, Soila. You can cut me off, but it will be on your conscience forever.

Soila, have you been to church? If you do nothing else, go to church.

Soila, God loves you. God doesn't want to see you like this.

It wasn't because she kept nagging that I did it. It wasn't even a longing. On the Sunday that I walked into St. Patrick's Old Cathedral, I wasn't going to see God. I wanted to photograph the catacombs, but then I learned that there were no tourist viewings allowed. Disappointed, I thought about turning back. But I was already there, and I had nothing else to do. Aisha had told me about the catacombs. We had stood on the street and watched as a happy couple was showered in rice on their wedding day. From the outside, it was an unremarkable church, but when I walked through the front door, I was astonished. The stained-glass windows, the carved wooden sculptures of the saints, Christ on a gold cruciform, as if he were floating from the ceiling above the altar—it was magical. Then I heard the sound of the organ, reverberating from the low-pitched rumbling of an earthquake to the delicacy of a string quartet, and I felt compelled to pray, even though I hadn't prayed in years. I found a spot in a mid-center pew and sat down, staring back at the gigantic organ. The sound washed over me. I felt I was drifting, levitating.

Mass was nearly finished by the time I came back to myself. When everyone had streamed out, I remained sitting in the pew. For the first time since losing Molly, my mind calmed. There were no more racing thoughts. I felt my anger dissipate.

I returned the next day and the next. It wasn't for the catacombs, or the history of a church that had survived riots and protests. It was for its unpretentious charm. It didn't have baroque designs, Gothic architecture, intricate artistry on sky-high ceilings, or priceless art. It was because something there, in that modest chapel, had made me want to pray.

In the days after the towers fell, I doubted God's existence. Then, I found peace again in that old church. I felt God's spirit stir inside of me. Even though I couldn't hear him, I could feel his love and mercy. For years, I had begged God for forgiveness for my abortion. I didn't know it until I sat in that old church, when I shut my mind to all the noise, and focused only on God's presence, that I was already forgiven. And there, I let go of the guilt. I let go of the unborn baby. I let go of my anger over not having been there for Molly. I opened my palms and saw the pain float away.

St. Patrick's Old Cathedral became my refuge. Since I was a child, I had been searching for that place where I could be just me. It wasn't at home in Kenya with Mother. Then, I came to a foreign land, which I loved, but I was still a stranger. I was different, even from the people with whom I shared a skin color and hair texture. I worried I would never find a place where I belonged. Then I stumbled into an old church and she asked nothing of me. My spirit was at peace. I had found home.

Chapter Eighteen

By the anniversary of September 11, an entire year I spent working miserably without Molly, I knew my life as a banker was over. I went to Angie to resign, but she didn't understand why I wanted to quit.

"Do you have a better offer? Is it the money?"

I laughed out loud, then tried to restrain myself.

"Angie, I just don't want to do it anymore. It's not for me."

"Is it about Molly? Soila, you have to let go."

"It's not about Molly," I said. "But yes, it's been hard. Losing Molly helped me see that I don't want to sit at that desk anymore. I don't love my job, Angie. I never have. I want to do something else."

I still hadn't talked to Mother in any real way for months. I talked to my aunts often, and sometimes Mother would get on the phone. I would offer a polite greeting then hang up. When I told Aunt Naserian I had quit my job, she wasn't completely surprised, but she said she hoped I had a plan.

"You know your yeyo can be spiteful when she is trying to prove a point," she said. "She won't help you out, if things don't work out for you. Remember how she refused to take Tanei back after she kicked her out, and Tanei was homeless at the YWCA?"

"I don't care," I said. "Make sure you tell her that I have quit my job. I'm done keeping secrets from her."

Akhenaten wanted to host a small dinner party to celebrate my new chapter in life. I was going to launch a photography career and it was surreal, finally being able to wake up in the morning to do something that I loved to do. That Saturday, I slept in all morning and woke up to find Akhenaten in the kitchen, standing over a boiling pot of udon noodles, next to which he was sautéing beef in ginger and lemongrass.

"I can't believe you're doing all this to celebrate me giving up a huge salary," I said. We both laughed. "I'm a little scared, to tell you the truth. But I'm also walking on air. I feel uncaged."

Akhenaten crossed to the record player and turned up the volume, and the jazzy Afrobeat of Fela Kuti crooning "Water No Get Enemy" drowned out the sputtering of his stir-fry. When he returned to the stove, he scooped a spoonful of sauce from the pan and brought it to the kitchen counter, where I sat between the toaster and the coffee machine.

"You're never going to regret going for what you really want in life," he said. "It'll be hard at first, no doubt. But in a few years, you'll be out of the trenches, and you'll be fulfilled in so many more ways."

He tilted my chin up and slipped the wooden ladle of sauce into my open mouth. I flinched a little from the heat, puffing air in and out to cool my tongue.

"I just feel so blessed that I have you while I'm trying to do this," I said. "I don't know that I would be brave enough on my own."

"Of course you would," he said. "You don't give yourself credit for all the incredible things you've been able to do before you're even thirty."

He traced his long thumb over the outline of my lips and kissed me. He rubbed his temples, and I could see he was exhausted. He'd been working hard for an upcoming gallery showcase and the fatigue was drawn around his eyes, and now he was cooking a Japanese dinner that seemed even more elaborate than his sculpting. He had marinated slivers of chicken breast with teriyaki, boiled sticky rice, and cut up raw salmon, tuna, and swordfish for a sashimi platter.

"I feel like you've been cooking all day and I haven't helped at all, even though you're doing this for me," I said, leaning in to kiss his temple.

"I love to cook, and I was the one who invited everyone over," he said, reaching out to trace along my cheek with his thumb. "Go take a walk or get a manicure—get outta here and maybe I can actually finish all this before six P.M."

I snuck two more kisses onto his cheek before leaving the kitchen to get dressed. I ventured outside with my camera. The oppressive heat of the summer was receding, giving way to the more moderate September temperatures.

I kept my eyes peeled, hoping to spot a celebrity walking about in the neighborhood, but instead, all I saw was a group of teen boys skateboarding across streets, meandering through traffic. The mood in the city wasn't as dark as it had been for months after the towers came down. With time, New Yorkers had done the best they could to take their city back and though some parts of the grid had closed, and everyone avoided Ground Zero as much as they could, human beings had proved their resilience and the ambience was gradually lightening up. I thought about what it must be like to grow up in the city. Would I consider raising a child in New York? I'd seen mothers ask strangers for help with carrying their strollers up and down the stairs to the subway, and cranky babies screaming their throats out inside the train, their little ears irritated by the rattling of the subway cars. Yet New York was the ultimate homeschooling canvas. Right in front of me were several galleries where I had learned to carefully look at art and appreciate the many layers behind every piece. Before living in the city, art wasn't something I'd ever imagined would be an active pastime. Now, I appreciated it as much as I did a good meal, or a good song. In New York, I learned a little bit about every corner of the world. A few blocks from me lay Chinatown, another encyclopedia. For me, Chinatown represented what it meant to be an immigrant in the United States. To come to a new place and make something of yourself. This was the significance of New York. This was the ultimate reason I would want to raise a child here.

After treating myself to an espresso and a walnut-fig gelato in a cone, I headed back to the loft. I found Akhenaten muttering to himself as he rolled dumplings. He'd folded little rice wontons with shredded vegetables inside, doing a little dance to his Afro-jazz each time he finished one.

The kitchen was so cluttered and countertops so smeared I didn't know where to start cleaning, though my heart was invested in helping. I collected the dirty dishes and stacked them in the dishwasher and we worked steadily and quietly.

Once I had cleared out the sink and wiped down the countertops, I started setting the table and lighting candles around the whole apartment. The afternoon had flown by, probably because I'd slept till noon.

"Okay. Everyone will be here soon. You need to go get ready," Akhenaten said.

He seemed jittery and nervous. I'd never seen him behave this way. He said he wanted it to be the perfect evening but I saw no reason why it had to be.

I wanted to tell him to sit for a while and have a sip of wine and calm himself. But once Akhenaten got going at something, he worked tirelessly to make sure it would be perfect. I had seen it with his art, the way he worked till dawn. He came to bed so wiped out that he could barely walk. He would fall into such a deep slumber that he wouldn't hear my pitter-pattering as I walked around the bedroom getting dressed for work. But that was who he was. I knew nothing I said would get him to stop obsessing over unnecessary details for this dinner party, so I let him be in his moment.

I got in the shower and let the water wash over me for a while before I even started to soap up my body. It was these little things, like allowing myself a long, hot shower, that made me realize I was gradually becoming my own person.

But even now at twenty-six, I still felt so unhappy that I couldn't get the approval of the one person who I most wanted to make proud. Sometimes the sadness became emptiness and doubt. What if she was right about everything? My love life, my career? For years, in those alone moments, in the shower, or on my six A.M. summer run, when the city was still waking up, I would hear my soul speak to my mind and I was always haunted by how much of my life I was not really living. But now that I had decided to live the life I wanted, I was haunted by how much I wanted Mother to be by my side in all of it.

Getting to know Aisha over the past year had inspired me to break out of the cage more than ever. She was out in the world doing exactly what she loved against the odds. I didn't want my birthdays rolling by, and every year promising myself I would do more of the things I loved and then never doing any of them. This was my chance to change things. But still, I was paralyzed. I shut my eyes tightly while the water ran down my face. I was afraid if I opened them, I would cry. Why couldn't Mother be happy for me? Why couldn't she accept the man I loved? How long would he live this way, loving a woman whose family rejected him? Would he get tired of waiting around and find someone who wasn't wrapped up in so much baggage? Mother and I were at an impasse. I had refused to play the game her way, and she had refused to give me the blessing that I yearned for to go off and fulfill my dreams. She knew how much I longed for her approval, and she knew not giving it would be the only way she could break me. I had chosen to wrangle myself from her suffocating grip and it should have been a relief but instead it was excruciating.

I got out of the shower in a bit of a daze. The mirror was clouded with steam as I towel-dried my hair. I wiped it off and saw my bloodshot eyes.

Akhenaten stood in the doorway, ready for his turn in the shower.

"Sorry," I said, feeling self-conscious. I grabbed another towel from the rail and wrapped myself up. "I know it's supposed to be a happy moment in my life right now, and I am happy. But I'm also so sad that my mother can't be on board. It makes me doubt myself. I'm afraid I'll fail at this, and she'll gloat and remind me what a huge mistake I've made leaving behind a decent career. I'm afraid you'll get tired of waiting for her to come around, and you'll leave, and she'll gloat and remind me that she'd warned me about you. I just can't get her out of my head."

He was leaning on the door, with his T-shirt off. "I hate that you constantly beat yourself up about all the things you're not doing and then when you find the courage to grow you beat yourself up about not making your mom happy. I feel so helpless in all this. You have to believe in what *you* want for your life. Are you enough for yourself? Am I enough for you?"

Then he knelt on the white bath mat.

My breath stopped in my throat. "What are you doing?" I asked.

"I wasn't going to do it this way," he said, bringing out a small jewelry box from the back pocket of his jeans. "I was going to wait until after dinner, in front of our friends, with candlelight. But . . .

you look beautiful in this light with your wet hair and I love you and I don't want to see you beat yourself up in this way anymore. You're the most amazing person I know. You've got a big heart, you are kind, you're generous, you're sincere, forgiving, loyal, you love your family, even your crazy mom, you challenge my bullshit every day, and make me want to be a better person. I never thought I'd want to get married. It just seemed so archaic and pointless, because why do you need a piece of paper, right? Then I met you and all I want is you by my side. I want you to live your authentic self—to see how incredible you really are, how talented and raw—and I want you to see it through my eyes. I want to go to Kenya with you and see it through your eyes. I'm inspired by the future you and I can have. I really want you in my life, like, officially. Will you marry me, Soila?"

Akhenaten opened the box. My body lurched forward and I quickly grabbed the edge of the sink to steady myself. Then I moved toward the toilet and sat heavily on the lid, thanking God it was already closed. It was only then that I realized I was covered in snot and crying and laughing all at once.

Why had I not seen Akhenaten in my dreams as a little girl when I thought about the man I'd marry? Kokoi often said that the joy and pain of life were unforeseeable. She said much of our lives would never make sense to us, even if we lived three lifetimes. I finally understood her. I didn't realize I had said I would marry him until I heard him say, "Thank you, thank you," as he held me close to him, making fun of the snot that was smeared over his bare shoulders. The ring was the exact one I would have picked out, if I had done it myself. A small sapphire cushioned by tiny diamonds on platinum. But once it was on my hand, I felt some guilt creep up, though I didn't want to complain.

"Don't worry, I did all the research on the jeweler," he said, reading the discomposure that was written on my face. "The diamonds are mined in Botswana, the sapphires are mined in Madagascar. All ethical and conflict-free."

. . .

Akhenaten always understood what was important to me. Clean jewels. Aisha. Earlier in the week, Aisha had messaged me to say that she would be in New York that month but she didn't have her dates set yet. I hadn't seen her in a year, since before 9/11, and I was looking forward to it more than anything. I had invited her to stay in our apartment while she was in the city and she said she couldn't wait.

That evening, Aisha was our first guest, and she would have been the highlight of my year had Akhenaten not asked me to marry him an hour before her arrival. I was ecstatic when I saw her small frame as I peeked through the front door. I loved Akhenaten even more. Knowing how much it would mean to me to have her there and organizing a dinner party around her schedule—it was everything I needed. The news of our engagement was received with a fireball of excitement. Aisha, Leticia, and Kevin gawking at the sapphire on my hand that night was surreal. Akhenaten's close friends were there too. We all congregated on our small balcony, drinking red wine and breathing in the warm air of the last remnants of the summer.

"Have you talked to your mom?" Leticia asked, still examining the ring. We were in my bedroom for some privacy.

"No, because this just happened, literally, an hour before you all walked into the apartment," I said.

"Are you scared?" Aisha prodded. She'd walked in, telling Leticia and me that she had suspected Akhenaten was going to propose after he told her he had an announcement and begged her relentlessly to be there.

"Yes, very," I said. "But I'm also exhausted with her. I don't think she'll be even slightly happy for me, but it's been a year since we moved in together and maybe she's had some time to digest the reality of this. Also, hopefully after the reality of 9/11, she's at a place where she sees that life is fragile and fighting with the people you love is time wasted. But who knows? She's extremely difficult."

"You're amazing," Aisha said. "Really brave. I'm so proud of you."

"I'm just so tired of hiding this really big part of my life away from her," I said. "My aunt kept her boyfriend a secret for years and years, and then dropped a bombshell that she was pregnant and getting married. I was honest with her from the get-go because I didn't want to do that to her all over again. But I don't think she even appreciates that. Anyway, she'll probably just hang up on me."

"Oh, please!" Leticia said. "Once she gets to meet Akhenaten she'll see. He's a dream son-in-law."

"I highly, highly doubt—no, I know for sure—my mother does not think that Akhenaten, who she has never so much as said hello to, is her dream son-in-law," I said.

Even though it wasn't funny, we all laughed.

I called Mother the next day after months of not taking her calls. This time, I let her know she couldn't control my life anymore.

"Yeyo, I can't keep going into that office every day when I absolutely hate this job," I said. "I'm going to lose my mind. I've resigned. Also, I'm engaged."

She cleared her throat. "Soila—you can't leave a big career like you're leaving a job at a dairy farm. What is your plan? What are you going to do?"

"Did you hear me say that I'm engaged? I want to get married to Akhenaten."

"Soila—I can't even talk about something so ridiculous. You're not marrying that man. I want to talk about what you want to do about your career."

“I want to go into photography full-time. I know you think it should be a hobby, some sort of pastime. But it’s more than that for me.”

“Soila, we’ve been through this. Photography is not a serious profession. We both know this is about your friend,” she said, and told me to look to God for strength.

“God has nothing to do with it and if you can’t understand me and you can’t be happy for me, for the life I want to live, then please just leave me alone.” I said goodbye respectfully.

For the next three months, Mother once again called me relentlessly and I refused to take her calls. Aunt Naserian was back at pleading her case.

“Your mother is distraught, your mother thinks she’s really lost you, your mother doesn’t seem well, just talk to her,” she said.

I didn’t care. I threw myself into photography, attending gallery openings and events with Akhenaten where I chatted with his art friends and made connections. I hoped I came across as knowledgeable and charming, but instead I felt desperately out of place. I was introduced to the editor in chief of a prominent feature magazine. He hired me as a freelance photographer. My pay was a pittance compared to my old banking salary, but the thrill of finally truly working as a photographer and the adventure of traveling around the country for stories made it worthwhile. I hoped it would be only a matter of time before I’d be working on international stories and it made my heart thump. By early December, I had found all of the happiness that had been missing in me since 9/11. Standing in the kitchen, watching an early snow fall over the city outside, my mind was on the shoot I had lined up for a small Muslim community in the Midwest who were being so racially victimized they were afraid to leave their houses. The buzzing arrival of a text message interrupted my musing.

Kayai, you have completely refused to take my calls since September and I am left with no choice. I don't know what's happening with you. I'm worried about you. I have bought a ticket to New York. I'll be there on the 15th of December.

I stared at the small screen. Mother would be here in a week. I had only days to figure out how I would convince the most stubborn, imperious, inflexible woman in the world to accept that there was no way she could stop me from living my own life.

. . .

Mother arrived in New York in heavy snow. I watched as she came through international arrivals at JFK, pushing a small suitcase on a cart and balancing a tan crocodile-skin handbag the size of a basket on her shoulder. I had always chafed against the contradiction between Mother's lectures about humility and modesty and her own expensive wardrobe. She was selfless with her time, generous with money for charity, and modest in her everyday living. But she also enjoyed expensive shoes and handbags and she'd always worn makeup, whereas I saw no reason to spend hundreds of dollars on a pair of shoes or a purse. She was dressed in black, head to toe—a thick black woolen coat, a black pashmina, black pants, and ankle-length black boots. Her once long, voluminous hair had been cut short like a young boy's. I realized I had no idea when she'd changed her hair. I hadn't seen her since my trip to Kenya right after graduation.

She walked toward me fast, with her arms wide open. I hugged her hesitantly, the duty of a daughter, but, in truth, I didn't want to see her at all.

"Sorry I took so long—I got lost," she said. "When did this airport become so big?"

"It's the same size it's always been; there's just more security." I noticed she was using a cart to lug only one suitcase and it was a carry-on. "Have you hurt your arm? Why are you using a cart?" I asked, lifting the small suitcase out of the luggage trolley.

"I have two suitcases," she said.

"No, you've got one."

She looked at me with a blank stare.

"Yeyo," I said, restraining myself from snapping at her. "Are you hearing me? Where is your other suitcase?"

"Oh no! You're right," she said, covering her face. The nails on her hands flashed a soft pink polish and she still wore the same ring she had worn on her ring finger since as far back as I could remember. Instead of a wedding band, she had a gold one with an emblem of Padre Pio and ten beads around it, one bead for each Hail Mary.

"I did take the other suitcase off the carousel, but I don't know what I did with it. I was so anxious not to keep you waiting, I must have forgotten it and then I got lost. What a mess I am today."

"It's okay, it's a long flight. Let's go find it."

The same airport, where only a few years back I had walked Mother right up to her boarding gate, was now restricted in every way. Two young cops walked up to us as we were trying to access the baggage collection and returned us like lost kittens outside the sliding doors. Our only recourse was to call the airline, report the bag forgotten, and have the airline drop it off at my apartment.

"Why all that?" Mother argued. "We're here now." The officer remained calm, reassuring her that her luggage wouldn't be lost. The other wasn't as tolerant. He started to lead Mother out of the doors, but Mother became more agitated, shouting, "Young man, take your arms off me. Can't you see I'm old enough to be your mother!"

"Ma'am, I don't care if you're old enough to be my great-grandmother," the agent said. "You gotta follow the rules."

Mother was never confrontational with authority. She had told me, growing up, to "always, always respect authority, even if you know you're right and they are wrong."

I quieted her down in Maa and apologized.

In the yellow cab on the way into the city, she started to complain about the policemen again, bitterly.

"You give a man a badge and he starts to think he is God himself," she said. "These white people!"

"Yeyo, may I remind you that the policemen in New York come in all different races, and many have recently given their lives," I said.

"Where are we going?" she asked, waving me off and staring out the window.

"To my apartment."

"In Brooklyn?"

"No, in Manhattan."

"Did you and Leticia move again? I didn't know this," she said, turning to me.

"Yeyo. We have talked about this. I moved in with my fiancé a year ago. We have been through this. No. Leticia has not moved. I've moved."

"Why? She's a great girl. Why are you not living with her, Soila?"

"Well, you know this already. Because I am engaged now. I live with my fiancé."

"What?" She raised her voice loud enough for the cabdriver to adjust his rearview mirror and steal a glance at us. "You're not serious. You're living with that man?"

"Yeyo," I said, signaling for her to lower her voice. "Do you see this ring?"

"Yes, I see a ring, but what does that matter? I have said you cannot marry this man."

"No, Yeyo. I am going to marry him, and I am living with him. Why did you come here anyway? To mock me?"

"Soila," she said, shaking her head vigorously. "I will not stay in a house with a man you're not married to. I won't participate. This is not how I raised you. Take me to a hotel."

My stomach cramped a little—a physical reaction to my fear of Mother. But I also had no patience left inside of me.

"Good. Maybe staying in a hotel will send you back home quicker."

"Soila, who have you become? This is the way you are talking to me, your own mother?"

She dug into her bag for a Kleenex and dabbed at her eyes. I ignored her. I told the driver we would be making a stop at the Four Seasons.

"Isn't that a very expensive hotel?" she asked, still wiping her eyes.

"It's the only place near my apartment that is big enough to have a room with no prior booking one week before Christmas," I said. "Tomorrow we can move you to another hotel. Or you can stay with me. It's up to you."

We stayed silent for the rest of the drive.

A cheery check-in woman at the tinsel-covered reception area of the Four Seasons signed Mother in quietly, trying to make small talk with her about the snowy weather, but all Mother would muster was a fixed stare. I smiled back at the woman on Mother's behalf.

When she received her room key card, Mother flipped it to the side to show me the number printed on it. She mumbled to me like I was a stranger in a deserted back alley and walked away.

When the tears started to cloud my eyes, I found my way through the marble-floored lobby decorated with a massive Christmas tree. "Have Yourself a Merry Little Christmas" piped softly in the background and I grew even more desolate. Everywhere around me, happy families prepared for a day of celebration and love. And I had just checked my mother in to a hotel because she pretended she didn't know I was living with Akhenaten even though I had told her about it a full year ago. She refused to be under the same roof as my fiancé, the man I loved, who loved me and supported me. I heaved a sigh, shook my head, and pushed out the doors into the snow. Mother could stay wherever she wanted. I was going home.

. . .

My phone rang at seven-thirty the next morning. I was lying in bed. I listened to the whir of Akhenaten's shaver, the shower, and then rustling. The phone buzzed twice again on the side table. I ignored it. Then it buzzed again and Akhenaten, walking past in a towel, looked at it.

"Babe, do you want to get this?"

"No," I said, turning my head away. I knew it must be Mother calling to scold me and I had no interest in answering.

The phone buzzed for the fifth time and Akhenaten took the call.

"It's some woman—she can hardly pronounce your name," he said. "She says she's a nurse. I think you should talk to her."

"Yes, hello, ma'am. I'm looking for a So-eela See-gee?"

"This is Soila," I said, flippantly, giving Akhenaten an eye-roll.

"Ma'am, I've got a woman here who says she's your mom," the nurse said. Her voice was so loud that I had to hold the phone slightly away from my ear. "You need to come get her."

"Is this the Four Seasons?" I sat up in bed and felt my heart pace a few beats too fast.

"Four Seasons? No. This is Lenox Hill Hospital. A young couple found your mom lost and confused on Fifth Avenue. We got your contact information from inside her purse. She's fine now. She's re-oriented. Here, talk to her."

Mother's voice came through raspy. "Soila, I'm not feeling so good, can you please come get me?"

I was already out of the bed, slipping on a pair of jeans. "I'm coming, I'm coming, Yeyo."

Akhenaten was standing at the door watching me.

"What's going on? Is she okay?"

"I have no idea," I said, while smearing a bead of paste on my toothbrush. "Sounds like she got lost. Some Good Samaritans took her to Lenox Hill."

"Do you want me to come with you?" he asked. "I can cancel with the gallery."

I mulled over his offer while brushing my teeth. Mother would have a fit, maybe even chase me out of the hospital. But I wanted the strength his presence beside me would provide.

"Yes. Yes, I'd like you to go with me."

Akhenaten's eyes lit up. I knew then that he hadn't been sure until that very moment that he wasn't going to lose me to Mother.

We rushed to the hospital, and when the nurse drew open the white curtain, I was shocked. Mother was sitting on a bed, barefoot and bewildered. Her jeans were wet, covered in salt from the knees down. She had bandages wrapped around her hands, covering her palms. She was hunched, fragile and shaky, like a rag doll. She looked about ten years old.

"Yeyo, where were you going? What were you doing on the street? Where are your shoes?"

"They're wet," she said, pointing at a pair of black boots lying tipped over under the bed.

I looked at Akhenaten. He was standing to the side, watching her like she was a creature behind a glass window at the zoo.

"Mom, this is Akhenaten," I said, directing him to shake her hand. "This is my fiancé."

"How are you doing, Mrs. Segeni? How are you feeling?"

Mother looked at his hand, then shrugged, and gave him her bandaged hand unwillingly. Akhenaten gave her a strong shake.

I signaled to Akhenaten to walk outside the curtain with me so that he and I could speak freely.

"I swear, I don't even know who that person is," I said. "Something's just not right with her."

We walked over to the nurses' station and I asked for help. They paged Dr. Anderson, who had examined Mother. He told us that her condition was troublesome.

"She had problems recalling basic information," he said. "Like counting back from fifty. She couldn't remember where she'd been staying. She even struggled to remember her name, until we prompted her with the information we got out of her purse. We were very lucky that she had a passport inside her bag. She did ask for you by name, though. She was lucid about having a daughter here in the city and we found your contact on her phone."

I looked across the room for a chair but couldn't find one.

"Are you okay?" said Akhenaten. "Do you want me to take your coat?"

I covered my eyes, too stressed to hear him.

"I know, it's a bit of a shock," Dr. Anderson said. "I'm not making a diagnosis today—I'm not a neurologist. But I'd really suggest you take her to see one as soon as you can." He scribbled a few names on the back of a card and handed it to me. "These guys are all good with Alzheimer's, dementia. . . ." he said.

"Alzheimer's? Dementia? My mom is fifty-five. There's no way," I said. I was flushed, my brow misting. I tried to pat down my forehead, but my hand was trembling.

"It could be anything—even a mini-stroke, which is fairly easy to recuperate from," he said. "That's why I don't want to speculate."

He excused himself from me and drew Akhenaten with him a few feet away. I stood stunned, but still in earshot of their words.

"Are you the husband?" Dr. Anderson whispered.

"About to be," Akhenaten muttered.

"You're going to have to step up here," he said. "I understand her mother is staying at a hotel. I'm afraid that's not going to work in her current state. Is there anywhere else she can stay? Can she stay with you?"

"Yes, yes, of course."

"Okay, that would be good. I wouldn't let her out of sight for now," he said. "I wouldn't let her travel back to Africa on her own either. She's very vulnerable right now. And call the doctors I told you about as soon as you can—they might be already heading out for the holidays. Good luck, man."

Akhenaten looked as the doctor turned to walk away, and I could see he didn't want to repeat the conversation with me.

"It's okay," I said. "I heard."

Back inside the curtain, I sat next to Mother while Akhenaten knelt beside the bed to reach for her shoes.

"Yeyo, you are going to have to come stay with me," I said. "We're going to find a good doctor."

"No, no," she said, holding her face in her hands. "I want to go home. Please, put me on the plane tomorrow. I want to go home."

"You can't go home," I said. "You have to come home with me for a while."

When we got home, I made up the second bedroom for Mother. It seemed like yesterday that Akhenaten's mom had stayed with us for months, and she was so easygoing. I knew this would be different. I called the airline about the suitcase. Akhenaten went over to the Four Seasons and checked Mother out. He went to the grocery store and stocked the fridge.

I called all three doctors on the list. The earliest any of them could see her was on the twenty-second of December. That was six days of not knowing what exactly was afflicting Mother. I called Naserian and told her everything—the emergency room, the lost luggage, the forgetfulness, the strange arguing with the policemen.

"I know," said Naserian.

"You *know*? What are you talking about?"

"Well, I don't *know,* really. But I have noticed strange things. She's been forgetting names, or forgetting faces, one or the other. She called me once from Westlands and said that she couldn't remember how to get home even though she's driven that route every day for twenty years. I was perplexed. Then later she dismissed it, but I could tell she was saving face. She's had a lot of stress the last few months, so I've brushed it off as that. She's been worried sick about you—saying you're clinically depressed, that you might kill yourself; saying you're about to throw your life away by leaving your job and marrying an American . . . all kinds of ridiculous things. She's been driving herself crazy. Do you want me to come to New York?"

"No, don't worry," I said. "You've got the businesses and Tanei—you can't just up and leave Laioni with all that by herself."

"How is your yeyo handling your relationship?"

"Terribly," I said, annoyed. "But then, she's not herself, so I'm not sure what's what."

"Okay, I know I discouraged you before, but Soila, if you love that man, stand up for him. It's your life. Besides, if it's about marrying foreigners, truth be told, Rarin is very happy. If she's found love with that strange Scottish man, I know you'll be happy too."

I hung up and went to check on Mother. When I didn't find her in her room, my heart raced all over again and I started to look frantically for her.

"I'm here," she called. "I'm in the kitchen."

"What are you doing? The doctor said you shouldn't be by yourself," I scolded.

"I wanted some tea."

She was the old Mother. It was becoming clear now that there were two different people alive in her. The pitiful, helpless soul whom I had rescued from the hospital only hours ago had taken leave, like an understudy, while the strong, unflappable, domineering woman had returned.

"Go sit," I said, unsure of how to handle her. "I'll make you the tea."

She moved away from the kettle and walked across the room looking at the photographs on the walls and on the mantel and bookshelves around the living room.

"Is this his mother?" she asked, looking at a framed photograph of Estelle smiling from ear to ear in a floppy beach hat. "She's very beautiful."

"She's lovely," I said. "And she loves me, like a daughter."

"Doesn't she have her own daughters?"

"No. He's an only child, and his father died too."

She looked around the room and circled back again, stopping at every black-and-white photograph. I had hung up all my favorites. The buildings on Wall Street shooting up like a Maasai moran's spears, schoolkids in Astoria playing double Dutch, my birthday triplets.

"Are these all your photographs?"

"Yes."

"Have you truly quit your job?"

"Yes."

"And you really want to marry this man?"

"Yes."

"Soila, the man has dreadlocks down to his back. How can I take this man to Kenya and introduce him as my son-in-law? How is this the man you will marry? I can't believe it. What's happened to you? I should never have sent you here. What about that Kenyan boy, the doctor? He was so decent."

"It didn't work out."

"Did you also sleep with him?"

"Mother, I am not going to talk about this. I'll be twenty-seven years old in a few weeks. I am a grown woman."

"Do you even go to church? When was the last time you were in church?"

"Actually, I do go to church," I said. "I have been going for a year, since my friend died."

"And why do you think that is?"

"I've found peace, just sitting in the quiet of the church," I said. "I just wish I could find some answers."

"There are no answers," she replied, with the authority of a woman who had been to heaven, then sent back to earth to give a report. "God is the answer and He's right in front of you. But we ignore Him, then run back when we need His grace and mercy. You're not going to know why all those people died that day, why your father died, why there's poverty, why there's disease and so much suffering. That's not for you to know, and it's arrogant of human beings to even think that it's their place. Death is inevitable and senseless, and all we can do is pray that, when it comes, we have enough faith to accept that everything in our lives is beyond our control. Tell me, does this boyfriend of yours go to church with you?"

"No. And I wouldn't force him to," I said.

"See, now, this is exactly what I'm talking about. You don't know how tough marriage is, Soila. You're living in a fantasy. How can you have a partner who doesn't share your beliefs? Have you talked about where you're going to live? What about when you want to come back home? Is he going to return with you? How will you raise your kids? Will they be Catholic? Will you have them baptized? Will you teach them your culture, your language? If you don't return, will you truly be happy here for the rest of your life? You know that they will put you in a nursing home. That is what Americans do. Your own kids will do that to you. Because they will never learn the value of caring for elders, helping your relatives who have less than you do, giving up your time to your community. How can they learn any of this when they grow up in a country where everyone is so individualistic? What about their history? Do you want to teach them about our chiefs and how we fought the British? Or do you want to teach them that they descended from slaves?"

I was shaking with anger. "Why can't you be happy for me?" I said. "It's the same reason you didn't want me to meet Aisha. You don't want me to find happiness anyplace else, except with you."

"That is ridiculous," Mother said. "Would you rather I had told you when you were a child that your father had another family and kept it a secret from me? That all his brothers, his friends, his colleagues at the mill—everyone else but me—knew. That I was the village idiot. Would that have made you happy?"

I took out a chicken from the fridge and set it out to marinate. I worked quietly, stuffing it with lemons and onions, and tied the drumsticks with twine. Mother stood by the windows and watched the city go by, the snow falling.

"I never thought I'd come here in the dead of winter—in all my years," she said. "I was happy to see snow on television. But you won't talk to me. I had no choice."

I ignored her and continued to prep dinner, cutting up potatoes and carrots to place in the oven with the roast.

"Who's paying for this apartment?" she asked.

"It's Akhenaten's. He owns it."

"So, on top of everything, you're now a kept woman?" She smirked. "What are you planning on doing for money, while you take photographs?"

"I do work already," I said. "I've been working as a freelance photographer and I get paid and I love it."

Akhenaten came home then, shivering a little, teeth chattering. As he removed his boots and unwrapped his scarf, he said the cold had gotten into his bones and I complained that he never dressed warmly enough. I saw him walking up to me as he unzipped his jacket and I knew that he was going to kiss me, because it was the first thing he always did when he got home. Mother was watching us, and her gaze was so piercing, I felt oxygen get sucked out of my lungs.

"Here," I said, shoving a chopping board between us. Akhenaten was befuddled until he turned to see Mother watching us and retreated. "Can you put this in the dishwasher for me?"

Mother left the room, dragging her house slippers on the hardwood floor so that it sounded like the floor was getting sandpapered.

"Oh my God!" I whispered. "What are you doing? You can't kiss me in front of my mother."

"Why not?" He looked partly bewildered, but mostly irritated.

"It's just not something Africans do in front of parents," I said.

"Okay, this is some bullshit," he said. "Are we in middle school? You're a grown woman and she's in our home."

"I know, but it's just a respect thing," I said.

"You know what, actually, I'm exhausted," he said, moving the chopping board back to me on the counter. "I'll go take a shower."

Mother returned. This time she was dragging her carry-on suitcase. I felt a headache stir up and stomp hard on my temples.

"What now?"

"I can't stay here, Soila," she said. "I just can't. It goes against everything that I stand for, watching my own daughter live in sin."

"Fine. You can go wandering about in the snow," I said, my tone acerbic. "I've had it."

"I don't care where I go; I just want to go now," she said. I watched her struggle into her coat, unable to bring myself to help her. When she'd given up, she hung it over her shoulders like they were a clothes hanger, then stood at the front door, holding her bandaged hands to her chest like a soldier in a marching troop. "I need help with my boots."

"Just give me a minute," I said. "I need to talk to Akhenaten."

When I walked into the bedroom, Akhenaten was on the phone.

"It's my mom," he whispered. I motioned for him to hang up. "She's asking to talk to your mom. What do you think—bad idea?"

"Yes, very bad idea," I whispered. "My mom is throwing another tantrum. Tell her some other time."

"Soila, you're being manipulated," he said, when he ended the call. "Can't you see that?"

"I don't think so. I think she honestly just can't bring herself to sleep on the other side of the wall when she thinks I'm in here having sex with you," I said, exasperated.

"So, what do you want me to do? Would you like me to take the sofa?"

"No, no," I said. "I'll take her to Leticia's and stay there with her for a while."

"Are you kidding me? You're seriously going to let her make you move out?"

"I'm not moving out," I said, overwhelmed. Akhenaten was so unfamiliar with the nuances of non-Western parenting. The realization that I'd have to explain the cross-cultural differences for the rest of our lives suddenly seemed exhausting.

"Honey, it's just different with African parents, okay? You have to respect that. If we're going to get through this visit, we're going to have to play it her way, just for a while."

That night, I left. I had a small suitcase, an extra bag with toiletries, and a laptop. "I'll come by and pick up my mom's other suitcase when the airline delivers it," I said.

"Don't do this. This is exactly what she wants," he said.

"You don't understand. You have a different relationship with your mother. I can't throw my mom out on the street, and I can't keep her here."

"And what about us? Don't you want to fight for us?"

"Of course I want to fight for us, but not like this. She'll just hate you even more. It's just for a little while," I said. "And hopefully she'll be well enough to go back home soon."

"And then what? Will she change her mind, when she gets home?"

"I don't know. . . . I can't think about all that right now."

Akhenaten sat on the bed, with his PowerBook on his lap and the screen's glare reflecting off his glasses. He said nothing; he didn't look up at me. It was as if I'd already ceased to exist.

The apartment was warm, but my hands and face suddenly felt desperately cold. Since I'd met him, Akhenaten had always been exactly where I needed him to be, to support me, love me, keep me standing. And now I had hurt him. All for Mother. All of it, always, because of Mother. I wiped away the tears slipping down my cheeks, wanting nothing more than to go to him. Then, I left the room.

. . .

Leticia's was the only place I could take Mother. I was desperate. Kevin, now living with Leticia, heard about the problems we had run into at my house and told her he was terrified the African woman would have a fit when she found him at the apartment. Leticia wasn't worried. She and my mother had always gotten along. As we walked through the door of Leticia's Brooklyn apartment, she was waiting to hug Mother warmly.

Mother left her suitcase at the door, as if a bellboy were behind her to carry it, and whisked herself to the kitchen to peek inside the pot boiling on Leticia's stove. I lugged the bag into the spare bedroom while Leticia took Mother's hand and introduced her to Kevin.

"Now, I'd like you to meet someone very special to me," she said. "This is Kevin."

Mother, looking taken aback, politely shook Kevin's hand and asked him where he was from and what he did. She said that she thought Leticia had found a very nice man and Kevin was very lucky.

"Kevin and I live together," Leticia said, matter-of-factly.

"Oh my," Mother said. "And your parents are okay with this?"

Leticia nodded and gave her an unapologetic yes.

"Well, if you know that this is the person for you, and it's not just a casual relationship, I suppose it's okay, if your parents are fine with it," Mother said.

I fumed silently. I couldn't believe the words coming out of Mother's mouth. She was willing to stay with Leticia, while Ticia was "living in sin," but she couldn't stand to be near Akhenaten for more than an hour. I lingered in the bedroom, too upset to go back to the kitchen. I heard them talking about the beef stew Leticia was cooking for dinner. Mother said it was the "kind of thing she'd cook at home on a rainy day." I shook my head to myself when I heard this. Another sign of Mother's mental decline: she had never cooked. Princess did all the cooking at home.

I hadn't been back in my old bedroom since 9/11. That was the last time I'd spent the night apart from Akhenaten. Akhenaten, with his long hair and jeweled fingers, who had snuck his way inside my life effortlessly, disrupting my rigidity and prodding me to take risks, daring me to reach for things I thought were meant for anyone else but me. And now, I was torn again between my love for him and my duty to Mother.

I went into the kitchen where Leticia was setting the table. She pulled out her treasured heirloom spoons and linen placemats, then returned to her simmering pot.

I busied myself filling up the glasses with water and cutting up a lemon I'd found in the fridge for the water.

"What are you cooking, my child?" Mother asked.

"Yeyo! She just told you she was making a beef stew. You looked at it."

"Ah! Beef stew. That's exactly the kind of thing I'd make at home myself on a rainy day."

Leticia and I met each other's eyes across the room. I shook my head.

"What's happening to her?" Leticia asked later, when Mother went to bed and we were sitting in the living room with Kevin. "It's not normal."

"She's already forgotten that she left her suitcase at the airport, and she's forgotten she had a big fight with the cops! She doesn't seem to remember how much time has passed since she arrived. It doesn't help that she seemed to have forgotten I lived with Akhenaten—or was she conveniently forgetting? She completely refuses to acknowledge him. I'm so mad at her, but then I'm also so terrified that something is horribly wrong with her."

"She'll come around to Akhenaten," Leticia said. "I would be the same if I had only one kid and they were going to be marrying somebody in a foreign country. She's afraid she'll lose you."

"There's more to it, though. Akhenaten doesn't understand how it is to grow up African," I said. "I'm not saying that I can speak for all fifty-four countries, but there are some basic rules that we all know and it's hard to explain it to a foreigner. The least he can do is respect that. He tried to kiss me in front of my mother. I was mortified."

"Okay, so why don't you maybe tell him everything you think he needs to know, so he's not constantly stepping on land mines?" Leticia said.

"Where would I begin? Our parents are revered. If an African parent says the sun orbits the earth, we will nod our heads and agree, at least in their presence. It's a level of respect so high it's illogical. African parents never admit they're wrong, and our grandparents are the only ones who can put them in their place, because they too wouldn't dare challenge *their* parents. There's this incredible hierarchy that only makes sense to an African who grew up in the midst of it."

"Soila, would it help if Akhenaten came to Kenya with you, and perhaps learned a little bit about the culture before you got married? Maybe that would help smooth things over?" Kevin asked.

I thought about it. Akhenaten in Nairobi, sitting with my grandmother, who would look at him like he was a different species, yet still pile his plate with nyama choma, grilled beef, because that's what the most important guests were served. Kokoi's feelings would vacillate between her love for me, her joy that I had found a man who made me happy, and, on the other end of the spectrum, the sense of loss she would feel because this man was so unrelatable that the only thing she could possibly say to him was "Eat, eat, eat some more. . . ."

"It's going to be weird in a way because the older generation, my grandmother's generation, has no problems with Black Americans," I said. "My grandmother, for example, will never warm up to white people. She'll tolerate them, but she'll never, ever trust them, not even my aunt's Scottish husband. Yet, white folks are familiar to her because of the colonials. She hasn't had much interaction with Black people from any other parts of the world. Can you see how it's a weird dynamic for an old lady? With Black Americans there is always going to be empathy and unspoken solidarity, but you guys are still the 'other.' There's a foreignness that cannot be bridged. Akhenaten is constantly going to be apart from the locals. It doesn't help that he's the opposite of what a 'decent' Black man should look like in Africa.

"My mother fears what her friends will think about Akhenaten. Where is the boy who grew up going to church like I did? Where is the boy who is a doctor, lawyer? And if I must love a Black American, why can't he be like Kevin, a neat-looking college professor? At least if I brought home a Kevin, she could brag. But I'm bringing home Basquiat."

Leticia and Kevin were laughing. I threw a cushion at them.

"Ticia, when I saw how she looked at Akhenaten at the hospital—how she had to force herself to shake his hand—I knew that I was in for a big fight. And yet, I can see that she's impressed by him. It's killing her that he is so successful. I saw how she admired the photograph of his mother, especially when I told her that Estelle is also a widow.

At least if he were poor and struggling, she'd have reason to say that he's a loser. She must know deep down that she's being completely selfish. But—she's already lost Rarin. I don't think she will survive losing me."

"Would it help if he shaved his dreads off and wore Dockers and a blazer?" Leticia asked.

"It would," I said. "But why should he have to change who he is? I would never ask him to do that."

"It's just hair," Kevin said. "All this superficial stuff shouldn't be such a problem. It will work itself out."

The next morning, Leticia and I circled each other in the kitchen, still groggy from a night spent detangling my life. She made coffee while I scrambled eggs and cut up slices of tomatoes, the way Mother liked. It had stopped snowing and I thought I'd try to convince Mother to go out with me and visit my cherished church in Little Italy. But Mother wouldn't leave the apartment. She stayed inside, mostly in bed, for days.

"She's usually awake at the crack of dawn, praying," I said, when Leticia asked if we should wake Mother up. I peeked my head in to check on her. Mother sat up as soon as I cracked the door open.

"Tanei, is that you?" she asked, looking directly at me.

"No, Yeyo. It's me, Soila."

"Where am I?"

Stunned, I shut the door and returned to the kitchen.

"What's wrong with you? Looks like you've just seen a ghost or something."

"Ticia, it's happening again," I said. "She doesn't know where she is, and she didn't recognize me."

Leticia walked past me, headed to the bedroom. I followed behind.

"Morning, Mrs. Segeni! We've made breakfast," Leticia said,

walking up to the window. She slid the curtains open and the room was bathed in a clear light.

"I don't think we've met," Mother said, scooting her body to the far side of the bed next to the wall. She was wringing her hands and rocking her body forward and back. She was like a nervous child shying away from a new teacher on the first day of school.

Leticia looked at me with the same stunned expression I wore on my face.

. . .

Eight days after Mother arrived in New York, we went to see Dr. Horsham, a highly regarded neurologist. Through that first session, he chatted pleasantly with Mother, asking her about her work in Kenya, the political climate, her friends, and she enjoyed the banter and kept up with the pace of their conversation. Afterward, he explained the battery of tests he would carry out. There would be an MRI, blood work, and several other things and Mother's next appointment would be after Christmas, he said.

Christmas came and went quietly with just Mother and me in Leticia's apartment after Leticia and Kevin went to her parents' house upstate. Akhenaten flew down to New Orleans to be with his mother. He said there was no reason to stay in the city if I wasn't going to spend time with him, and it felt like a veiled ultimatum.

"Half the time she's foggy about what day it is," I tried to tell him before he left New York. "She gets rattled and angry about the smallest things. This isn't a good time for us to be pushing our relationship in her face."

Mother and I attended the midnight Mass on Christmas Eve at Old St. Patrick's. The organ piped, the choir crooned the carols, and the priest talked about rebirth. Leticia returned to work, and Akhenaten came back to New York.

On an evening when Leticia was going to be home with Mother, I snuck out to spend a few hours with Akhenaten, all the while worrying that Mother would leave the apartment and go wandering around Brooklyn and get hit by a bus. Akhenaten listened. He made love to me and he let me cry.

"I think I have to go back to Kenya," I said. "The reality of it all is coming down hard. What kind of a daughter would I be, to abandon her with a terminal illness? How would I forgive myself if she died and I wasn't there with her?"

"But what does that mean for us?" I could hear trembling in his voice. He was asking a question he didn't want an answer to.

"We can't have a relationship like this," I said. "Me in Kenya, you here. Long-distance . . ."

"It doesn't have to be," he said. "I'll visit, I'll stay in Kenya, whatever you want. I can work from anywhere."

"It's not that easy." And then the tears would come again.

"Well it is, actually," he said. "It is, if you want it to be. I choose you, and all your baggage. I choose your difficult, ill mother. I choose everything about you. Why is it so hard for you to choose me?"

"Why is it so hard for you to quit being so idealistic?" I snapped. "A Kenyan guy would never put this much pressure on me. A Kenyan guy would just get it."

"Well, why don't you call up your ex and let's see how that works out for you?"

When I left his apartment, we didn't even hug goodbye.

"It's so unfair," I said to Leticia that night. "I finally found someone who I can really be with. Why is this happening?"

Akhenaten didn't call me for the rest of the week. Then, the doorbell rang, and he was standing there, unexpected. He took off his boots like he always did at the door, then he walked in and sat on the couch, next to Mother. Neither one of them spoke to the other. Instead, they spent an afternoon in silence watching figure skating on television. A few hours later, he stood up, his tallness towering over Mother on the couch like a baobab tree.

"It's like her eyes are glazed over," he said, when I walked him outside. "She's watching it, but she's not really. It's weird."

"The funny thing is, she struggles to remember everyday faces, like Leticia," I said. "But she never forgets you. Your face is stamped permanently in her memory, her permanent nightmare."

We laughed like we used to. We stood close, feeling the cold air slice through our bones and we hugged for a long time, with no words said.

"I don't know what I'm supposed to do. I don't know what's going to happen," I said. "I've never felt so lost. I'm so scared."

He put his hand on my cheek and I saw in his eyes that he didn't have an answer either.

. . .

On the twenty-seventh of December, less than a week after our first appointment with Dr. Horsham, we were back to see him again. This time, his office didn't seem bright and cheery. Instead, I felt like I was in a dark tunnel without a flashlight. The doctor's casual manner had vanished. He was stiff and subdued. He wouldn't look me directly in the eye and didn't want to have a friendly chat with Mother.

"The tests were all conclusive," he said, in a measured tone. "It confirms what I suspected. I'm sorry to tell you that it is early-onset Alzheimer's."

Mother started crying loudly, unabashedly, her hands cupped over her face.

"There's no way," I said. "She's only fifty-five, are you sure? My grandmother is seventy and she's lucid. How is this even possible?"

"Well, it's not always in the family. There are many factors and risks, but it might be worth having genetic testing yourself."

He started to hand me brochures and cards about support groups, networks, associations, and therapists. His words bounced off my ears and hit the walls, becoming echoes I couldn't understand. Beside me, Mother was curled into a ball, crying hysterically. Mother, stoic, a mountain, a thundering storm—she had come apart in an American neurologist's office, sobbing in my arms. I looked at her like she was a sweater that had been knit inside out. I couldn't make sense of it. She was the one who'd always been in control.

"No, it's fine," I said. "I don't need any of the information here. I'm going to take her back home."

"That is the best thing you can do for her eventually," Dr. Horsham said. "She'll find she's happier being around people with whom she's familiar. But for now, she'll still need active treatments and support groups with other patients, and I'm not sure this kind of medical support is going to be available in Kenya."

"I want to go home," Mother cried. "Please just take me home."

"I will, Yeyo. I will."

That evening, the only place I knew to find refuge from the chaos that had become my life was St. Patrick's Old Cathedral. Dr. Horsham had prescribed a sedative for Mother to calm her nerves and though she'd fought me, she finally agreed to take it and was groggy by the time our cab pulled up in front of Leticia's front door. I put Mother to bed and went to the place that had always granted me peace in the moments when I so needed it. And this time, while kneeling in the empty church, in the very back pew, I cried more than I'd ever cried before.

It was grief, it was anger, and everything in between. I was being punished but I didn't know why and the silence in my quiet place that had always been a haven was now haunting. The nuns, Mother, every

Christian I knew, had told me as a child that if I prayed in earnest, put all my faith in God, he would answer my prayer. But God wasn't answering my prayers. He was completely silent. He had turned his back on me and I didn't know why.

I had been growing more furious and desperate every day since Mother arrived in New York. I was furious that she lost her luggage at the airport, got lost on the streets, refused to show even a little bit of acceptance for Akhenaten. I was furious with her for being diagnosed with an illness that had no hope for a cure. I was furious that God would take away my happiness right when I'd finally discovered it. I was furious that I couldn't have the life I wanted. But then after all the fury came the shame. Shame that I would even have such horrible thoughts. Mother was sick. She had raised me on her own. She had always done everything she could to give me the most privileged life. I owed her everything. But none of it made sense to me. I didn't know what God's plan was for my life. I wished He would answer me, give me a compass. But the only sound that I heard in that silent church that evening was the sound of my tormented sobbing.

The conversation that night with Akhenaten was so difficult that I was mostly silent. I let him speak because it was easier than trying to put words to my devastation.

"Your life doesn't have to get cut off because you have to care for her," he said. "You can care for her and we can still be together."

"How can I do that?" I asked hopelessly. "How can I live here with you, and care for my mother back home?"

"I'll come be with you," he said.

"Akhenaten, please! This is impossible for me right now. This isn't about you or us right now."

When I gave him back the ring, the pain was immeasurable. It was like another death.

Chapter Nineteen

When I got on the plane with Mother, I was on the cusp of turning twenty-seven and leaving everything I had known in my adult life. It was the same experience as seven years before, when I got on a plane and left behind my childhood. Mother was capricious on the journey back home. She cried when she said goodbye to Leticia. She thanked Leticia for caring for her only daughter. On the plane, she smiled sweetly with one stewardess then verbally attacked another. Her disease had no guidebook, no instruction manual. I didn't know how to fight for her without brawling against the rest of the world.

Back in Kenya, caring for Mother was harder than I'd imagined it would be. Dr. Horsham had been right—there were no support groups of any kind, no treatment facilities for Alzheimer's patients. Old people with senility were disregarded by their families, by society. Disregarded, not discarded, everyone told me, over and over.

"Africans—we don't discard loved ones in care homes. We care for our own until the very end." But what good did it do to hide our loved ones away when they needed help, I asked. Weren't they still worthy of friendships, of human connection?

I faced barriers even with simple communication. Swahili had no translation for dementia except "disease of the mind," which could mean any type of mental illness. As I searched for support, I found that everyone knew someone living with symptoms of dementia, but no one knew what to do with them. Their struggles were shrugged off as advanced age.

I met a grandmother whose family bathed her every morning and brought her out to sit in the sun, where chickens clucked and walked by her feet as she had long chats with no one in particular. And I was introduced to a grandfather who wore his farm boots every morning even though his farm had long been sold off and turned into a development property by his adult children. I spent time with a sixty-year-old mother who sat in front of the television speaking to it as though the people on the screen were sitting in her living room. I saw how she scolded her daughter, telling her that she had abandoned her, despite the fact that the woman lived in her daughter's home.

These encounters gave me shivers. This was what was coming my way. I had no access to a fancy treatment facility, like in America, where I could outsource Mother's care, and there were no support groups. I knew she needed better and decided it was up to me to do something. So, I worked to create a group that brought affected families together. I visited South Africa, which was years ahead, to understand how they had rolled out their programs. But Kenya was different. Most Kenyans couldn't afford healthcare. Every time I believed I was making headway, I hit another roadblock.

"This is why it's so hard to get things done in Africa," Aisha commiserated when I phoned her to share my frustrations. We spoke at least once a week since I had returned to Nairobi. "It's impossible to get anything off the ground without donor money, but soon enough the donors will want you to do things their way."

I dreamed of a state-of-the-art treatment and care facility. But I was only one person and had no experience in this kind of work. I had to start with something modest—a weekly support group for families held in churches around the country. I rallied a small group of neurologists who agreed to visit the support group pro bono once a week. The work gave me a cause I was passionate about—if I couldn't help Mother, maybe I could make a difference for the next generation.

In the meantime, as days rolled on—six months, nine months—I watched Mother's brain deteriorate. On the outside she was aging beautifully at fifty-six. But on the inside, she was half gone. She had once been razor-sharp, so astute that not even the butcher in town would dare to add half a gram on the weighing scale when she bought meat. Now, only a year after her diagnosis, her mind was spotty. She remembered intricate details about strange events. She retold stories of Tanei's youthful shenanigans, but she didn't know where she had put her keys or whether the kettle was turned off. In the mornings, she demanded a notebook and a pencil and wrote pages of shorthand none of us could make out. In her mind, she had returned to her early career as a secretary. In the early evenings, she was hopeless. The doctor had warned us about it. He called it sundowning. She got our names wrong, and complained, as if to an imaginary friend, about all of us. It broke my heart to hear her mutter, "They don't care, they're never home."

On rare occasions, she would bring up Akhenaten. I suffered through those conversations.

"Why don't you just say that you blame me for your American boyfriend breaking up with you? Go ahead. Say it. Don't worry, I'll be dead soon anyway, and then you can marry him." As she ranted, I turned my face to hide my tears.

I called Akhenaten only a few times after I left New York. I could tell in his voice that he had barely any spirit left in him. He sounded robotic, obligatory. If I were anyone else, he would have told me never to call him again. My emails to him went unanswered. So, I made the decision not to cling to him.

"He's just trying to move on as best he can," Leticia said, when I asked about him on the phone. "You won't marry him, you won't let him see you in Kenya, you won't come back—he's completely helpless in this. Soila, you've got to let him go because he is completely broken."

"*I* am broken," I replied. "I don't think I can ever be with someone else."

Just like that, I had lost him, like the sun setting into the horizon, except there'd be no sunrise. To help make the silence between us bearable, I drowned myself in medication. Ambien because the insomnia was crushing, antianxiety pills, antidepressants—anything to help me stand on my feet.

One day, Naserian and Laioni asked me out to lunch. To discuss Mother's long-term care, they said. When I arrived at the restaurant, my aunts introduced another woman as the best psychiatrist in town, recently back from England.

"Look, I'm sure you're very smart," I said, turning to the psychiatrist, "and would be a great resource, but my mother has already been diagnosed. There's not much else we can do here except support and care for her." A waiter came by with a menu and asked me what I wanted to drink. I told him I wasn't staying for lunch, impatient with my aunts for inviting this woman who could be no help to Mother.

"Soila, my baby, we didn't ask her here to talk about Yeyo," Naserian said gently.

This was an intervention, I realized. All of the broken pieces that I couldn't put back together were about to be pecked at in a busy restaurant in the middle of the day. I had refused to talk about the details of our breakup with my aunts, the way it hurt when I gave back the ring, the look on Akhenaten's face when I told him our relationship couldn't work.

My hands trembled from sheer anger. "How can you ambush me like this? You think that by bringing this woman here to a public place you can get me to talk about my issues?"

"Soila, we are just trying to help," Laioni said. "We can't watch you continue to suffer like this. You don't eat a thing. You're hooked on pills. You don't have any friends. You don't sleep. All you do is work. When you're not on the phone, you're on your laptop, or you're in meetings, or you're traveling. Or you're screaming at the nurse because she didn't draw the curtains all around the house at six P.M. sharp. Even Princess is afraid of you."

"So, this is supposed to be helping? Bringing a stranger to lunch to get me to talk about my private life?" The trembling in my hands had spread all over my body. I held every muscle together as tightly as I could to keep from throwing the table settings across the room. Instead, I stood up and politely, coldly, thanked the psychiatrist for her time.

"Soila, don't leave," Naserian said. "She can help you."

"Naserian—stay out of my life."

. . .

A little over a year had passed since I brought Mother back to Kenya when on a pouring day in March, Leticia called me with news.

"I'm getting married!" she screamed, blasting my ear through the phone. She told me about Kevin's proposal and how relieved she was because it was coming up to five years and she had been very nearly about to walk away.

Leticia said the wedding would be in six months. She didn't want to wait much longer. True to herself, Leticia said she was determined to throw the classiest wedding on a tight schedule and a medium budget. I smiled remembering how she would spend weekends hunting for designer clothing in the city's thrift shops, and I knew the wedding, however big or small, would be beautiful. "Soila, will you please be my maid of honor?" she asked. "I hate to ask you to leave your mom, but you're my best friend."

"Of course I will!"

I walked into the living room to tell my family the news. Since Mother's illness, everyone came around every evening. I was happy to announce Leticia's engagement news to Mother and my aunts that night. But I also felt my spirit sinking as I watched their excitement. I would never have Leticia's kind of luck.

"It's going to happen for you, Soila," Naserian said, when she found me lying in my bed that night. "It scares me when you get so dark like this. I think of what happened to your father."

I shook my head and turned away. "Who will I marry? The man I still love is long gone."

. . .

Later that year, I arrived in New York for Leticia's wedding the day before the ceremony, on a crisp October day. I rented a car to drive to Rochester from New York and as the miles rolled past, I could think only of Akhenaten. I knew he would be attending the wedding, and I didn't want to see him in public without having a private conversation first. I dialed his number from the road and he picked up on the first ring.

"I honestly didn't think you would want to talk to me," I said. "You don't call me anymore or respond to my emails. Leticia asked me to give you space. . . ."

"I'm glad you called. I'm not sure if Leticia told you, but I'm bringing a date tomorrow. I thought you should know."

I didn't want him to hear me break down. I thanked him, though unsure what for, and hung up. The drive to Rochester was the loneliest one of my life. But after living in a dusty, smoggy city for so long, I had forgotten how clean the air could be. I stopped every hour along the way and got out of the car to stretch, listening to the rustling of the red and yellow leaves. I breathed the air in deeply, as if I could store it up for when I went back to Nairobi.

The next morning, as Mrs. Hopkins and I helped Leticia get ready, we gossiped about what Akhenaten's date would be like. "I bet you she's a white girl," Leticia said. We were dressing her in her mother's wedding dress and veil. "Successful Black men *always* end up with a white woman on their arms."

"He's not the type to be caught up in skin color," I said. "He dated a Japanese girl before me. But how could he move on so quickly? I still cry like it happened yesterday. On my mother's lucid days she thinks I'm just trying to get her attention if she sees me crying. She says, 'Oh, I know you can't wait to bury me, so you can marry that foreigner.'"

"Your mother has Alzheimer's and still hasn't changed. What will it take?" Leticia asked sympathetically.

"Death," I said, matter-of-factly.

"Oh, girls, please don't talk like that," Mrs. Hopkins said. "You'll be mothers one day yourselves, and you'll see how difficult it is to part with your kids. Hopefully, Soila, your mom will come around before it's too late."

Despite my heartache, Leticia's wedding was a fantasy. It was held on a large estate, in a romantic garden. Against the fall foliage with her red roses, Leticia looked perfect.

I didn't see Akhenaten until I was walking down the aisle ahead of Leticia and her father. He wore a black suit with a black button-up shirt and a navy-and-red silk neck scarf layered over them. His six-foot-four-inch stature suddenly seemed more than seven feet. His dreadlocks were held neatly back. He looked at me the same way he had in the gallery when we first met, and in the bathroom when he knelt on the floor to propose to me. He was still in love with me. Standing beside Leticia when all the guests sat down, I caught a glimpse of his date. She was a tall Black woman with big hair and long teardrop earrings. She had a hand laid casually on his lap. It was only as the guests walked away from their seats that I realized just how tall she was.

"Do you think she's a model?" I whispered to Leticia, helping her adjust her dress. "Her legs don't end."

"Now, Soila, I love you. But I just got married two seconds ago. Can we not talk about Glamazon over there for a minute? We gotta take pictures!" Later, we moved inside for the reception, the space decorated with soft drapery and glowing chandeliers. We had a buffet-style dinner of soul food: pulled pork sliders, fried chicken, mini pot-pies, green beans—all the things Leticia loved.

I sat at the top table, anticipating the toast I had to make as the maid of honor and reworking it in my mind. Across the room, Akhenaten and his date were immersed in conversation. I could tell, from the way he leaned all the way back when he laughed, that he was at ease. He was happy. I was so overwhelmed I felt sick.

Kevin's brother was clinking a glass for a toast. He talked about Kevin being shy and studious, never getting into trouble like his brothers. "Kevin was being flaky and eventually we had to sit him down and say, 'You need to marry this girl. You lucked out to have a girl like Leticia even look at you twice. . . .' "

As he finished, everyone clapped and Kevin hugged his brother. Leticia gestured to me. My turn. I tried to push thoughts of Akhenaten and his girlfriend to the back of my mind even though he was all I could see. Then, he met my eyes and mouthed, "You've got this."

"Leticia was there for me from the minute I came to this country," I said, the words suddenly falling out of my mouth with ease. I kept my eyes on Akhenaten as I spoke, watching him nod, so subtly that not even his date sitting next to him noticed. He willed me on, giving me strength.

"I didn't know anyone. She was kind to me; she protected me fiercely, as if I were her sister. She deserves all the happiness." I realized that I truly was happy for Leticia. The envy I had felt since she first called me with the news lifted. After the toast, when she hugged me, I cried so much I had to leave the room. My best friend, my ex-fiancé, everyone who was important to me outside of my family, was heading away from me, their lives continuing, while I was right where I started. Still planted with Mother. Still in the same house I grew up in, with my aunts and grandmother. Nothing had changed for me. I sat outside on a bench in the garden, lost in my thoughts. Then out of nowhere, Akhenaten was sitting next to me. Just being in his presence, I was sure I would faint from the scent of him.

"I've been looking everywhere for you," he said. "I wanted to make sure you're okay. That was a lot of crying back there." He shook his head. "Look at you literally freezing to death," he said. "Where's your coat?" He took off his suit jacket and placed it over my shoulders.

"I've missed you," I said. I hadn't planned to, but with Akhenaten, my mind and my body had always betrayed me. "I've really missed you."

He didn't say it back. Instead he asked how I was doing, how I was coping with Mother's illness. He said I had lost weight.

"You don't like your Kenyan food?" he asked, laughing, but I could see real concern in his eyes.

"Is that woman your girlfriend?" I blurted out. If she was, I could finish off the night and go home with some closure, I thought. I'd know that he's moved on.

"Who? Candice?"

"Well, who else? Your date."

"I wouldn't use the word 'girlfriend,' but yeah, I'm dating again," he said. "A few people. You?"

"Me?" I scoffed. "No."

"Look, I didn't want to start dating again, but I had to make peace with the fact that you said you could never be with me," he said.

"You don't have to apologize, Akhenaten. But seeing you now, after so long, is really hard. You've moved on and I haven't been able to."

He was interested in my Alzheimer's projects and we talked about the uphill challenges, the stigma of dementia, and how much I wanted to change things in Kenya.

"I mean there's just absolutely no support, at all," I said. "The very wealthy folks have assisted-living homes, hidden out in the suburbs—and sure, I can stick my mom there and move on with my life, but that's not what I want. I want to make an actual change. I want to start a foundation like they have in South Africa and in developed countries. There's just nothing now. Once you get your diagnosis, you're on your own."

"What can I do to help?" Akhenaten said. "There's got to be something."

"I'm just doing it one step at a time—trying to figure out her long-term care when she really, really is mentally gone, helping organize her estate. I even did a home makeover. I couldn't bear to look at the same yellow kitchen I grew up in!"

Akhenaten laughed out loud then said he was very proud of me.

"You're so resilient, so strong," he said. "Most people would have already buckled from the burden of all this."

What I couldn't tell him was that I really wasn't strong and that in the nearly two years since our breakup, I had mourned our relationship like a death. I cried most nights, and dangerously self-medicated. No matter how hard I tried, I couldn't move on. The only thing that had kept me sane was the chaos brought on by Mother's diagnosis. Somehow, the pain that came from her illness had helped wash over the pain of losing Akhenaten.

"It feels like I have no one to talk to," I said. "Aisha and I talk nearly every week, but it's not the same as having someone with me, like I did with Leticia, or you. My aunts are busybodies. They mean well, but they just want to fix me. Some things can't be fixed."

"So, your mother still won't see Aisha?"

"Nope. Aisha hasn't even visited me in Kenya. She doesn't want to antagonize a sick woman. Rarin still lives in Europe, my two other aunts don't live at home, and Tanei is disabled and my grandmother is aging too. I don't travel much except in and out for work, but I did go to Ghana. I met Aisha's daughter. She's so beautiful. I felt so alive, to just have some time for myself. I took photographs for the first time in God knows how long."

"I miss you, Soila," he said finally, putting his hand over mine.

"Thank you," I said. "I really needed to hear you say that."

The party went till late and Akhenaten and Candice, who I learned later was a model, left for their hotel. Leticia and Kevin went to a hotel too, after Leticia threw her bouquet. I returned to Leticia's childhood home, where I lay in her old bed, tossing and turning until dawn.

I spent the morning with the Hopkins extended family—Leticia's aunts and grandmothers—helping in the kitchen to prepare a big lunch for Kevin's family, who had all stayed in hotels and motels downtown. The kitchen conversations reminded me of being with my aunts. The laughter, the teasing, it was all the same.

Leticia and Kevin arrived in the early afternoon. Leticia said they had barely slept. They couldn't turn off their excitement motor, she said. They'd talked all night.

"Let's hope that's not all you did," one aunt yelled from the back of the room and everyone laughed. Leticia was the one who brought me my phone. She said she'd gone into her room to put away some things and saw it buzzing on the bed. There were five missed calls. First, my stomach dropped, thinking something had happened to Mother. But all the calls were from Akhenaten.

"What's going on?" I said, walking outside. "Did you get home okay?"

"Yeah, that was the longest drive of my life," Akhenaten said. "Candice got into a stink because you and I spent so much time talking."

"That's awful," I said. "We didn't plan to. We just haven't seen each other in so long."

"Can you come to my apartment tomorrow? I know you're leaving tomorrow night, but we can spend a few hours . . ."

"No. You have a girlfriend," I said. "I can't do that."

"I don't mean like that. Anyway, she's not my girlfriend, and frankly, I don't think I'll be seeing her again after that fight."

"Let me think about it."

Akhenaten's plea was all I could concentrate on for the rest of the afternoon, as I dried Mrs. Hopkins's china and cleared more dishes out of the dishwasher.

"Soila! Can you hear me? Where is your mind?" Leticia was standing in front of me, looking at me like I did Mother when her memory lapsed.

"Sorry, I'm just thinking about Akhenaten. He wants me to go see him tomorrow, but what about Candice?"

"Who's Candice?" Leticia said, with her arms stretched out.

"His date."

She scoffed. "Screw Candice. That's *your* man."

"Not anymore," I said.

"Well, can you blame him? You broke his heart. You have no idea what Akhenaten was like the first maybe six months after you left. If he weren't self-employed, he'd have had his ass fired. Soila, what do you want to do? Decide before you leave here what it is you want with this man. If you really can't have a relationship you need to walk into his apartment tomorrow and end it. You both need to move on. If you want to be with him, you need to be with him."

I took a deep breath. "I think I want to go now," I said. "To the city."

"Now?" Leticia looked at the clock. "It's more than five hours to Manhattan, it's too late to leave now."

"I'll be fine. I'll call you along the way, every time I need to make a pit stop, just so you know where I am," I said. "Is it okay? Will you hate me if I go?"

"Don't be ridiculous," Leticia said. "You just flew halfway across the world for my wedding. Get packed and go get your man."

It rained a lot that night and my eyes were blurry from jet lag and my sleepless night. Leticia's dad called several times asking for my whereabouts and the condition of the roads. I could hear the screams and laughs in the room behind his voice; the party hadn't slowed down.

"Now, you call me on this phone when you get to the city, you hear?" he said, with a firmness I had known only from Mother. "Don't call Ticia's phone. Call me."

It was nearly midnight by the time I reached Akhenaten's apartment building, circling the block four times searching for parking. I finally found a spot three blocks away and hauled my suitcase to the doorstep in the freezing rain. I pressed Akhenaten's buzzer over and over before his sleepy, hoarse voice came through the intercom.

"Who is it? It's midnight, man."

"It's me."

"What?"

"It's me, Soila, and I'm freezing to death. Please let me up."

Akhenaten opened his apartment door and walked down a flight of stairs to help me with my suitcase. Looking up at him standing in front of me in sweatpants and a torn T-shirt, the light behind him coloring him in warm shades of gray—I knew that I was going to marry him.

"What's going on? How did you get here?" he said, dragging my suitcase up the stairs.

"I drove my rental."

"That little Fiesta, in the middle of the night? I'm surprised Mr. Hopkins let you."

The first thing I did when I got inside Akhenaten's apartment was telephone Mr. Hopkins. I thanked him and he told me to keep well and sent his warm greetings to my family. After I hung up, I walked straight into Akhenaten's arms.

. . .

When I got home from Leticia's wedding, I told Mother that Akhenaten was coming for a visit, and that eventually we would be married. I said that if she wanted to be nice to him, it would make me happy. But if she didn't want to be nice, that was fine too. He was coming to see me either way.

"I don't know how you can invite that man here to my house, when I have told you that I won't accept this relationship," Mother said. I ignored her and left the room.

"Let it be, Nalu," I heard Kokoi say to Mother. Her voice broke as if she was about to cry. "I can't watch this child suffering like this anymore. She hardly eats. She cries in her sleep. Imagine, if I had told you back then that you couldn't marry her father?"

It could have been the disease. It could have been that she was finally tired of fighting. But just before Christmas, Akhenaten was sitting in Mother's living room and she was a little warmer to him than she'd been in New York. In turn, he was gracious and well-mannered.

He remembered the things that were important. He bowed when he greeted Kokoi. She was talking to him on the couch in Maa and broken Swahili about the morans, Maasai warriors, and he was listening attentively, even though he didn't understand a word.

"She's telling you that you remind her of the Maasai warriors, the morans," I translated. "Because you're so tall and statuesque. She admires your hair and that it must take a lot of commitment to grow hair that long. She's saying that the morans keep their hair in braids too."

"Thank you so much, Kokoi," Akhenaten said, and he clasped her hand.

My aunts watched the strange dynamic unfolding and giggled like schoolchildren in the kitchen, where they pretended to be busy boiling masala tea.

"Ah, Soila, he is too sweet," Naserian said. "The way he sits there, smiling and nodding like he's been there his whole life. Isn't it amazing? He fits right in, even though he really doesn't."

I told Mother that Akhenaten and I were taking a holiday. First, we would go down to the coast for Christmas break and then later, we'd go north to the Mara. Akhenaten had never been on a safari.

"You need a holiday," Kokoi said. "You do too much around here. I'm happy your friend is here."

Mother stayed quiet.

"He's a good boy," Kokoi whispered to Mother. "I can't talk his language, but I can see his heart."

...

"What is it that you want with my daughter?" Mother asked, when Akhenaten and I returned from our holiday. "You two have been apart as long as you were together. Surely you cannot feel the same way after so much time has passed. Isn't it time you let go of each other?"

Akhenaten was quiet for a long time.

"What will you do here?" Mother asked, before he had a chance to respond.

"I can work from anywhere, Mrs. Segeni." Akhenaten shrugged. "That's not an issue for me. I'll travel back and forth."

Mother stared at him for a long time, then turned to me. "Soila, is this truly the man you want to marry?"

"Yes. Absolutely."

"Will you go to church with my daughter?" she asked Akhenaten.

"Sure," Akhenaten said, again shrugging.

"Will you marry her in a Catholic church?"

"Sure."

Mother stared at him for a long, silent moment. Then she left the room without another word.

During Akhenaten's visit, Mother faded in and out of memory lapses. He saw just how far her illness had advanced and he said he couldn't bear the thought that I had to see my mother this way. Still, he was determined to stay in Kenya until he got the answer he wanted from Mother. When Mother was lucid, Kokoi and my aunts would persuade her to accept Akhenaten, to make me happy. Finally, on a warm evening while Akhenaten and I were getting ready to leave the house for an early dinner, Mother called for me and asked to sit down with me under her lemon tree. She reached out and took my hand.

"Kayai," she murmured, "I will never understand why you must have only this man. I have only ever wanted you to be happy. But I can see that you hate me."

"I don't hate you," I said. "But I love only him. I don't want to be with anyone else. Why can't you just be happy with that?"

Mother sat quietly for a while and I feared she had once again gone into a lapse and wouldn't remember the conversation we were having.

"The way you've given up your whole life to take care of me . . ." she said, then started to cry. "I couldn't have asked God for a better daughter. So, if this is what you need to be happy then I'm going to accept it. Besides, his heart is good. I can see it."

"He loves me, Yeyo," I said.

"Call him out here."

I rushed into the house to find Akhenaten. He let me lead him out to the lemon tree. Mother pointed at a chair next to her. Akhenaten sat quietly and I could see the resignation on his face. He was sure Mother was going to ask him to leave.

"I can see that your heart is in the right place," Mother said, firmly, with the tone of her old self. "But there are some things you should know. Soila won't move back to America. She has to hold down all the things this family has struggled so hard to build. If you're willing to make that sacrifice, to be here more, to learn the culture and do all the things that are important to this family, then you can marry Soila. But if these things are too difficult for you to commit to, then you need to let Soila go now."

Akhenaten breathed out heavily. His sigh was relief, but also the utter frustration and loneliness of the past two years since Mother crashed into our lives and ruined our engagement with her toxic stubbornness and disease. Our heartache was finally over.

"You don't have to worry about all that," he said. "I understand it all. I just want to marry her."

Mother nodded.

Then Akhenaten stood up and knelt in front of me. He took my hand and removed the little ring box from his pocket. For the second time, he slid the sapphire ring onto my finger.

"I can't believe you kept the ring," I whispered in awe.

"I really did try to get rid of it, but I just couldn't," Akhenaten said.

"It's settled then," Mother said. "We will have a small wedding, and, if God is good to me, I'll see my grandchild before it's too late."

. . .

On a warm day in March 2005, we stood at the altar of Mother's beloved St. Francis of Assisi Church on my wedding day.

Only our closest family was there. It's what Mother wanted. Since her disease, she enjoyed the solace and the quiet of a small world. She would not grant me my wish for Father Emmanuel not to officiate my wedding. She needed to know why. Why would a man who saw me grow up in the church not be allowed to marry me? I couldn't give her an answer.

"It's completely ludicrous that this guy will do our vows," Akhenaten said. "I mean, I just want to punch him every time he looks at you. I literally get sick just looking at him."

"I won't break her heart over this," I said. "I just can't do it. It's one hour of our lives, and then we never have to deal with him again."

Aunt Rarin was there with her Alisdair. Her freckled twin boys flanked me like baby swans. Aunt Laioni fussed over my simple gown. Aisha had helped pick it out—a white lace dress with subtle cleavage and capped sleeves. I felt more beautiful than I had in my life.

Aisha was there too. Mother had laid down all her grudges the day she gave her blessing to Akhenaten and me under the lemon tree.

The day was already perfect. Then, as if by magic, Leticia was standing at my bedroom door that morning. The surprise made me so happy that I felt light-headed. Everyone I loved was there. Estelle wore a red-feathered hat and a bold red African dress she'd had made back in the States with fabric that I sent her from Kenya. She told us that her friends were quivering with envy at the thought of her being in Africa. Akhenaten said he didn't doubt it. Later, while we stood around for photographs, Akhenaten tapped my shoulder to get my attention, then pointed at Mother.

"Look how happy she is."

Mother stood alone, off to the side, in her feathered hat. She was looking up at the sky and the tall blue gum trees. She smiled in a way that I had never seen her smile before.

EPILOGUE

Kokoi turned seventy-six today. She sits like a queen in the garden, in the shade of Mother's lemon tree. As Mother wished, she got to see her grandchild. My daughter was born in the East African monsoon. The rain was so heavy outside that her newborn cry was drowned out by the sound of wind pounding on the windows. She had a round, plump face and a shock of wavy hair, so we named her Kulthum—"chubby, rosy cheeks."

She's two and a half and she loves it when I help her make Mother a crown with roses. Her tiny fingers, pricked mercilessly by thorns, are wrapped in kiddie plasters that I administer over mountains of feel-better kisses. Before Mother fell ill, she loved those roses. In the hot summers, she knelt over the bushes, misting them with water bottles and shielding them from the African sun that threatened to burn their delicate petals away. If Mother were here, she would chase Kulthum away from her rosebushes. Or maybe she wouldn't. Maybe she would love her differently than she loved me. Maybe she'd hug her. Maybe she'd even tell her that she loved her.

I tell my daughter that I love her every day. Akhenaten does too. He's the best father I could have wished for. Kokoi tells me that Akhenaten reminds her of my papai, the way he dotes on our daughter and does all the things that a traditional man would refuse to do. When Kulthum was a baby he changed her diapers and mashed peas by hand to spoon into her mouth. Now that she's almost three, he plays games of pretend, acting the part of an ogre or a prince. When he travels for his work, he calls to tuck her in over the phone. Every summer, we take her to New Orleans to visit Estelle, who shows her off to her friends like a prized jewel.

I take photographs of everyone around me all the time. Tanei laughs so much now. In every photo her head is tilted up to the sky, her hand to her chest, as if the laughter is choking her. It's the joy all the children around her bring, she says. It's also her work as a counselor with trauma victims. Naserian has a child too, a little boy she adopted on her own after her marriage to Kamau ended. Laioni is here too. Still never married, still happily in love. Aisha's daughter, Nuru, is the one who looks most Maasai.

"Those long limbs—she'll be as tall as a jacaranda tree," Kokoi says, while she watches Nuru run around the garden.

"That's the nicest thing anyone can say to me," Aisha says. "To know that I carry something of my father."

Mother is here. But she's not really here. She sits in her wheelchair beside Kokoi in the shade of her lemon tree. She watches us, but her eyes have long turned to stones. She's still tall; she's still beautiful. But the gravitas and the stoicism have melted down, a diminished candle. Frail neck and a hanging head, like a newborn baby. Drool. She lives in a galaxy of her own mind, in quiet solitude.

"Soila! Where's my Soila? Why won't she visit me?"

I say to her, "Yeyo, I'm right here."

Everyone is showering Kokoi with gifts and gratitude.

"Gratitude? I'm the one who is grateful," Kokoi says, throwing her hands up to the sky. "God's given me good health, five daughters who have made me proud, four grandchildren, one great-granddaughter."

Kokoi is the one who has held us all together. Mother's meltdowns, verbal abuse, the horrible way she smacks and bites at us. Kokoi is the only one who can ever calm her down.

I have missed Mother more than I thought I would when she first got ill. But over the years being back home, my life has been full of love and happiness. I treasure my family, Akhenaten and our daughter. I have my aunts and my kokoi. I have work that I love.

I still take photographs and I'm proud of my art. Finally, after so many years of seeking out my identity, Mother's affirmation, and unconditional love, I'm at peace. I feel truly lucky.

Mother and I have spent many afternoons under her lemon tree in these final years. It is where we exorcised our demons. I told her that I had struggled to understand her love for me. She told me she was sorry, to forgive her. I told her despite it all, I loved her and I would have made the same choice again if I had to relive choosing to care for her over my heart's desire.

It is under the shelter of Mother's lemon tree where Akhenaten and I first brought Kulthum to meet Mother. The newborn was swaddled like a mummy. I laid her on her kokoi's lap like a Christmas present and Mother was so overjoyed that she wept.

The shadow of the tree has sheltered us in the past few years while I showed Mother all the photographs of her life in the family album. Some things she remembered. The photograph of me as a toddler sitting on my father's shoulder as he posed for the camera at the large canyon of the Great Rift Valley. Her wedding. His funeral. Some things she couldn't remember. Some things brought tears, whimpers. The photographs of Aisha's mother passed down to me by my uncle Oldonyok—my father on his wedding day with his bride by a lake in Purdue, him holding his infant daughter. I saw how

Mother closed her eyes for a few minutes, and I knew the pain was still raw.

Still, over the years, she continued to flip over the pages of the album, and I knew that she'd finally forgiven my father. Then, she was gone.

ACKNOWLEDGMENTS

In loving memory of Melanie Richards. Your love, light, and encouragement are sprinkled through the pages of this novel. I know you would have loved *Lucky Girl*. I will cherish your memory for a lifetime. Rest in peace, my beautiful friend.

I will forever be thankful to my literary agent, Maria Cardona Serra, who believed in a raw and rugged manuscript written by a no-name author. You gave me the shot of a lifetime and made my dream come true.

Thanks to my editors, Rose Fox and Whitney Frick, for helping me untangle these complex characters and breathe life into them. I have multiple copies of this novel from when it first landed on your desks to when it finally left mine and wow—it took three years but the work we have done together is beyond imaginable. To all the unseen staff at The Dial Press who work behind the scenes to make a story a beautifully designed storybook—thank you.

Thanks to my mentors, especially Imraan Coovadia and Consuelo Roland, who have guided and encouraged me during this current phase of my career. For years I dreamed about creative writing but was too afraid to put one foot in front of the other. Finally, I did it at the whopping age of forty and I'm a true testament to "it's never too late to try." I see now that the truth is that most of us are late bloomers. But when we finally bloom, we bloom beautifully.

To every rock-solid girlfriend and one special male friend (you all know yourselves) who have had to hear for years about my doubts, my fear of failure, my frustration throughout the editing of this novel, and especially to the ones who said, "Just do it already!" I wouldn't have done this without you, and I am so blessed to have you all in my life.

Thanks to my extended family. Jimbob, only you can make me laugh so hard that I literally cry; Betty, your prayers are magical. My sweet granny, whose name I carry, Aunt Dorothy, cousin Wangash, you always think of and pray for me. I'm so grateful. And to my mom-in-law, who always has me in her heart and carries me in her prayers throughout my health battles.

To my three monkeys—Myles, Makena, and Maya—you're not little monkeys anymore. I'm so glad I took the time to stay home with you and watch you bud into the kind, generous, industrious, and most hilarious human beings you have become. And now that you're big monkeys, I hope when you look at me, you feel that I've made you proud.

To my millennial girls' army: Tanya, Terry-Maya, Mary, Stacey, Lucy, Lynette, Melissa, Imani, Tessa, Ivy, Crystal, Rehema, Maisha, Layla, and all the others who I have watched grow up from gap-toothed and diapered little girls to phenomenal young ladies, I hope as a woman that I inspire you. Remember—it's okay to fail, and it's never too late to chase after your most scary dreams and to reinvent yourself.

Finally, I thank my partner in life for his incredible support. With hand on my heart I can assure you, Nick, that I truly would not have started, written, or endured three years of punishing editing without your steadfast love for me. I don't know what I did in my past life to deserve you. I thank God every day for the blessing you are in my life.

PHOTO: © GOSIA WYER

Irene Muchemi-Ndiritu was born in Nairobi and moved to the United States to attend college in 1998. She has an MA in journalism from Columbia University and has worked as a journalist in New York City, Washington, D.C., and Boston. She later received an MFA in creative writing from the University of Cape Town, graduating with distinction. Her fictional work has been published in *The Yale Review* and *adda,* and she has been shortlisted for the Commonwealth Short Story Prize. She currently lives in Cape Town, South Africa. *Lucky Girl* is her first novel.

Twitter: @indiritu

ABOUT THE TYPE

This book was set in Bembo, a typeface based on an old-style Roman face that was used for Cardinal Pietro Bembo's tract *De Aetna* in 1495. Bembo was cut by Francesco Griffo (1450–1518) in the early sixteenth century for Italian Renaissance printer and publisher Aldus Manutius (1449–1515). The Lanston Monotype Company of Philadelphia brought the well-proportioned letterforms of Bembo to the United States in the 1930s.